SHERRYL WOODS

Beach Lane

**Doubleday Large Print
Home Library Edition**

MIRA®

business establishments, events or locales is entirely coincidental.

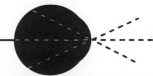

This Large Print Book carries the Seal of Approval of N.A.V.H.

Dear Friends,

From the very beginning, not only the O'Briens, but all the rest of us, have been befuddled by the not-dating stance determinedly taken by Susie O'Brien and Mack Franklin. Finally these two are getting their act together in *Beach Lane.* This book will also give you a glimpse into Susie's side of the family—father Jeff and his ongoing tense relationship with his brother Mick; his mother, Jo; and Susie's brothers, Matthew and Luke.

As if Mack and Susie's relationship hasn't been difficult enough, they're about to be thrown a major curve, which has the power to pull them together or tear them apart. To his everlasting credit, when those very scary chips are down, Mack doesn't even hesitate to step up. For me he's the ultimate hero! I hope you'll agree.

Beach Lane will hopefully make you laugh, but it's almost guaranteed to have you shedding more than a few tears, so keep the tissues handy! And be attuned to the next budding romance in this series between two very unlikely people. It will play out in *An O'Brien Family Christmas,* scheduled for fall 2011 from MIRA Books.

All the best,

Sherryl Woods

1

Men were the bane of Susie O'Brien's life. She was surrounded by them, all of them stubborn in the extreme, beginning with her father, Jeff. Add in her uncles Mick and Thomas, her brothers and, the very worst of all, Mack Franklin, and it was a wonder she could get through a day without screaming.

Today, in fact, already seemed likely to test the limits of her patience in never-before-imagined ways. Before she'd even had the first sip of her coffee, her uncle Mick came charging into the Chesapeake Shores real estate management company that she ran with her father.

"Where's Jeff, that—" At her frown, he cut off the disparaging epithet he'd apparently been intent on using. "Your father, where is he?"

"Dad had an appointment with a client," she said, then chose her next words about her father's whereabouts carefully. She knew that this particular piece of property was a hot-button issue for Mick. "He's showing her a house on Mill Road. It's the third time she's gone through the place. He's almost certain she's going to sign a contract today."

Mick frowned, obviously clicking through his own mental data bank of properties on Mill Road. Then astonishment dawned. "The Brighton house? He's finally going to unload that old eyesore? How'd he get the listing? Last I heard, no one in that family would even speak to an O'Brien."

Susie hid a smile. It still stuck in her uncle's craw that old Mr. Brighton had refused to sell him a key piece of shoreline property when he'd been developing Chesapeake Shores. Apparently the refusal had something to do with a Brighton-O'Brien family feud several generations back that neither coaxing nor big bucks had been able to resolve. For all Susie knew, some great-great-uncle's rooster had chased a Brighton, who'd lopped off its head and cooked it for Sunday dinner. In her family that was all it would take to start a feud that could last for eons.

"Seems that way," she confirmed. "Apparently Mr. Brighton's heirs don't have the same aversion to dealing with an O'Brien that he did."

"Stubborn old coot," Mick muttered.

"Why did you want to see Dad?" Susie asked. "Is there a problem?"

For years now the only things that brought the two brothers together were problems and the entreaties of their mother. Nell O'Brien insisted that even the sparring brothers and their families had to spend holidays under the same roof. Susie couldn't recall a tension-free holiday meal in her entire lifetime. The antacid business probably thrived thanks to the O'Brien dynamics.

Mick and her dad could be civil for an hour or two, which was more than she could say for Mick and her uncle Thomas, at least until recently. Lately they'd apparently struck some kind of accord, which was akin to achieving peace in the Middle

East. Like those treaties, Susie suspected this one didn't have a lot of hope of lasting, though now that Thomas was with Connie Collins she seemed to have a soothing effect on him. She also seemed determined to maintain the détente.

"There's water leaking in Shanna's bookstore again," Mick told Susie, referring to his daughter-in-law's business on Main Street. "And, frankly, the plumbing in Megan's gallery should be checked, too. The last thing she needs is a flood ruining all that expensive art."

Susie gave him an innocent look. "Isn't the art hanging on the walls?"

Her uncle scowled. "What's your point?"

"Only that it would take quite a flood to ruin the paintings." She beamed at him. "Besides, since you gave Megan that space for a dollar a year, didn't you agree to take care of all the upkeep? I can look at the lease, if you like. We kept a copy here—at your insistence, as I recall."

Mick gave her a sour look. "If your daddy stayed on top of details the way you do, he'd be a better businessman."

"He doesn't need to," Susie retorted. "He has me. I will get the plumber over to Shanna's today, though. The last thing we need is another insurance claim. And I can send him by Megan's as well, as long as the bill comes to you."

Though he looked disgruntled, Mick nodded. "That'll do." He studied her. "You'll be at the house for Thanksgiving dinner?"

"Of course."

He eyed her speculatively. "You bringing Mack?"

Susie stilled. "Why would I? I've never brought him before."

"I've seen you around town with Mack Franklin for at least three years now," Mick replied. "Maybe longer. Isn't it time the two of you either got serious or called it quits? What kind of man drags his heels this long, and what sort of woman lets him? You deserve better than that, Susie. You're an O'Brien, after all, even if you're not one of mine. Nobody would have gotten away with treating one of my girls that way."

"Mack and I aren't dating," Susie said stiffly. "We're friends. Besides, how he treats me is none of your concern."

Mick just shook his head. "Damned waste, if you ask me. Reel the man in or move on, that's my advice."

"Not that I asked for it," Susie said. She'd heard some version of the same advice for a couple of years now from just about everyone in her family, and a few outsiders to boot. It was getting tiresome, mostly because it was sound advice she didn't particularly want to heed.

Unfortunately, as crazy as she'd been about Mack for most of her life, she was also a realist. Handsome, sexy ex-jocks who dated sexy, sophisticated, powerful women weren't going to be seriously interested in a woman who was ordinary on her very best day and downright pitiful when the sun freckled her pale skin and her bright red hair refused to be tamed. Despite a college degree and a few family trips to Ireland, Susie was basically a small-town girl, not Mack's type at all.

Though Shanna, who was married now to Susie's cousin Kevin, had suggested that Mack was as infatuated as she was, Susie didn't entirely believe her. She'd also discovered it was next to impossible to break a non-dating pattern once it had been established. With Mack and her, it was practically carved in stone. Other than one kiss under the mistletoe that had gotten decidedly out of hand, their relationship was strictly platonic. That kiss, however, had given her enough hope to give things between them more time to heat up.

"Maybe I'll ask Mack to dinner myself," Mick said, studying Susie intently as if to gauge her reaction. "How about that?"

She shrugged. "Up to you." Being around Mack wasn't the problem. They were together all the time. Turning it into anything romantic, *that* was the problem. Tying him to her bed and having her wicked way with him seemed extreme, though she was getting desperate enough to consider it.

Beyond that, she didn't have one single idea about how she could change things without risking total humiliation. She wondered what her uncle would have to say if she asked him straight out how to get Mack to make love to her. Her lips curved just thinking about Mick's reaction to such a query.

Mick regarded her suspiciously. "What are you smiling about?"

"I was just wondering how far you'd be willing to take your meddling," she said, studying him curiously.

"Meaning?"

"You pride yourself on getting all five of my cousins happily married. What do you think you could do to get Mack and me to the altar?"

At the immediate glint in his eye, she reconsidered her question. "Not that I'm asking you to intervene," she said hurriedly. "I'm just wondering."

Mick pulled up a chair and sat down, his expression suddenly serious. "Okay, let's think about this. I imagine I've still got a few tricks up my sleeve that might work."

The daring side of Susie's nature failed her at the eagerness in his voice. The status quo might well be better than the disaster her uncle might unleash. "Never mind, Uncle Mick. I think I'd better deal with Mack myself."

"You sure about that?" he asked, looking disappointed. "Like you said yourself a minute ago, I have a track record."

Susie knew for a fact that most of her cousins had found true love despite their father's interference, not because of it. "I'm sure," she said.

He shrugged. "Up to you, but I'm around if you change your mind. It's obvious your father's no help, but you can count on me."

Susie fought to hide her smile. Once again, her uncle's competitive spirit had reared its head. She might not know a lot about what the future held with Mack, but she knew with absolute certainty that the very last thing they needed was having her father and Mick in the middle of their relationship, vying for control of their future. Somehow she'd just have to figure out a way to get Mack to stop seeing her as a pal and realize that she was a desirable woman.

As Mick left the office, Susie glanced ruefully at her reflection in the window. First, though, she had to learn to see herself that way.

Mack walked into the managing editor's office at his Baltimore newspaper a week before Thanksgiving, took one look at Don Richmond's face and sat down hard.

"You're firing me," he said before his boss could. He should have known that being summoned into the office this morning couldn't mean anything good.

"I hate this," Don said, which wasn't an outright confirmation, but it certainly wasn't a denial.

He met Mack's gaze with an earnest expression that begged him to understand. "I don't have a choice, Mack. You know how it is. We're making cutbacks in every department. The newspaper business has been going downhill for quite a while now, and we're not immune."

Don scowled at the computer on his desk. "It's because of this," he grumbled. "Darn things are taking over. I know the world is changing, but I didn't think I'd live to see the day when newspapers would be all but obsolete."

Mack had been anticipating the possibility of being fired for a while now. His sports column was widely read and sometimes controversial. The publisher didn't always like dealing with the fallout after Mack had called some local athlete or team management on a boneheaded move. He said it was ruining his digestion when he had to face those same people at some benefit or other and defend Mack's words.

Worse, of course, was that Mack was the highest-paid writer in the sports department. By firing him, they could hang on to a couple of low-paid interns and turn them into reporters. As the theory went these days, what they lacked in experience they'd make up for in energy.

"I'm sorry," Don said, looking miserable. "You'll get a decent severance package that should give you some time to look around for something else. Not that someone as good as you are will need them, but I'll give you glowing references and every contact I have in the business."

"But the bottom line is that I'm going to run into the same cutbacks anywhere I go," Mack said realistically.

He'd tried to plan for this. The handwriting had been on the wall for months, but getting the news was still a blow. And none of his ideas for the future so far had excited him.

Still, as Don said, he'd have some time. It wasn't as if he was going to be destitute. He was, however, going to be unemployed. Even though it was through no fault of his own, it left him feeling like a failure. He wondered if this was the way his own father had felt when he'd been jobless. Was that why he'd taken off before Mack was even born?

"How soon?" he asked Don. "Will they keep me on through football season?"

"Nope. End of the week. The publisher thinks keeping people around once they're fired is bad for morale."

Or maybe he was just afraid that if the body count became obvious, the remaining employees would cut and run. That's what a few had done immediately after the last round of cutbacks.

Mack wasn't sure he had the stomach for finishing out the week, much less football season, anyway. "How about I write a couple of columns from home this week?" he suggested. "Wrap things up from there?"

Don looked torn. "You want to just slip away? People are gonna be real unhappy about that. You should at least stick around long enough for the kind of blowout party you deserve down at Callahan's."

"No, thanks," Mack said, shuddering at the thought. Being fired sucked, no matter the reason. He didn't want to wallow in the humiliation in front of his colleagues. He didn't much want to commiserate with them, either.

"Okay, then, whatever works for you," Don agreed with obvious reluctance.

Unfortunately, what worked for Mack was

keeping a job he loved in a business that was disappearing practically overnight.

At home that night, as the news really sank in, along with all of the financial implications for the short term, Mack stared morosely at the black velvet box sitting on his coffee table.

He'd finally decided to take a huge leap of faith and ask Susie O'Brien to marry him, even though she'd always said she'd rather eat dirt than even go out on a date with a promiscuous player like him. He'd figured several years of dating without acknowledging it ought to just about equal officially courting her for a few months.

Maybe she'd overlook the fact that they'd shared only one memorable, bone-melting kiss in all that time. He doubted she'd forgotten it. He certainly hadn't. The heat and sweetness of it were burned into his memory. He'd never anticipated falling in love, much less with a vulnerable bundle of contradictions like Susie, but it had happened. It had caught him completely off guard.

Now, however, with his financial prospects in doubt, proposing was out of the question. He couldn't even think about marrying anyone until he figured out what he was going to do with the rest of his life. And right this second, with a couple of glasses of scotch dulling the pain of his firing, he didn't even want to cross paths with Susie, who'd been telling him for weeks now that he was in a dying profession. Not that he'd ever contradicted her—how could he?—but he wasn't quite ready for an I-told-you-so.

When his phone rang repeatedly that night, he ignored it. When his cell phone rang off and on the next day, he ignored that, too. Messages were accumulating on both lines, but he wasn't interested. Normally an upbeat, positive guy, he was in an unparalleled funk. He figured he was entitled to wallow there for a few days at least.

Unfortunately, his friends Will Lincoln and Jake Collins had other ideas. After one day of not joining them for their regular lunch at Sally's, they were banging on his door. Since each of them had a key for emergencies, Mack wasn't surprised when they barged right in two seconds after knocking. Both of them stopped and stared at the mostly empty bottle of scotch and the box of half-eaten pizza, then took in his disheveled appearance.

"What the devil happened to you?" Will demanded. "You're not answering your phone. You didn't show up for lunch. You didn't call. And, sorry to say, you look like hell."

"Actually you look worse," Jake added, regarding him speculatively. "When was the last time you shaved? I don't think I've ever seen you looking less than immaculate. Did you and Susie have a fight?"

"Susie and I don't fight," Mack said wearily. "This has nothing to do with her."

"Then explain," Will said, sitting down and regarding him patiently.

Mack knew that as a shrink, Will was perfectly capable of sitting there exactly like that for the rest of the evening, waiting him out. "Lost my job," he said eventually. "I'm not taking it well."

Neither of his friends reacted with shock, which proved that they, too, had seen the handwriting on the wall.

"Why would you be expected to take it well?" Jake asked. "Nobody likes being fired. I'm really sorry, man."

Mack sighed at the sympathy. It was

exactly what he'd been hoping to avoid, but now that he couldn't, it felt good knowing that his friends were in his corner.

"I loved that stupid job," he told them mournfully. "I was good at it."

"And you'll find one that's even better," Will said. "Like you said, you're good."

"Newspapers are a dying breed," Mack lamented, taking another sip of scotch. "If I stay in the business, I'll just be prolonging the inevitable."

"Now, that's a cheery attitude," Jake said, this time without a hint of sympathy. Taking his cue from Will, he'd apparently gone into booster mode, as well. "Can I tag along on your first job interview?"

"Bite me," Mack retorted, smiling despite his sour mood.

"You have any more of that scotch?" Will asked.

"Why?"

"If you're going to sit here and get drunk, we're not going to let you do it alone," Will insisted. He found two glasses, then poured the drinks.

Jake took a sip and grimaced. "I hate this stuff. Tastes like medicine. Do you have any beer?"

"Of course," Mack said. "Why do I suddenly feel as if I should be playing host? I'm supposed to be sulking."

"Was the sulking helping?" Will asked.

Mack shrugged. "Not that much."

"Then leave it to us to cheer you up," Will said. "Or would you rather we call Susie? I'm sure she'd be happy to come over if she knew what was going on."

"Absolutely not," Mack said at once. "I don't want her to know about this."

Both men regarded him incredulously.

"That's crazy," Jake said. "You can't keep a secret like this, not in Chesapeake Shores."

"I want to have something new lined up before I see her," Mack insisted. "I will not have her pitying me or hovering over me. Besides, she's been predicting something like this for a long time now and, in her own less than subtle way, trying to get me to plan for it. I'm not up for the gloating."

"Gloating?" Will shook his head. "Do you really think that would be Susie's response?"

"Probably not, but even gloating would be better than pity."

"Has it occurred to you that Susie has a pretty level head on her shoulders? She could help," Jake said. "I think she'd want to."

"No," Mack said flatly.

"How are you planning to avoid her?" Will asked reasonably. "You two have practically been joined at the hip for a very long time. If you check your messages, I'm quite sure you'll find that several of them are from her. I'm sure she's already worried. She's called both Jake and me to see if we know what's going on."

"You could let her know I'm okay," Mack suggested. "Tell her I had to go out of town or something."

Jake immediately shook his head. "I don't think so, pal. The way I hear it, Mick is inviting you to the family Thanksgiving next week. Turn him down at your peril."

"Why?" Mack asked, feeling panicked by the thought of his news coming out amid all those well-meaning O'Briens. "I mean, why me? Why this year? I've never been invited before."

"Bree's theory is that Mick's decided it's time for you and Susie to get off the dime and move this relationship forward," Jake said, obviously quoting his wife. "Bree thought Mick ought to wait for Jeff to do it, but you know how Mick loves trumping his brother on anything. Sadly, you also know what Mick's like when he starts matchmaking. His tactics have as much finesse as a bulldozer."

Mack moaned. "Can I get out of this? Maybe I really will go out of town."

Will chuckled. "Bad idea. I don't see how you can get out of this, at least not without offending Susie, which I don't think you want to do."

"If she knew what was going on, she'd understand," Mack said, a note of desperation in his voice.

"But you don't want to tell her," Jake reminded him. "You're pretty much between a rock and a hard place here."

It was a catch-22, all right. If Mick officially issued that invitation to Thanksgiving dinner, Mack would have to be there. And while everyone else was counting their blessings, he could be praying that his news didn't leak out with a serving of humble pie for dessert.

Or he could bite the bullet, call Susie and fill her in. Maybe she wouldn't hover over him as if there'd been a death in his family. He supposed in some ways losing a job could rank right up there with the loss of someone important, but he didn't need pity or well-meant advice right now. He didn't know what he did need, but it wasn't that.

The third option would be to get out of town tonight so the invitation could never be issued in the first place. That one held the most appeal, but it smacked of cowardice. Mack might be an unemployed member of a dying profession, but he was no coward.

Suddenly Will's gaze landed on the jewelry box sitting on the coffee table. His expression brightened. "Is that what I think it is?"

Jake followed the direction of his gaze. "An engagement ring? You bought an engagement ring? Is it for Susie?"

Mack scowled at the question, "Who else would it be for? I haven't been out with another woman for a long time now."

Jake shrugged. "You could be dating a whole slew of them. People have secret lives that not even their best friends know about. I heard about it on *Oprah*."

Will and Mack both stared at him. "Since

when do you watch daytime television?" Will inquired, his eyes alight with amusement.

"Bree has it on at the flower shop sometimes," Jake responded defensively. "I see it when I make deliveries there. It's not like I race home to watch every afternoon."

Mack grinned. "Good to know."

"Hold it," Will said. "How'd we get away from the real question here? Are you planning to ask Susie to marry you?"

"Not anymore," Mack said, sinking right back into despondency. "How can I? The timing sucks."

"I doubt Susie would agree," Will said. "She's been waiting for a very long time for you to wake up and see the light. I don't think your temporary unemployment would deter her from saying yes."

"It wouldn't be right," Mack insisted. "I need to get my life back in order first." He frowned at his friends. "And if either of you mention a word about this to anyone, I swear you'll live to regret it. Am I clear?"

"Got it," Jake said.

"No one will hear it from me," Will agreed. "Thank you."

"But I am going on record telling you that waiting is a mistake," Will said. "Life's short. Don't waste a minute of it."

"Says the man who took forever to get around to asking Jess O'Brien to go on a date, much less marry him," Jake commented.

"Different situation entirely," Will claimed, then grinned. "But, yeah, I wasted too much time. Don't follow my example. Learn from my experience."

"The timing's all wrong," Mack reiterated. "And I don't want to talk about any of this anymore. What do you guys think about that backup quarterback the Ravens picked up? He's looking good, don't you think?"

Will and Jake exchanged a look, then sighed.

"Real good," Jake agreed.

"I was planning to write a column about him next week . . ." Mack began, but his voice trailed off. He reached for his scotch again. It didn't seem to matter what they talked about. Right this second, his entire life sucked.

"You guys might as well go," he said. "I'm lousy company."

Both men shook their heads.

"Doesn't matter," Jake said. "We stick together."

"Jake's right," Will said. "But if I'm going to drink any more, we'd better think about ordering a pizza. This disgusting day-old glob sitting on the table is starting to look downright tasty to me. And if I don't eat, I'll wind up falling asleep on your floor, and Jess will be on the warpath."

"Ditto with Bree," Jake said.

Mack saw the determination on their faces and sighed. "I'll make the call."

"Extra sausage," Jake said.

"Extra cheese," Will added.

Mack chuckled. "I know you two don't order like that when your wives are around. Last I heard, you were limited to the veggie specials."

"Sadly true," Jake said despondently. "That's why we love you. You don't judge us for our disgusting eating habits."

"Who knew that pizza was the bond that would keep us together for a lifetime," Mack said wryly.

"That, and knowing too many of each other's deep dark secrets," Will added. He held up his glass of scotch. "To friends."

Mack and Jake tapped his glass with

their own. Maybe there was one part of his life that didn't suck, after all. He had some of the best friends around.

That one of them also happened to be the woman he loved was just a bonus. He'd have to think about that after these two went home. Maybe talking to Susie about all this wouldn't be quite the disaster he'd been envisioning.

Then again, a man had his pride.

2

Susie had to admit she was a little freaked-out when she didn't hear from Mack as usual. He'd gotten into the habit of calling on his way back from Baltimore. Most nights they made plans to have dinner together. Sometimes she cooked. More often, they grabbed a bite to eat at one of the cafés along Shore Road, then went for a walk or sat somewhere by the bay and talked. Once in a while they played Scrabble or cards. It always astonished her how competitive Mack could be over a silly game.

As quiet and relaxed as they were, she'd

grown to count on these evenings. Of course, that had probably been a mistake. It wasn't as if they had any kind of commitment, for heaven's sake. It was just dinner and conversation, night after night, for what seemed like forever.

Though she felt thoroughly foolish doing it, she swallowed her pride and walked into Sally's at lunchtime to see if Mack was there with Will and Jake. The three of them had been claiming the same booth ever since Jake and Bree had split up years before. Will and Mack had done it to support their friend during the roughest period of his life. And the tradition had stuck. Only after lunch did Mack occasionally make the drive to Baltimore to put in an actual appearance at the newspaper office.

Since he did his interviews from home or in team locker rooms, then emailed his columns, going into the office was purely to remind people what he looked like, or so he claimed. Since the paper had plastered his face on billboards and bus benches, it seemed unlikely to Susie that there was a person in the region who wouldn't recognize him, but Mack thought it was important to show up in person from time to time.

She thought he enjoyed the interaction with his colleagues and the bustle of the newsroom more than he wanted to admit.

At Sally's, she found Will and Jake in their usual spot, but Mack wasn't with them. His absence alone was enough to give her another disquieting twinge. She slipped into the booth and studied them intently.

"Why do the two of you look hungover?" she asked bluntly. "Now that you're married, I thought your carousing days were behind you."

"Just a late night," Will said with his usual circumspect caution.

"With Mack?" she inquired pointedly. She noted that Jake and Will were a little too careful to avoid each other's gazes. "Okay, what's going on with him? I know you know. Maybe you didn't when I called to ask you, but you do now. I can see it in your faces. Heaven help either of you if you ever decide to play high-stakes poker. You couldn't bluff worth beans."

"Susie, anything I know, assuming I do know something, would be confidential," Will said piously.

Susie rolled her eyes, then turned to

Jake. "And you? Have you taken some oath of confidentiality, as well?"

Jake simply held up his hands. "No comment."

She glowered at the pair of them. "This is ridiculous. I haven't been able to reach him for two days now. It's not like Mack to vanish without a word. Can you at least assure me he's alive?"

"Of course he is," Jake said. "I'm sure he'll give you a call soon." Though he sounded certain, his expression showed unmistakable skepticism.

"Of course he will," Will added. Unfortunately, his upbeat tone sounded forced, as well.

"Has he started seeing someone else?" Susie asked, laying her worst fear right out there. These men might be Mack's friends, but they were hers, too. It wasn't as if they didn't know how she felt about Mack. Maybe asking for reassurance made her sound pitiful, but she needed to know the truth. If it was time to move on, she'd rather hear it from them than from someone else.

"Absolutely not," Will said with satisfying conviction. "Don't let your imagination run away with you, Susie. Mack just needs a little time."

"Time for what?" she wanted to know. It wasn't as if Mack were prone to long periods of introspection. To the contrary, he generally talked everything to death, then moved forward or put it behind him. He wasn't all that complicated, except when it came to figuring out how he felt about her. That seemed to elude him completely.

"Susie, just give him a little space," Jake advised.

She frowned. "Time? Space? From me?"

"No," Will said. "This has nothing to do with you."

"It does if he's shutting me out," she said, then shook her head. Talking to these two was pointless. They'd apparently sworn some oath of silence, which they were unlikely to break no matter how many ways she asked all the questions they'd stirred up. "Never mind. I suppose he'll fill me in whenever it's convenient for him. I guess it was too much to hope that he'd consider me the kind of friend who'd want to support him if he's in some kind of trouble."

She stood up.

Will regarded her with alarm. "Susie,

please, don't get the wrong idea here. You know how Mack feels about you."

She met Will's concerned gaze. "No," she said softly. "Actually, I don't, and that's precisely the problem."

She walked away before either man could see the tears that were building in her eyes. Crying in front of them would be just too darned humiliating to bear.

"They were lying to me," Susie told Shanna after she'd left Sally's and walked to the bookstore down the block for moral support. "Right to my face."

"I don't think they were lying," Shanna said reasonably. "I think they were following Mack's wishes, as misguided as those might be. You put them on the spot, sweetie. What were they supposed to do? Betray their friend?"

"I'm their friend, too."

"Of course you are, but they're guys. There's some kind of loyalty oath they all take when they're, like, eight. We don't stand a chance." She set a cup of coffee, heavily laced with cream and sugar, in front of Susie. "What are you really worried about?"

"That Mack has made a decision finally

to cut me out of his life," she said. "What if he's just working up the courage to tell me?"

"Has there been even the tiniest indication lately that he's tired of spending time with you? Last I heard you were still inseparable, which has caused no end of confusion for the rest of us."

"Not really," Susie admitted. "But come on, Shanna, this can't be normal. We're supposed to be friends. It's the one thing I've been able to count on all this time."

Shanna shook her head. "Now, that's the part that's not normal. How the two of you have gone this long deluding yourselves that you're nothing more than friends is beyond me. It's beyond all of us, for that matter. Sometimes I want to lock the two of you in a room—preferably a bedroom—and leave you there until you figure out what the stupid bed is for."

Susie smiled despite herself. "I'm pretty sure Mack has sufficient experience with beds to know what to do in one. I'm kind of counting on that," she said wistfully.

"And yet how many times have you reiterated to him that all that experience is precisely why you won't date him?"

"I have done this to myself, haven't I?" Susie said despondently. "It started out as a defense mechanism, but Mack took all those protests to heart, and now neither one of us knows how to change the dynamics between us."

"It's pitiful, that's for sure," Shanna said.

"What do I do?"

"You could start by telling him what you really want," Shanna suggested. "I hear that's the mature way to go about these things."

Susie winced. "And risk total humiliation?"

"Or get exactly what you want," Shanna countered.

"I'll think about it," Susie said eventually. "Of course, telling Mack what I want when he's not even answering his phone could prove to be tricky."

"Then go over to his apartment," Shanna suggested.

"Will and Jake said he needs time to deal with whatever is going on."

"They're men. What do they know? At the very least, keep calling until he can't stand listening to your voice on his answering machine and either takes your call or calls you back. This is no time to be faint of heart, Susie. Go after what you want."

"And if I fail?"

Shanna gave her a commiserating look. "Will you really be any worse off than you are now?"

"What if I lose him for good? At least now we're friends."

"I repeat, will you really be any worse off than you are now? No matter how often you say it to me or to yourself, it's obvious that just being his friend isn't cutting it for you anymore." She looked into Susie's eyes. "Or am I wrong about that?"

Susie sighed. "No, you're not wrong. I want more. I want it all, everything you have with Kevin, everything Abby, Jess and Bree have found with the men in their lives. I even grew up with perfect examples all around me, at least when it came to my parents. Even Uncle Mick and Megan finally got it right."

"Okay, then, do whatever it takes to get what the rest of us have. Personally, I don't think there's the slightest risk in hell that Mack is going to reject you. In fact, I think he'll welcome you taking the initiative."

"Maybe," Susie said, though she still had her doubts. Hundreds of them, in fact.

Then again, something had to change. Limbo had been bad enough. She certainly wasn't going to let herself wallow in misery.

"Thanks, Shanna," she said, giving her friend a hug.

"Keep me posted, okay? I'm here anytime you need me. The whole family's on your side, you know." She grinned. "Especially your uncle Mick. In fact, if you need motivation, just remember that resolving this yourself will be a whole lot better than letting Mick work up a full head of steam as a matchmaker."

"I'll definitely keep that in mind," Susie said. As Shanna had said, it was the best possible motivation.

Mack sat in the dark listening to what had to be Susie's twentieth message in the past forty-eight hours. She was starting to sound just a little frantic. Or maybe angry. He couldn't recall ever hearing Susie sound quite so fit to be tied before.

"So help me, Mack Franklin, if you don't surface soon and tell me what's going on,

I'm calling the police and putting out an all-points bulletin on you."

Mack winced. He knew she'd do exactly that. Susie might appear shy and vulnerable, but she had a spine of pure steel and a glint of determination in her eyes that could scare a man half to death. It might take a while for that gutsiness to kick in, but once it did, she was formidable. Normally Mack considered that admirable, but tonight it made him shudder.

She was still ranting when he picked up the phone. "No need to alert the police," he said calmly. "I'm right here."

She breathed an audible sigh of relief. "Well, thank God," she said, then immediately started berating him. "Why haven't you picked up all the other times I've called, or at least called me back?"

"Most women would already know the answer to that question."

"Is this one of those he's-not-into-you things?" she asked, "Because if it is, that is so not the point. I was worried about you."

"No, it's one of those I-don't-want-to-talk-to-anybody things. And I'm sorry if I worried you. Maybe I should have checked in before going into seclusion."

"Yes, you should have," she said fiercely. Then her voice softened. "What's going on, Mack? Talk to me."

He chuckled despite himself. "Did you not hear what I just said?"

"That you don't want to talk to anybody, blah-blah-blah. I'm not anybody, Mack. I'm your friend, just like Will and Jake. I'll bet you've talked to them."

There was a note of hurt in her voice that twisted him up inside. "You are nothing like Will and Jake," he said.

"I see," she said stiffly. "Okay, then. I'm very sorry I bothered you."

She hung up before he could tell her she'd misunderstood. He muttered a curse and called her back. It took ten rings before she finally answered.

"Now *I* don't want to talk," she said heatedly. "You know what that's like." She hung up again.

Mack redialed. "Will you just listen to me for ten seconds?" he said. "Then you can slam the phone down in my ear if you want to."

"It will be my pleasure," she retorted. "Okay, talk."

"I just meant that the relationship you

and I have is different from the one I have with Will and Mack."

"Friends are friends."

"Come on, Susie. You know that's not entirely true. I'm not saying men can't be friends with women, but the dynamics are not the same."

"You're talking about sex," she said bluntly. "Since we've never had sex, then it's exactly the same."

"No," he insisted, a little startled by the fact that she'd even mentioned sex. It wasn't a topic they discussed. Since she'd brought it up, though, he couldn't seem to stop himself from saying, "We always have the potential for sex."

Silence greeted the comment.

"Is that so?" she said at last, amusement now threading through her voice. At least she no longer sounded insulted or furious. If anything, she sounded intrigued. "Just how great do you think that potential is?"

"That's always depended on you," he said before he could stop himself. Going down this road now with his professional life in turmoil was a very bad idea. While starting to think about or even to act on the idea of sleeping with Susie would be a fascinating distraction, that wasn't the way he intended to get through this rough patch. It would be too unfair to her.

Mack realized just how big a mistake he'd made when she sucked in a deep breath and murmured, "Oh, really? It's up to me? I had no idea I had that kind of power over you. I'll have to think about exploring some new possibilities."

"Susie, you don't want to sleep with me," he said, as if the idea were ludicrous.

"Maybe I do," she said, sounding dead serious.

Mack almost swallowed his tongue. "Susie, you don't even want to date me, much less get seriously involved with me. How many times have you told me that?"

"Possibly a few too many," she said candidly.

"Meaning?"

"You're not dense, Mack. It means I might have changed my mind."

"It's the *might have* part that worries me. Men wind up in jail over *maybes* and *might haves.*"

"We could get together and talk about it," she suggested.

"Oh, no," he said at once. "You're obviously having some kind of mental lapse tonight about the kind of man I am. In fact, you're starting to sound downright reckless, which isn't you at all. I don't want to take advantage of that."

She sighed heavily. "I was afraid you'd say that. Are you ever going to try to seduce me, Mack? It's giving me some kind of complex that you'll apparently hook up with every other female on earth except me."

"I do not hook up at all," Mack said indignantly. "At least not recently."

"What's recently?"

The pitiful truth was that he'd lost interest in all other women the minute he and Susie had started hanging out together on a regular basis. She was in his head all the time. In his heart, too. It had taken him a while, but he knew it now. Talk about lousy timing!

"It doesn't matter," he said. "Look, I'm going to let you go. We'll talk about this next time I see you."

"Which will be on Thanksgiving at Uncle Mick's, right?"

He hesitated. "I don't know about that,

Susie. It's probably a bad idea. Besides, Mick hasn't mentioned it to me."

"He will," she predicted. "And you will say yes. Even if he doesn't track you down, I'm asking you now, and again, the correct answer is 'Yes, thank you very much, I'd love to come.'"

To Mack's surprise, she sounded awfully determined. "Why?" he asked.

"Because I haven't had a date for one of these family shindigs since I turned eight and dragged Joe Campbell along. It was his second Thanksgiving dinner of the day and he threw up. After that, nobody ever encouraged me to bring someone."

"Joe Campbell always did have a weak stomach," Mack said. "You had lousy taste in boyfriends back then."

"Did you not hear me say I was eight? What did I know about boys?"

"And now?" he asked, suddenly on edge. Had he missed something? Was Susie interested in someone else? He'd seen no evidence of that, but maybe she was as sick of living a totally celibate life as he was. Maybe Thanksgiving was some kind of test. If he failed, was she ready to cut him out of her life for good? Was that what this whole conversation was about?

"Apparently I'm still on shaky ground when it comes to figuring out men," she said. "Which makes it even more important that the next man I turn up with at a family function is the kind of solid guy my family will approve of. They all like you, and I'm pretty sure you won't throw up before the pumpkin pie."

"Not even after," he promised. He cursed himself for his inability to stick to his guns. There were way too many ways this could go badly. Even so, he said, "Okay, I'll see you there."

"Maybe you should pick me up," she said. "That way you aren't as likely to chicken out."

"And your family will think it really is a date," he speculated. "Is that wise? I gather Mick is already getting ideas about taking our situation in hand."

"He is, which is annoying, but not unexpected. Frankly, though, the non-dating thing really isn't working for me anymore," she said, startling him. "I think it's time for a serious attitude adjustment."

Once again he heard that bold, reckless note in her voice. What on earth had gotten into her? And why, heaven help him, now?

"Susie, maybe we should rethink this," he said urgently. "I might not be around for Thanksgiving, after all. I have some things I need to take care of."

"More important than showing up for dinner with friends?" she asked. "Are these things so important that you're willing to let me down?"

There was a warning note in her voice that caught him off guard. It strengthened his suspicion that this dinner was, indeed, some kind of a test.

"Okay, what's going on here, Susie? You've been saying stuff all night that's not like you. Now you're issuing some kind of subtle warning. What's that about?"

"Maybe I've decided it's past time to shake things up," she said. "Maybe I'm sick of all this dancing around we've been doing for way too long now."

"And you've just had this epiphany this week?"

"Yes," she said flatly. "Just tonight, in fact. Deal with it."

The blunt order was so unlike Susie, he had no idea how to respond to it.

"Have you been drinking?" he asked, because he couldn't come up with any other explanation.

"Have you ever known me to drink more than an occasional glass of wine?"

"No, but there's a first time for everything," he said. "Has somebody been talking to you, putting ideas into your head?"

He envisioned Will having some kind of heart-to-heart with her and getting her all stirred up to take charge of things. It would be just like him, since he knew Mack was having second thoughts about the whole proposal thing.

"Have you seen Will?" he asked suspiciously when she remained silent.

"I saw him earlier today, but he didn't give away any of your closely guarded secrets, if that's what you're worried about. He and Jake are more tight-lipped than some international spy. I'm sure they could give lessons to the CIA."

"Good to know," he said with relief. Of course, that still raised the question of what had gotten into Susie tonight. Maybe he should invite her over and get to the bottom of this.

Then, again, given her reckless, unpredictable mood, that could be dangerous . . . for both of them.

"I'll give you a call before Thanksgiving," he said eventually. "We'll make plans."

"And in the meantime, what?" she demanded. "You're going to be in hiding?"

"Something like that. Like I said earlier, don't worry about me. I'm fine."

"Whatever you say," she said. "But don't even think about standing me up on Thanksgiving. If you try to, I will come over to your apartment and drag you out, if necessary. I will bring my brothers, Will, Jake, whoever I need to, to get you to Uncle Mick's—is that understood?"

Mack laughed. "What's not to understand? I have to say, though, that this bossy side of you could take some getting used to."

"Something tells me you're going to have plenty of opportunities to do just that," she said, her tone unexpectedly sassy.

She hung up before Mack could come up with an adequate reply. Whether it was alcohol or something in the water, this was

definitely Susie as he'd never seen her before. Despite its emergence at the worst
possible time, he couldn't help being fas-
cinated. He'd never before thought of her
as having a devious bone in her body, but
perhaps he'd been wrong. Perhaps intriguing him had been exactly what she'd been
counting on.

On the day before Thanksgiving, Laila
Riley sat in her office at the bank, staring
out the window, her mood dark. The upcoming holiday weekend promised to be
the most depressing ever. Her parents had
decided to take a spur-of-the-moment trip
to London. Her brother would be with Abby
and the twins at the O'Briens, leaving her
to do what? Nothing, as usual.

She glanced up as Jess O'Brien—Jess
Lincoln, she corrected—walked into her
office without being announced.

"Just as I suspected," Jess said. "You're
sitting here in a funk."

"Who says I'm in a funk?" Laila demanded,
sitting up straighter and trying to look more
cheerful. "I have a four-day weekend
stretching out ahead of me. I have all sorts
of plans."

"Oh, really? To do what?"

"You know, the usual Thanksgiving holiday things. I'll eat a little turkey, hit all the holiday sales on Friday and Saturday."

"Let's say I buy that for a single minute," Jess said. "With whom are you having that turkey dinner? Your parents have already left for England, and Abby tells me you turned down their invitation to join us."

"You can't possibly shove another person around that already overcrowded table," Laila said. "Besides, I'm getting tired of the pity invitations."

Jess regarded her indignantly. "Since when has anyone in my family made you feel as if you were being included out of pity? It's a well-known fact that we invite you for your scintillating personality."

Laila knew what her friend was trying to do, and on some level she wanted to say yes. Spending Thanksgiving on her own would be more depressing than any of the other meals she'd eaten alone since she'd sworn off dating after the whole online dating fiasco, when she'd wound up being stalked and harassed.

"Look, I appreciate the invitation, but I'll be okay," she insisted.

"Okay, then, I'll back off," Jess said a little too readily. "On one condition."

Laila regarded her with suspicion. "What condition?"

"You tell me what your other plans are— and they'd better be good. Frozen turkey and dressing heated in the microwave and eaten all alone doesn't count."

Defeated, Laila sighed. "What time is dinner?"

"Three o'clock," Jess said, obviously happy over her victory. "Will and I will pick you up at two so you can help with the preparations. That's part of the fun."

"Says the woman who lets the chef at her inn fix all of her meals."

Jess grinned. "I don't want my husband to starve, do I? Or to die from my cooking?"

"Exactly what does your grandmother let you do to help prepare Thanksgiving dinner?"

"Last year I dished up the stuffing and the cranberry relish and put them on the table," Jess said proudly. "This year I'm pouring the wine that Will picked out from the inn's wine cellar."

Laila laughed. "Well, I have no idea how I'll compete with that, but since the standard's pretty low, I suppose I won't fall flat on my face. There's bound to be some task at which I can excel."

Jess grinned back, but then her expression sobered. "You do know we all love you like family and that you belong with us, right?"

Unexpected tears stung Laila's eyes. "Thanks."

"Don't you dare cry," Jess ordered. "Just be ready on time tomorrow."

"Promptly at two," Laila promised.

Maybe Thanksgiving wouldn't turn out to be half as depressing as she'd envisioned after all. Or else, once again, she'd feel like a fifth wheel among all those exuberantly happy O'Brien couples.

3

Thanksgiving turned out to be one of those perfect fall days in Chesapeake Shores. The sky was a brilliant blue, the air crisp and cool. There were whitecaps on the bay, churning the surface to a froth.

It was, in fact, an ideal day for playing touch football, which almost all of the O'Brien men and the spouses of the women had gathered for on the lawn. Before heading outside, they'd claimed—as usual—that it was the absolute best way to work off the huge meal. The women knew better. It was a way to get out of cleanup. Not that there was room in the kitchen for another person to squeeze in, but it might have been nice if at least one of them had offered, Susie thought as she stood at the kitchen door staring at them.

She had a dish towel in one hand and a Waterford crystal goblet in the other. She'd finished drying the glass long ago, but she couldn't seem to take her eyes off Mack, who was in the thick of the game. Nor could she stop thinking about how well he fit in, as if he were already one of the family. Just the thought created a twinge of longing.

Her grandmother came over to stand beside her. Nell O'Brien was known for her insight and for her good sense. She also spoke her mind.

"He's a good-looking one, isn't he?" she said, her eyes alight with mischief.

"Who?" Susie asked.

Nell gave her a disbelieving look. "Don't play coy with me, young lady. Mack, of course. You haven't been able to keep your eyes off him all day. For what it's worth, he seems to have the same problem."

Susie felt a faint spark of hope. Surely her grandmother wouldn't say what she knew Susie wanted to hear. Surely Nell, if no one else, would tell Susie the unvarnished truth. "Do you really think so, Gram?" she asked, unable to keep the plaintive note from her voice.

Gram gave her a chiding look. "Come now, girl. You know the answer to that as well as I do. I've seen a lot of men fall in love through the years. Mack looks as smitten as any of them. He's looked that way for a long time now," she added pointedly.

"I want to believe that," Susie admitted.

"Then believe it," Gram said briskly. "I'm glad you finally brought him around to join us for dinner. I was beginning to think you were going to let him get away. That would have been a real pity."

"Mack's not really mine to lose."

"Nonsense!" Gram responded with asperity.

"No, it's true. We've been friends a long time," Susie said, a wistful note in her voice. "That's as far as it's gone."

"But you want more," Gram surmised. "You're certain of it?"

Susie nodded. "I really do."

"What's stopping you from reaching for it?"

"Habit," Susie said at once. "And fear. I'm afraid if we try and don't make it, I'll lose my best friend."

"If Mack's friendship is that important to you, you'll find a way to make it work, even if having a more intimate relationship fails," Gram said confidently. "One thing I know for sure—if you truly love this man and don't try to have the relationship you really want with him, you'll regret it for the rest of your life. When you're as old as I am, the one thing you know is that it's too late to make up for the things you didn't do."

Susie hugged her grandmother, felt her frailty that was belied by her strong spirit. "You're very wise."

"I should hope so," Gram said. "After eighty-some years, I hope I've learned a thing or two."

Susie grinned. "Eighty-some? You're finally admitting to being eighty?"

"At some point it was going to be obvious to anyone looking at this wrinkled old face that I couldn't pass for sixty or even seventy anymore. Why not own up to the truth?"

"You're going to be young when you're a hundred and two," Susie predicted.

"If I live that long, I hope it's with my wits about me and the ability to work in my garden. Otherwise, what's the point?" Nell's expression turned wistful. "And I'd like to see Ireland one more time. If that doesn't happen soon, I fear it will be too late."

Something in her tone worried Susie. It was the first time she could recall hearing her grandmother come close to admitting that she didn't have a whole lifetime left to her.

"We'll make it happen," Susie assured her, determined to find a way. If the others knew this was Gram's dream, they'd want to make it come true before it was too late. "I'll see to it."

"Don't you worry about an old woman's daydreams," Gram chided. "Concentrate on making your own come true." She took the glass and towel from Susie's hands. "Now go out there and get into that football game. You could always run as fast as most of the men in this family." She gave Susie's hand a squeeze. "Just be sure you don't run so fast that the right man can't catch you."

* * *

Susie had always been a bit of a tomboy, but Mack hadn't expected her to throw herself into the family's touch football game with such enthusiasm. In fact, he'd been counting on her staying inside with all the other women, while the men blew off steam. He'd needed some distance. Being caught up in an O'Brien celebration had been a little bit like a fantasy for him. It made him yearn for things that right at this moment seemed out of reach.

Okay, it was more than that. His wish for her to remain safely inside might hint at a disgustingly sexist attitude, but it was also a matter of self-preservation. Being around her today had stirred up some totally unexpected responses. It was as if all that talk about sex the other night had taken root in his brain—or in his libido—and the only thing he saw when he looked at her was a desirable woman whose clothes he wanted to strip off.

Now she was out here in the yard in an old pair of snug-fitting jeans she'd apparently borrowed and some kind of soft, touch-me sweater in a shade of red that should have looked ridiculous with her hair, but instead simply looked daring and downright provocative.

Standing just to the left of one of her brothers, a former college quarterback, she had her hands on her hips, a spark of mischief in her eyes and the kind of challenging expression that was giving Mack all sorts of ideas that had nothing to do with football. He almost regretted playing for the opposing team, since playing behind her with a clear view of her delectable backside held a lot of appeal.

Trace suddenly nudged him in the ribs. "Hey, pay attention! You do know that you can't wimp out and go easy on Susie just because she's a girl, right? If they hand the ball off to her, you take her down. You know that's what they're going to do because they think you'll go easy on her. Do not let them get away with it," he commanded.

Mack frowned at him. "I thought we were playing a friendly game of touch football."

"We were until ten minutes ago, when Susie joined their team. They're out to win. So are we." Trace looked him squarely in the eye. "Do I need to move Will into your position?"

"Will hasn't made a tackle since grade school," Mack scoffed. "Who are you kidding?"

"Hey!" Will protested. "The game isn't always about brute force. Sometimes it's about finesse."

"Tell that to the National Football League," Mack said. "I'm sure the commissioner will be interested in your point of view."

Jake joined the huddle. "Are we going to play or not? We can't let their bringing in a girl psyche us out. Susie's been playing in these games for years. She can take care of herself."

He paused and glanced at Trace. "How about your sister? Maybe Laila would want to play. She's tall and it would even things up. It would freak Matthew, Luke and Kevin out if the shoe were on the other foot and we had a woman playing for us."

Trace frowned. "I am not letting my sister get pummeled by that team. Laila was never the tomboy that Susie was."

"Hey, it was just a thought," Jake said defensively. "You don't have to go all macho and protective on us." He turned back to Mack. "Okay, then, you can't let Susie get past you. The woman runs like the wind. Remember high school? She blew away every other sprinter in the region when she competed in track."

Mack frowned at the whole lot of them. "Oh, for heaven's sake, which one of us made all-American all through high school? No girl is going to get the better of me."

"Not even Susie?" Trace asked doubtfully.

Mack gritted his teeth. "No, not even Susie."

"Okay, then," Trace said as their players fell into position.

"About time," Susie's brother Matthew taunted. "I was starting to think I had enough time to go back inside for more pie."

He called a play, the ball was snapped and, sure enough, it was handed off to Susie, who made a remarkable move to her right to avoid Jake's tackle. Mack streaked after her, picked her up off her feet and fell to the ground, cushioning the fall with his own body. Her expression startled, Susie stared into his eyes.

"You tackled me," she said with an indignant huff.

"Just following directions," he said. "You okay?"

She scrambled up. "Of course I'm okay, but this is touch football, you idiot."

Mack stared at her. "I was told the rules had changed."

She stepped closer until she was toe-to-toe with him. "Is that so?"

"Swear to God."

She looked around at the other players, then nodded. "Okay, then. You won't catch me off guard again, Mack Franklin, I promise you that."

She stomped back across the yard to join her own team. Mack got the distinct impression he'd stirred up her temper in ways he couldn't possibly envision.

Fortunately, the last play had been fourth down and his team had the ball back. He took the hike from center and started to run, only to have 110 pounds of fury cut him off at the knees. This time when he hit the ground, Susie rolled with him. She jumped up before he could catch his breath.

"Okay, now we're even," she said. "I feel better. How about you?"

He stared at her incredulously. "You're a little crazy. You know that, don't you?"

She grinned. "I've spent a lot of time being one of the guys. Don't sell me short, Mack. I have moves you can't possibly imagine," she boasted, then grinned. "On and off the field."

Suddenly heat flared in Mack's belly. All of the moves he envisioned were in a bedroom, not in the middle of a yard with her entire family surrounding them. He reached out, snagged her hand and pulled her into his arms, then leaned down to whisper in her ear.

"Do not taunt me, Susie. You'll be asking for trouble."

Amusement lit her eyes as she stared right back at him. "You don't scare me. You're all talk. I have years of experience to testify to that."

"I beg your pardon?"

"*All* talk," she taunted again.

It was Matthew who walked over, gave his sister an odd look, then broke up the standoff. "Hey, guys, we're playing football."

Susie blinked and looked away, her cheeks flushed. Mack dropped his hold on her and walked back to his own team, not sure if he was more disconcerted by her taunt or infuriated by it.

Will and Jake were grinning. "This O'Brien holiday tradition has just gotten interesting," Jake commented. "You might want to keep in mind, though, that Jeff and Mick are sitting right up there on the porch watching. I'm not sure how thrilled they're likely to be if you decide to seduce Susie right here and now. I know Mick, especially, talks a good game, but at heart, they're pretty old-fashioned guys."

"Seducing Susie never crossed my mind," Mack said with grim determination. Making her take back her words, now, that was something entirely different.

Jake rolled his eyes. "Just like I didn't pine away for Bree all those years she was off in Chicago writing plays."

Mack just stared him down.

Across the yard he overheard Susie's brother Luke arguing heatedly with Matthew.

"You've got to stop giving her the ball," he told Matthew. "She's not exactly a secret weapon right now."

Susie marched right up to her brothers. "I am in this game to win it," she declared fiercely. "Give me the ball."

Mack had to hide a grin at the family squabble. He could hardly wait to see how it turned out. His money was on Susie. She was determined to run the ball past him and score. That grit was another aspect of her never-say-die spirit that he enjoyed. At least until today, when she seemed determined to use it to drive him wild.

On their next two plays after they got the ball back, Matthew tried passing downfield to Kevin, but Connor broke up the plays. On the next play Susie took a handoff and tried sprinting around Mack's blind side. He caught her by the waistband of her pants and tumbled to the ground with her.

"You are so annoying," she grumbled, but she didn't scramble away from him quite as quickly this time. In fact, as she looked into his eyes, she suddenly seemed a little out of breath. He didn't think it could be blamed entirely on her run or their fall.

Mack reached over to brush a streak of dirt from her cheek. To his astonishment, his fingers trembled as he touched her skin.

His own breath hitched.

"Susie," he murmured softly.

She couldn't seem to tear her gaze away,

either. "Uh-huh," she said in a distracted whisper.

"We should stop this before you get hurt."

She blinked for a second, then punched him in the ribs. "Me? What about you? Or Will, or any of the others?"

Mack held her in place, his gaze never leaving her face. "You're the only one I'm worried about."

"Just because I'm a girl," she said, as if it were a curse.

"Just because you're the girl I care about," he said. He hesitated, scant inches from her mouth. He could kiss her right here and now. He wanted to. One look into her blazing eyes told him that was what she wanted, too.

"Mack?" she said, a questioning note in her voice. "What's going on here?"

"I wish I knew," he said with frustration.

Before he could do something they'd both regret, he scrambled to his feet and held out his hand. "Let's go for a walk."

"Now?" she said, regarding him incredulously. "You want to go for a walk now, in the middle of the traditional football game?"

"I do."

She looked around at the speculative

looks on the faces of the men in her family, then nodded slowly. "Okay."

Grateful that she wasn't going to give him an argument, Mack tossed the football back to Trace. "Count us out. We're going for a walk on the beach."

"In the middle of the game?" Matthew demanded, staring at his sister as if she'd betrayed him.

"Seems like as good a time as any to me," she said.

Matthew turned to his brother. "Do you have any idea what is going on with her?"

Luke laughed. "Oh, yeah, and if you ask me, it's about time."

All the way across the endless expanse of Uncle Mick's lawn and down the steps to the beach, Susie clung to Mack's hand and cast sideways glances at his unexpectedly grim expression.

"Was there something you wanted to talk about?" she asked eventually, when the silence had gone on way too long.

"Not really," he said. The soft sand made walking difficult, but he was eating up the distance as if he had some destination in mind.

"Are we going someplace specific?" she asked, glad for her track experience and long legs. She had no problem keeping up with him, even though she would have preferred a leisurely, romantic stroll.

"Nope."

"Are we on a deadline?"

He scowled. "Of course not."

"Then could we slow down? I know I ran track in high school, but I stopped competing years ago."

He glanced at her. "Sorry," he said, slowing his gait.

"Mack, if you don't mind me saying so, you don't seem happy about going on this walk. Why did you suggest it?"

"Because I didn't like what was happening back there."

She studied him in confusion. "Me getting tackled?"

He shook his head. "I knew I wasn't going to hurt you."

"Then what?"

He heaved a sigh, stopped and met her gaze. "I came within a heartbeat of kissing you."

She blinked at the shock in his voice.

"Would that have been so terrible? Do you think the world would have come to an end or something?"

"I can't just start kissing you because I feel like it," he said angrily. "Not after all this time."

"Maybe you should leave that decision up to me. Maybe I want you to kiss me. Maybe I think we've been waiting way too long to start kissing like crazy."

"No way," he said adamantly. "Not now."

"Why?"

"Because the timing's all wrong."

"Because we had an audience?"

"Don't be ridiculous. What makes you think I've ever cared what anyone else thinks?"

"Okay, then, if it's not because you were afraid that Will, Jake, my brothers and all the rest of them would give you a rough time, what was going on?"

"I told you the timing was bad," he practically growled. "Now leave it alone."

"No," she said fiercely. If he'd wanted, even for a second, to change things finally—and hallelujah for that—and she wanted to change their relationship, why shouldn't they? They were both consenting adults, for heaven's sakes. "I'm half of this equation, and I get to have a say in what happens, too."

"Not now," he insisted grimly.

"Are you worried because my dad and Uncle Mick were there? Do you not want the pressure of getting those two all worked up, because believe me, I get that."

"It's not that," he insisted.

"Then enlighten me, because I am totally confused."

"You just have to take my word for it that this isn't a good time for us to be thinking about getting any more involved than we already are."

"I'm sorry," she said, stopping and looking directly into his eyes. "But I happen to think it's way past time, so if there's something I'm missing, you need to fill me in."

"No," he said. "Once I've worked everything out, we'll talk. Until then, you just have to give me some space, Susie. I mean it. It's the only thing that'll work right now."

She scowled at his edict. He'd obviously made yet another arbitrary decision and was expecting her to go along with it without argument. Well, not this time.

"You want space?" she said heatedly. "You've got it. But don't count on me being at home waiting when you've worked everything out to your satisfaction. That's not how it works, Mack. Either we're friends or we're not. Either we're something more or we're not. Whatever you want to call what we have, we both need to be all in. Otherwise, what's the point?"

He regarded her miserably. "Susie, please don't pick now to start issuing ultimatums."

"Why not? Isn't that exactly what you just did? Give me space, or else, Susie. That pretty much sums it up, doesn't it?"

"Okay, yes. If you can't accept that I know what's best, then I won't have any choice but to walk away."

Fighting tears, she simply nodded. "Your decision," she said quietly.

But despite his words, she was the one to turn and walk away. At least she was able to cling to her dignity, if only by a thread, by not letting him see her tears start to fall.

Back at the house, Susie managed to slip around to the parking area without anyone noticing her. Fortunately she'd driven earlier, and her car keys were tucked in her pocket. Mack could get home under his own steam. It would serve him right, though, if every one of the O'Briens declined to give him a ride.

She was about to pull out of the driveway when Shanna tapped on the window, a worried expression on her face.

"Why are you leaving without even saying goodbye?" she asked. "Did you and Mack have a fight? Everybody inside has been speculating about what's going on ever since the two of you took off together. Add in the fact that Laila and Matthew got into some kind of argument and she left in a huff, and it's turning into an interesting day."

Momentarily distracted by that bit of news, Susie said, "Laila and Matthew argued? What on earth would they argue about?"

"I have no idea," Shanna admitted. "But it caused quite a stir when she left. Now you're doing the same thing. Curiosity is at a fever pitch."

"Then is it any wonder I don't want to come inside?" Susie asked wryly. "I'm not in the mood for talking right now."

Shanna studied her face, clearly saw the dampness on her cheeks and sighed. "Then you did have a fight," she said with real regret. "I'm so sorry."

"Not really," Susie replied wearily. "Mack doesn't fight. He just makes decisions and expects me to abide by them with absolutely no explanation at all. I'm sick of it. If he has all these secrets he suddenly doesn't want to share with me, that's his right, I suppose, but it makes me feel like an irrelevant outsider."

"Oh, sweetie, I'm sure that was never his intention. He's just the kind of guy who's used to relying on himself. Isn't that what he's had to do for years now?"

It was true, Susie was forced to admit. Mack's family had been a far cry from the O'Briens. He didn't even know who his father was, and from an early age he'd been more of a grown-up than his irresponsible mother. As his confidante through a troubled adolescence, she knew better than anyone how tough it had been on him to maintain a facade of good cheer when his home life was a shambles.

College would never have been an option if it hadn't been for an athletic scholarship.

He'd taken any odd job available to pay for extras, and he'd worked as an unpaid stringer for the Baltimore paper just to prove himself. His work ethic as much as his knowledge of sports and his writing ability had earned him his coveted column.

"You're right," Susie reluctantly admitted to Shanna. "I know Mack isn't used to leaning on anyone, not even Will and Jake. I guess I just hoped I was different, that he trusted me enough to let me help. He used to."

"Maybe that was before you were the problem," Shanna suggested gently. "Besides, what did you do the second he trusted you enough to say he needed time? Instead of taking him at his word and giving him time, you got in a snit and bolted on him."

"I'm not in a snit," Susie said, not liking the characterization.

"Really?"

She sighed. "Okay, maybe a little bit of a snit." She regarded Shanna plaintively. "You're not saying I have to go over to his place and wait for him and apologize, are you? I don't think I could do that right now."

Shanna laughed. "Heavens, no! That

would definitely be asking too much. I'm just saying that when he does come to you, and he will, you should keep an open mind. Really listen when he decides to talk."

"I've always listened." She regarded her friend curiously. "I don't suppose you have any idea what's going on, do you? Has Kevin said anything?"

"Not a word, but he's the last to know anything. He's so wrapped up with his work with the foundation and their attempts to protect the bay, he has no idea what's going on with me and the kids, much less the rest of the family or this town. Trust me, when I do manage to snag his attention, local gossip is not on my mind or his. We're trying to make a baby."

Susie finally had a reason to smile. "Really?"

Shanna nodded, though she didn't look especially happy. "Sadly, accomplishing that requires two people to be in the same room, preferably in the same bed, and awake. It's not as easy as you'd think."

"It will work out," Susie assured her. "You two are such wonderful parents for Henry and Davy. Any child you have together will be totally blessed."

"Thanks. Now, as for you and Mack, be patient, Susie. I know things will work out with the two of you the same way you know Kevin and I will find a way to make that baby. It's just destined to happen."

"Patience isn't my best trait, but I suppose it won't kill me to give it a try," Susie replied.

"Mack's worth it, don't you think?"

"I've been waiting all these years, so I must believe that," Susie said.

But after a thoroughly frustrating day like today, it was really, really hard to remember why.

4

Jeff O'Brien felt as if he'd always lived in the shadow of his older brother. Mick was like a force of nature, the kind of man who was confident in his own skin, a talented architect with amazing vision. Though Jeff had worked with him on the development of Chesapeake Shores, he'd merely overseen the construction details and ultimately the sales. The town had been built according to Mick's specifications and modified to fit with Thomas's ideas on doing the least harm to the bay. They were the visionaries behind it.

The three O'Brien brothers had butted

heads repeatedly. Mick won most arguments through an absolute sense of self-confidence that couldn't be shaken by law or reason. The only time he'd been trumped was when Thomas had used legal means to ensure that Mick adhered to the strictest interpretation of environmental regulations. Mick had never entirely forgiven him, or Jeff for siding with him. He'd labeled Thomas a traitor and told Jeff he had no backbone. Jeff hadn't bothered trying to contradict him, which had only further infuriated Mick.

Things were easier among the three of them now that they'd wisely decided against working together. Ma insisted that some level of family obligation bring them together on Sundays and holidays and, over time, they'd managed to handle the occasions with a certain amount of grace and goodwill.

Still, Jeff couldn't deny that it grated when he'd heard about Mick threatening to interfere in Susie's relationship with Mack Franklin. Now that Mick's own children were all happily married, apparently he'd decided to take on Jeff's.

Personally Jeff had never understood the need to meddle in someone else's life. He and Jo had raised Susie with good values and good sense. Whatever was going on between her and Mack, he trusted her to get what she wanted out of it. Susie had never been some shy little wallflower. She was every bit as stubborn and determined as anyone else in the family.

At least, he'd felt that way until he'd seen her with Mack on Thanksgiving, recognized the sparks flying during that traditional family football game, and then seen his daughter come back from a walk with Mack with tears on her cheeks. For the first time, he'd wanted to throttle a man for making his little girl cry. He'd told Jo about it that night.

"She has a good head on her shoulders," Jo insisted. "And she's loved Mack as far back as I can remember. All we can do is be there for her if things don't work out the way she wants them to."

"I suppose," he'd said. "Are you sure I can't sit him down and knock some sense into him?"

She laughed. "You could, but then you'd be just like Mick. Is that what you want?"

The suggestion had been enough to keep him away from Mack. For now.

He glanced at the list Susie had given him of things he needed to do on Saturday morning. Bringing her into the real estate management company had been the smartest thing he'd ever done. She could organize an army battalion without batting an eye. He could easily see her with a houseful of kids underfoot, handling the chaos with total competence and ease. A part of him longed for the time when she'd do just that. Watching his older brother with his grandkids had made Jeff just a little envious.

"Are you heading over to Shanna's now, Dad?" Susie called out to him. "I told her you'd be there first thing to check on that plumbing. Dwight's good, but we don't want to take any chances that he missed something."

"On my way," he assured her, then paused after taking a closer look at her pale complexion. "You okay?"

She looked startled by the question. "Of course. Why wouldn't I be?"

"You don't look so hot, and you took off pretty suddenly on Thanksgiving."

"I . . . I didn't feel well," she said, then hurriedly added, "Then. I didn't feel well *then.* I'm perfectly fine now."

"Something you ate? I haven't heard about anyone else feeling ill."

"Maybe nobody else got thrown on the ground as many times as I did right after dinner," she retorted with a faint grin.

Jeff recognized the perfect opening. "About that," he began.

"Dad, leave it alone," she said tersely, her expression forbidding.

"You sure? If you ever want to talk, your mother and I, we're always on your side. You do know that, don't you?"

She managed to pull off a reassuring smile that Jeff didn't entirely buy. "Of course I know that," she promised. "Now, get started. It's going to take you all day to get through that list I gave you, and Mitzi Gaylord is coming in at five to sign the contract for the Brighton house."

"On my way," he said, still oddly reluctant to leave his daughter.

A few minutes later, though, he was in the bookstore when he overheard someone make a comment about Mack's column not being in the paper. He realized he'd noticed the same thing this morning at breakfast, but hadn't seen any reason to be alarmed by it.

"Well, I heard he was fired," one of the women said. "That's why he's been hiding out the past few days. Who can blame him? His whole identity was wrapped up in that job. I think he was convinced it was his ticket to respectability—not that he needed one as far as I'm concerned. Still, after all he went through as a boy, this had to be a blow."

"Fired? Are you sure?" a second woman asked. "The paper's been making a big fuss about him for a long time now. Have you been up to Baltimore? Everywhere you look, his picture's right there. It's even on the sides of buses. He's like some kind of sports columnist superstar."

Jeff stepped out of the back room and looked around to identify the speakers. One of them was Ethel, whose nearby shop specialized in souvenirs and local gossip. He glanced around and caught Shanna's eye, then beckoned her to the back.

"Did you hear them?" he asked.

She nodded. "But I have no idea if what

they're saying is true. I only know Mack's been really upset. He wouldn't tell Susie why. That's why they fought on Thanksgiving."

Jeff nodded, absorbing that news. "I see."

"Please don't tell her I told you about the fight," Shanna pleaded. "She'd hate having you worry about her."

"Yeah, Susie never wants anyone to worry," he said. "Thanks, though, Shanna."

After he'd finished checking to make sure the plumbing had been fixed, he was about to leave when he saw Will browsing through the nonfiction section. Jeff confronted him. If anyone would know what was going on, Will would.

"Have you got a minute?" he asked Will.

"Sure. What's up?"

"Outside," Jeff commanded, not wanting Ethel to overhear anything she could pass along to her customers.

When he and Will had walked to one of the benches along the bay and sat down, Jeff asked, "Has Mack been fired from his job? That's the talk going around town this morning."

Will's uncomfortable expression was answer enough. Jeff sighed. "Then it's true?"

Will nodded. "It happened the week be-fore Thanksgiving. It's really rocked him."

"I can imagine," Jeff said, feeling a cer-tain amount of pity for him. Like everyone else in town, he know how much the job had meant to Mack. It had been his dream, and as Ethel had noted, it had given him the respect he'd always craved. Of anyone Jeff knew, no one had been more deserv-ing of finding a little happiness.

"Has he told Susie?" he asked. "She hasn't mentioned it to us."

Will frowned. "I don't think she knows. Can you leave it alone, Jeff? She should hear it from Mack."

"I don't know. Seems to me it's some-thing she deserves to know before ev-eryone else in town starts blabbing about it. From what I overheard back at the book-store, it won't take long for the word to get back to her. Ethel has a pipeline that those TV tabloids would envy."

"I agree with you. I'll see if I can get Mack to talk to her today, but frankly, he hasn't wanted to discuss it with anyone. Jake and I found out only after going over to his apartment and confronting him."

"Tell him to do it today," Jeff said. "Or I'll see to it she finds out tomorrow."

Will nodded. "Fair enough. I'll do my best, but Mack's not exactly listening to reason right now."

"While Mack has my sympathy, he's not the one I'm worried about," Jeff said grimly.

And whatever it took, he was going to try to make sure Susie wasn't the one who wound up getting hurt because Mack didn't have the guts to own up to what was going on in his life. There was no shame in losing a job. But there was something wrong with not sharing that news with someone who supposedly mattered.

Susie had been living on her own in a small apartment above the shops on Main Street ever since she'd graduated from college and gone to work for her father. It was convenient to her job, which was just downstairs, and in the heart of downtown Chesapeake Shores, which was lively in the summer and quiet this time of year.

Though the apartment wasn't spacious— just an open kitchen, living room and dining room area, plus a single bedroom and bath—it suited her, or at least it had until it filled up with her parents and her brothers, as it did on the Sunday after Thanksgiving.

It wasn't as if she'd been expecting them. They'd all turned up uninvited, armed with coffee and croissants from Sally's, apparently staging some sort of intervention. She was still trying to get a fix on what had them in such an uproar.

"Okay, slow down," she finally shouted, hoping to be heard over the commotion. "I can't even think, much less understand a word any of you are saying."

Thankfully, they all shut up and looked to her mother. Josephine O'Brien had been a high school and college athlete who, as a physical education teacher, had encouraged Susie's love of sports and who'd coached her on the high school track team. She'd been the perfect mother for two energetic, athletic boys, and an even better one for a tomboy daughter. When she had something to say, they all listened.

"We're worried about this ongoing infatuation you seem to have with Mack Franklin," her mother began. "Especially right now."

Susie frowned. "Why especially now?"

Rather than giving her a direct answer, Matthew said, "We all like the guy, but he has a lousy history with women, Suze. You know that."

"Yeah, we thought that's why you'd refused to date him," Luke chimed in. "We all thought you'd made a smart decision."

"Okay," Susie said slowly. "All this is old news. Mack and I have been friends for a long time now. You've never objected to that. And I still don't know what Mom meant when she said something about it being a bad time for our relationship to change." She gave them a defiant look. "Not that I'm admitting it has."

Her brothers exchanged a look as if deciding who should respond to that point.

It was Matthew who stepped in. "You let him tackle you on Thanksgiving," he said as if it were a crime. "More than once."

Susie frowned. "I didn't exactly do it by choice."

"But you didn't even try to get away from him," Luke countered. "No one has ever tackled you before. So, what? Did you want to roll around on the ground with him? That's how it looked."

Susie's temper stirred. "Are you mad

because I didn't fight Mack off or because I didn't score a touchdown? Since when is it all up to me to win a stupid family football game?"

"Well, we do count on you," Matthew admitted. "None of us like losing."

Luke scowled at him. "So not the point. Susie, you looked like you wanted to kiss him, right there in front of everybody."

"If I hadn't come over to help you up, I think you would have," Matthew added. "Are you crazy? This has gone too far, Susie. Or it's about to. That's why we're here, to stop you from doing something you'll regret."

"And you think I'd regret kissing Mack?" she inquired, her voice like ice. "Or is it sleeping with him that really worries you? Maybe falling in love with him? Well, I have news for you—it's too late." She avoided looking at either of her parents when she said it. She didn't want to see any sign of shock on either of their faces, but she had to put a stop to this nonsense.

Matthew regarded her with alarm. "You've already slept with him? I'll kill him. I swear I will. He should not be taking advantage of you. We've all told him that."

Susie froze. "Excuse me? Who's warned Mack to stay away from me?"

"We all have," Matthew said. "Well, me and Luke, anyway. I think maybe Kevin and Connor have said something, too."

Susie couldn't believe what she was hearing. "How dare you interfere in my life like that! If and when Mack and I decide we want to sleep together, believe me, it will be none of your business."

"Then you haven't slept with him already?" Matthew asked, sounding relieved.

She groaned at his persistence. "No, I have not slept with him, though I would have if I'd had the opportunity."

"Then what?" Luke asked suspiciously. "You said it was too late. So, have you kissed him? I guess that's not so bad. People kiss all the time and it doesn't mean anything."

"This is so not about kissing," Susie declared. "It's about all of you meddling in my business. Who I kiss or sleep with is none of your business. Haven't any of you noticed that I'm in my late twenties? In most worlds that's considered old enough to make my own decisions." She turned

toward her mother, who gave her a commiserating look.

"We're just concerned, dear. None of us
want to see you get hurt," Jo O'Brien said
gently.

Susie didn't buy the sudden onset of
parental or sibling concern. "Oh, come on,
this thing between Mack and me, if there is
anything, has been coming on for a long
time. If you all were so dead set against
it, why didn't you speak up sooner?" she
demanded, then waved off the question.
"That's irrelevant. I'm a grown woman. I get
to choose my own dates."

She looked to her father for support. Unlike her uncle Mick, her dad wasn't known
for meddling in his children's business.
They'd grown especially close since they'd
been working together. He trusted her
judgment. She knew he did. "Dad, you've
been awfully quiet. Do you have an opinion about this? If you do, I'd like to hear it."

He regarded her with an uncomfortable
expression. "You have a good head on
your shoulders," he began. At a nudge
from his wife, he faltered. "That said, this
might not be the best time to consider get-

ting closer to Mack. Circumstances have changed."

Her gaze narrowed at his careful choice of words. The comment suggested he knew more than she did, perhaps even the very thing that Mack had so determinedly been keeping from her.

"Why not now?" she asked, keeping her gaze steady on her father. "What circumstances have changed? Has he run off and married someone else?"

Though she asked her father, it was her mother who responded. "He's unemployed," she said bluntly, startling Susie.

"He is?" she said before she could stop herself.

"There you go," Matthew said triumphantly. "He didn't tell you, did he? What kind of man keeps that kind of thing a secret from someone he cares about? It's pretty significant news, don't you think? It's the kind of news friends share with each other."

Susie couldn't deny that. It explained a lot, in fact, especially the dark funk of a few days ago, the repeated comments about the timing for starting up a real relationship being all wrong.

She wasn't sure exactly what she was feeling—anger at Mack keeping such a huge secret or pity over him losing something that mattered so much to him—but she did know this wasn't where she needed to be. She stood up, grabbed her coat and her purse, then turned to her family.

"Sorry. I need to go."

"You're leaving?" Luke asked incredulously. "Nothing's decided."

"Believe me, I've heard everything I need to hear. Lock up when you leave." She brushed a kiss across her mother's cheek, then another on her dad's. "Love you."

Though they both looked worried, they didn't try to stop her.

All the way across town to Mack's, she stewed about being blindsided by news this monumental. She was torn between wanting to kill him for keeping her in the dark and wanting to hug him to take away the pain he must be feeling. No matter what, though, he should have told her. Her family was right about that.

Of course, she could guess exactly why he hadn't: pride. Mack had a boatload of it. But friendship should have trumped pride. She would have helped or just listened, whatever he wanted.

Halfway to Mack's, it sank in that maybe he simply hadn't trusted her with the news, that he didn't even think she had a right to know. It was also possible that he'd been embarrassed to tell her, especially after all the conversations they'd had about newspapers being a dying breed. He might have worried she'd gloat, instead of offering a shoulder to lean on.

Or maybe Matthew had been right for once in his mostly insensitive life. Maybe she didn't really count as a true friend with Mack after all, not enough to be his sounding board in a crisis this big.

She pulled to the side of the road as she considered that possibility, then pounded a fist on the steering wheel in frustration.

A friend wouldn't care about his reasons. A friend would charge right in and offer support. The woman who didn't quite know her own place, however, hesitated.

And then, filled with too many questions and no answers, she turned around and drove back home, relieved to find that her family had gone. She'd have all the privacy in the world to wrestle with what she should be doing next . . . or with accepting the fact that she wasn't the one who could do anything at all.

"You know the word is out about the newspaper letting you go," Will said to Mack at lunch on the Monday after Thanksgiving. "Have you said anything to Susie?"

Mack grimaced. "No. How'd the word get around this fast, anyway? It's not as if it was worthy of a big announcement on *Entertainment Tonight.*"

Will simply stared at him. "You really don't get it, do you? We've always thought you had this rock-solid ego, but you have no idea how people talked about your columns, especially in this town. Everyone here has always been so proud of you, especially those of us who know what you overcame to get there."

"You're exaggerating," Mack said.

Will shook his head. "I'm not, am I, Jake?"

"Absolutely not," Jake agreed. "Which is why people noticed that you didn't have a column about the Ravens in Saturday's paper. Somebody else did. And somebody else also wrote about yesterday's game.

People have drawn their own conclusions. Speculation was running wild by the time I stopped by here for coffee this morning."

"I hate to tell you, but the news gets worse," Will told him, his tone dire. "On Saturday I stopped by the bookstore to pick up a book and ran into Susie's dad. Jeff was there checking on some plumbing repair, I guess. Anyway, he cornered me and asked point-blank if I knew what was going on. Said he'd heard some talk about you losing your job. What was I supposed to do, lie?"

Mack sighed. "No, but you could have warned me on Saturday."

"Don't you think I tried? I called your apartment and your cell phone. Not only didn't you answer, but I couldn't leave a message because both voice mailboxes were full."

"You should have come looking for me," Mack said, knowing that the real fault wasn't Will's, but needing to blame someone. "Maybe there would have been time for me to get to Susie. I'm sure by now her dad's filled her in."

"No question about it," Will said. "He told me he intended to do it if you didn't. He was pretty insistent about that."

"Call her now," Jake said. "Better yet, stop by the management office. She's probably there. You should tell her something like this face-to-face."

"I'm not sure I'd be able to take it if she starts pitying me or saying I told you so," Mack said, though he wasn't sure that was his real concern. He was more worried that she'd lose faith in him, walk away before they ever got the chance he wanted for the two of them.

"Why would she say I told you so?" Will asked. "The woman's crazy about you."

"I told you a while back that she's been warning me that I ought to be planning ahead," Mack said. "I guess she's read all the stories about newspaper cutbacks."

"Well, I seriously doubt she's going to throw that in your face," Will said. "Susie's not that kind of woman."

Mack thought about the way their discussion had veered off on a tangent about sex the week before, about the way she'd looked into his eyes when he'd tackled her on Thanksgiving, holding his gaze until it had required every last ounce of willpower he possessed to keep from kissing her.

Then he thought about the fight they'd

had on the beach when she realized he was keeping something from her. Now that she knew what it was, she was likely to be even more furious. He could even understand her point of view. He'd be livid—and hurt—if she kept a secret this huge from him.

"I'm not sure I know what kind of woman she is lately," he said despondently. "She seems to be changing."

"Well, she's not mean," Jake said. "We all know that. Talk to her, Mack, before this becomes some huge issue between you. If it gets blown all out of proportion, you'll both wind up being miserable. Fix it now. That's my advice." He turned a sheepish look on Will. "Not that I'm the expert."

"Couldn't have said it better myself," Will said. "Go. Fix."

Mack sighed when they left him on the street, just a few paces away from the Chesapeake Shores Real Estate Management Company. He had a hunch both of his friends were sitting in their respective vehicles watching to see if he took their advice or chickened out.

Since he'd been humiliated enough lately, he sucked in a bracing breath and walked into the office, wishing he had even the first clue about what to expect or what to say to her. Susie might have a cheery, live-and-let-live demeanor most of the time, but facing her right now was no less intimidating than walking into a lion's den. Something told him that whatever happened in the next few minutes would decide his future . . . and whether or not Susie was likely to be a part of it.

5

At the sound of the door opening, Susie glanced up from the contract she'd been reading for the past hour without one single word registering. An automatic smile had her lips curving up until she recognized Mack.

"Oh, it's you," she said, her tone flat. To her chagrin, her pulse skipped several beats despite her mood. Apparently chemistry was slow to catch on to reality. Thankfully, Mack couldn't possibly know all the conficting emotions churning inside her.

Mack winced. "I gather you've heard the news."

"From my family," she confirmed accusingly. "Why would you let me find out something that monumental from my family, Mack? How could you do that to me? You had to know how humiliating it would be."

"Sorry," he said, looking genuinely contrite. "Really. The honest-to-goodness truth is that I just couldn't work up the nerve to tell you. I've dealt with my share of humiliation since this happened."

On some level she understood his reluctance, the blow to his pride, but she couldn't let it pass. Communication was the one thing they'd always had going for them. If they lost that now, she was afraid they were doomed.

"Mack, we keep saying we're friends, but it doesn't seem like it to me right now. If you can't even tell me that you lost your job, then what kind of friendship do we really have? Is it some superficial thing that's good for a few laughs? Am I just some woman you hang out with to keep from being bored?"

His expression pleaded for understanding. "Susie, this isn't about you and me, what we are or aren't to each other. I'm the one who lost a job that meant everything to me. Don't try to make it about something else. I can't fight that battle right now."

"I'm sorry," she said. "I have to. This is like some huge turning point for us on so many levels. Can't you see that?"

He sat down on the chair beside her desk. Though he obviously still didn't want to have this conversation, he settled in, apparently ready to have the talk they should have had days ago.

"Okay, hear me out," he said, a coaxing note in his voice. "This just happened a little over a week ago. I was trying to absorb the news, work through what it meant for the future."

"Thus the funk," she said.

"Exactly." He regarded her earnestly. "I wanted to have a plan before you found out. I needed to feel as if I was in control of the situation."

"Mack, I adore you, but you don't think that fast." When he was about to protest the insulting comment, she added, "What I'm saying is that you ponder things, think them through from every angle. It's a good trait in many ways, but it's not a fast track to decision-making. You had to know the gossip mill in this town would beat you to the punch." She couldn't keep the hurt out of her voice when she repeated, "I should have heard this from you, not from my family, who heard it on the street."

"Okay, you're right," he said apologetically. "I knew I was taking a huge risk, but I didn't want to see that look in your eyes, the one you have right now."

She couldn't imagine what he meant. "What look is that?"

"You feel sorry for me. No man wants a woman's pity."

Susie rolled her eyes. It was such a guy comment. "I do feel sorry for you, but certainly not because I think you're some kind of failure, if that's what you mean."

He shrugged. "More or less."

"Well, here's a news flash. I feel bad for you because I know how much that job meant to you. You live and breathe sports. That column was all tied up in who you are. It gave you a very public professional identity. Losing it has to be killing you."

He looked vaguely relieved by her words. "That's exactly it," he said.

"You don't have to sound so surprised

that I get it," she said wryly. "I've had a lot of years to figure out what makes you tick."

He met her gaze. "I really am sorry about how you found out about this."

She gave him an amused look. "Do you actually know how I found out? Not just that it came from my family, but the circumstances?"

"Your father filled you in?" he guessed.

"*And* my mother *and* my brothers," she said. "They staged an intervention to warn me against getting involved with you right now."

For the first time, he looked truly guilt stricken. "Geez, Susie, I am so sorry."

"They forced me to consider for the first time that I must not mean much to you if you'd keep such a huge secret from me."

"You know that's not true," he said emphatically, then studied her closely. "You do know it, don't you?"

"Actually, no, I don't. And to make this little intervention of theirs even more fun, Matthew also mentioned that he and Luke had warned you to stay away from me. Why on earth didn't you tell me about that? I was horrified."

He waved it off. "Trust me, it was no big

deal. They were just being protective brothers."

"Then what they said had nothing to do with why you and I, well . . ." She couldn't quite bring herself to put it into words. "Why we haven't, you know, done anything?"

He blinked in apparent confusion, then caught on. "No," he said quickly. "Hell, no. We've just had these boundaries between us. I guess I always knew the rules. Heaven knows, you were clear enough about them, made sure I understood that we had this totally platonic thing going on."

Susie sighed. "Forget the stupid rules, Mack," she snapped impatiently. "I'm sick to death of them."

Looking a little stunned by her vehemence, he stood up and started to pace, then paused to meet her gaze. "We talked about this on Thanksgiving, Susie. Now's not the time—"

"Who says?" she challenged.

"I do," he told her. "And your whole family, for that matter. Didn't you listen to what they said?"

"They don't get a say."

"I just think it's for the best," he insisted stubbornly.

Susie knew better than to push too hard right now, no matter how badly she wanted to. As she'd told him earlier, she sensed they were at a turning point, but with Mack's career in turmoil, he wasn't ready to make another life-altering decision. She had to respect that.

"Okay, then, let's figure out what comes next for you," she said briskly, letting the rest go for now. They'd get back to it. She made a promise to herself to be sure of that.

He paused in his agitated pacing and stared at her. "You sound as if we can do that between now and your next appointment," Mack said, sounding vaguely disgruntled. "It's not going to be that easy. Right now I'm thinking I might have to put out feelers, see what else is out there and then move to wherever I can find a job opening."

Susie didn't even attempt to hide her stunned reaction. "You'd leave Chesapeake Shores?" she asked in dismay.

He nodded, though he looked almost as miserable as she was feeling. "I might not have a choice."

"No," she said flatly, determined not to

have things end between them before they'd even gotten started. And if Mack left now, they would surely end. Distance, especially with their undefined relationship, would kill whatever chance they had.

"That's not going to happen," she added even more emphatically. "You love it here as much as I do. Granted your experiences growing up in Chesapeake Shores were far different from mine, but this is your home, Mack."

"Susie, it's not that simple," he argued. "Good jobs in journalism don't grow on trees, especially not these days. Haven't you been warning me about that for months now? I was the one who was an idiot. I thought my column was so successful, I'd be immune from cutbacks. Instead, it made me the perfect target. Even if I could find another newspaper job, the salary probably won't be what I was getting in Baltimore."

"Then create your own," she blurted. "Your own job, I mean."

Mack blinked at the suggestion. "Excuse me?"

"You heard me. Create a job for yourself."

"Did you have something specific in mind?" he asked, sitting back down, his expression curious.

This was exactly why he should have talked to her the minute he was fired, she thought. Mack plodded through lists of pros and cons. She was quicker and much more creative, especially, it seemed, when it came to holding on to someone she didn't want leaving her world.

Thinking on her feet, she said, "You could blog about sports on a national scale. That's the big trend these days, isn't it? Everything's going on the internet. You have the experience and reputation. You'd have a built-in following."

Though he looked intrigued, he shook his head. "I don't see how it could bring in much money."

"Build up a subscriber base, paid or unpaid," she said, thinking off the top of her head. This might not be her usual area of expertise, but since Mack was in journalism, she'd been paying attention to the field recently. "The point would be to get hits. You get enough hits, you can find advertisers. Who knows, maybe you'd even be picked up by newspapers in syndication or something. I don't know. It just seems like it could work. The internet is the future, isn't it?"

"So my boss told me as he was kicking me out the door," Mack said wryly. "Any other ideas?"

Her expression turned thoughtful. "Well, speaking as someone who wants to get real estate listings in front of a targeted local audience, what about starting a weekly newspaper right here? I know that seems counterintuitive, since newspapers are dying, but I think the local ones will continue to be in demand, if only as a vehicle for advertising."

"I'm a sports columnist, not a publisher," Mack argued. "Or even an editor. I haven't had to worry about getting a paper out on time since college."

"Have you forgotten everything you knew back then?" she asked.

"No, but . . ."

She frowned at his negative attitude. "These are just ideas, Mack. Don't dismiss them out of hand or make excuses for why they won't work. Think about the independence you'd have with your own blog. Or imagine how exciting it could be to start something brand-new, something that's needed in this community. You could shape it into the kind of newspaper you always dreamed of working for."

Mack continued to look skeptical. "I don't know," he murmured.

"Just think about it," Susie ordered. "That's my contribution for now," she said. "I have an appointment. Go home and do what you do best, ponder. I'm not saying these two ideas are the only possibilities, but even you have to admit they're interesting options. And either one is better than packing up and leaving your home."

"True," he conceded. "I knew there was a reason I came by here today."

She gave him a chiding look. "You came by here to apologize for leaving me out of the loop," she corrected. "Now that you've seen what a help I can be, next time maybe you won't be so reluctant to talk to me."

Mack grinned at her. "Of course, if I follow your advice and take on either of these challenges, I'll be my own boss, and there won't even be a next time."

"Mack, there will always be a next time when you'll need to make a choice about either trusting me or keeping something to yourself," she said. "If this incident is an indication of some pattern, I'll tell you now that I won't stand for it."

She was relieved to see that her comment actually seemed to shake him a bit.

She stood up, planted a kiss on his cheek, then walked out of the office. "Lock up when you leave," she called back over her shoulder, not bothering to wait for him.

The man had a lot of thinking to do, and they both knew he'd do it best without her hovering over him.

She'd hover tomorrow. Or the next day. And probably for days after that.

Mack was too restless to sit around in his apartment. Over the past few years he'd gotten used to spending his evenings with Susie. Now that the truth was out and she understood his situation, there was no reason for that habit not to resume.

Okay, there was one reason. Things were obviously changing between them, and the timing for that still sucked, but he couldn't seem to keep himself from walking over to her apartment around dinnertime. He needed a booster shot of her eternal optimism.

When she opened her door, he shoved his hands into his pockets and inquired casually, "Have you eaten yet?"

Her expression brightened. "You've seen my refrigerator. What do you think?"

Relief spread through him. Things weren't going to be awkward between them, after all. Thank goodness for that. "Italian? Chinese? French?"

"Pizza?" she asked hopefully.

He shook his head. "Between you, Will and Jake, that's my primary food group these days."

"Are you complaining?"

"Not really, but I'd wanted to take you someplace a little fancier. How about Brady's instead?"

She shook her head at once. "No way."

He studied her with a narrowed gaze. "You don't need to be worrying about the expense, Susie. I'm not destitute yet."

"It's not that," she insisted. "We never go to Brady's, except to the bar from time to time. It's one of those places that people reserve for special occasions."

"Maybe tonight's a special occasion," he said, suddenly determined to go to Brady's for reasons that had more to do with pride

than any real desire for an excellent crab-
cake.

"What are we celebrating?" she asked,
looking suspicious. "You haven't found
some new job in Alaska or someplace else
halfway across the world, have you? Are
you going to stuff me with crabmeat and
fine wine, then break the bad news to me?"

"Hardly. I thought we could celebrate
getting past what happened."

"If we start celebrating every time we
move on after a disagreement, you'll go
broke."

"A risk I'm willing to take. Now, are you
really going to argue with me about going
to the best restaurant in town?"

She held his gaze, then finally shook
her head. "Not if it means so much to you."

"Thank you," he said solemnly. "That was
easier than I'd expected."

"Are you implying that I'm difficult?" she
demanded, immediately irritated all over
again.

He grinned. "You are," he said without
hesitation. "But it keeps things interesting.
I've always been fond of a challenge."

"I should think you have enough challenges on your plate right now without deliberately turning me into one."

"I'm not responsible for your being a challenge. You just are."

"Then I'm surprised you want to have dinner with me at all," she said testily.

Mack laughed. "Come on, Susie. Let's go before you work yourself up into a bad case of indigestion without having the first bite of food."

She frowned but went with him. "I have no idea why I bother with you," she muttered as she walked down the steps to the alley where his car was parked.

"Because I'm charming and sexy," he suggested.

"No, those are the reasons I should steer clear of you," she countered.

"Then it must be because I make you laugh."

She smiled. "I'm sure that's it."

As he started the car, he glanced over at her. "Want to know why I bother with you?"

She looked flustered by the question. "I'm not entirely sure I do."

"You need to hear this," he said, suddenly

solemn. "Because you ground me, you fascinate me and you make me feel like a whole person, someone worth loving."

When she met his gaze, there were tears in her eyes.

"Oh, Mack, of course you're worth loving," she said softly. "You're surrounded by friends who prove that, not just me. You have to let go of the past. Your father— whoever he was—was obviously a worthless jerk, and your mother did the best she could. You're worth a hundred of either one of them. When are you going to believe that?"

"I do sometimes," he said, then added, "When I'm with you."

And that's why, no matter how this job mess worked itself out, he couldn't let himself lose her. No matter what it took.

That one sweet moment in the car when Mack had admitted how she made him feel sustained Susie for the next week. She'd sensed that there was more he wanted to say. A lot more. But as always, he'd quickly made a joke that had altered the mood at once. And he'd keep things light all through dinner at Brady's, casting a warning look in her direction any time she tried to turn the conversation to anything serious, or even remotely personal. She'd gone along with it, knowing he needed laughter right now more than he needed advice or even consolation.

Oddly, she'd concluded that evening feeling more hopeful about the two of them than she had for a long time. Not even Mack's absence over the past few days had thrown her. He'd called regularly to let her know he was okay, but the brief conversations hadn't been terribly revealing about how he was spending his time or what he was thinking about his future. She'd told herself to accept his need to work through things on his own. It was a struggle, but she was mostly succeeding.

In an odd way, it helped that she hadn't been feeling all that great. In fact, today she'd actually gone home from the office, suffering from the worst cramps she'd ever had. She crawled into bed with a heating pad and slept most of the day away. She'd always had terrible periods, so she knew the drill.

When she woke up in the morning and the pain had gotten worse, she felt a momentary glimmer of concern. Something about this time felt different, but maybe she was just on edge about everything these days. At least, that's what she told herself when she called her father and told him she was taking another sick day.

An hour later, there was a brisk knock on her door. Then a key turned in the lock before she could even think of stirring from bed, and her mother came in.

Susie immediately sat up. "Mom, what are you doing here? You're supposed to be at school."

"Your father called me. What's going on?"

"Cramps. You know. It's no big deal. Nothing to bring you racing over here."

"Have you seen your doctor recently?" Jo inquired, worry creasing her brow.

"There's no need. I had my annual checkup a few months ago. Everything's fine."

"How often have you had pain this severe?"

"It's a little worse this time, but I've always been this way. Remember how often I had to stay home from school?"

"I thought you'd gotten over that long ago."

"I guess when I started on birth control pills, it did get a little better," she admitted.

"Are you still on them?" Jo asked matter-of-factly.

Susie blushed. "I haven't had any reason to be. I took a break."

"Well, maybe you shouldn't have, if they were helping. Let's call your doctor and get you checked out."

Susie felt too lousy to argue. "Fine. I'll call and make an appointment."

"It'll take weeks to get in, unless you tell him it's an emergency. Where's your address book? Do you have the number in there? I'll call."

"Mom, it's not an emergency. By tomorrow I'll be perfectly fine."

"I'll feel better if a medical professional tells me that."

Susie regarded her mother curiously. "Why are you so worked up about this?"

Jo sat down on the edge of the bed, her expression drawn. "I've never really felt any need to get into this with you, but it's obviously time I did."

Susie regarded her with concern. She sounded so somber. "Get into what?"

"After I had Luke, I had to have a hyster-ectomy. For years I'd had symptoms very much like yours. After Matthew the doctor suggested I have one, but I refused. Your father and I wanted more children, and the symptoms weren't that bad. I looked at the research on hyperplasia—that's what I had, some abnormal cells in my uterus—and was convinced I could afford to wait. But when Luke was born, it was worse. They couldn't stop the bleeding. They found the abnormal cells had spread. There was no longer any choice."

Susie stared at her mother in shock. "You had cancer?"

"I suppose you'd call it precancer. The abnormal cells hadn't spread beyond the uterus, and with that gone, along with my ovaries, the prognosis was good. I didn't even need chemotherapy or radiation. You were much too young to be aware that any of this was going on. Since then, I've never really seen the need to talk about it, but I don't like what's going on with you right now. I think you need to get checked out. Will you do this for me?"

Susie nodded at once. "Of course, but you're worrying for no reason. I promise."

Her mother squeezed her hand. "I'm counting on that."

She made the call to the doctor's office, waited while Susie dressed, then insisted on driving her to his office.

Alone in the examining room, Susie sat on the cold, hard table and told herself that she was here only to put her mom's fears to rest. There was no reason to panic. She'd been dealing with the same symptoms for years, and they hadn't meant anything. They were more of a nuisance than anything else.

When Dr. Kinnear came in, he gave her a warm smile. "Under the circumstances, I'm glad you came in."

Susie managed a wan smile in return. "I had no idea until today that there was any family history to be concerned about."

"I'm glad your mother finally filled you in. Better to be safe than sorry," he said. "Now let's do a quick examination and see where we are."

Gynecological exams had never been at the top of Susie's list of favorite things, but this one proved more uncomfortable than most. At one point she nearly yelped out loud in pain.

Dr. Kinnear glanced at her. "Tender there?"

She nodded.

He patted her knee. "Okay, then. That's it for now, but I'd like to have you go in for another test."

Susie regarded him with alarm. "You found something?"

"Maybe," he hedged. "I can't say with certainty without more tests. There's no need to start worrying yet. An ultrasound will be more definitive."

An ultrasound wouldn't be so bad, Susie thought. "And then?"

"Perhaps a biopsy."

She swallowed hard, trying to force the words past the sudden lumps in her throat. "What?" she asked eventually. "What do you think's going on?"

"There could be a problem with one of your ovaries. More than likely it's nothing more than a cyst, but we don't like to fool around with this. We'll want answers as quickly as possible."

Susie read between the lines and

guessed what he wasn't saying. "It could be ovarian cancer?" she asked, stunned.

"Let's not get ahead of ourselves, okay?" he soothed. "I'll get you in for that ultrasound in the next day or two. My receptionist will make the appointment and call you."

All Susie knew about ovarian cancer was that it could be deadly, because it was generally caught too late. This morning she'd thought she was simply having a particularly painful period, and now she could die? She couldn't even begin to process it.

Again Dr. Kinnear gave her a reassuring look. "One step at a time, young lady. If you have questions at any time, call me. We'll find the answers, and whatever the situation is, we'll deal with it."

She nodded. After he'd left the examining room, she sat there frozen.

A few minutes later, her mother stepped into the room. Susie met her gaze.

"He told you?"

Her mother nodded. "He told me there's no cause for alarm yet. You are not to panic, okay? Neither one of us is going to panic."

Susie nodded, then gave her mother a plaintive look. "Is it okay to be scared out of my wits?"

Her mother gathered her into her arms. "We can be scared together, but we are going to think positively, Susie. I mean it. No negative thoughts. People do beat ovarian cancer, and we're not even sure yet that you have it. It could be nothing more than a cyst, okay?"

Susie blinked back tears. "Got it." She hesitated. "Mom, can we keep this just between us for now? It's not as if we know anything. I don't think I could stand having Dad and everyone hovering."

"If that's what you want," her mother agreed. "I do wish you'd consider telling your grandmother, thought."

"Why Gram? It'll only worry her."

"But she's the one with the direct link to God," Jo said with a smile. "I think her prayers are exactly what you need right now."

Susie smiled back. The whole family counted on Nell O'Brien to save them. The rest of them might be believers, they might be churchgoers, but it was Gram's faith that was steadfast, no matter what the crisis.

"Let's see what happens with the ultra-sound," Susie said. "If there's a problem with that, then we'll call in the big guns."

Her mother met her gaze. "What about Mack?"

"What about him?"

"I think he'd want to know."

Susie shook her head. "It's not like that between us."

"Remember how upset you were that he'd kept losing his job from you? How do you think he'll feel if he finds out about this later?"

"I can't tell him," Susie said simply. "Not until I know more."

Because if she needed to have surgery, if she couldn't have children, it would change everything between them. And, of course, if she wasn't one of those who beat the odds, they'd have absolutely no future at all.

6

Mack didn't like Susie's pale complexion or the dark shadows under her eyes. It had been evident for a few days now that she was worried about something, and he was very much afraid it was him. He didn't want to be responsible for making her sick.

"Okay, we need to get out of here," he said after taking a good look at her when he stopped by her office at lunchtime. If anything, she looked worse than she had when he'd seen her the day before.

Before she could argue, he marched into Jeff's office and announced, "I'm taking Susie away from here for the afternoon. You can manage without her for a few hours, right?"

Jeff frowned. "Of course, but I haven't heard her say she wanted to go anywhere with you."

"I'm not giving her an option," Mack responded. "She needs some sunshine and a long walk on the beach. Haven't you noticed her color's not good?" He lowered his voice. "Any idea what's going on with her?"

Jeff shook his head, then cast a worried glance in his daughter's direction. "Not a clue. She took a couple of sick days, which isn't like her, but she swears she's fine, and Jo's backing her up. I'm at a loss."

Mack glanced in Susie's direction. "No offense intended, but they're both lying. I want to know why. I'm worried, Jeff. Something's not right."

Her father nodded. "I agree. If you can get to the bottom of it, I'd appreciate it. She's not herself, that's for sure. I thought it had something to do with you."

"Maybe it does," Mack admitted. "If so, I'll do whatever it takes to fix it. That's a promise."

Just then Susie appeared at Mack's

side, her cheeks flaming. "I do not appreciate the two of you whispering behind my back as if I'm not right here." She directed her scowl at Mack. "Nor am I happy about you making decisions for me. I have work to do, Mack. I'm not going anywhere."

"The work can wait," Mack countered, leveling a look into her eyes that matched his determination against her stubbornness. She looked as if she were wavering, so he cajoled, "If you won't do this for yourself, do it for me. I need an outing and a fresh perspective. You can boss me around and tell me what I need to be doing. It'll cheer you up."

Her lips curved, but the smile never quite reached her eyes. "Well, when you make such an appealing offer, how can I possibly resist? But we'll just go for a couple of hours, okay?"

"We'll see how it goes," Mack responded, his tone noncommittal.

Mack usually walked into town, but today he'd brought his convertible. When they'd settled in the front seat, he turned the heat up full blast, then put the top down. Susie just stared at him.

"Are you crazy? It's almost December."

"Riding around with the top down is the quickest way I know to blow the cobwebs out of your brain. I think it encourages the absorption of oxygen or something."

She looked justifiably skeptical. "I can't wait to see the scientific proof of that. Until then, maybe you should put the top up. I'd hate to refresh all those brain cells and then die of pneumonia."

He gave her a disappointed look. "You sure?"

"I'm sure."

"Okay, then," he said. He put the top up, then turned the car toward Annapolis. "Maybe we can convince Kevin and your uncle Thomas to treat us to lunch. One of the advantages to being unemployed, I've discovered, is that people can't wait to buy me meals."

She shook her head. "You've gone from having too much pride to being totally shameless. How did that happen?"

He winked at her. "I've always been just a little shameless. Didn't you notice?"

"I thought that was only with regard to your dating history."

He shrugged. "Apparently not."

"You're in an odd mood today," she assessed. "What's gotten into you?"

He glanced over and met her gaze. "I could ask you the same thing. You haven't been yourself for a couple of days now. You're obviously worried about something. Is it me?"

"There's that streak of modesty we all know and love," she commented acerbically. "Not everything is about you, Mack."

"Then what is going on?"

She turned away. "Nothing that concerns you."

Something stilled inside him. "What does that mean? If you have something on your mind that's making you look like death warmed over, then yeah, it concerns me."

"Thanks for the lovely compliment," she said sourly. "If I look that awful, I'm surprised you want to be seen with me."

Mack counted to ten. He knew all her defense mechanisms, probably even better than she did. She resorted to jokes or turn-the-table attacks when things were cutting a little too close to home.

"Don't pull that garbage with me, Susie.

This isn't about me. It's about you. What's on your mind? Something obviously is. Even your dad recognizes that something's not right. If it's not me, then what?"

"Absolutely nothing," she said with a stubborn set to her jaw. "Leave it alone, Mack."

He might have ignored her and kept pressing, but there was an oddly imploring look in her eyes that cautioned him to let it go for now. Unlike him, Susie wasn't used to keeping secrets. Sooner or later she'd reveal the truth.

"Mack?" she said eventually.

"Yes?"

"Do you really want to have lunch with Kevin and Uncle Thomas?"

"It was just an idea. Why? Would you rather not?"

She nodded. "I'm not all that hungry, to be honest. Maybe we could just go for that walk on the beach you mentioned earlier."

He didn't even hesitate. "If that's what you want, sure."

He turned the car back toward Chesapeake Shores, then drove south of town to a rare undeveloped area along the water. He turned onto Beach Lane, a narrow, rutted dirt road that was barely more than a wide path cut into the woods. At the end, it opened onto a sliver of beach. Like Moon-light Cove on the other side of town, it was secluded and almost always deserted. Its advantage over Moonlight Cove was that it could at least be reached by car.

The weak late-autumn sun filtered through the old oaks, weeping willows and pine trees. Leaves crunched underfoot as they walked down to the beach.

"I always thought I'd buy this piece of property and build a house here someday," Mack said. "Not one of those huge places that Mick builds, but something cozy and warm and just big enough for a family. Hardwood floors. Maybe a big fireplace that opens to the living room on one side and to the kitchen on the other."

"It sounds amazing," Susie said, an oddly wistful note in her voice.

He held his hand out to help her over a few boulders that blocked their way.

"It's peaceful, isn't it?" she said in a tone of near reverence. "It's as if no one else knows about this place."

"Someone must. They put a road in."

"My father," she revealed. "He owns it."

Mack didn't even attempt to hide his surprise. "He does?"

She nodded. "Back when he and Mick were fighting, I think he had some idea of starting his own development along here, but his heart wasn't really in it. He kept the property for me, Matthew and Luke, in case we ever wanted to build along the bay. He knew the land would be worth a fortune someday."

"You've never mentioned that before," he said, not sure whether to be disappointed or delighted by the news. It meant he'd never get his hands on the land, but at least it belonged to someone who'd treat it with respect.

"I never knew how much you cared about it," she said. "Funny how things turn out, isn't it? Maybe I'll put in a good word and Dad will let you buy my parcel someday."

There was a note in her voice he couldn't interpret. Regret? Sorrow? He wasn't intuitive enough to figure it out. "Why on earth would you ever let him sell it?"

"Because you want it so badly," she said simply.

Mack shook his head. "Absolutely not. I

could never let you do that. It's your legacy, Susie. You could build the home of your dreams right here."

There was a faraway look in her eyes, and once more Mack had the feeling there was something important he was missing.

"Susie, is everything okay?" he asked yet again, hoping that this time she'd open up about whatever was bothering her.

"I told you it was," she said, her tone once more defensive.

He studied her with a penetrating look. "And you wouldn't lie to me, would you?"

"I never have."

Until now. Mack heard the words as clearly as if she'd spoken them aloud. But looking at her, he couldn't bring himself to press for answers—she suddenly seemed so fragile, not at all like the vibrant, fight-to-the-finish woman who usually challenged his every word. He had this sinking feeling in the pit of his stomach that if she responded, he wouldn't like what she said one bit.

Susie hated lying to Mack, especially in light of her own reaction to his recent evasions. She simply couldn't tell him what was going on with her health. Not until she knew more. She'd have the ultrasound in a few days. After that, things would be clearer.

It had almost killed her when he'd told her his dream of owning the Beach Lane property. For years now, ever since her father had told her a piece of it was to be hers, she'd envisioned a home there for herself, Mack and their children. A whole houseful of children. It was what she wanted more than anything.

She'd always thought it was Mack who'd stand in the way of making that dream come true. Now it could be her. Even if she lived, children might be out of the question. How would Mack feel about that? They'd never really talked about it. In fact, the whole subject of fatherhood was a touchy one because of his own history. Ironically she knew that past was what would make him the best possible father, because of all people, he knew exactly what not to do. He'd be the kind of steadfast man his own father hadn't been.

Thinking about what might or might not happen in the future was too depressing. If she stayed in her apartment worrying, she'd go crazy. She wished she'd maintained closer ties to her cousins, but the discord between their fathers had always made her feel like a traitor if she spent much time with Abby, Bree or Jess. Especially Jess, in fact, who was closest to her own age. Jess had always had some kind of oddly competitive thing going on with her, likely because Jess's attention deficit disorder had made learning difficult, while school had come easily to Susie. At any rate, the family dynamics had made the forming of any bonds awkward.

She had, however, grown close to Shanna, Kevin's wife, who had none of the O'Brien baggage. She knew if she revealed to her what was going on, Shanna would keep it to herself and offer sage advice, if asked.

Even though the bookstore was closed by now, she knew Shanna stayed late to tally the day's receipts before heading home to her family. Susie walked downstairs and around the corner to her shop, then tapped on the front door.

Shanna emerged from the back, spotted Susie and flipped on lights as she came to the door. "Hey, what brings you by here this late?" she asked, stepping aside to let Susie in. Then she frowned. "You don't look so hot."

"That seems to be the consensus of the day," Susie said, forcing an upbeat note into her voice. "Nothing like hearing that from a bunch of people to perk up a woman's ego."

"Was one of those people Mack?"

Susie gave her a weary look. "It was."

"I thought the man was known for his charm," Shanna muttered.

"He apparently used it all up on other women."

"Okay, so bottom line, you're feeling low and need a pep talk," Shanna said. "Want to come to dinner at my house? I guarantee you an hour or two with Davy and Henry underfoot will make you happy to go home to the peace and quiet of your own apartment."

"There's nothing wrong with those boys," Susie said, jumping to their defense. "They're just energetic, typical kids."

"Don't I know it!" Shanna grinned. "And to think Henry was this shy, studious little boy when I first became his stepmother. Now that my ex has allowed Kevin and me to adopt him, Henry's suddenly blossoming into a wild child. It would be wonderful to see, if it weren't so exhausting."

"You and Kevin are responsible for the transformation," Susie said. "Having a sick, alcoholic dad for so long had that poor child tiptoeing around in fear of doing anything to upset his father."

"True enough," Shanna said. "Of course, Davy didn't come into my life with any baggage. His mom died when he was just a baby, and Kevin was always an amazing father. Plus he was surrounded by all those O'Briens. He's just a rambunctious little kid, exactly the way he's supposed to be. Funny how I thought Henry would be a quieting influence on him, but instead it's been just the opposite."

She studied Susie. "So, do you want to join us for dinner? It might actually be a quiet meal, if Kevin's managed to get the boys bathed and in bed by the time I get home."

Susie regarded her with humor. "So that's why you hang around here after hours, so your husband will settle your children down for the night."

Shanna laughed. "Guilty. Bedtime stories are my favorite part of the day. All the rest—getting soaked to the skin during their baths, fighting with them about going to bed—not so much."

"I wouldn't mind reading a bedtime story tonight," Susie confessed. "Would that be okay?"

"It's a deal. You do that, and I'll make us something spectacular for dinner." Her gaze narrowed. "Or would you rather stay here and talk? Is there something on your mind? Are you really after a sounding board, rather than a distraction?"

"No, this is nothing that a good distraction won't cure," Susie insisted. "As long as you're sure I'm not imposing."

"Friends can't possibly impose," Shanna assured her, then impulsively gave her a hug.

"What was that for?" Susie asked.

"You looked like you needed it. I've learned to read the signs."

"Thanks," Susie said, smiling. "I really did."

Even without saying a single word about her problems, the burden suddenly felt a thousand percent lighter.

* * *

Davy streaked naked through the foyer as Susie and Shanna arrived at Shanna's house.

"Get back up those stairs right this second," Shanna ordered, trying unsuccessfully to hide her laughter. She turned to Susie. "Told you it might be a little wild around here."

"I'm drying off," Davy claimed as he raced past again.

Shanna closed her eyes. "Heaven help me," she murmured, then shouted up the stairs, "Kevin, your son is down here naked in front of company!"

Kevin peered over the railing. "It's Susie, not company. I'm sure she's seen naked kids before." Even so, he managed a stern look for Davy. "Up here, now!"

Davy flew up the stairs, giving Susie and Shanna an irrepressible grin as he went.

"Are you sure you want any part of reading bedtime stories tonight?" Shanna asked. "If I were you, I'd run for the hills."

"Nope, I'm still game," Susie said, then followed Shanna up the stairs.

Though the house had rooms for both

the boys, Henry had been so intrigued by the prospect of having a little brother and Davy so adoring of his new big brother, they'd insisted on sharing the larger bedroom for now.

"Okay, you two," Shanna announced after kissing them both and reserving a longer kiss for her husband, "I've recruited new talent for storytime."

Davy, now clad in SpongeBob SquarePants pajamas, bounced on his bed. "Yay! I have a book all picked out. It's about trucks."

Henry groaned. "You want that book every night. I thought it was my turn to pick. I want the next chapter about Percy Jackson."

Davy shrugged. "Okay," he said readily. "But I get the truck book tomorrow night."

"Fine," Henry said grudgingly.

Susie sat down on the floor between their twin beds and accepted the book from Henry. "Okay, you'll need to fill me in on what's happened in the story up till now," she told them.

Their words tumbled over each other as they brought her up to date.

"It's a really good story," Henry concluded.

Shanna grinned. "They only get to hear one chapter," she warned Susie. "Do not let them try to talk you into more."

"Absolutely not," Susie told her solemnly, then winked at Henry, who giggled.

Shanna merely shook her head, then left the room. "Dinner's in a half hour," she called back.

Susie looked at the two boys. "I guess I'll have to read fast."

She began the book on the designated page, less caught up in the story than in glancing at both boys as they listened. Davy soon curled up with his pillow and fell asleep, but Henry was on the edge of the bed eagerly absorbing every word. He sighed when she reached the end of the second chapter.

"Do we really have to stop?" he asked wistfully.

"We really do," she said, giving him a hug and tucking him in. She pressed a kiss to his cheek. "You need lots of sleep so you can go to school tomorrow and get very, very smart."

He regarded her solemnly. "I'm already smart."

"Trust me, kid, there's a whole universe of stuff you don't know yet. Even I'm not caught up on everything, and I've been around a lot longer than you have."

"I guess," he said. "Thanks for reading to us."

"It was fun. I wish I'd had a mom with a bookstore when I was your age. You guys are so lucky."

"The luckiest," Henry said, his eyes drifting closed.

Susie tiptoed from the room, then leaned against the wall outside the door, trying very hard not to cry. She wanted nights exactly like this, putting her own kids to bed, then going downstairs to her husband, to Mack.

What if that could never be?

"Susie, dinner," Shanna called, snapping her out of her moment of self-pity and panic.

"On my way," she called back, wiping the tears from her cheeks and plastering a smile on her face.

"Please God," she murmured as she

went downstairs, "don't take this away from me. Please."

For just an instant, she regretted not filling Gram in on what was going on. Gram would know exactly the right words to use, the ones God would hear.

She'd also remind Susie that God always knew what was in her heart.

A few days after his disquieting conversation with Susie, Mack learned the details about yet another investigation of steroid use among top-ranked baseball players, one of whom had been especially outspoken in his criticism of players who'd been caught in the past. The hypocrisy irked him, as did the crash of more sports heroes. He was itching to take on the topic, but without his column where was he supposed to find an audience?

He recalled Susie's suggestion that he blog, went online, set up an account and wrote the kind of scathing column that once might have gotten him into hot water at the newspaper.

He had no idea what to expect. For all he knew, his words were going out into cyberspace, unread by anyone. When he logged on the next day, he had half a dozen comments, most of them from people who'd sometimes emailed him at the Baltimore paper.

"Happy to see your voice hasn't been silenced forever," one wrote. "Welcome back!"

A couple of days later, he had a call from a local sports radio show inviting him to come in and discuss the topic. The gig didn't pay, but it was exposure for his views and, he thought with a sense of amazement, for the blog he'd started with little hope of drawing any attention.

By the end of the next week the hit counter he'd installed on his site was surprisingly active. It didn't rival his old paper's circulation yet—and probably never would, he realized—but at least he'd found a way to keep his name and his views out there.

"The man is back," Jake said, giving him a slap on the back when they met for lunch. "That blog you wrote today was on the mark."

Mack regarded him with surprise. "You read it?"

"Sure," Jake said. "I heard about it from a guy I met on a job a couple of days ago.

What I want to know is why you didn't tell Will or me about it?"

"It wasn't a big deal," Mack said. "More like a hobby till I figure out what I want to do next. In the meantime, I've been fielding a few calls from newspapers that might be interested in hiring me."

"Where?" Will asked, regarding him worriedly.

"Right now the most promising are in California and Colorado," he admitted.

"Too far away," Will said succinctly. "Couldn't you make this blog into something?"

"I don't know if I want to," Mack admitted. "It feels like the same old thing, but with a smaller audience."

"I thought you loved that job," Will said, looking confused. "Wasn't that what all the moping and scotch were about?"

"I did," Mack said, then admitted, "But when Susie and I were talking about all this, she planted another idea in my head, and I can't seem to shake it. It would be a real challenge. Something new and potentially exciting."

"Doing what?" Jake asked.

"A Chesapeake Shores weekly newspaper," Mack said, looking from one friend to the other and trying to gauge their reactions. "Is that insane, especially these days?"

"When has insane ever bothered you?" Will asked. "You've always thrived on doing things people tell you are impossible. If you're excited about it, dig into the details, put a plan on paper and decide if it's financially feasible."

"I, for one, would be thrilled to have a place to do cost-effective, targeted advertising for the nursery," Jake said.

Mack studied him. "Seriously? On a regular basis?"

"Absolutely," Jake said. "Sign me up now."

"What would you consider cost-effective?"

Jake threw out some figures, which Mack jotted down on a napkin. It wasn't much on which to base a business plan, but it was a starting point. He began making more notes, oblivious to everything around him.

When he looked up eventually, Will and Jake were gone and Susie had taken their place.

"Where'd you come from?" he asked, blinking at her in surprise.

"I've been here awhile."

"Why didn't you say anything?"

"It was nice watching you so absorbed in something." She reached for the pile of napkins he'd accumulated before Sally had given him a pad of paper and scolded him for wasting her supply of napkins.

Mack wanted to snatch them back, but he recalled the way he'd sworn to Susie that he'd stop keeping things from her.

He kept his gaze on her face, noting exactly when she realized what his notes were about.

She looked up, a smile spreading across her face. "Seriously?"

"I think so. What do you think?"

"There are a lot of questions here. What if you don't like the answers?" she asked.

He shrugged. "Then it's back to square one, I guess."

But as he caught the hope shining in her eyes, he knew he had to find some way to make this newspaper thing work. Not only would it provide a challenge he could sink his teeth into, but it would pave the way toward the kind of settled, secure future he wanted with Susie. For now, those papers in California and Colorado were simply out of the question.

7

Susie wasn't sure how much longer she could stand waiting around to get the ultrasound done. The test had been postponed twice, ironically once by her.

Something had come up at work, and she hadn't wanted to reveal to her father why she couldn't attend a meeting he'd scheduled. At least that's what she'd told herself as she'd changed the doctor's appointment. Her mother had been livid.

"You know how important this appointment is," Jo had scolded. "Why would you do that?"

"Dad really wanted me at this meeting,

and I couldn't think of any way to get out of it without telling him the truth. I wasn't ready to do that."

Her mother didn't look as if she believed her. "I think it's because you're terrified of what they'll find."

"Well, of course I'm terrified," Susie had retorted. "Aren't you?"

"Knowing is better than not knowing," Jo said, which didn't answer Susie's question. Then again, maybe it did.

Her mother regarded her sympathetically. "Once you have answers, you'll know what you're dealing with."

"I'm not ready to know," Susie said stubbornly, then admitted, "That'll make it real. I'll have to face the possibility of surgery, radiation, chemo and who knows what else? I might have to accept that I'll never have children of my own. I don't know if I can handle that."

Jo brushed Susie's untamed hair back from her face. "You're a strong woman, Susie. You'll face whatever needs to be faced with courage. And who knows? It could be good news, and then you'll have worried longer for no reason."

"We both know the news isn't going to

be good," Susie said direly, refusing to give herself false hope.

"I know no such thing!" Jo replied fiercely. "Neither do you. What happened to our vow to keep a positive attitude?"

"I've been reading up on all the latest symptoms, research and likely outcomes," Susie said. "It's enough to strike terror in anyone's heart."

"Honey, there's nothing wrong with being well-informed, but you're unique," Jo reminded her. "Worst-case scenarios don't necessarily apply to you."

"But they could," Susie replied, not daring to leave herself even a sliver of hope that might be dashed later.

"Enough of that," Jo commanded. "When is the next appointment?"

Susie told her.

"I'm going with you. You won't be able to back out then. I'll rally the family troops and drag you there, if need be."

Susie knew she meant it, too. In the end, though, the doctor's office had called to reschedule.

Now the time had come. There could be no escape or excuses. Her mother was on the way over, and there wasn't a single

way Susie could think of to keep from going. She understood her mother well
enough to know that she really would en-
list help from Susie's father and brothers,
if need be. Maybe even Mack.

Thankfully Mack had been so caught up
in making his own plans lately that he hadn't
commented on her odd moods or lacklus-
ter energy again recently. She certainly
didn't want him finding out what was going
on from her mother. The only way to ensure
that wouldn't happen was to drag herself to
the doctor's office and have the test done.

As it turned out, the ultrasound itself was
no big deal. She wasn't even in the office
very long. She'd tried to read answers on
the technician's face, but the woman had
obviously learned to keep her expression
neutral.

"Can't you tell me what you found?" she
asked when the test was over.

"Your doctor will discuss the results with
you," Paula Marcus said. "He'll probably
have the report by tomorrow. Give him a
call then."

"Not even a hint?" Susie pleaded.

The ultrasound tech gave her a sympathetic look. "Sorry. Hints aren't in my job description," she said lightly. Her expression sobered. "I know the waiting sucks, hon. I'll see if I can't hurry the report along. Try your doctor later this afternoon."

Susie sighed, knowing it was the best she could hope for. "Thanks."

She met her mother in the reception area and gave her a wan smile. "All done."

Jo studied her face. "Any idea what they found?"

"Not even a tiny hint," Susie admitted glumly. "The tech said she'd try to get the report to Dr. Kinnear later today."

"Then let's go out for lunch," Jo suggested. "Someplace we've never been before. Want to drive to Baltimore and try something at the Inner Harbor? That's always fun."

Susie shook her head. "Thanks for trying, Mom, but I'm not hungry."

Jo's gaze narrowed. "Something tells me you've been feeling like that ever since you first saw the doctor. You're losing weight you can't spare. If you don't want anyone guessing that you might be ill, you need to eat. Now, Baltimore or someplace here?"

Susie heard the steely resolve behind her mother's words. "Sally's is fine."

"You're up for running into Mack?" her mother asked, looking surprised.

Oddly enough, she was. "He won't bug me if I don't eat every bite on my plate."

Her mother smiled. "Fortunately, I'll be right there to do that."

"You'd stick around even if Mack is there?"

"Sweetie, I'm stuck to you today like a burr that's embedded in your skin, unless I feel you're in someone else's capable hands."

"Well, that just sucks," Susie commented, then chuckled. "And now I sound like a petulant five-year-old." She tucked her arm through her mother's. "Come on. I promise to behave and to eat every spoonful of soup."

"And a grilled cheese sandwich?" Jo coaxed.

Susie rolled her eyes. "Maybe."

"How about a hot fudge sundae?"

"Now you're just getting downright pushy."

Her mother laughed. "That's my prerogative, if not my duty."

Susie stopped and faced her mother, noted the real worry in her eyes. "Thank you for coming with me today, and for bugging me to eat, and for being my mom."

"Always, kiddo. That's what I'm around for."

Mack was just finishing up lunch with Will and Jake when Susie came into Sally's with her mother. The sight wouldn't have been so surprising were it not the middle of a school day. Something was up, if Jo had taken off. He had this gut-sick feeling it had something to do with whatever was going on with Susie these days. He'd pushed his own alarm down deep, but it resurfaced now, with all sorts of warning bells going off in his head.

"Does Susie look okay to you guys?" he asked Will and Jake. It was a ridiculous question since Jake, at least, was one of the least observant men he knew. Will, however, might have picked up on something.

Will glanced over his shoulder. "She's a little pale, but it's early December. Everybody's looking a little pasty these days."

"And Jess hasn't said anything?" Mack pressed.

Will shook his head. "You know how things are between those two. Jess always felt as if Susie did everything better than she did. Family or not, they're not exactly best buddies."

Mack turned to Jake. "What about you? Any thoughts?"

Jake shrugged. "She looks about the same to me. And before you ask, Bree hasn't mentioned Susie recently. Between the baby, the flower shop and her theater's Christmas production, she barely has time to say hello before she falls into bed at night."

Mack sighed. "A big help you are." He studied Susie more intently. "Will's right. She's pale, and it looks to me as if she's lost weight, too."

"Have you asked her if everything's okay?" Will wanted to know.

"Of course," Mack said. "She swears she's fine, but I'm not buying it. Now she's in here with her mother in the middle of a school day. Why isn't Jo at work?"

Mack's concern finally registered with Jake. "You're really worried about this, aren't you?"

Mack nodded.

"Well, we're not the one with the answers," Will said. "Go over there and join them. See what you can find out. Be sure to let us know if there *is* something going on. If Susie needs anything at all, let me know."

"Sure," Mack said distractedly, already out of the booth and heading in Susie's direction. Jo met his gaze, and there was no mistaking the look in her eyes: She was worried sick. That alarmed Mack more than anything. Jo O'Brien was the most unflappable woman he'd ever met.

"Hey, ladies," he said, sliding into the booth next to Susie. "You all take the day off to go shopping or something?"

"Just grabbing a bite of lunch," Susie said with forced cheer. "Isn't that right, Mom?"

"That's right," Jo said, then suddenly stood up. "Since Mack's here to keep you company, though, I think I'll take off."

"Don't let me chase you away," Mack said, though he was actually relieved by her departure. He'd have better luck getting straight answers from Susie without her mother there as a buffer.

"Oh, you're not chasing me away at all," Jo insisted. "I should probably check back in at school. I left my classes with a substitute. By now they've probably terrorized her."

Susie gave her mother a pleading look. "Mom?"

Jo kissed her cheek. "You're in capable hands."

Before she left, she leaned down and whispered in Mack's ear, "Make sure she eats something."

"Will do," he promised.

After she'd gone, he studied Susie quizzically. "What's up with your mom?"

"Nothing," Susie said a little too quickly. "She's just a bit distracted today."

"By what?"

"There's a lot going on."

"Such as?" Mack pressed.

Susie gave him a warning glance. "Leave it alone, Mack. I need to grab a quick bite to eat and get back to work myself. In fact, maybe I'll just get some soup to go."

He shook his head. "I don't think so."

She scowled at the response, but since he had her exit from the booth blocked, she could do little beyond complain. "Who made you my guard dog?" she asked irritably.

"Your mother, and I take my promises to her seriously. Always have."

"What about your loyalty to me?" she inquired, sounding even more disgruntled.

"Somehow I have a feeling that in this instance, it's one and the same thing. Why's your mom worried about you, Susie? Are you sick?"

"No," she said. "Do I look sick?"

Now, there was a minefield if ever he'd seen one. There was the chivalrous answer and the truth. "You're pale. You've lost weight, so yeah, you don't look well. It's not the first time I've mentioned that, either, so don't be scowling at me as if I've just insulted you. I'm concerned."

"Don't be," she said, then gave him a bright smile that was too obviously forced. "Now tell me how the plans are going for the newspaper. I want to hear all about it. You've been hiding out for days now, so you must have something concrete put together."

Mack considered calling her on the deliberate change of topic, but settled instead for seeing that she ordered soup and a sandwich.

"I can't possibly eat all that," she protested. "Soup's plenty."

"Hey, I didn't even mention the apple pie you're going to eat for dessert," he said.

"Forget it. No way."

"We'll see," he said. "It's the price for changing the subject."

She gave him a weary smile. "A small price, then. Now talk to me."

He filled her in on some of the information he'd been able to pull together from talking to the owners of half a dozen local weeklies in Maryland and nearby areas of Virginia.

"Business is tough," he said. "Every one of them agreed about that."

"And yet you still sound excited," Susie said as she ate a spoonful of the steaming crab soup Sally had brought, along with a grilled cheese sandwich. "How are the numbers looking?"

"Scary, to be honest. I have no idea if I can come up with that kind of money. Just hiring a staff will be outrageously expensive, and then there's the cost of engaging a printer. I don't know, Susie, this could be more than I'm ready to tackle. Every last bit of common sense I have is screaming at me to forget about the idea."

She grinned. "But you're not going to,

are you? Admit it, Mack, this is the happiest you've been since you lost your job. You're dying to take on the challenge."

"I am," he confessed. "I started roughing out a business plan last night, projecting costs and potential income. I can't imagine that any bank will take a risk like this. I have some money of my own. I've been pretty frugal with my salary and I have my severance package, but that's just the tip of the iceberg."

"Talk to Laila," Susie suggested. "Her father's as conservative as they come. He wouldn't even approve a loan for Megan to open her art gallery unless Mick backed her, which she refused to let him do, but Laila's a different story. She'll understand what a huge investment this will be, not just in you, but in Chesapeake Shores. A newspaper's needed here. She has the vision to see that."

"Maybe you're the one who should be selling her on the idea," he suggested. "You seem to know exactly what to say. Want to be my business partner? I don't want your money, just your enthusiasm."

"Hey, you've been charming women into doing what you want for years. Just think

of Laila as one of your potential con-
quests."

He frowned at the offhand comment.
"The stakes are very different," he pointed
out. "I wanted to sleep with those women.
I wasn't asking them for huge amounts of
money."

"Going after sex and money aren't all
that different," Susie insisted. "Ask any of
those guys who managed to talk very
smart investors out of their life's savings
what it took to do it. Charm was a big part
of the package."

"Plus a lot of rosy projections on paper,"
Mack replied. "My projections are realistic.
They're not all that rosy. I'm not going to
get rich doing this."

"What do you want most? Money or satisfaction?"

"Some of both," he said candidly.

"Won't these projections of yours give
you that much?"

"I think so. I'm not convinced the bank
will."

"You won't know until you've talked to
Laila." She met his gaze, her expression
earnest. "Do it, Mack. Life's too short to

play it safe. If this is something you want, do whatever it takes to make it happen."

He studied her intently. "Why do I have a feeling you're talking about more than me starting a newspaper?"

"Because you think you know me so well," she retorted. "But not this time, Mack. This is all about you and what's right for your future."

"It'll take me a little longer to pull everything together, but I'll at least talk to Laila before I throw in the towel. I promise."

"I can't ask for more than that." She met his gaze. "You know, I think I might be able to eat that piece of pie, after all."

He watched as she dug into the warm apple pie with melting vanilla ice cream on top, then shook his head. "And here I thought you'd leave at least a bite or two for me," he teased.

"Get your own," she said. "This piece is all mine."

Mack felt strangely relieved by her sudden burst of appetite. And yet the fact that he felt that way said way too much about just how worried he was about her.

* * *

Spending the afternoon with Mack, while a bit stressful, had been just the distraction Susie had needed. She'd almost forgotten about the ultrasound results. When she stopped back in the office, though, there was a message on her desk, taken by her father, to call Dr. Kinnear's office.

She could feel her father's gaze on her as she read it.

"What's that about, Suze?" he asked, worry creasing his brow. "Why is the doctor's office calling you?"

"Nothing to be concerned about, Dad. They just want me to schedule an appointment."

He stepped out of his office and crossed to her desk, then perched on the chair beside it. "I've been married to your mother a lot of years, you know. When it's time for her to make an appointment, she gets a notice in the mail."

"And she probably does it right away," Susie suggested. "I didn't. Thus the phone call."

"You're lying to me," her father said bluntly. "Don't even try. You're not that good at it. I grew up playing poker with your uncles. I learned to spot the signs of a bluff years ago."

Though she refused to meet his gaze, Susie felt her eyes brimming with tears. "I can't talk about it, Dad. Not right now."

He stood up and suddenly she was in his arms, her head buried on his shoulder. She let the sobs come, soaking his shirt, while he murmured soothing words to her.

"I can let you cry, sweetie, but I can't help unless you talk to me," he said. "Would you rather I get your mother over here? Does this have something to do with why the two of you have been huddled together so much recently?"

"Don't call Mom. I'm okay," she said, though she clung to his hand. "Could you just sit here with me while I make the call? Then we can talk, okay?"

He nodded. "Whatever you need."

Her hand shook as she dialed the number. "Is Dr. Kinnear available?" she asked. "I think he has my test results."

"He's with a patient, but I know he wants to speak to you right away," the nurse said. "I'll get him. Just sit tight, okay?"

Susie nodded, then realized the woman couldn't see her. "Sure," she managed to murmur.

As she waited, she avoided looking at her father's face. She knew how frantic he must be. She was probably scaring him to death.

Then the doctor was on the line.

"It's as I suspected, Susie. There's a mass of some kind. Could just be a cyst. We could do an MRI that might tell us more, but I'd rather go straight for a biopsy. It'll be more definitive, and we're probably going to have to do it eventually anyway."

"I see," she said, hearing the words, knowing what they meant, but somehow unable to process all of the implications. "You're pretty sure it's cancer, aren't you? That's why you want to jump ahead."

"I didn't say that," he said, his tone deliberately calm and soothing. "I'm just trying to cut out an intermediate step that will only give you longer to worry about this. We can get the biopsy scheduled by next week, more than likely. Getting you in for an MRI could take a lot longer. And, like I said, you'd most likely wind up in an O.R.

down the road, anyway. Do you want to come in and talk about this? I'll have Jane fit you in this afternoon, if you like."

"No, that's okay," she said dully. "Go ahead and schedule the biopsy. What you said makes total sense. I want answers sooner rather than later." She drew in a deep breath. "What's actually going to happen? If the biopsy results are bad, will you do surgery right then and there?"

"Probably not. We like to do it that way with breast cancer, but with this we like to think about all the treatment options depending on what we find, then schedule the surgery. We'll want to get a surgical oncologist involved, as well. I have someone I usually recommend, if that's okay. I'll work with him on the scheduling."

"That's fine," she said, feeling mostly numb. All she could sense was her father's reassuring grip on her hand. It had tightened as he listened. She knew he must be devastated by what he was hearing.

"Jane will call you when she has a time for the biopsy."

"Thank you."

"Susie, I know it sounds impossible, but

try not to worry," the doctor said, doing his best to reassure her. "Approach this one step at a time, okay?"

"I'm doing the best I can," she told him. And that was true. It was just that at the moment, her best wasn't very good. She felt as if her head were about to explode, and her pulse was racing a mile a minute.

When she'd hung up, she couldn't seem to bring herself to meet her father's gaze.

"Suze, what is it? What's the biopsy for?" His voice hitched. "Is it breast cancer?"

She shook her head. "Worse. It's possible that I have ovarian cancer," she said in a choked voice. "I might never have kids, Dad." Then it hit that not having children was far from the worst-case scenario. "I . . ." She blinked back fresh tears. "I could die."

Her father sucked in a shocked breath, but he didn't let go of her hand. "That is *not* going to happen. Do you hear me? It's not. Whatever it takes, wherever we have to go for the best treatment, that's what we'll do. There are specialists at Johns Hopkins in Baltimore. Call Dr. Kinnear back and tell him that's where you're going. I insist on your seeing the best."

She almost smiled at the force behind his words. "Do you know you sounded exactly like Uncle Mick then, as if you could command the world to do your bidding. I'm okay with Dr. Kinnear and the oncologist he's recommending, at least for now, Dad. I'd like to be with someone I know, okay?"

"Whatever you need, Suze," he said with obvious reluctance, then muttered, "I wish to God you and your mother had told me about this sooner."

"So you could do what? Worry with us?"

"Exactly." He frowned. "Does Mack know?"

"No one knows besides Mom and now you. I want it to stay that way," she said emphatically. "You know how our family is. They'll hover. I don't think I could take that right now."

"Okay, I get why you might not want to drag the whole family into this, but you need to tell Mack."

"No," she repeated.

"Aw, Suze, come on," he coaxed. "The man would want to know."

"Dad, you know the kind of guy Mack is. He keeps things light and casual. This is anything but that."

"He loves you," Jeff said adamantly. "Anyone can see that. He's going to be furious if he finds out about this later. He'd want to be with you, right by your side."

"I'm not so sure about that," Susie said, wishing she could believe in Mack's devotion as fervently as her father did. "I don't want to put him to the test, especially now when he has so much else on his mind. Once I know how this is going to turn out, I'll tell him. That's soon enough."

Her father looked disappointed by her response. "I think you're making a mistake—not just for Mack, but for yourself. You need him in your corner, possibly even more than you need your mother and me."

She frowned. "What do you mean?"

"Let's face it, honey, that man can give you a reason to fight. He can give you the will to live, no matter how dark things appear."

Susie shook her head. "No, I won't put that kind of pressure on him. I don't want him with me out of pity, or as some kind of cheerleader."

"I'm not suggesting you have to marry him. Just let him be there for you the way I know he'd want to be there. Shutting him out is the kind of behavior that he might never be able to forgive."

There was a tone in his voice that rattled her. "Why do you think that?"

"Because your mom almost didn't tell me what was going on with her after Matthew was born. When she finally had to fill me in because of the problems she had with Luke's delivery, well, it tore me up inside thinking of her going through that all alone, making the decisions about our future without any input from me."

"What did you do?"

"I'm ashamed to say I walked out," he admitted. "It was only for a couple of days, but I had to wrap my head around the fact that your mother could keep something so important from me. In the end I realized she'd done it, at least in part, to protect me, but that didn't seem to matter. It took me a while to trust in what we had again. Mack could feel the same way, that's all I'm saying."

He met her gaze, gave her a weary smile. "Just think about what I'm telling you, okay? Think about how you felt when he kept his job loss from you. Don't wait too long to bring Mack into the loop on this."

"I'll think about it," she whispered, shaken. "I promise."

But though her father had raised a lot of very valid points, she was almost as scared of talking to Mack as she was of facing the biopsy next week.

What if she was right? What if go-with-the-flow Mack couldn't handle the kind of devastating news she might be facing? She thought she knew him better than that, better than he knew himself, but right now being wrong wasn't a chance she was willing to take.

8

Mack's blog had been up and running for a couple of weeks when his old boss called.

"Hey, pal, I saw the blog. It's good to see you're still writing," Don Richmond said. "One of the guys in the sports department told me about it. Based on the comments flowing in, it looks as if you still have your knack for stirring up controversy."

"Just trying to keep my finger on the pulse of the sports world," Mack said.

"So, are you making any money at this or are you still actively looking for another job?"

"I've sent out a couple of feelers, heard from a few papers, but I have some other things I'm following up on in the meantime."

"Such as?"

Mack wasn't ready to share his idea for starting a newspaper with anyone outside his immediate circle of friends. "I'll fill you in if it works out."

"Does that mean you'd still be open to another suggestion?" Don probed.

Mack knew it would be foolish not to be open to anything and everything right now. "Why? Do you have a lead on a job?"

"It's not a job. More of a freelance assignment."

"That might be a real possibility," Mack said, thinking of the income it would provide while he was waiting to see if he could pull together the newspaper. "What's the deal?"

"I had a call from a publisher the other day," Don explained. "They're looking for someone to ghostwrite a book for a sports figure. They want someone who knows the sports world and can spin a good story. The book's about someone big, though they don't want me to mention the name.

They'll pay a sizable flat-fee advance. You'd be perfect for the job. Are you interested? If so, I'll pass your name along. I didn't want to do that without discussing it with you first."

"I'd be writing anonymously, basically putting this person's words down on paper?" Mack asked.

"That's the way I understand it."

Mack hesitated. He recalled a friend spending months on one of those deals, only to have the book pulled because the athlete in question balked at the last minute. "What if the person's not being candid and I know it? Or what if I write the book and the guy won't okay it?"

"All things you'd need to discuss with the publisher," Don told him. "It's worth a conversation. You could fly up to New York next week and sit down with the editor, then meet the celebrity to see if it's a comfortable fit."

"Any idea what kind of money they're talking about?"

Don named a figure that would fatten his bank account nicely and would allow him to remain here in Chesapeake Shores while he wrote. Or at least he thought it would.

"Would I need to relocate?"

"I'm sure you'd have to spend some time with this guy, and he's not local, but I imagine you could do the bulk of the writing anyplace you wanted to."

"What's the timetable?"

"The way I understand it, they're hoping to jump on a current news situation. That's one reason they were looking for a journalist who's used to writing under deadline pressure."

The idea was intriguing and lucrative enough that Mack knew he couldn't possibly dismiss it out of hand. "Sure, tell the publisher I'm interested," he said.

It didn't mean he had to forgo the whole newspaper thing, especially if this project required a tight turnaround. It would just give him something to do while that plan came together, assuming it did. He told himself it was smart to hedge his bets, since getting financing for the newspaper was far from a sure thing.

But later, as he made the arrangements to fly up to New York for the meetings, he couldn't help wondering if Susie would see the opportunity as he did, as a means to an end, rather than as the first step to moving on to an entirely new life.

That evening, as Susie helped Mack decorate the small Christmas tree they'd bought for his apartment, she listened as he explained his upcoming trip to New York.

"I see," she said eventually, her heart sinking. "It sounds like a terrific possibility."

Mack frowned. "You don't sound all that thrilled about it. I wouldn't be moving away, Susie. If anything, this could be a way to stay right here and build an entirely different career."

She shrugged. "I guess I'd let myself get too excited about the whole newspaper thing," she said. It had been a surefire way to keep him close.

"Is that it, or are you worried that once I'm off traveling or whatever for the book, I might find someplace I like better than Chesapeake Shores?" Mack asked perceptively.

"Maybe so," she admitted. "Do you want to write this book, Mack? If you do, then that's all that really matters."

"Frankly, I see it as a way to get an infusion of cash that would tide me over until I see how this newspaper thing comes together, or even *if* it does. If it opens the door to other book deals, that might be good, but that's not how I'm looking at it. It's a onetime thing."

"The newspaper will never fly if you're not a hundred percent committed to it," Susie argued. "Laila will see right away if your time's going to be too scattered. She'll never approve a loan then."

"You probably have a point," Mack conceded. "But it's a couple of days in New York. I'll know more by the time I come back. Then I can make an informed decision."

Susie didn't want him to guess there were other reasons she didn't want him out of town right now. She forced a smile. "Right. Just a couple of days. When will you go?"

"Day after tomorrow," he said.

It was a struggle not to reveal her dismay. "Good," she said with forced cheer. "Then you'll know something by the end of the week."

"More than likely." He studied her intently. "Susie, am I missing something? You're saying all the right words, but I can tell you're not wildly enthused about any of this. Is it the book? The trip? The timing?"

"Don't be silly," she said, faking a smile she hoped Mack wouldn't be able to see through. She'd had enough practice at fooling him over the years, at not letting him see what was really going on inside her. He'd probably hurt her inadvertently a hundred different ways and never had a clue. She intended to keep it that way.

She looked up from the strand of lights she'd been clutching so tightly they'd marked her palm and forced a smile. "I can't wait to hear how it goes and who this mystery athlete is. Any ideas?"

"Not a one," he confessed. "Don wouldn't even give me a hint."

"Not even about the sport?"

"Nope. Not even that."

She grinned, and this time it was genuine. "What if it's some obscure women's lacrosse player?" she teased. "Are you up on all the details about the lacrosse world? Or a swimmer? Maybe you'll get to hang out in a pool all day, till your skin withers up like a prune."

He laughed. "Given the advance they were talking about, I doubt it's anybody obscure, no matter the sport. And I'm going to be less of a journalist and more of a writer on this one. I think my job's going to be to write this person's story, not investigate all their deep, dark secrets."

"What fun will that be?"

Mack's expression wavered. "Not much, to be honest," he admitted with candor.

"Then why even consider it?" she asked before she could stop herself from once again questioning his decision.

"It's a financial choice, Susie. I can't afford to turn my back on any options right now. And who knows, like I said before, it could open doors for me to other book projects."

"You've never mentioned wanting to write a book."

"Frankly, I'd never even thought about it, but now seems like a good time to look at everything before I decide what I want for the future."

"I suppose," she said.

He regarded her curiously. "There it is again, that sense I'm getting that you are really not okay with any of this."

"You're imagining things," she insisted, then stood up and pressed a kiss to his cheek. "Look, let's leave the tree for now. I need to run, anyway. I have an early appointment in the morning and you probably have things you need to do to get ready for your trip. I'll see you when you get back."

She thought she'd injected just the right, breezy note into her voice, but Mack latched on to her arm and held her in place, a frown creasing his brow. He stood up, then leveled a look into her eyes that had her glancing away.

"What about tomorrow, before I go?" he asked.

"I'm busy," she told him. "I might not have time to get together."

His frown deepened, proving just how badly she was handling this. She was stirring his suspicions rather than allaying them.

"Busy doing what?" he asked, his skeptical tone proving her point.

"I have appointments all day," she said. It was true as far as it went. She was doing a pre-op test, then going from that to outpatient surgery so they could do the biopsy.

"Want to have dinner tomorrow night?"

"Sorry, I can't make it," she said. "We'll do it when you get back, okay?"

Mack nodded slowly. "Sure, if that works for you."

"Have a safe trip," she said, relieved that he'd stopped pressing her about tomorrow. "Call me from New York if you get a chance. Otherwise, I'll see you Friday."

"I'll call," he said.

Though his expression was still perplexed, he actually let her go this time. Only after she was outside and was sure his door was closed did Susie release the breath it seemed she'd been holding ever since they'd started discussing this whole book thing.

And then she cried.

She'd wanted so badly for Mack to be by her side when she walked into the hospital for the biopsy, but how could she possibly blame him for not being there when she hadn't had the gumption to tell him? He would have postponed the trip to New York. A few days would hardly have mattered. She was sure of that, but she hadn't been able to bring herself to ask it of him, even though she could hear her father's words echoing in her head that she was making a mistake.

Come on, she chided herself. She'd handled most of the crises of her life totally on her own, or with her parents' backup. This would be no different, she told herself bracingly. Her mother would be with her. So would her father, Gram, her brothers, if she decided to tell them. Right now she didn't think she would. It would only increase the chances of Mack finding out, and she didn't want anything to spoil this business trip for him. She might not be happy about it, but it *was* a fantastic opportunity. He needed to be focused and at the top of his game, not worrying about her biopsy and the potentially devastating results.

There would be time to fill him in on his return. Maybe by then she'd have real news, rather than conjecture and speculation. Maybe it would even be good news.

For just a minute she let herself bask in that possibility, that the news would be good and all this fear would be behind her.

And whether Mack got this book deal or went ahead with the plan for the paper, they'd both be able to look toward a brighter future.

One thing for sure, if the news *was* good, she didn't intend to waste another minute where Mack was concerned. They'd lost enough time already. She was going to fight for what she wanted. If she blew it, if things simply didn't happen between them, well, so be it. At least she would have gone down fighting, instead of sitting on the sidelines hoping for something that was never meant to be.

When Mack got back from New York, he was bursting with excitement about the book deal. Everything had clicked into place. He already knew the football player, whose long career was winding down amid a scandal over a DUI accident in which a pedestrian had been killed. The victim's family had been paid a huge sum of money, and the charges had been reduced. The athlete had been suspended from play by the league, which meant instead of leaving the game in a blaze of glory, he was going out with a whimper.

His hope was that this book would clear his name and allow him to move forward with all of the charitable goals he and his wife hoped to meet with their foundation.

"We won't be able to ignore the controversy," Mack told Brock Hunt. "If we do, if people think this book is just blowing smoke, it won't accomplish what you want."

"He's probably right," Brock's agent agreed. "Deal with it head-on."

Next to Brock, his publicist rolled her eyes. "Now you're on board," she said sarcastically. "I've been telling him to be straight with the media from the beginning."

The agent didn't look remotely chagrined. "Now the real scoop will sell books."

Mary Long scowled at him. "You are such a sleaze."

"But I know how to work an angle," the man retorted.

"Oh, quit squabbling, you two," Brock's wife snapped. "For once, let's just do the right thing." Kelly Hunt turned to her husband. "It's time for the truth to come out."

Mack studied the soon-to-retire quarterback. "What is the truth?"

Brock hesitated, looking miserable. "I hate saving myself by taking someone else down."

"What kind of friend would have let you

take a fall for him in the first place?" Kelly asked reasonably, then turned to Mack and blurted, "Coop Mitchell was driving the car that night. That's the truth."

Mack stared at her. "That wasn't in any of the police reports. I read them when the incident happened. His name wasn't even mentioned as being at the scene."

"Because he's the team's bright young hope, Brock told him to take off. Coop was long gone by the time the police arrived. At that hour of the morning, there were no witnesses. Brock stuck around to deal with the situation."

"Who paid off the family?" Mack asked. "The speculation was that Brock did."

"It was the team," Brock admitted. "They knew the truth. Coop told them. He wanted to turn himself in, but they said they'd come up with a way to get me off." He shrugged. "And they did. The story should end right there. I don't need redemption."

"You do if you want anyone to contribute to this foundation of yours," Mary said. "You and Kelly are doing good things, Brock. The foundation isn't just your legacy. It's providing hope for a lot of kids and their families."

"The truth needs to be in the book," Mack said forcefully. "If you can't agree to that, I'm out."

The room was absolutely still while Brock thought about what they'd all said. "Okay, fine, but it's not the main thrust of the book, and we're not going to sensationalize it, is that clear?"

Mack nodded. "That works for me."

The editor who'd brought them all together looked around the room. "Then we have a deal?"

Mack reached out and shook the player's hand. "We have a deal. How soon can we get together?"

While everyone else left the room, Mack and Brock worked out a timetable that would enable Mack to meet the publisher's deadline. It promised to be a time-consuming few weeks, but the challenge was more exciting than he'd expected it to be. He'd left the meeting anxious to get back to Chesapeake Shores to fill Susie in. Maybe they could even go out and celebrate tonight. He might even take out the engagement ring that was hidden in the back of his drawer. He finally felt as if his fortunes were turning around.

Now that he was back in town, though, he couldn't seem to track down Susie. She wasn't answering her home phone or her cell. Nor was she in the office. Not even Jeff was there to fill Mack in on her whereabouts.

Thoroughly frustrated, he popped into the bookstore. Shanna looked startled and vaguely uneasy when she spotted him.

"What brings you by?" she asked, sounding less than welcoming. Actually, she sounded as if she could hardly wait for him to be on his way again.

"I'm looking for Susie. Any idea where I might find her?"

"Have you tried her cell?"

He nodded. "She's not at home, or the office, either."

"Then I'm afraid I can't help," Shanna said, avoiding his gaze.

During his years as a journalist, Mack had honed his skills at reading people. Shanna, bless her loyal heart, was lying through her teeth.

"I have the distinct impression that you know more than you're saying," he said, leaning across the counter to gaze directly into her eyes. "What's going on, Shanna?"

"I have no idea what you mean," she said, clearly flustered.

"Sure you do. You know exactly where Susie is, but for some reason you don't want to tell me."

She hesitated, then turned an unexpected scowl on him. "If you were any kind of friend, you'd know what's going on," she said, an accusing note in her voice.

He was taken aback by her sudden anger. "I have no idea what you're talking about."

"No, of course you have no idea, because you don't ask questions. That way you can tell yourself later it was everyone else's fault for not filling you in." She stepped out from behind the counter and got in his face. "Do you love her, Mack? If so, now's the time to step up and be a man."

He stared at Shanna in shock. She was probably the least confrontational woman he knew, and she was clearly furious with him. He had absolutely no idea why. He knew, though, that he'd better find out in a hurry.

"Okay, slow down the train till I can get on board. What are you so angry about? And why are you taking it out on me? I haven't even been around the past couple of days. If something's going on with Susie, I know nothing about it because she didn't tell me."

"That's exactly what I mean. She didn't spill her guts to you, so you can wring your hands now and say, 'Oh, so sorry, but I didn't know.'"

"Didn't know what, for God's sake? Is Susie okay or not?"

"I don't know. None of us know. The results aren't back."

Mack's heart started pounding so hard, he was sure it would fly right out of his chest. He couldn't seem to catch his breath. "Results?" he asked weakly. "Shanna, I swear to God, if you don't tell me what's going on, I'm going to flip out and start throwing things."

His outburst had her regarding him with surprise. "You're really scared, aren't you?"

"Terrified," he admitted. "You've made your point. I'm an insensitive jerk. Now please tell me what's going on with Susie. I'm feeling a little desperate here."

Suddenly, after accomplishing what she'd clearly wanted, she looked guilty. "I can't," she said.

He stared at her. "What do you mean you can't? Do you know something or not?"

"I know, but Susie doesn't want a lot of people fussing over her. She didn't even tell me till last night, and then she swore me to secrecy." She hesitated, then added, "I will tell you this much, though. You need to talk to her, Mack. And this time don't let her gloss anything over, okay? Make her tell you the truth. Whether she'll admit it or not, she needs you right now." She frowned at him again. "And so help me, if you don't step up, I will have Kevin take you out in the middle of the bay and dump you overboard."

"Won't be the first time," he commented, though the moment definitely didn't call for humor. It was obvious how worked up she was, and how worried. "Where is she?"

Shanna didn't answer immediately, looking torn over having revealed so much already.

"I can't tell you that, either," she said eventually.

Mack stared at her, not comprehending. "Excuse me?"

"I've said too much already."

"So help me, Shanna . . ." he began, only to have her expression completely shut down.

"You know Susie, Mack. Where do you think she's likely to go if she's hurting?"

That was the thing. There were plenty of people Susie might turn to. He'd always thought he would be one of them, but she hadn't even been taking his calls since he'd gone to New York. He'd left half a dozen messages, and she'd returned none of them. Now he knew exactly how she'd felt when she hadn't been able to reach him after he was fired.

"Never mind," he said, understanding the position he'd put Shanna in. "I'll find her."

She gave him the first genuine look of sympathy she'd shown him since he'd turned up at the store. "I'm sorry, Mack. If it were up to me, I'd tell you. Susie's the one who insisted that none of us tell you anything. I have to respect her wishes."

"I get that. I really do," he admitted. "It's frustrating as hell, but I'm glad you're in her corner."

"Always."

"I am, too, you know."

Shanna nodded. "I think I get that now. Good luck, Mack."

The minute he was in his car, he headed for Jeff and Jo O'Brien's house. When he rang the bell, it was Matthew who answered.

"Is Susie over here?" Mack asked.

"Nope. I haven't seen her for a couple of days," Matthew said, his expression guileless.

Whatever was going on, Matthew was as clueless as he was, Mack concluded.

"Are your folks here?"

"No, they drove up to Annapolis for some kind of event Uncle Thomas is hosting for the foundation. I think Uncle Mick and Megan went, too."

"Would Susie have gone with them?"

Matthew just shrugged. "No idea. Sorry."

"Okay, thanks," Mack said, thoroughly frustrated.

He sat his car and called Jake to see if Bree knew anything, then tried Will. He drew a blank with each call.

Where else would Susie go if she was sick or in trouble? The answer dawned on him at once. It should have been the first

place he'd thought of. She was at her grandmother's. She had to be.

Now he just had to pray that Nell O'Brien
was feeling kindly toward him, because
when it came to protecting a member of
her family, she could be the fiercest person around.

9

"Mack has been turning the town upside down looking for you," Shanna told Susie when she arrived at Nell O'Brien's cottage.

"He can't have looked that hard. The town's not that big," Susie said, wrapping one of Gram's quilts from Ireland more snugly around herself. She couldn't seem to get warm, despite a blazing fire in the fireplace.

"It is when the O'Briens present a united front of silence. Your parents are in Annapolis tonight. Matthew and Luke don't know anything. There's no one who'll give Mack a clue that you're over here at Nell's."

For once the whole family-solidarity thing seemed like a good thing. "Yay, O'Briens," Susie said halfheartedly.

Shanna merely frowned at the jest. "Of course, if he were half the reporter I've been told he is, he would have followed me straight here. He had to know I'd come looking for you the second he left the bookstore."

"I don't think his mind works like yours," Susie said wryly. "Or maybe he doesn't want to find me as badly as you think he does."

"Okay, that's it," Shanna said, clearly losing patience. "You love this man. He loves you. This game you've been playing has gone on long enough. This is the big moment of truth, the turning point. You owe it to Mack to fill him in on everything that's going on, not just with your health, but your feelings. Get it all out there and let him help you through this."

Susie winced under Shanna's impatient scrutiny. "Okay, I admit that I love Mack, heaven help me, but come on, Shanna, there is absolutely no evidence whatso- ever that he loves me. And what do I have to offer him, anyway? The chance to watch me go through surgery and who knows what kind of treatments after that?"

Shanna looked at her as if she'd lost her mind. "Why on earth would you say something like that? First, right this second you have no idea if surgery will even be necessary. Second, you're a wonderful woman. Any man would be lucky to have you. And everything Mack has done has been about how much he loves you. For heaven's sake, Susie, he's planning to start a newspaper so he can stay here to be with you. I'd say that alone suggests how devoted he is."

Susie wasn't convinced. Or maybe it was just the depressed mood she was in that made her doubt everything. "Who knows if that will ever happen," she said glumly. "Did you know he went to New York to talk about a book deal? If that comes through, he could leave."

Shanna looked startled. "He never mentioned any book thing to me. Isn't that something you'd tell a bookseller, especially one who's practically family? Maybe it didn't happen. I still say he's going to start a paper so he can be with you. If you didn't matter to him, why would even consider taking such a huge financial risk? It would have been a lot simpler and more financially rewarding just to take another newspaper job in some other city. He's had offers. A couple of really good ones, in fact. Kevin told me. Mack didn't even go for the interviews. He turned them down flat because they were too far away."

Susie hadn't realized that. "Good papers or lousy papers?"

"Does it really matter? The point is that he chose to stay here, rather than leave you behind or ask you to make a move with him. He knows how much this town means to you."

"But I have no idea what the future holds for me, or if I even have a future—"

"You will," Shanna said, cutting her off. "Everyone has a future. We just don't know how long it might be, which is why we need to live every minute as if it could be our last. You've heard that Tim McGraw song, haven't you? All of us should live like we're dying."

"Now, that's exactly what some man wants to hear. Make love to me because I could be dying and I really want to know what it's like before I go."

Shanna scowled at her. "Now you're just being maudlin. What I *know* is that there are sparks between you and Mack. And it's a crying shame that the two of you haven't done anything about those. For a man who could get any other woman into bed with a single glance, he seems to be terrified to take that step with you. Want to know why that is? Because you really matter."

"Nice spin," Susie said, though she desperately wanted to believe Shanna was right.

"It's not spin," Shanna replied. "Change the dynamics, sweetie. Take a risk before it's too late, and I don't mean because you might be sick. I mean before you lose him. It's time. Seduce the man."

Susie stared at her incredulously. "Now? With everything completely up in the air?"

"No time like the present," Shanna said.

Susie laughed. "As if I know how. I think three years of celibacy is proof enough of that."

"Get Mack alone," Shanna said. "Set the scene. Light some candles. Play romantic music. Something tells me the rest will take care of itself."

"It hasn't before," Susie said disconsolately. "We've been alone plenty of times. We've even been in situations that were totally romantic, and nothing. Well, except for one kiss under the mistletoe."

"And it was hot, wasn't it?"

Susie blushed. "Well, yes, but—"

"It's a start," Shanna said, not letting her finish the protest she'd been about to utter. She reached for a bag she'd brought along. It couldn't contain much, because it had been tucked inside her purse. "Maybe that's because you weren't wearing this." She dangled a sexy scrap of black silk and lace in front of Susie.

Susie stared. She wasn't sure what it was supposed to cover, but obviously it wouldn't conceal much.

"I would have gone for red," Shanna continued, "but with your coloring it would have been all wrong. Now take this, go back to your own apartment and call Mack. Put the man out of his misery."

Susie took another look at the lingerie. She tried to imagine herself wearing it, tried to envision the glint of desire it would stir in Mack's eyes, but her imagination failed her. Besides, the timing was all wrong.

"I can't do it," she told Shanna. "Not until I have the test results."

Shanna regarded her with sympathy. "I understand your instinct to wait, but I think it's wrong. I think you need to know how Mack feels before you get those test results. Otherwise you'll always wonder why he's with you. I know you. You'll convince yourself he's only with you out of pity."

"But it would feel like cheating to seduce him without telling him what's going on."

"What do you think is going to happen if you fill him in? Do you think he's going to walk away from you?"

"He might. He likes things casual and uncomplicated."

Shanna looked dismayed by her assessment. "Susie O'Brien, this is the man you love. Do you honestly think he's that shallow? If so, why on earth would you want to be with him?"

"Okay, deep in my heart I certainly don't think Mack is shallow, but right now I'm too scared to find out if I'm wrong," Susie admitted. "I don't think I could handle it if he turned his back on me. I need him. He's my best friend, aside from you, of course."

"Then he should be with you," Shanna said stubbornly. She handed Susie her cell phone. "Let's forget about the seduction for the moment. Obviously you need to resolve whether he's the kind of stand-up guy you need in your life. Call him now. If you don't, I will. I have a lot more faith in him than you seem to."

Susie held Shanna's unrelenting gaze, hoping she'd back down, but she didn't. Susie sighed and dialed. He answered on the first ring.

"Mack, I need to see you," she said, her voice barely above a whisper. "I'm at Gram's."

"Is he coming?" Shanna asked when Susie gave back her phone.

Susie nodded. "He said he'd just pulled into the driveway."

Shanna smiled approvingly. "I guess the man is brighter than I was giving him credit for," she said. "Or else he's just determined to cover every base. That should tell you something about how much he cares for you."

"You can go now. Your work is done," Susie said wryly. "I can take it from here."

Even as she spoke, though, she stuffed the lingerie behind a pillow.

Shanna looked disappointed by the gesture, but she stood. "I'll let him in on my way out. Tell him everything, Susie. Don't sell him short."

Susie felt as if her entire future were riding on this conversation with Mack, which was ironic since it was really riding on the outcome of the medical procedure she'd had yesterday.

When Mack arrived at Nell O'Brien's cottage, he was surprised to see Shanna emerge and head straight for him, a scowl firmly in place. He matched it.

"Don't you dare make me regret insisting that she call you," she said fiercely.

"You were behind the phone call?" he said, surprised. "A couple of hours ago you wouldn't even tell me where she was."

"Because that's the way she wanted it. I persuaded her she was wrong." She gave him a long look. "I also thought maybe I'd lead you straight to her without having to spill her secret."

He shook his head. "I should have

guessed. It would have saved me running all over the place and making a bunch of wasted phone calls."

"Then your instincts brought you here," she said approvingly. "That's a good sign."

"I'm asking you one more time, Shanna. Please tell me what's going on. I know something's very wrong."

She shook her head. "She'll tell you herself. If she doesn't, if she hedges, come see me. I don't want to break her confidence, but I will if I have to."

Mack knew she would never offer such a thing lightly. Something in her tone caused dread to once again settle in the pit of his stomach. "Maybe you should give me a clue here, so I don't blow this."

Shanna smiled sadly. "I don't think you're going to blow it, not if you love her half as much as I think you do. But for once, the two of you need to be really straight with each other. No more of these stupid games, okay? Promise me. They've gone on long enough."

Mack nodded. It was the one thing on which they were in total agreement. He leaned down and impulsively pressed a kiss to Shanna's cheek. "Thanks for being her friend."

"You're the friend she needs right now."

Mack stared after her as she walked away, then drew in a bracing breath and went inside.

He found Susie at the kitchen table holding a cup of steaming tea. When she set it down, her hands shook. It was apparent she'd been crying, too. His heart clenched at the sight.

He pulled a chair closer and sat down facing her, then took her hands in his. Hers were ice-cold. "Tell me what's going on. Please, Susie. I'm going a little crazy here."

She lifted her gaze and he saw something he'd never expected to see in the eyes of this intrepid woman—genuine fear. "Susie," he pleaded, "you have to talk to me."

"I know," she said, then fell silent. When she spoke again, her voice was heartbreakingly weak. "I'm scared, Mack. Really scared."

He brushed a tear from her cheek, then another. "Tell me. Just start at the beginning and tell me everything."

She hesitated for a very long time, but he waited.

"I've had some problems lately," she said eventually. "A little pain in my abdomen, cramps, that kind of thing. The doctor's run a couple of tests. He . . ." She swallowed hard. "He thinks it could be ovarian cancer."

Mack's pulse pounded. Cancer! He didn't know much about ovarian cancer, except that it could be deadly. Symptoms often appeared only after it was too late. "Has the diagnosis been confirmed?"

Susie shook her head. "He keeps telling me it could be nothing more than a cyst, but the biopsy will tell the real story."

He nodded slowly, trying to process all of this without panicking. "You need a biopsy. Okay. When?"

"I had it yesterday."

As her words registered, he stood up abruptly, unable to keep his temper in check. "Yesterday? And you're just telling me about this now? How long have you known about all this?"

"A few days."

"Before I went to New York?"

She nodded.

"And that's why you were acting so strange when I was telling you about the trip," he guessed.

"I didn't want to spoil it for you."

"Spoil it!" he exploded before he could stop himself. "Don't you know that you're more important to me than any stupid book deal?"

She leveled a look into his eyes. "No, Mack, I don't know that. How would I?"

"Because . . ." He thought of the ring back in his apartment. She was right. How could she possibly know how deep his feelings ran? "We've been together for three years now, Susie."

"We've been *friends* for three years. You were very clear about that. There's a difference, Mack, and you made sure I knew it."

"Because those were *your* terms, Susie. *Your* rules." He sat down and ran his hands over his head. "How have we made such a mess of things?"

"It's not too late to fix things," she suggested tentatively. "If you want to."

Mack looked into her eyes, saw the undisguised longing there and understood with absolute certainty that she wanted exactly what he'd always wanted, a life together. Please, God, they would have time. . . .

"Aw, Susie," he said, scooping her into his arms.

"Where are you taking me?" she asked, though she didn't struggle to get down.

"Just into the living room. I want to sit in front of the fire with you in my arms and figure out where we go from here."

She touched his cheek. "I can think of a better alternative," she whispered in his ear.

He stared into her eyes. "Here? You want us to have sex for the first time in Nell's house? Not a chance! She could be home any minute. Where is she, by the way?"

"She went to Annapolis with the rest of the family for Uncle Thomas's big fund-raiser. She won't be back for hours."

"I am still not making love to you in her house on her sofa," he said, though the temptation was strong to do just that.

"We could go to my place," she suggested hopefully. "Or yours."

"I don't think so. I think we need to work on our other communication skills first."

She frowned at him. "When did you turn so stuffy?"

"When I fell for an impossible woman."

"I am not impossible. In fact, at this moment I am very, very possible."

She reached behind a pillow on the sofa and extracted some scrap of black lace that had him nearly swallowing his tongue.

"That's yours?" he asked, not sure if he was more shocked or intrigued.

"Shanna bought it for me. She thought it might come in handy."

Mack fingered the revealing lace, then shook his head. "I'm sure it will, but not tonight. You put that on tonight and there will be no talking."

"That works for me," Susie said. "I'm tired of talking."

"You also had a medical procedure yesterday. You're probably not thinking clearly. I imagine whatever anesthesia they gave you hasn't worn off yet."

She scowled at him. "Did you make all these excuses to avoid sleeping with all those other women? Is that why they kept coming around because you were a challenge? I always thought it was because you were easy, to say nothing of sexy and very skilled."

"Gee, you think a lot of me, don't you?"

The glint of amusement in her eyes died, and she nodded solemnly. "Always have."

Mack settled on the sofa with Susie in his lap. Despite his resolve, the situation was more arousing than he'd anticipated. While the prospect of sex had always been in the back of his mind—he was a man, after all—he'd sublimated the desire beneath a ton of very rational reasons for sticking to the friendship boundary that had seemed so important to Susie. Tonight it was clear the boundaries no longer applied. That made it trickier to remain rational.

"Maybe this isn't such a good idea, after all," he said, his mouth dry.

He set her at the opposite end of the sofa. "There. That's better."

She gave him a wry look. "Really? It's not actually working for me."

"What has gotten into you tonight?"

"The realization that I might not have much time left," she said a little too brightly. "I intend to go after what I want."

Her words slammed into Mack like a freight train. "Stop it!" he commanded.

"Don't you dare say that. We haven't even started to fight this thing. We don't even know if there's something to fight."

"I know," she said. "I think that's why I was so scared to see the doctor. I already knew."

"And you got your medical degree where?"

She frowned at his sarcasm. "Women know their own bodies, Mack."

"Then I'm surprised you bothered with the biopsy. Do you already know the outcome, too?"

"Of course not."

"When will you get the results?"

"I have an appointment tomorrow."

"I'm going with you," he announced.

"But, Mack—"

"No arguments, Susie. I'll take you or I'll meet you there, but I am going to that appointment. I have a stake in this, too."

"I was just going to say that Mom's going with me."

"Fine, then you'll have plenty of backup."

"Have I ever mentioned how stubborn you are?"

He laughed. "This, coming from an O'Brien?"

"Well, you are."

"Which makes us a match made in heaven," he told her.

She studied him quizzically. "Do you really think so?"

He looked into her eyes, saw the traces of fear lingering there and pushed aside his own panic. "I think we're going to have years and years to find out for sure."

He prayed that God was listening and would make sure this one prayer, above any others he'd ever made, would be answered.

Susie fell asleep in Mack's arms. Admittedly, she'd crawled back into them after he'd fallen into a sound sleep, but when she'd shifted ever so slightly, his arms had tightened around her. She was still in place, listening to the sound of his heart, when her grandmother got home from Annapolis. Thankfully Nell had come into the cottage alone.

She regarded Susie with a lift of her brow and a faint smile on her lips.

Susie pressed a finger to her own lips and managed to extricate herself from

Mack's embrace. She followed her grand-mother into the kitchen.

"I leave for a few hours and come home to find you snuggling on my sofa with a man," Gram said, though she clearly ap-proved.

Susie grinned. "Not just any man. Mack."

"The two of you have worked things out? You've told him what's going on?"

Susie nodded. "He's been amazing. He insists on going with me to see Dr. Kinnear tomorrow." She blushed. "And I think maybe he really does love me."

Nell shook her head. "Well, of course he does. The man has good sense, doesn't he?"

Susie looked into her grandmother's sparkling blue eyes, which were filled with compassion and wisdom. "What if there's not enough time for us, Gram?"

"There's never enough time," Nell told her. "So you treasure every minute you do have."

"I don't remember very clearly when Grandpa died. He was older than you, wasn't he?"

"He was."

"Was it a shock when he died?"

"A shock? No. He'd been sick for a while, but that doesn't make the loss any easier. There are still days when I think I can smell the scent of his pipe tobacco. I'll turn around, expecting to see him."

"It must make you unbearably sad all over again, when you realize it's just your imagination."

Gram smiled. "Or is it? Maybe for just an instant God's reminding me that your grandfather is still right here, looking out for me."

"Have you ever thought about marrying again?"

"Thought about it? Not really. I do enjoy making your uncle Mick a little crazy by talking about wanting a few new gentleman callers."

"Was Grandpa your one and only love? Was he your soul mate?"

"I don't think I ever thought of it in those terms, but I suppose he was. My parents chose him, but we were well-suited. Once we married, I never looked back. I made myself forget all about the man I'd met on my last summer in Ireland."

"Do you still miss Ireland?"

Nell's expression turned wistful. "More lately. I'd like to see it again before my time comes."

"Then we should go," Susie said. "Let's plan on it. Just you and me, if no one else can get away. You'll show me all of your favorite places."

"As soon as you're well, we'll do just that," Gram agreed, then gave her a sly look. "Of course, it would be a lovely place for a honeymoon, as well. Something to think about if things are progressing with Mack."

"They haven't progressed that far," Susie said.

Gram gave her hand a squeeze. "They will. Just you wait and see."

Susie felt as if she'd already been waiting a lifetime, but tonight, sitting here in Gram's cozy kitchen with Mack asleep in the next room, she felt hopeful for the first time ever. Even with so much uncertainty in her future, she still felt hopeful.

10

When Mack awoke the next morning and realized that Susie was no longer in the room, he wandered into the kitchen, following the scent of coffee. But instead of Susie, he found Nell O'Brien at the stove, stirring a pot of oatmeal.

Drawn to the coffee, he glanced at Nell. "May I?"

"Help yourself. I made it for you. Never touch the stuff myself. I prefer tea."

"Where's Susie?"

"Sleeping. She needs her rest." She gave him a knowing look. "I gather she told you what's going on."

He nodded. "Finally. She should have told me the second she suspected there was a problem."

"I think she was afraid you'd run off." Her gaze seared him. "Will you?"

"Absolutely not," he said, speaking with firm conviction. The future might be terrifying, but he was in this for the long haul. "I love her, Mrs. O'Brien."

She gave him a chiding look at the formality. She'd long ago told him he could call her Nell, or even Gram, but he'd never felt comfortable with either one. When it came to family, he'd never quite understood the dynamics. His own had set a terrible example. As for the O'Briens, as welcome as they'd made him feel, he'd held himself aloof, afraid to want too much what they had.

"I think your love for Susie was plain to everyone except the two of you," she responded wryly. "Now what?"

"I'm going to see her through this, then marry her if she'll have me."

Nell nodded approvingly. "Mind a suggestion from me?"

"Of course not."

She looked him directly in the eye.

"Marry her now, Mack," she said earnestly. "Don't wait. You've waited far too long already. Be totally impulsive and romantic for once. Don't give her even a second's doubt that you'll be by her side no matter how all this turns out."

He was shaking his head before she'd completed the thought. "She won't hear of it," he said, though he had to admit he was intrigued by the idea. "She wants to put her life on hold until she has answers about the biopsy."

"Are those results going to make a difference in how you feel?" she asked pointedly.

"Of course not."

"The only way to prove that to my granddaughter is to marry her before the results are in." She gave him a sly look. "I'd like to see her married in the church, but I don't think God would frown on the two of you eloping under the circumstances. I've made a few calls, if you're interested."

He grinned at her. "When it comes to matchmaking, Mick has nothing on you, does he?"

"No matchmaking involved," she replied. "Fate handled that. I'm just trying to give the two of you a little push to speed things along, though frankly after all this not-dating nonsense, speed doesn't really describe your courtship, does it?" She waved off the comment. "Water under the bridge. The important thing is to act quickly now, when it truly counts."

Mack still had his doubts. "Her appointment with the doctor is today. How on earth could we possibly get married before that?"

She chuckled. "Like I said, I've made a few calls. Want me to go in there and wake her up? Or you could do it yourself. Something tells me your powers of persuasion are up to the job. Your charm, after all, is legendary around here."

He hesitated to remind her that his so-called legendary charm was what had stood between him and Susie for all these years, slowed down any chance of her taking him seriously.

Now, though, he thought of everything Susie was facing. She needed to know he was in her corner all the way, no matter what. Nell O'Brien was right. This was a way to prove that. And he did have the ring back at his place. The timing might be lousy in a lot of ways, but in one critical way it was exactly right.

"I'll be back," he said, pushing away from the counter. "Don't let her slip out of here."

She smiled. "Not a chance of that. But you hurry up, young man. Too much time's been wasted already."

Mack nodded. He couldn't have agreed with her more, and he regretted those wasted years more than he could say. What if—?

He cut himself off before the thought could fully form. No negativity. Not now.

What Susie needed more than anything was positive energy, support and hope. And maybe just this once—after a lifetime of questioning his own merits as the son of two totally irresponsible people—he was exactly the right man for the job.

Susie wandered into the living room, discovered Mack was missing, then headed for the kitchen.

"Where'd Mack go? Did you see him leave?" she asked her grandmother, not even trying to hide her disappointment. She frowned. "You didn't run him off, did you?"

"Now, why would I do that?" Nell inquired testily. "I've always been in Mack's corner when it came to you, and vice versa."

"So where is he, then?"

"He had an errand or two," Nell replied, her eyes twinkling mischievously. "He'll be back."

"Or maybe he's come to his senses and taken off for good," Susie said. "Who could blame him?"

"I would, for one," Gram said. "But I don't think that's the case."

Just then the front door opened and Mack called out. Gram gave her an I-told-you-so look. "I'll leave the two of you to talk," she said. "I have some things to do." When Susie regarded her suspiciously, she added, "Over at the church."

Susie was almost positive her grandmother was improvising. "Since when? This isn't one of your regular days to help out."

"Just pitching in for one of the other women, and I'm already late," Gram said, then pressed a kiss to her cheek. "Whatever Mack has to say, listen with your heart and act accordingly. Understood?"

Susie gave her another suspicious look but nodded, her gaze already drawn to Mack, who was standing in the doorway looking oddly uneasy, even though he was dressed impeccably in one of those expensive designer suits that always made her feel underdressed.

"Everything okay?" she asked him. "Where'd you go?"

"To my place. I wanted to shower and change."

"Into a suit? You look very handsome, by the way, but I don't think going to my doctor's appointment calls for dressing up."

"We have a stop to make first," he said.

She balked. "I don't know, Mack. I'm awfully nervous. I'd rather just get there and get it over with."

"We have time for this," he insisted.

Out of the blue he dropped to one knee in front of her, then pulled a jewelry box out of his pocket. As she grasped his intention, Susie's heart hammered so hard, she thought it might jump right out of her chest. "Mack, what are you doing?"

He grinned. "And here I thought I was going about this the old-fashioned way, the way every woman dreams of."

"You're proposing?" she asked, a breathless note in her voice.

"I am if you'll give me two seconds to get the words out," he said. "Now, hush, and let me say this. I've been rehearsing for a while now."

She fell silent, mostly from shock.

"Susie, I have loved you for a very long time," he said, gazing earnestly into her eyes. "I've waited far too long to tell you or to show you, but I think in your heart you've always known we were meant for each other. I want you to marry me, right now, this morning."

She swallowed hard, still staring at the box in his hand. "Now?" she whispered.

He flipped open the box to reveal a diamond solitaire with emeralds—her birthstone, a match for her eyes, some said—set on either side. He couldn't possibly have found something that exquisite, that perfect, on short notice. He had to have had it for a while. Given how Mack pondered things, it had to have been quite a while.

"How long have you been thinking about this?"

"I was going to ask you weeks ago," he told her. "But then I lost my job and decided

the timing was all wrong. I know you probably think the timing is all wrong for entirely different reasons, but it's not. It's the
perfect time."

She wanted to say yes, to jump in with
both feet. He was offering her the one thing
she'd always dreamed of, a life with him.

"How can I?" she whispered.

"One word is all it takes," he said. "Just
yes, and we're standing before a justice
of the peace an hour from now. When we
walk into your doctor's appointment, we'll
officially be a team, facing whatever's ahead
together."

Her lips trembled and her eyes watered.
"I want that, Mack. I really do, but—"

"No second thoughts, Susie. I know you
love me."

"I do."

"Then hold on to that and the fact that I
love you. I may not be the man you deserve, but I'll love you and protect you
with everything that's in me. Not a day
will go by that you won't know I'm in your
corner."

Before she could stop him, he took the
ring from the box and slid it on her finger.
It fit perfectly.

"Well?" he prodded. "Does it stay?"

She wanted to say no, to argue that the timing was all wrong, just as he'd predicted she would say. That would be the right thing to do, the fair thing, but she couldn't force the words past her lips. She wanted this so desperately, especially now, with so much uncertainty ahead.

"Yes," she said at last. "It stays."

"And we elope right this second?"

Blinking back tears, this time of joy, she nodded. "I do want to put some clothes on, though. It was never my dream to get married in my pajamas."

"All taken care of," he said, going into the living room and holding a whispered conversation with someone.

He reappeared with her mother and Gram in tow. She stared at the two of them in amazement. "You knew?"

"I knew," Nell confirmed. "And I knew you'd want your mother and a lovely dress." She held out a garment bag. "This was mine. I think it'll fit you perfectly, if it suits you."

Susie threw her arms around first one woman and then the other. "You two are incredible."

"Well, of course we are," Nell said. "We're O'Briens."

"Now, let's hurry," Jo said, beaming. "Your father's probably worn a hole in the carpet at the justice of the peace's office by now."

"Dad knows, too?"

"Of course," Mack said. "I had to ask his permission, didn't I?"

For a moment, Susie seemed rooted in place. "This is all happening so fast."

At that, everyone else in the room hooted, which made her laugh, too. "Okay, maybe it's not that fast. But five minutes ago all I could think about was my doctor's appointment, and now I'm getting married. Who does that?"

"Two people who belong together," Nell said.

Maybe this was wrong. Maybe it was totally unfair to Mack. But with her heart filled with indescribable joy, Susie could only be thankful that she would have time with Mack, after all. It might be short—or an eternity—but she knew it would be the happiest time of her life.

* * *

Mack knew he would remember forever the shadows in Susie's eyes when the justice of the peace read the vow about love lasting in sickness and in health. For just an instant he saw the near panic and squeezed her hand reassuringly. "Forever," he murmured. "We're going to have forever."

After lunch, there was barely enough time for Susie to change out of Nell's wedding gown and into her usual slacks and a blouse before they headed for the doctor's office.

At Dr. Kinnear's somber expression, Mack knew the news wasn't what they'd hoped for.

"It's cancer," Susie said dully, obviously sensing the same thing.

"I'm afraid so," the doctor said. "And the sooner we can schedule the surgery, the better, if we want to give you the best possible shot at a full recovery."

Susie had been holding Mack's hand so tightly, he'd lost feeling, but at the doctor's words, she released it. Her mother stood behind her chair, her hands on Susie's shoulders.

"What exactly does that mean?" Mack asked, regretting that he hadn't had time to do the kind of research he should have before coming here today.

"We'll do a complete hysterectomy," Dr. Kinnear said.

Already pale, Susie seemed to turn ashen at the words. "No children?" she whispered.

Mack knew they'd never discussed their future—there'd been no time—but in his mind he'd dared to envision children down the road. This was an unexpected twist. He hoped he was able to keep his expression neutral at the news.

Dr. Kinnear nodded in response to Susie's question. "There is the possibility we can harvest some of your eggs. We'll have to take a look at that situation and see if it's feasible given the need to get this surgery done quickly."

"Couldn't we postpone the surgery to make it feasible?" Susie pleaded. "Or what about only taking out the affected ovary? Couldn't we try that first?"

Dr. Kinnear shook his head, his expression sympathetic. "I wouldn't recommend it. With ovarian cancer, early treatment is critical. I understand your desire to hold on to options, but the oncologist and I have discussed it, especially given your young age, and we feel this will give you the best chance to survive for a long time. I promise you, Susie, we wouldn't recommend this if we didn't think it to be the best possible solution."

Mack reached for Susie's hand again, but she shifted away. "Susie," he said, all but commanding her to look at him. "It's okay. There are plenty of kids in the world who desperately need a good home. We'll find a way to have a whole houseful, if that's what you want."

His remark didn't seem to cheer her in the slightest. If anything, she looked even sadder.

"I need to think about all this," Susie said, standing up and heading straight for the door.

"Susie," the doctor protested.

Jo gave him an apologetic look. "Let her go. This has been a shock." She turned to Mack. "I should go after her."

"No, I will," he said, already on his feet. "Could you stay and maybe schedule whatever we need to do from here?"

Jo looked relieved to have something

concrete to do. She nodded at once. "I'm so glad she has you, Mack. She's going to need you now more than ever."

Mack thought about his entire lifetime of avoiding commitments, of loving and leaving anyone who threatened to cut through his defenses. Now, just when he'd decided to risk his heart with the only woman he'd truly dared to love, she could be snatched from him. Talk about a cruel twist of fate.

"I'll do the best I can for her," he promised Jo.

She gave him a watery smile. "I know you will. You're one of the good guys, Mack. It's time you started believing that about yourself. Don't let the past shadow the rest of your life. I've known you a long time, and you are nothing like either one of your parents."

"Thanks for saying that," he said, meaning it. He just didn't entirely believe her, because right this second he wanted nothing more than to run as far from Chesapeake Shores as he possibly could. He wouldn't, though. He knew that much about himself. So maybe Jo was right, after all.

* * *

Susie had run track in high school. She still had a lot of speed. Of course, she'd run in sneakers, not high heels, and the track hadn't been slick with rain most of the time, either. Today, after a sunny morning that had seemed to bless her wedding, clouds had rolled in. The sky was dark and gloomy, mirroring the shift in her own mood.

She was soaked and out of breath by the time she reached Beach Lane on the other side of town. She found her favorite boulder along the shoreline and sat, holding her painful side. Her tears mingled with the rain.

She wasn't all that surprised when Mack arrived and sat down beside her, seemingly oblivious to getting his suit ruined. He sat shoulder-to-shoulder with her, staring out to sea, not saying a word, just there. His heat, his nearness offered comfort. It was also a stark reminder of what she'd come so close to having.

"We're not getting this marriage annulled," he announced eventually.

Susie stared at him for a long time. "How did you know that's what I was thinking? It's the only fair thing to do. You didn't sign on for this, Mack."

"I signed on for *you*," he said emphatically. "For better or worse, in sickness and in health. Have you forgotten so quickly?"

"I just didn't think it would be this much worse," she said, unable to keep her eyes from filling with tears. "I know I never said much, but I wanted babies, Mack. I wanted *our* babies."

"Any children we have, whether by a surrogate or through adoption, will be ours. Biological parenting isn't all it's cracked up to be, Susie. You lucked out, but me, not so much. Maybe my gene pool isn't the best to draw on, anyway."

"Don't be ridiculous," she retorted. "You're one of the finest men I know."

He smiled at that. "You didn't always speak that kindly of me."

She waved off the comment. "I didn't much care for your carousing, but I understood exactly why you did it. With so many women in your life, there was little danger of falling for just one, right?"

He frowned. "You think you're so smart."

She allowed herself a faint grin. "When it comes to you, I'm a freaking genius. I've had a long time to study you, Mack. I doubt there's a single thing about you I don't know or haven't figured out, even when you've done your best to hide it from everyone."

"Did you know how I felt about you?" he asked.

"That," she said with a sigh, "I wasn't so sure about. I wanted to believe the feelings were there. I think what scared me wasn't that you didn't love me, but that you might never admit that you did."

"There was a good chance of that," he conceded. "Believe me, I fought against the feelings, and your brothers reinforced my belief that staying away from you was the way to go." He shrugged. "In the end, *not* loving you was impossible."

She smiled at the hint of regret in his voice. "Sorry to mess up your big life plan," she said, nudging him in the side.

He looked around at the bay and the nearby property. "Given any thought to what kind of house you'd like?" he asked.

Despite the fear coursing through her whenever she let herself stop to think about the future, Susie laughed. "Mack, we were engaged for what? Maybe an hour. And we've been married for maybe three hours with a diagnosis of ovarian cancer thrown in. I haven't had a lot of time for daydreaming about a house."

"No time like the present to start, then," he said briskly. "I'm thinking two stories with the master bedroom over the living room, so both rooms have views of the water. Maybe there ought to be a view from the kitchen, too."

Again she chuckled. She couldn't help herself. "And which one of us do you envision in there cooking?"

He laughed, too. "I'm pretty good with eggs and toaster waffles," he said. "We can sit at a big table on Sunday mornings, look out at the bay and relax while we read the paper."

"The Chesapeake Shores paper?" she inquired slyly.

He gave her a wry look. "Subtle, Suze. Very subtle. No, that'll probably come out at midweek."

"So you're still thinking about it?"

"Of course."

She studied him worriedly. "Mack, is it really something you want to do? It's not just because I want you to stay here, is it? Because who knows how long—"

"Don't you dare go there," he said fiercely.

"You're going to beat this, Susie. Anything else is unacceptable. And I'm going to pull this paper together because the idea appeals to me. It'll be a challenge."

"What about the book deal?"

He hesitated. "I've been thinking about turning it down."

She frowned immediately. "Because of me?"

"I just don't think I should be doing a lot of traveling right now," he said, avoiding her gaze.

"Because of me," she said again.

"Okay, yes. The timing's not good," he conceded. "It's no big deal."

"But it could lead to other books," she said. "You can't walk away from it, Mack. I want you to do it. How much traveling will there really be? The deadline's pretty tight, so it can't be much."

"True."

"Then do it. There will be plenty of people around to make sure I'm doing everything I'm supposed to be doing."

"But looking out for you is my job now," he said.

"Believe me, you'll have plenty of opportunities to hold my head when I'm sick or to make sure I'm eating properly. And you can boss me around to your heart's content when you're here."

He lifted a brow. "You're honestly telling me I can get away with bossing you around?"

She grinned. "You can certainly try."

He draped an arm around her shoulder and pulled her close. "We're going to have a long life together, Susie O'Brien Franklin. I'm counting on that."

She leaned against him, let herself imagine a real future with this man she'd loved forever. "I'm counting on it," she whispered. "I'm really counting on it."

In fact, during all of the likely dark days ahead, she was going to hang on to that with every fiber of her being.

11

Under the circumstances, Mack had no idea what to do about a honeymoon. Obviously they couldn't take an extended vacation right now. Susie needed to deal with her surgery and treatment as quickly as possible, to say nothing of his own financial constraints. Still, he would have blown his budget to smithereens if it would have made her happy.

After they left the beach, he'd driven to her place so she could shower and change into something warm and dry. He was worried sick about the lack of color in her cheeks and the dullness in her eyes. Even though he thought they'd had a good talk and clarified a lot of things, he knew she still had more than a few doubts about whether they were strong enough as a couple to weather whatever lay ahead. He had plenty of fears of his own, certainly more than he dared to admit to her.

By the time she was out of the shower and wrapped in a thick terry-cloth robe, he'd started a fire and made a pot of tea. "Would you rather have a drink?" he asked. "It seems as if we should be toasting with champagne."

She shook her head. "Not now. To be honest, I'm exhausted."

"Why don't I run home and change, then come back here?" he suggested. "That way you won't have to get dressed."

She regarded him blankly. "Why?" She sounded genuinely mystified.

"Because it's our wedding night," he reminded her, not allowing himself to be offended by how little that seemed to matter to her. "I'm not saying we have to make a big romantic production out of it, if you're not up to it, but we should at least spend it together, don't you think?"

She actually hesitated. "I don't know, Mack."

This time he really did have to work to keep his temper in check. He held her gaze. "Okay, Susie, spill it. What are you thinking? You're not back to the annulment thing, are you?"

"I don't know," she said guiltily. "Maybe. I know there are ways to get an annulment once we've slept together, but it will be more complicated."

The fear in her voice was real. She was convinced they ought to end this now, that he'd want to end it. He thought he detected, though, just a hint of wistfulness. An annulment wasn't what she really wanted. She was simply trying to be fair. He had to make it clear that ending their marriage before it had even begun wasn't an option.

"No annulment. No divorce," he said flatly, reiterating what he'd basically told her earlier. "We can postpone the honeymoon. We can even postpone the wedding night, but I want to be absolutely clear that there's no turning back from this marriage, Susie. Loving you, being with you, it's what I want—I wanted it before I had any idea you might be sick—and I know it's what you want, too. You're just scared."

"Of a wedding night? Don't be crazy."

He allowed himself a smile. "No, I imagine that wouldn't shake you at all. I'm talking about what comes after, the living together, trying to be a couple when we've had so little practice at it, to say nothing of dealing with the cancer."

She sighed. "Okay, yes. I'm terrified of all that," she admitted. "I feel as if I trapped you or tricked you or something. You married me thinking you were getting this healthy person with a reasonable life expectancy, and now there's this cloud hanging over the future."

"You seem to have forgotten that I knew you might have cancer when I proposed. I understood exactly what I was bargaining for—a lifetime with you, however long that may turn out to be."

Tears welled up in her eyes. "But you hadn't heard the words yet. Neither of us had. They're pretty stark, when you actually say them out loud." She met his gaze, her chin trembling. "I have ovarian cancer, Mack."

Her tears began to fall in earnest now, breaking his heart.

"Don't you see? After the surgery I won't be a whole woman," she added, her voice barely above a whisper. "Most likely that means never having kids of our own."

"Your ability to have kids or not isn't a deal breaker for me," he said emphatically. "And if you dare to describe yourself again as anything less than whole, I will . . ." Words failed him. The idea that she was anything other than a wonderful, complete, incredible woman was absolutely ridiculous. How could she not know that?

Still, his idle, incomplete threat seemed to do what his prior words hadn't. It got through to her just how serious he was about sticking with her.

"You'll what?" she asked sweetly, her eyes suddenly twinkling. She swiped at the tears with an impatient gesture, as if determined to rid herself of any sign of weakness. "Challenge me to a duel? Tickle me till I take it back?"

"Both excellent options," he replied. "Or maybe I'll just kiss you till you shut up."

She drew in a deep breath. "You could

kiss me anyway," she said daringly. "You've only kissed me once, you know. That doesn't seem right, since we're now married."

"I've kissed you lots of times," he said, thinking of the frustratingly chaste pecks on the cheek that had been a staple of their friendship.

"Only once like you really meant it," she insisted, heat in her eyes.

Mack smiled at the memory. "Under the mistletoe."

She nodded. "I don't know if you'd had too much champagne or what, but it gave me hope."

"Me, too," he said, drawing her close. He looked into her eyes and saw everything he'd ever wanted—her steadiness, her love, the passion she'd so carefully kept in check to give him the room she'd thought he needed to breathe.

His first kiss was soft, tender, a little tentative even. It felt as if it were the first one ever. And then she sighed and he was lost. His tongue touched her lips, then dived inside her mouth. She melted against him, stirring the kind of heat he'd been imagining for months now. No, longer than that. Practically since the first time he'd seen her as something other than his dearest friend. Their friendship was unmistakably different from the one he shared with Will and Jake, not just because she was a woman, but because she was *the* woman. The bond was deeper somehow, perhaps because it tapped in to emotions he'd never expected to feel.

His breath turned ragged. Hers hitched, and still she clung to him, matching him with a desire that fueled his own.

Eventually he pulled back, searched her eyes. "Is this what you want? Now, tonight?"

"I think it's what I've wanted since the day we met," she whispered against his lips, then smiled. "Well, maybe not then, since we were kids, but for a long, long time." She looked into his eyes. "And, Mack?"

"Uh-huh," he said, already lost to the feel of her surrendering in his arms.

"Tonight is just about us, just about this moment, okay? Not one single thought about tomorrow or the next day or the day after that. Agreed? You're making love to me, not to a woman with ovarian cancer. Can you do that?"

"Agreed," he said, knowing that they

couldn't postpone reality forever. But this, too, was reality, one that had been a very long time coming. They deserved this moment out of time, this happiness at its most basic level.

Of course, they deserved many more moments like it, but as Susie had requested, this wasn't the time to worry about whether they'd have them. The only way for them to live right now was as if each precious moment might be their last.

Tears stung his eyes at that thought, but he blinked them away. And when he looked into Susie's gaze, he managed a smile and a promise. "Tonight I'm going to love you like there's no tomorrow," he said, then cupped her chin. "But just so you know, there are going to be plenty of tomorrows. We'll make it happen, Susie. Whatever it takes, we'll make it happen."

He swept her into his arms, then carried her into the bedroom he'd never before shared, settled her amid the mound of lace-trimmed feminine pillows that were such a contrast to her matter-of-fact personality. He smiled at the image of her mussed hair, strands of red silk against that sea of white

and turquoise. She'd brought the sea inside.

And the fire, he thought as she reached
for him, snagged the edge of his shirt and
ripped it open, sending buttons flying.

"I owe you a shirt," she murmured as she
pressed her hands against his bare chest,
exploring, not with the tentative touch he'd
expected, but with a woman's long-denied
passion. They were anxious, restless
touches that stirred his blood and had him
counting backward from a hundred in his
head in an attempt to slow things down.

"Um, Suze, you might want to give me a
chance to catch up here," he said.

Laughter sparked in her eyes. "I think I
like being in charge. I like knowing I can
drive you a little crazy. I never imagined
that."

"You've been driving me crazy for years,"
he corrected with a smile, then lay back.
"Have your way with me, then."

She gave him a surprised look. "Really?"

"Really," he said. "I hear there's a bal-
ance of power in any good marriage. If you
want to take over tonight, I can handle it."

But as she explored, caressed and kissed

her way over his burning skin, he wondered if that was true. Could he handle it? Could he handle her? Or in this, as in life in general with this woman, was he in way over his head? He'd never wanted any woman the way he wanted this one, never felt the need to show anyone the tenderness and passion that Susie deserved.

When she reached for the zipper on his pants, he stilled her hand. "Not just yet," he murmured. "Let's get you caught up."

For an instant she looked disappointed. "But you promised . . ."

He grinned. "Changed my mind. Come here, my beautiful, redheaded temptress."

Delight lit her eyes. "Temptress?"

"Don't play coy. It's obvious the effect you're having on me. Now it's my turn."

With quick, sure fingers, he removed her blouse and bra, then sucked in his breath at the sight of her breasts. "If I'd had any idea how gorgeous you are, we'd have done this long ago."

"You mean my mistake was not running around naked?" she asked, an impish glint in her eyes.

Mack choked on a laugh. "Yeah, that

probably would have done it, but then I'd have had to kill anyone else who caught a glimpse of you."

His laughter died as she reached for his hand and placed it over her breast.

"Feel my heart beating?" she asked, a catch in her voice.

Mack nodded.

"You've made it beat that fast," she said solemnly.

"It's a strong heart," he told her, hoping to reassure her, reassure himself that it would be beating like that for a long, long time. A fair and loving God would give them that time.

"I love you, Susie. I wasn't sure I'd ever be able to say those words to anyone, ever be able to feel the kind of love I feel for you. Let me show you."

And then, with a tenderness he hadn't known himself capable of, he taught her desire and passion and, he hoped, the depths of his love for her.

"We could skip Sunday dinner at Uncle Mick's," Susie said as she watched Mack dress. It had become one of her favorite pastimes, watching this man she'd wanted for so long as he put on his clothes. She thought he deliberately turned it into some kind of reverse striptease just to torment her. "We could stay right here and spend the afternoon in bed."

That was another thing. She seemed to have become addicted to making love with him. He was very, very good at it. She only rarely allowed herself to consider that he'd gotten that way through lots and lots of practice.

"We're expected for dinner," he said, though desire darkened his eyes as he met her gaze. "I'm not going to disappoint everyone. And you know your parents will worry if you're not there. Your mother's still a little freaked that you put the doctor's appointment off until tomorrow."

"I told her that I'd spoken to Dr. Kinnear Friday morning," Susie said. "A couple of days weren't going to make a huge difference. I wanted this time for us." She frowned at him. "Didn't you?"

"I'd say the fact that we haven't left your apartment since the day we got married speaks for itself. Even the pizza delivery guy is finding it difficult not to smirk when he comes by."

Susie laughed. "Poor Teddy. I think he had high hopes that one day I'd give up on you and say yes when he asked me out."

Mack paused and scowled. "Teddy asked you out?"

She nodded, hiding a smile. "Lots of times."

"Isn't he, like, sixteen?"

"Nineteen," she corrected.

"That's it. From now on, the only take-out we order is Chinese."

Susie chuckled happily at the unmistakable note of jealousy in Mack's voice. She'd never expected that. "That hardly seems fair," she chided. "I'm pretty sure Teddy's being consoled by your huge tips. Now, let's get back to the idea of spending the afternoon right here." She reached for him, managed to slip her hand past the waistband of his pants. "I think I could make a good case for it."

Mack laughed and removed her hand, then backed a safe distance away. "Sorry, kid. It's not going to happen. This is a command performance."

"Says who? And how come it's more important than my command?"

"Your mother, your grandmother and Mick, among others. In this instance, they outrank you."

"When have you had time to speak to all of them?"

"During those rare occasions when you've let me out of bed long enough for you to soak in another of those bubble baths you seem to love."

"I invited you to soak with me," she reminded him.

"And come out smelling like roses or lilacs or whatever?" he said with an exaggerated shudder.

"You're man enough to pull it off," she countered.

"Thanks, but I'd rather not take any chances."

Susie walked over to him and put her hands on his shoulders. As tall as she was, she still had to stand on tiptoe to touch her lips to his. "I love you, Mack."

"I love you, too."

"We might want to remember that this afternoon," she said direly. "I think once word gets out that we had a wedding and didn't invite the family, both of our names are going to be mud."

Mack shook his head. "Oh, Susie, do you know nothing of your family or this town? The word was out about five seconds after the ceremony. This is just our official family debut."

She should have known it, of course, but she'd hoped there could be one secret that would be safe for a few days. "Everyone knows?"

"Based on the messages on my cell phone and your answering machine, I'd say yes."

"Why didn't you tell me?"

"Why let the outside world intrude? This was our time. It wasn't much in the way of a honeymoon, but we deserved a little privacy. We'll take that real honeymoon as soon as you're finished with surgery and treatments," he promised. "Anyplace you want to go."

"Ireland," she said at once. "I promised Gram I'd take her."

He shook his head as if he despaired of ever understanding her. "You honestly want to take your grandmother on our honeymoon?"

"The whole family," she corrected.

"You O'Briens are a strange lot," he said.

"Sorry you married into the family?"

He touched his lips to hers. "I will never be sorry I married you. Now let's go deal with the fallout from our elopement."

Susie tried to imagine the furor that lay ahead, but she couldn't. Still, after so many years of being predictable, it was going to be fun to be the one who'd shaken things up.

Even though he'd tried to hurry Susie along in order to avoid making a grand entrance, the entire family had assembled at Mick's by the time they arrived, slightly disheveled from Susie's final attempt to distract him.

Despite the wintry chill in the air, Will and Jake were on the porch waiting for them.

"Well, if it isn't Mr. and Mrs. Franklin," Will said, grinning. He slapped Mack on the back, then scooped Susie up in a bear hug and twirled her around. "You two might be slow out of the gate, but once you decide on something, you don't mess around, do you?"

Jake winked at Susie. "So, how'd you finally talk him into getting married, Susie? Did you ply him with scotch, have your wicked way with him and then sneak off to a justice of the peace before he sobered up?"

"Not even remotely close to the truth," Mack said. "The justice of the peace was my idea. And you know perfectly well I'd had the ring for ages. The two of you saw it."

"In the box," Will reminded him. "I, for one, wasn't sure it would ever see the light of day."

"Thanks for the vote of confidence," Mack grumbled. "Susie, let's go inside. Maybe the rest of the family will behave more civilly than these two."

"Hey, we're civil," Jake protested. "And we're your best friends. Those people in there . . ." He leaned in close. "They're O'Briens, man. And some of them are fit to be tied that they missed the wedding of the century."

Susie flinched. "This isn't going to be pretty, is it?" she said to Mack. "How are we going to explain?"

He knew what she was really asking—if

they needed to tell everyone the truth.
They'd agreed to keep the cancer diagnosis a secret, at least until she'd had the
surgery and they knew more about her
prognosis.

He gave her hand a squeeze. "We're
not telling them a thing. Don't worry about
it. Everything's under control."

She looked doubtful. "How?"

"You'll see." He'd called Jo earlier and
made a suggestion she'd seized gratefully. By now, she would have run with it,
he hoped.

He smiled as they walked inside and
almost no one so much as looked their
way. All of the women were huddled together in the living room. Susie might have
slipped right on by them, but Mack coughed
to catch their attention.

"You!" Shanna said, leaping to her feet
and running over to gather Susie into an
embrace. "You sneaky thing!" She punched
Mack in the arm. "Congratulations!"

Within moments, Susie was surrounded
by the O'Brien women, laughing as they
bubbled over with plans for a reception to
be held in a few weeks at The Inn at Eagle
Point, Jess's hotel just up the road.

Mack watched from the sidelines until Jo slipped over to stand beside him.

"Look how happy she is, Mack," she said softly. "Thank you for that. No matter what happens from here on out, you're responsible for putting that glow on her face. I'll be forever grateful to you for that."

"No need to be. It's what she deserves. I just hope I can make it last."

She gave him a sad look. "It's not entirely up to you, is it? It's in God's hands now." Then she patted his arm. "Run along. This planning is going to take a while."

He wandered down the hall toward Mick's study, where the men were watching football. Before he could enter, though, Will met him in the hallway, his expression somber.

"Okay, pal, spill it. What's really going on? A couple of weeks ago you'd decided against asking Susie to marry you right now. And here you are not just engaged, but married. I doubt it's because she's pregnant, since I know for a fact the two of you were too stupid to sleep together, even though it's what you both wanted."

"What a lovely characterization," Mack retorted. "Why does something have to be going on? When a situation is right, it's right."

"It's been right for years," Will reminded him.

Mack shrugged. "We finally acknowledged it, then decided it was time to get on with what we wanted."

Will shook his head. "Still not buying it. Look, you're going to need to talk to someone. I can see something's off just watching the way you look at her."

"Don't men in love stare at their new wives?" Mack asked irritably.

"Not as if they might vanish in a puff of smoke," Will said, then shook his head. "Okay, you want me to back off, I'll back off. Just know I'm around if you need me. Some people pay me big bucks because I'm a great listener. For you, the service is free."

"Thanks," Mack said. "I mean that. And I know the day will come when I'll take you up on it. I just can't right now."

Will nodded. "Can we expect you back at Sally's tomorrow?"

Mack shook his head, thinking of the pre-op meeting with Dr. Kinnear. "Probably not this week, but I will be back," he promised. "There are some things I have to take care of first."

"Is it the book deal?"

Mack shook his head. Even though Susie had protested vehemently, he'd canceled that. He'd set them up with another reporter who'd do an outstanding job, a man whose life wasn't as complicated as Mack's was right now.

"I dropped out of that. I want to meet with Laila, get things started on this whole newspaper idea. My future's right here. It's time to get that moving."

Will seemed surprised, but as he'd promised, he didn't press with more mostly unanswerable questions.

Just then Nell and Megan O'Brien came out of the kitchen and called everyone to the table.

"You're right here, sweetheart," Nell said to Susie, gesturing to the chair next to hers. "And Mack, you're next to her. Try to keep your hands to yourselves during the meal."

Susie laughed. "Way to spoil it for us, Gram."

"You can behave for an hour in company," Nell scolded, though her eyes were twinkling. "If you can't, then head on home."

Susie turned eagerly to Mack. "Now, that's an idea I can totally get behind," she said. "What do you think?"

"I think if we try to leave, there are people here who'd block the exits." He took her hand and saw that she was seated, then pulled out the chair next to her and sat.

As soon as everyone was in their places, Mick stood up. He looked around with satisfaction at his family. "I see we have a full house today, but something tells me Ma's pot roast isn't the main attraction." He turned to his brother. "Jeff, do you have something you'd like to say?"

Susie leaned over and whispered into Mack's ear. "That has to be a first, Mick ceding the spotlight to my dad."

Jeff picked up his glass. "I imagine there are quite a few of us here today who thought this day would never come." He grinned. "You know, Mick letting me get a word in edgewise."

When the laughter quieted, his expression sobered. "I doubt there's anyone in this room who didn't know that one of these days my daughter and Mack would wind up together. We just had no idea that a former quarterback who could run like the wind could possibly take so long to catch her. I mean, Susie ran track, but let's face it, she practically slowed down to a crawl to give him a fair chance."

"Thanks, Dad," she said, her cheeks flaming.

"Okay, I'm going to be serious now," Jeff said. "There's no one around who could possibly make Susie as happy as Mack does. And if that changes, I'll be first in line to see he pays."

"Count me in for that," Mick chimed in.

Susie again leaned close. "Scared yet?"

"Not of them," Mack said. "You're the one who terrifies me."

She grinned happily. "Good."

Jeff raised his glass. "To Susie and Mack, who took a long time getting here, but are ready for a whole . . ." His voice broke. He turned to his wife, his expression shaken. Jo stood up and linked her arm through his.

"To my daughter and her new husband and a lifetime of happiness," she said when Jeff couldn't continue.

"To Susie and Mack!" The salutation echoed around the table.

If anyone noticed that Jeff continued to look shaken or that there were tears in Jo's eyes, they didn't comment. Everyone was a little sentimental at wedding toasts, after all, so what was there to say? Mack didn't dare meet Susie's gaze for fear his own emotions might be revealed. Instead, he took her hand and gave it a squeeze.

"I love you," she whispered. "And this will be over soon."

Not soon enough for Mack. He'd thought she would be the one who'd have trouble facing all of the family scrutiny, but it seemed he was the one most in jeopardy of losing it. If Jeff had fallen completely apart during that toast, Mack would have been right on his heels.

And then there would have been a huge amount of explaining to do.

Susie had almost made it out of Mick's and back to the car when Shanna caught up with her. One look at her friend's shaken expression and Susie knew Shanna had figured out everything.

"It's cancer, isn't it?" Shanna asked quietly. "That's why you and Mack rushed to get married."

"I'd like to think we got married because we suddenly came to our senses," Susie said, then sighed. "But yes, he proposed before the diagnosis and convinced me to elope."

"So you didn't really know before the wedding?" Shanna said, looking surprised. "Wow! That should tell you something."

"Mack's pretty amazing," Susie said, trying to spot him amid the men hanging out on the porch. It was easy, since he was taller than most, except for Will and her cousin Connor.

Shanna chuckled. "I doubt there's anyone in the universe who didn't know how highly you've always thought of Mack."

"I'm serious. He's an amazing man," Susie reiterated. "Who else would willingly jump into a marriage with someone who might have no future? When we found out it was cancer, I offered him an out, but he turned me down flat."

Shanna's eyes widened. "You did what?"

"We got the diagnosis just after the wedding. I was willing to get an annulment. It would have been the fair thing to do.

Assuming I even survive, we'll never have children. Or at least I won't."

Shanna looked stunned. "Surrogacy?" she asked.

"A possibility, but not a very good one, from what I gather. Dr. Kinnear doesn't want to postpone surgery until I have viable eggs. And he refused to consider the more cautious approach of removing only one ovary for now. I could get a second opinion, but I trust him and the oncologist who's on the case. They know the research better than I do."

Shanna hugged her tightly. "Oh, sweetie, you must have been devastated, but it's not the end of the world. I'm sure Mack reassured you about that."

Susie nodded. "But I'd wanted to carry his baby inside me. That has to be the most intimate, amazing thing, and now neither of us will ever know what it's like."

Shanna paled just a little, enough to tell Susie that she had news of her own she hadn't shared.

"You're pregnant," Susie said dully, wishing she could muster genuine enthusiasm. At the moment she simply couldn't. "I know how much you and Kevin want to have a child together."

"We do," Shanna admitted, trying to contain her joy. "I just wish you hadn't figured it out right now. The timing sucks for you to get this kind of news."

Drawing on some inner strength, Susie found the words she needed. "I'm so happy for you," she said, almost sounding totally sincere. She touched Shanna's cheek. "I really am, you know. And one day soon I'll be able to say it and it'll sound like I mean it."

"I know," Shanna said, holding her tight. "I wish it were you, instead."

"No," Susie said emphatically. "Don't say that."

"But we already have Henry and Davy. We've been doubly blessed, even if neither boy is ours together."

"It doesn't work that way," Susie scolded. "Things turn out the way they're meant to. If Mack and I are meant to have children, we'll find a way, even if they're not biologically ours. Right now, I'm living one day at a time. I have to focus entirely on beating this cancer so that Mack and I will have a future."

"You're going to do it," Shanna said with confidence. "Have you ever known an O'Brien who didn't get exactly what they wanted out of life? You guys are indomitable. This is just a little bump in the road, Susie. And it's already brought you and Mack together the way you were meant to be. I'm not saying cancer's ever a good thing, but maybe it was just the wake-up call you and Mack needed to realize how deeply you loved each other."

Susie gave her friend a wry look. "If you think I'm going to jump up and down and say, 'Yay, cancer!', you're certifiable."

Shanna laughed. "Well, maybe not that, but you're married to Mack! As perks go, it's not a bad one."

Susie glanced again toward the group of men on the porch, watched as Mack broke free and strode toward her. Just knowing he was her husband made her breath catch.

"No," she said softly. "It's definitely not a bad perk at all."

12

It had probably been too much to hope that the news of Susie's surgery could be kept from the rest of the family. When Mack had given her a last kiss before she was wheeled off to the operating room, he walked with Jo, Jeff and Nell O'Brien toward the waiting room. There they found the rest of the family already assembled. Even Thomas and Connie had come down from Annapolis. Given how widespread the O'Brien reach was in the fabric of the community, Mack had to wonder if any business at all was being conducted in Chesapeake Shores this morning.

"She's going to be fine," Mick said gruffly, giving his brother a rare hug. "She's an O'Brien, isn't she?"

"Of course she's going to be fine," Nell said. "Which makes me wonder what all of you are doing sitting around in here when you should be out living your lives. That's what Susie would want."

"We're here for moral support," Abby declared. "You'd all be here if it were one of us." She gave her grandmother a defiant look. "And we're staying until Susie's back in her room."

Mack looked around. The only person missing was Jess. Her absence was telling. She and Susie had this oddly competitive relationship, which somehow needed to be mended. Now that Jess was married to Will, one of his two best friends, it was going to be awkward if Jess and Susie were constantly sparring like the rivals they'd been back in high school.

As if he'd read Mack's mind, Will came over to sit beside him. "Jess wanted to be here," he said.

"Really?" Mack was skeptical.

"Honestly, she did," Will insisted. "She had a group of tourists arriving this morning and couldn't get away. She'll be by later."

Mack continued to look at him doubtfully.

"Come on, man. Give her a break," Will pleaded. "She knows this whole thing she's had going with Susie all these years is ridiculous. We talked about it last night."

Happy to have a distraction that would keep his mind off whatever was happening in the operating room, Mack studied his friend. "What's that about, anyway? Do you have any idea?"

"Susie aced high school. She was a track superstar. She graduated summa cum laude from college."

Will recited the familiar facts as if Mack ought to be able to add them together and come up with an answer. He couldn't. "So?"

"Jess was the screwup. Bad grades. Close to suspension so many times, only Mick's influence saved her. Of course, the attention deficit disorder was to blame, but no one recognized that for years. Even though she more or less got her act together and finished college, it was a struggle. And unthinking people, even in the family, kept throwing Susie's successes in her face. No one did it intentionally, of course, but to someone with Jess's insecurities, it was like rubbing salt in a wound."

Mack recalled some of those occasions himself, times when the family was lauding Susie for her outstanding grades or a track win. Jess was always on the sidelines, looking lost and sometimes angry. He'd attributed it to simple jealousy, but he realized now it had been much deeper than that.

"We need to find a way to mend those fences," he told Will. "Susie's going to need everyone in her corner. Something tells me Jess could be the best one to reach her. She learned how to be a fighter. For all the rest of the O'Briens, Susie included, things have come too easily."

"Good point," Will said. "To say nothing of the fact that it will be darned awkward for us if those two are at odds." His expression sobered. "You doing okay? This can't have been part of your plan."

Mack managed a dry laugh. "As if I ever had a clear-cut plan where Susie and I were concerned. I've been flying by the seat of my pants for years now, trying to

prove myself to her or maybe trying to convince myself I was good enough for her.
Frankly, I'm surprised she married me, because she was clearly certain I'd bolt the
second I heard the news."

Will frowned. "You didn't marry her just
to prove a point, did you?"

"Of course not. I love her, Will. If anything happens to her . . ." His voice trailed
off before he gave Will a determined look.
"One thing for sure, I'm not going to take
off on her."

"Never thought you would," Will said with
total confidence. "You don't run from problems. You never have. When your mom was
a total mess and my folks invited you to live
with us, you didn't consider it for a second.
You said your mom needed you. You were,
what? Maybe twelve? And it never got any
easier, but you stuck right in there."

"Hating every second of it," Mack said.
"And her." He shook his head sorrowfully.
"I hated my own mother, Will. What does
that say about me?"

"That you were the strongest kid I knew.
However you felt about your mother, you
understood that the problem she had with
drugs and alcohol was a sickness, and

you did what you knew in your gut was right. That's the kind of moral compass that'll get you through this situation with Susie."

The certainty in his friend's voice should have bolstered his spirits, but Mack shuddered. "I don't know, man. This diagnosis is terrifying. It's not just never having kids. That's never been that big a deal for me. Susie could *die!* And look at all the time we will have wasted. It makes me sick when I think about it."

"Then don't think about it," Will advised. "You can't change the past."

"Well, it's not as if gazing into the future's all that rosy, either," Mack said, then added angrily, "Dammit, Will, she doesn't deserve this."

"No one deserves to have cancer," Will said. "It just happens. Facing it proves the kind of inner strength we have."

"What if I'm not strong enough?" Mack asked. "I've never doubted myself the way I have the past week or so. I thought losing my job was the worst thing that could ever happen to me, but that's a blasted picnic compared to this."

Jake approached and took the vacant chair on his other side. "You need anything?" he asked, his expression somber. "Coffee? A stiff drink?"

"I could use the drink about now," Mack admitted. "But I don't want Susie waking up to scotch on my breath. She'll figure out just how scared I am. I need to keep her convinced that I'm a hundred percent certain she's going to have a full recovery."

"And that's what everyone in this room is going to believe," Will said. "All that positive energy matters, Mack. I believe that. I've seen it work."

Mack regarded him gratefully. "You're not just saying that to keep me from freaking out?"

"You ever known me to say anything I don't mean?" Will said, his gaze level. "Hang on to that, Mack. And if you can't, then just hang on to us. There's no shame in letting your friends see you're scared. If it were Jess in that O.R., not a one of these words I'm saying would matter a hill of beans. I'd be freaking out, same as you."

"Ditto if it were Bree," Jake said, his gaze seeking out his wife. Every bit of the love he'd always felt for her was in the tenderness of his glance.

"I have no idea what I'd do if you two

weren't in my life, if you hadn't been all these years," Mack said with total sincerity. Even as kids, they'd instinctively shown him the kind of support and backup he'd never had at home. Along with Kevin and Connor and the rest of the O'Briens, they'd made up his family.

Jake gave his shoulder a squeeze. "Lucky for you, you'll never have to find out. Now, why don't I go grab some coffee for everyone? Mack, you want to help? From what I gather it's going to be a while yet before there's news. I imagine keeping busy will help the time go by more quickly."

Mack nodded. Anything to get out of this crowded room and into fresh air. Anything to avoid sitting around thinking too much.

"I'll come, too," Will said. "I'll let Jo know where we're going."

"Thanks," Mack said, heading for the door.

Only when he was outside in the frigid December air did he draw in a deep breath.

"I think if I'd stayed there one more minute, I'd have lost it," he told Jake.

"No, you wouldn't have," Jake said. "I heard what Will said earlier, and he was right. You always do what needs to be done, no matter how much it's killing you inside. Right now you need to be strong for Susie, and trust me, you're going to nail it."

Mack hoped his friends weren't mistaken, because it had never been more important to get it right.

The holidays, always Susie's favorite time of the year, came and went in a blur. She'd barely recovered from the surgery when she had to begin chemo. Though she'd known it intuitively, she now had proof that cancer didn't take breaks for Christmas or the New Year. The fight was nonstop.

There were days when she felt so crummy she wondered if it was all worth it, but Mack was by her side with whatever she needed—ginger ale, broth, a joke or simply to hold her in his arms, letting her soak up his strength.

That didn't mean she hadn't noticed the shadows under his eyes or his drawn expression. The day after the New Year dawned, she told him to sit beside her on the bed, then leveled a look directly into his eyes.

"Enough of this," she said flatly.

"Enough of what?"

"You putting your life on hold for me. Where's that business plan you promised to put together for Laila?"

He looked vaguely uneasy. "I've been working on it," he claimed.

"Great. Then let me take a look at it while you schedule an appointment at the bank."

"It can wait a little longer," he protested. "Let's get you through treatment first. We're okay for money for now."

She gave him an impatient look. "Money is not the point. You need to focus on something other than me. You're hovering, and while I might bask in the attention, it's starting to get on my nerves."

He looked taken aback, and maybe just a little hurt. "I'm getting on your nerves? I've been trying to help."

She grasped his hand. "Of course you're helping, but you need to have your own life, Mack."

"And I will," he insisted.

"I want to see that business plan," she repeated. "Now, please."

He gave her a wry look. "Boy, are you bossy!"

"You knew that about me long ago," she said. "And stop with the evasions. Do you have a plan or not? And I don't want to see those napkins and notes you made weeks ago at Sally's."

He laughed. "Fine. Give me a minute."

When he returned, he did, in fact, have several pages of carefully thought out ideas, organized into sections: potential costs for start-up, staffing, printing and so on, along with projections for advertising revenue. Even to her untrained eye, it looked like a shaky proposition.

"Can't you boost these ad revenues some?"

"Not if I'm being realistic," he said.

"Maybe you'll have to get by with fewer people," she suggested.

"I don't see how. Believe me, I've talked to a lot of publishers in the region. This is the bare minimum." He met her gaze. "Not so promising, is it? We'll certainly never get rich this way."

"Rich doesn't matter," she said. "Satisfaction and fulfillment are the goals." She held his gaze. "Do you want to do this, Mack? Really and truly? Or was this just an exercise to pacify me?"

To her relief, his eyes lit up. "At first maybe that was it, but the more I thought about it and talked to other people, the more excited I got. It'll be a challenge, no question about it, but it could be my chance to do something that matters for this community."

He gave her a look that told her just how much he needed that, to do something that mattered.

"For so many years I got by around here by being a superjock and then a hotshot columnist," he explained. "People gave me a pass, maybe even a little respect, even though behind my back I know there were always a few saying 'Poor Mack, just look where he's come from.' I don't want anyone's pity anymore. I want to be someone they look up to because I've actually accomplished something important."

"Being a superjock was an accomplishment," Susie argued. "So was your newspaper job. Don't downplay them."

"I'm just saying this newspaper could be something that makes a difference, something that lasts and makes the community stronger."

She saw it through his eyes and wanted that for him. "Then we'll make it happen," she said confidently. "We could talk to my dad, or to Uncle Mick," she began, only to have him silence her with a look.

"Not a chance," he said at once. "If the bank won't back me without either of them, then I'll figure out something else."

"Come on, Mack. Be reasonable. There's nothing wrong with finding backers for a business."

"Not your family," he said emphatically.

"What about Abby? She puts investment deals together. She did it for her mother, so Megan could open that gallery."

He gave her an incredulous look. "She did that with family money," he reminded her. "And Megan wasn't one bit happy when she found out about it. Remember that?"

Susie sighed. Yeah, Megan had been ticked, but the gallery had been a huge success. She'd paid back every dime the family had invested. Mack would do the same. Arguing, though, when his jaw was set like that, was pointless.

"Fine. I'll forget it for now. Just know that it's a possibility if things don't work out at the bank."

Mack leaned down and kissed her. "I

love you for believing in me, but I'll handle this on my own. Your only job right now is beating cancer."

Susie frowned at the comment. She knew he'd meant it to be supportive, but the lecture was getting old. Whatever lay ahead, she wanted to have a full life now. She didn't want to spend whatever time she had so focused on cancer that she'd have no memories of actually living. She was a newlywed. She wanted to enjoy that. She wanted to celebrate it.

She faced Mack. "There's something else we need to discuss."

"Not now," he said, already standing up and backing away from the bed. "You need to rest."

"What I need is for the family to throw that huge party they started planning weeks ago after we eloped. I know you talked them into delaying it, but I want it, Mack. I want to dance with you and toast the two of us."

He frowned. "I'm not sure—"

"Well, I am. Dr. Kinnear says it's fine. I'm not an invalid, Mack. You have to stop treating me as if I am. I'm calling Mom this morning and telling her to set the date. We know when the chemo effects are the toughest. We'll work around that."

"But your immune system," he protested. "You shouldn't be around so many people."

She caught his hand and insisted he sit once again beside her. "Here's the deal. I love that you want to take care of me, but I want to live my life. I'm not going to do anything stupid, but I will not look back at this period of time and regret that I didn't make more memories while I still could. I don't want the cancer to define my life, Mack. I want to *live* my life."

"But—"

She shook her head. "No buts. This is my decision, Mack."

"And I have no say?"

"About a thousand and one things, you do, but not about this one." She looked into his eyes, saw the worry there. "Please don't fight me on this. It's one night, Mack. That's all I'm asking for."

"But I know you. If I give in, first it will be this party, then you'll want to go back to work, then you'll start taking dancing lessons or something."

She laughed. "I think you're safe when it

comes to dancing lessons. I have two left feet." She sobered. "But we could talk about me going back to work part-time."

He sighed heavily. "See what I mean? Okay, I'll agree to the party, if it means that much to you, but forget going back to work."

"I could do paperwork here at home," she suggested.

He shook his head, then chuckled. "You're going to do it no matter what I say, aren't you?"

She beamed at him. "Pretty much."

"Okay, then," he said, his expression resigned. "You have my blessing on all counts."

"Thank you," she said solemnly. "Now, go and fine-tune your proposal and make that appointment with Laila. I'm going to take a much-needed nap. Battling wits with you takes a lot out of me."

"Me, too," he commented drily, then kissed her. "Love you."

She watched as he left the room, then sighed deeply. She'd waited a lifetime for those words to come from him so easily. She prayed she'd have just a little longer to truly savor them.

* * *

When Susie woke again, there were shadows in the room and someone was sitting in a chair near the window. Even though she couldn't make out the features, she knew instinctively that it wasn't Mack.

"Suze, are you awake?"

It was her brother. "Matthew, what are you doing here? Mack didn't recruit you to babysit me, did he?"

"Are you kidding me? He wouldn't dare. You'd never let him live to tell the story."

"Then why are you here?"

"I just wanted to check on you," he said. He walked over to the bed. "You mind?" He sat down on the edge before she could reply. Susie flipped on her bedside lamp, took one look at his haggard expression and demanded, "What's happened? Is it Mom or Dad? Luke?"

His lips curved slightly. "Everybody except you is just fine."

"Well, I'm going to be fine, too," she said. "Now, tell me what's wrong. You look as if you've lost your best friend."

He gave her a wry look. "Leave it to you to nail it on the first guess."

Susie tried to recall who the love of her brother's life had been last week, or the week before, for that matter. Matthew changed girlfriends as frequently as he did shirts. She'd always thought he was trying to model himself after Mack.

Eventually she gave up and asked, "Which one was it this time?"

He shifted uncomfortably. "I can't really say."

"That's going to make the conversation a little tricky, don't you think? I need details if I'm going to help."

"We've kind of been flying under the radar. It's probably better to keep it that way."

"Is this someone I know?"

"Sorry. I can't say."

"Which means it is," she concluded. "Why were the two of you keeping it a secret?"

"It seemed wise, that's all. Under the circumstances, I guess she was right about that."

"Is it over, then?"

"She says it is," he said, his expression miserable.

"What happened?"

"That's the hell of it," he said heatedly. "I

have no idea. One minute everything was fine. Better than fine, in fact. The next it was 'Thanks for a good time. See you later, pal.'"

"I see."

"Do you think it was only about the sex for her?" he asked, sounding like a lost kid rather than the relatively sheltered but otherwise fairly experienced twenty-six-year-old man he was. "I mean, I know guys are supposed to always be about the sex, but I didn't think it was like that for women."

She gave him a rueful look. "I'm probably not the best person to ask about this. Mack was always the one for me. I didn't date a lot, and my sexual escapades could be counted on one hand." She touched his arm. "Do you really care about this woman, or is your ego just bruised?"

Heat flared in his eyes. "I was falling in love with her," he replied. "I told her I was."

Ah, Susie thought, maybe he'd set off a panic attack. It usually happened in reverse, with the man running off in a tailspin, but she supposed women could freak out, too.

"Maybe she thought you were getting too serious too quickly."

"But I've known her, like, forever."

"And were dating her for how long?"

"A couple of months, I guess. It just sort of happened, you know? We got together a few times for drinks, then things changed, and we *got together,* if you know what I mean."

Susie managed to contain a smile. "Yeah, I know what you mean. I think you're talking to the wrong person, though. You need to be having this conversation with her. If she means that much to you, sit down and talk it out. Find out what's really going on in her head."

"I guess that makes sense," he said, though with obvious reluctance.

"I know men hate to have these deep, emotional conversations, but it's the only way to clear the air and try to get your signals straight."

He gave her a penetrating look. "Do you and Mack have your signals straight these days?"

Susie frowned at the question. "Of course we do. Now that we're married, we're better than ever at communicating. We're not fighting all those doubts I used to have about whether he could ever have a serious relationship."

"You do know I'm glad for you, right?" Matthew asked earnestly. "Mack's the best. Luke and I only told him to stay away because, well, we knew his history. We didn't want you to get hurt."

"I know that, and I appreciate that the two of you were being so protective. It's all good now."

"Except for the cancer," Matthew said. "That sucks."

She nodded. "That definitely sucks."

Her brother stood up, his shoulders squared, his jaw set with determination. She smiled, looking up at him. "When did you go and grow up on me?" she asked, a little wistful for the days when she'd been able to torment her kid brother.

"I did it while you were busy mooning over Mack," he told her drily. "Somehow you missed the fact that I've been moving up in the ranks at Uncle Mick's company. Some people even think I'm almost as good an architect as he is."

She heard the note of pride in his voice and knew she'd done far too little to encourage him on the career path that had put him smack between his father and his uncle. "You and Dad worked out your differences over your deciding to work for Mick?" she asked.

He shrugged. "He might not be overjoyed, but Dad's a pragmatic man. He knows I'll get the best experience in the world with Mick." He grinned. "And I've promised to design some outstanding houses for some of the property he owns outside town, so we're all good."

Susie suddenly sat upright. "Beach Lane," she said excitedly. "Would you design a house there for me and Mack? We might not be able to afford to build it right away, but I'd like to see the plans on paper."

Matthew grinned at her. "Done," he said at once. "I'd been wondering what to give you for a wedding present. Now I know. We'll get together soon and you can tell me exactly what you want."

"I want to pay you," Susie protested.

"Not a chance." He pressed a kiss to her brow. "Thanks for the advice, Suze. I'll be in touch about the plans for the house."

"Advice is available anytime. And if you

work things out, bring this woman around, okay?"

A guilty expression flitted across his face, then was gone before she could question it.

"Will do," he mumbled on his way out the door.

"You know there are no secrets in this town," she called after him.

"There's at least one," he shouted back, laughing. "Bet I can keep it, if I work at it."

"Matthew O'Brien, get back in here," she commanded.

He poked his head in the doorway.

"Why would you want to? Maybe you should be asking yourself that."

His expression turned solemn. "Not my decision," he said. "If it were up to me, the whole world would know."

"Then why would you want to be with a woman who's embarrassed to have anyone know about your relationship? That's not healthy, Matt."

"You'd understand if you knew," he insisted. "I get where she's coming from. I might not like it, but I get it."

Susie regarded him worriedly. "This situation is giving off all sorts of warning bells.

Maybe you should think about it some more. Take some time off."

"Nope. It's nothing I can't handle," he insisted, suddenly sounding sure of himself again. "Love you."

"Love you, too."

But that didn't mean she didn't intend to get to the bottom of this. And if some woman was planning to make a fool of her brother, she'd be faced with the full fury of the O'Briens. Nobody messed with an O'Brien, not in Chesapeake Shores, at any rate.

13

After his conversation with Susie, Mack had wasted no time in putting the finishing touches on his business plan. When he'd called Laila Riley at the bank, she'd told him to come straight over. Surprised by her eagerness, he'd rushed to get there within minutes.

"First, I want to hear how Susie's doing," she said after they were seated across from each other in her office with its splashes of brightly colored modern artwork on the walls. Compared to the rest of the bank with its stodgy furnishings, the room was bright and cheerful, much like Laila herself. As tall as she was, she made no attempt to disguise it. She chose bright colors and bold patterns, and heels that emphasized her height and her shapely legs.

"Susie's tolerating the side effects of the chemo a whole lot better than I would be," Mack said candidly. "She's sick as a dog right after the treatments, but she's never uttered a single complaint, at least not around me."

"Susie always did have an amazing amount of inner strength," Laila said. "I don't think we realized it because she was just so darn good at everything she ever tackled. We all thought she'd just cruise through life accomplishing whatever she put her mind to."

Mack gave her a thoughtful look. "Don't tell me you have the same issues with Susie that Jess has always had."

Laila laughed. "Heavens, no. Competitiveness is an O'Brien trait. I've been blessedly exempt from it."

"Except when it came to this job and Trace," Mack said knowingly. "You had quite a thing going with your brother for a long time, as I recall."

"Ironically, Trace and I never saw it as a competition. He never wanted the job. I did. It was my father who thought his only son should inherit the bank presidency, after serving a dutiful internship period as vice president, of course. Me, he offered a position as a clerk. I was so disgusted by his sexist attitude, I pretty much took myself out of the competition for a lot of years, till my sneaky brother did what I hadn't been able to do. Trace convinced our father I was better at banking than he was."

"Now that you have the job, are you happy?" Mack asked, sensing that Laila wasn't quite as fulfilled as she was pretending to be.

"With my job? Of course," she said at once.

"And outside of work?"

She shrugged. "We can't have it all, can we?"

"I don't see any reason why not," Mack said. "Anything I can do?"

She waved off the offer. "You didn't come over here to talk about my personal life, or the lack thereof," she said, injecting an upbeat note into her voice. "Let me see that business plan of yours."

Mack took the bound pages out of his briefcase and handed them over. "I've never put one of these together before, so feel free to rip it to shreds and tell me what I'm missing. I want this to work, Laila, so I'm willing to do whatever it takes to prove to you that I'm a good risk."

He started his spiel about the important role a local newspaper could play in town, but Laila interrupted.

"You don't have to sell me on the idea," she told him. "The town has needed its own paper for a long time. That's one reason I was so eager when you finally called. I've been hearing rumors about this for a while now, and I'll admit I'm intrigued. You just have to convince me that the numbers make sense. Give me a few minutes to take a look."

Mack waited anxiously as she flipped through the pages, jotting notes on a legal pad as she went. When she'd looked it over carefully, she met his gaze, her expression neutral.

"Mack, as much as I'd personally like to see this happen, it's not without some serious risks. Are you sure you want to tackle something this challenging? You've made it look good on paper, but we both know the newspaper business isn't exactly flourishing these days. Frankly, your figures are worrisome."

He understood her reservations. He'd had many of the same ones, but he also had faith he could pull this off. "I wanted to be conservative," he explained. "Pie-in-the-sky projections wouldn't have fooled you. I should remind you, though, that this is a new business model. It includes the on-line aspect of the paper, which can give advertisers more bang for their bucks."

"How are you going to make that work?" she asked with more curiosity than the skepticism he'd feared.

"If we can work out the financing, the first person I hire will be the web coordinator. I already have someone in mind, a woman I worked with in Baltimore. She's really talented, and I think the challenge of starting something like this from scratch will appeal to her. She's experienced and smart. I think she'd be a huge asset to the project and to the town."

Laila looked unconvinced. "I don't mean to come across as being negative, because I do love the whole idea, but do you really think you can lure somebody away from a major newspaper to work here? You don't have that kind of budget, Mack."

"I can give her a piece of the action," he contradicted, "and a chance to do something fresh and innovative, instead of trying to turn a bulky, uncooperative beast around. Look, I'm willing to invest a lot of my own money in this, but it's going to take more than I have to get it off the ground."

"You believe in this that strongly?" Laila asked.

"I do."

"Have you thought about going after other investors?"

He frowned at the question. "I'm not asking the O'Briens for backing."

"What about Abby? She puts deals together all the time. It would be strictly business."

"Really?" Mack said skeptically. "Unfortunately, I think I know just where she'd start on this, with the family. Let's not forget the Megan debacle."

She laughed. "Actually my father is still kicking himself for not fighting harder to get that loan approved by the committee.

Megan's gallery made a lot of money for her investors, probably because she was highly motivated to pay them back."

"Well, I'm highly motivated, as well, but I don't want my fate in the hands of Susie's family."

"Any particular reason, other than pride?" she asked.

He smiled at the question. "I can't deny that's probably part of it, but I also don't want any of them to have a moment's doubt about the reason I married Susie. It's because I love her, not so I can get the rest of the family to back me on some business deal."

Laila nodded, looking pleased by his reply. "Good point. I can respect that. How about this? You get your web expert on board, add in some of her ideas and review your figures. Once you've done that, I'll take another look at your proposal."

He shook his head. "Not good enough. I can't ask her to commit, then have you yank the rug out from under both of us."

"All I need is an agreement in principle," Laila told him. "She doesn't have to quit her job or make the move down here. This can all be handled discreetly, so her job's not at risk if this doesn't work out."

Mack stood up. "Then we have a deal," he said holding out his hand. Instead of shaking it, though, she came from behind her desk and hugged him, then took a step back.

"Just one thing, Mack."

Something in her expression gave him pause. "What?"

"Is this dynamite woman going to cause problems for you and Susie?"

Mack frowned. "Why would you even ask that?"

"Because you have a track record, my friend, and I care about Susie's feelings. I don't want her heart broken because you're out trying to seduce some other woman into working for you."

"Believe me, seduction, the way you mean it, won't come into play. I do have some boundaries," he replied, offended. "Whatever courting I do of Kristen Lewis will be strictly professional. Susie has nothing to worry about."

"Did the two of you have a relationship in the past?" she inquired with the kind of directness Mack had to respect, even if the question made him squirm.

He wanted to tell Laila it was none of her business, but he understood her point. "It was a long time ago, and it was never a big deal."

"Does Ms. Lewis understand that?"

"We managed to stay friends, if that's what you're asking."

"And Susie knows about this past?"

He shook his head. "I don't think Susie was ever interested in knowing the names and faces from my past."

"She might care now, especially if you intend to bring this woman to town. Think long and hard before you make that decision, Mack. Susie's self-esteem is bound to be a little fragile right now."

"Susie knows she has nothing to worry about," Mack insisted.

But even as he said the words, an image of willowy, blonde Kristen came to mind. Too many people focused on her flawless cover model beauty and missed her sharp wit and intelligence. Normally that wouldn't be an issue with Susie, who had an innate ability to read people, but given her insecurities where he was concerned and the current state of her health, he wondered if maybe Laila had a point.

"I'll fill Susie in, then make a decision," he said eventually, knowing he had no choice. He wasn't going to undercut Susie's confidence, especially now. "I'll be in touch."

"Soon, I hope," Laila said. "Despite the reservations I've expressed, Mack, I think this is an exciting idea. I want to help you pull it together."

"Thanks for the encouragement," he said. "And the advice."

"Just looking out for a couple of people I care about," she said. "Give Susie my love."

"Will do," he promised.

He was on his way out of the bank when he ran into Matthew just outside.

"Hey, bro, what are you doing here?" he asked his brother-in-law.

A surprising burst of color flooded Matthew's cheeks. "I just needed to have a word with Laila. Did you happen to notice if she's in?"

"Yep. I just left her office."

Matthew paused, clearly struggling to

gather his composure. Mack regarded him curiously. He'd never seen his brother-in-law rattled like this.

"Something going on, Matt?"

"Like what?" Matthew asked defensively.

"I have no idea, but you seem a little uptight."

"I'm fine," Matthew insisted. "Were you here to talk about the newspaper thing?"

Mack nodded.

"How'd it go?"

"Let's just say Laila has some justifiable concerns. I have a lot of things to work out before she's likely to take it seriously."

"Maybe I can put in a good word," Matthew said.

Mack regarded him curiously. "Really? Why would Laila listen to you?"

This time there was no mistaking Matthew's embarrassment. "Old family friends, you know. She's Trace's sister, Abby's sister-in-law, all of that."

Mack wasn't always attuned to the nuances of things, but there was no mistaking what was really going on here. He'd once been a master of evasion when it came to his social life. He latched on to

Matthew's arm and steered him down the street to Sally's.

"Talk to me," he commanded as they sat in a booth and ordered a couple of Cokes.

Matthew feigned innocence. "About what?"

"You and Laila," Mack said. "Please tell me the two of you are not having some kind of fling."

"If we were, it wouldn't be any of your business," Matthew said indignantly. "You're my brother-in-law, not my keeper."

"She's at least ten years older than you," Mack said.

"More than that," Matthew said. "So what?"

"Look, under any other circumstances, I'd say your personal life is absolutely none of my concern, but I don't need to have whatever's going on with you two get in the way of this business proposal of mine."

"Why would it?" Matthew said. "I just told you I'd put in a good word for you."

"And when this whole crazy relationship goes up in flames, I could wind up caught in the cross fire," Mack said, not caring how selfish that sounded. If he'd thought for an instant that there was something serious between those two, he'd have backed off, but how could there be? Laila was no cougar who made a habit of dating younger men. Matthew, however, had a track record that rivaled Mack's when it came to loving and leaving women. This had disaster and heartbreak written all over it.

"I don't see how what I do or don't do could possibly hurt your business deal," Matthew said stubbornly. "Besides, the relationship isn't going to go up in flames. I came over here to get things back on track."

Mack nearly groaned. "*Back on track* implies they've already derailed once."

"Oh, give it a rest," Matthew said impatiently. "Don't try to convince me you lived a life of complete virtue when you were my age. We all know better."

"I wouldn't dream of it," Mack said. "But you're the one who pointed out that Laila is like family, which means you don't mess around and risk hurting her. Just imagine the chaos that would stir up."

"I'm not going to hurt her," Matthew insisted. "This isn't some immature game to me, not like the ones you used to play."

Mack winced at the direct hit. "Okay. Just don't say I didn't warn you when Trace and Abby descend on you and drag Mick and your father into the battle."

"Duly noted," Matthew responded. He hesitated, then said, "By the way, don't mention any of this to Susie, okay? She has enough on her plate. I talked to her about the situation earlier, but I deliberately didn't mention Laila's name. I knew it would freak her out."

"She won't hear it from me," Mack assured him. But he knew the O'Briens and Chesapeake Shores well enough to know that she would hear it, and when that happened, who knew what kind of hell was likely to break loose.

Susie had managed to shower and change into a sexy negligee—another gift from Shanna, who clearly had a romantic heart—by the time Mack got home from the bank. She'd opened a bottle of sparkling cider and started dinner.

"What are we celebrating?" he asked when he walked in.

"Me being out of bed," she said at once,

then grinned. "Though I'm hoping this will get us right back into it." She lifted the filmy lace so candlelight shone through it. She saw Mack's eyes darken with desire.

"Really?" he said, his voice thick.

"Oh, yeah," she said, slipping into his arms. "How's it working?"

"You definitely have my attention," he said. "Are you—?"

She silenced him with a kiss.

His usual calm facade looked a little rattled by the time she released him. "Um, Susie, don't you think we should eat a little something?"

"Do you seriously want dinner more than you want me?" she inquired in a way that dared him to say yes.

"Of course not," he said wisely, "but—"

She grinned at him. "You're starting to get on my nerves."

Whatever his reservations were, they fled. "Okay, then," he said, scooping her into his arms. "You first. Dinner later."

"Sounds like a plan," she said happily.

For just a little while, in his arms, she could almost forget about her cancer, about the chemo, about being sick at all. She could be nothing more than a woman who was finally with the man she'd always wanted. And nothing else mattered.

Only after they were cooling down and curled together did she think to ask, "How'd things go at the bank?"

"We have a lot to talk about," he said evasively.

"What does that mean?"

"It means we have a lot to talk about," he repeated. "We can do that over dinner. Did you sleep all afternoon?"

"Mostly," she said. "Then Matthew came by."

Mack stilled, his expression guarded. "Really? Any particular reason?"

"He wanted advice about relationships, if you can believe that."

"Did he give you any details?"

"Not a one, darn it. I do think it's serious, though. He seemed really upset. I guess the woman dumped him, and he had no idea why. It must have been a huge blow to his ego. Matthew hasn't been dropped by a lot of women over the years. He's always been the golden boy." She grinned. "He's a lot like you. I think I was the only woman who ever said no to going out with you."

He laughed. "And look where we wound up," he reminded her. "For some of us, *no* must be some kind of aphrodisiac."

"I wish I had some idea who this woman is. I hope it's someone who's worthy of my brother."

"Did you ever stop to think it might be Matthew who's not worthy of her?"

She frowned at the suggestion. "Why would you even ask something like that?" she inquired with sisterly protectiveness. "I always thought you liked Matthew. I know he idolizes you."

"I think *idolizes* is probably too strong a word. We get along just fine. He's a good guy at heart. I just wonder if he's not in over his head in this situation."

She studied him with a narrowed gaze. "That almost sounds as if you know something about this that I don't. Do you?"

Mack leaned in and kissed her thoroughly. "Not at liberty to say," he said. "And I'm starved. Let's have dinner."

Susie's stomach rumbled. "Obviously, I'm starved, too," she said. "Otherwise I'd never let you get away with an evasion like that. We'll take this up again after dessert."

"Not if I can help it," he said. "I have much more interesting plans for after dessert."

"Boy, you must really want to avoid this subject," she said, studying him intently. "Makes me wonder why."

"You don't think it could be because I find my new wife ever so sexy and desirable?"

She laughed. "Well, of course, I know I'm all that, but there's something else going on here. You might as well fill me in, because I'll figure it out sooner or later."

"I don't doubt it for a minute," he said. "But I look forward to the challenge of not being the one who tips you off."

"Now you're just taunting me," she responded.

Mack winked. "Yes, I am."

She met his gaze, saw the twinkle in his eye and marveled at how quickly they'd moved from being friends to having the kind of easygoing, loving marriage she'd envied between her parents.

Sobering, she touched his cheek. "Do you have any idea how much I love you?"

"Back at you," he said softly. "I'm sorry it took us so long to get here."

"But we did get here, and that's what counts," she said. "And we're going to be exactly like this always."

He pulled her back down onto the bed with him, dinner forgotten. "Always," he murmured against her lips.

It was a promise she knew she would hold in her heart all during these horrendous treatments she was undergoing. Because in the end, it gave her a reason to fight.

Laila looked up from Mack's business proposal to see Matthew O'Brien standing in the doorway to her office. To her annoyance, her heart leaped at the sight of him.

"I thought I told you it was over between us," she said, trying to keep her voice cool and distant. She knew that giving this particular man the slightest opening would only lead to heartache. "I thought I made myself very clear at dinner at Mick and Megan's a few weeks ago."

"You did," he said, walking into the room and settling into a chair across from her. He crossed his long legs at the ankles and surveyed her with a frankness that made her blood heat. "I decided to ignore you."

"Matthew," she protested. "This thing between us, it's crazy."

"Possibly," he said. "But that doesn't mean it's not incredible."

"It can't possibly go anywhere," she continued. "I'm too old for you."

"I hadn't noticed."

She frowned at his flippancy. "See, right there, that's the problem. You don't listen to a word I say."

"I listen to *everything* you say," he corrected. "And to what you don't say, as well."

"What is that supposed to mean?" she asked in frustration.

"It means that you're saying what you think is appropriate, even though what you want is something else entirely."

She scowled at his presumption. "You have no idea what I want."

"Sure I do," he said, grinning. "Want me to prove it?"

To her annoyance, her pulse scrambled the way it always did when he made some outrageous proposition designed to rattle her.

"Matt, this is my office. You can't come

in here and have this kind of inappropriate conversation. It just shows me how immature you are."

Sparks of annoyance flashed in his eyes. She thought for an instant he'd turned the comment into some kind of a dare, and she knew from experience what a mistake it would be to let that happen.

"Don't get any ideas," she added quickly.

He laughed. "You always give me ideas."

"Well, I shouldn't. I don't mean to," she said, sounding a little desperate even to her own ears. "Go away. I have work to do."

"So do I. I've been out of the office most of the afternoon, but I'm not leaving here until we've reached some kind of an understanding."

"About what? It's over, Matthew. It was a mistake. I don't know how to be any clearer than that."

Even as she said the words, a part of her was screaming that she was the one making the mistake. She hadn't felt so desirable, so carefree, in years. Matthew had breathed new life into her stodgy, boring existence. If only it hadn't felt so wrong. Then again, maybe that was part of his appeal, the idea of how shocked people would be if they knew about the two of them.

He leveled a look into her eyes that gave her goose bumps. "And I can't make myself any clearer, either," he said quietly. "It's not over, Laila. Not by a long shot. You can tell me to go a hundred different ways, but I'm not letting you run me off."

"Matthew, this is crazy," she repeated.

"So you've mentioned. Nonetheless, I'm in it for the duration. I think we owe it to ourselves to see where this takes us."

"Nowhere," she said staunchly. "It'll take us nowhere."

He shook his head. "I'm not convinced of that."

"Why are you being so stubborn about this?"

"I'm an O'Brien. Stubborn is just who we are."

"But you're supposed to be from the sensible side of the family," she said in frustration.

"Have you met Susie? She waited around for years for Mack to get his act together. No one thought there was a chance they'd ever get together. Just look at them now. Their relationship might be implausible, but it's working."

"You're suggesting that you and I have a similar fate in store for us?" Laila asked, unable to hide her astonishment.

"We won't know unless we give it a chance," he said. "Look, I'm willing to play by your rules for a little longer and keep this whole thing a secret, but I'm not willing to walk away without a fight."

"But why? There are dozens of women in this town, in this region, for that matter, who'd be a whole lot less complicated than me."

"That's just part of your charm," he said. "Apparently I like complicated."

Laila sighed. It was clear she wasn't going to get him out of here unless she agreed to whatever he wanted. Which was what exactly?

She studied him with a narrowed gaze. "Matthew, what's it going to take to get you to leave?"

"You agreeing to let me fix dinner for you tonight," he said at once.

"You can cook?" she asked, surprised.

"Well enough to keep us from starvation. So, is it a deal?"

"I suppose," she said, desire trumping all of her very sensible reservations.

"Your place or mine?"

She hesitated, knowing that dinner was far from the only thing on the menu. "Your place," she said eventually. There was something about having him in her space that made her start picturing the future, a future that simply couldn't be.

"Seven o'clock?" he asked.

"I'll be there," she said.

He stood up then and brushed a lingering kiss across her lips. "That wasn't so hard now, was it?"

She gave him an exasperated look as he walked away, looking thoroughly satisfied with himself. The man had no idea just how hard it had been. Another five minutes and she might very well have locked her office door, swept everything off her desk and dragged him into her arms right there.

It seemed Matthew O'Brien had the ability to rob her of common sense, reason, logic—all of those things on which she prided herself. And that made him not only the most inappropriate man she'd ever dated, but the most dangerous.

14

Mack had intended to tell Susie about Kristen Lewis over dinner, but the evening had gotten away from them. He hadn't wanted to spoil Susie's rare upbeat mood and seductive overtures by introducing a topic that was bound to ruin the moment.

At least that's what he told himself to justify putting the discussion on hold. But when he mentioned his meeting with Laila to Will and Jake, both men regarded him skeptically.

"You didn't tell Susie because you were scared of her reaction," Will argued. "You know she's going to hate the whole idea of bringing one of your ex-lovers to town, no matter how innocent you claim it's going to be."

"Bree would tear me apart if I ever tried something like that," Jake said.

"Ditto with Jess," Will added. "It's a really bad idea, Mack, especially now, with so much of Susie's future up in the air."

Mack wasn't quite ready to concede defeat, despite the validity of their arguments. "But Kristen has skills that are critical to making this whole newspaper proposition fly," he said. Even as he heard the words, he acknowledged they were outweighed by what Kristen's presence might do to Susie's fragile self-esteem right now.

"You can justify it all you want, and your intentions may be a thousand percent honorable, but look at it through Susie's eyes," Will persisted. "It has the potential to be seen as betrayal written all over it. Do you really want her worrying every second about whether you're starting up again with this woman?"

"Come on, Susie's reasonable," Mack protested. "She's going to understand."

"Maybe," Will said. "Theoretically."

"But she's a woman," Jake said. "They don't think like we do."

"Isn't there another person in the entire world of journalism you could recruit for this job?" Will asked.

"Probably," Mack said. "But Kristen's the one I know, and she's damn good at what she does."

"Is having her here worth risking your marriage?" Will asked pointedly.

"Come on," Mack protested. "It's not going to come to that. Susie wants this paper to happen as much as I do. She'll go along with this once I explain how important it is. I'm not going to give her a single reason to doubt me and my love for her."

"You can try," Will agreed. "And I can tell your mind is made up, but if you want my advice, kill this idea now."

Mack looked to Jake for support.

"Sorry, pal. I'm with Will on this. It's just begging for disaster."

Mack sighed heavily. He heard what they were saying. He'd known in his gut ever since his conversation with Laila that involving Kristen would be a risk to his marriage, but he also trusted in Susie and their feelings for one another. He didn't have any doubts. Why should she? Even with the cancer in the mix, surely she would be able to take a pragmatic view of what was necessary to get this newspaper up and running.

He scowled at his friends. "I thought you'd be my backup on this," he grumbled.

"We both get where you're coming from," Will said. "We just think you're delusional where Susie's concerned."

"Big-time delusional," Jake confirmed.

With those discouraging words ringing in his ears, Mack headed back home. At least he would run the idea past Susie. If she was uncomfortable with it, he'd drop the idea of hiring Kristen and find someone else for the job. He even promised himself he'd be attuned to more than the words she spoke. He'd watch and listen for the subtext, all the things she wasn't likely to say for fear of letting him see her insecurities.

"Susie, you here?" he called out when he entered the apartment.

She came to the doorway of the bedroom, looking vaguely green, her eyes dull.

"Where else would I be? I haven't been able to get ten feet from the bathroom this morning."

Mack winced. He should have realized the chemo aftereffects could have kicked in with a vengeance by this morning. Sometimes she was fine for hours after a treatment, sometimes even for a day, and then she'd get sick as a dog. A few days later the nausea would be a thing of the past . . . until the next time.

"What can I do?" he asked at once. "Want some crackers? Ginger ale?"

She shook her head.

"Get back in bed and I'll get a cool washcloth for your head."

She gave him a wan smile. "Thanks."

He went in to sit beside her on the edge of the bed, putting the cool cloth on her brow. "Better?"

"For now," she said. "I hate this, Mack. It's not how I envisioned our first year of marriage going, with me so sick I can barely sit up in bed some days."

"There are plenty of other days when you can get up and even out of the house," he reminded her. "The chemo won't last forever. And you need to stop focusing on what it's costing you and remember that this is the treatment that's going to cure you. Concentrate on the goal. View all those nasty chemicals as your friends."

She gave him a wan smile. "Whoever knew back when you were lighting up a gridiron that you also had amazing talents as a cheerleader, too?"

Mack laughed. "Just get me some pom-poms and I'll do one of those old routines here and now. I'm pretty sure they're burned into my memory."

"Because you hardly ever took your eyes off Emma Martin," she teased. "Or was it Bee-Bee Leggett?"

"Depends on which year you're talking about," he responded.

"Or which month," she said.

"I was a cad, no question about it," he admitted. He smoothed her hair back from her face. "But no more. You know that, don't you? I'm all yours."

"I want to believe it," she said, a faintly wistful note in her voice.

"You can," he said firmly. He drew in a deep breath, wondered if this was a good time or possibly the worst, but plunged in anyway. "There's something I need to talk to you about. Are you up to it?"

"Sure. Anything to keep my mind off the fact that my stomach is dancing a particularly energetic jig at the moment."

"We talked a little about my meeting with Laila yesterday, but we didn't get into all of it." He grinned. "You were having your wicked way with me, and I got sidetracked."

"You said Laila had reservations about the loan."

"She does, but I pitched an idea to her that seemed to relieve some of her concerns."

"What idea?"

"There's someone I'd like to hire to create the paper's online presence, a woman I worked with in Baltimore." He regarded her earnestly. "She's good, Susie, one of the best in the business, and she's way ahead of the trend. She'd be a huge asset. Laila agrees about that. In fact, she pretty much made it a condition of the loan."

She nodded, studying him intently. "Okay," she said slowly. "Then why not hire her, if it could clinch the deal at the bank? Why are you hesitating? Why even run it past me? The newspaper's your baby,

Mack. You certainly don't have to get my approval for something like this."

"I think I do," he said.

"Why?"

Mack could hear the trepidation in her voice and knew she already suspected there was much more to the story. He looked away, drew in a deep breath, then said, "Because I slept with her."

"I see," she said softly, looking shaken.

"Sweetheart, it was a long time ago, before you and I started spending so much time together. It never meant anything to either one of us. There wasn't a relationship, not even a short-term one. It was nothing more than a fling. You have to believe that."

"Then why the big production about it?"

"Because I didn't want you to find out about it later and wonder if the only reason I brought her here was because we still had something going on. I swear to you it was over practically before it got started, and it was way before you and I began spending all this time together. It's been years, Susie, so you have to believe it's truly over."

Susie frowned, but she didn't burst into tears. He considered that a positive sign.

"Okay," she said softly. "Thank you for being up-front with me."

"So how would you feel about it?" he prodded. "If it's going to make you uncomfortable in any way or make things tense between us, it won't happen."

Mack saw the struggle she was having with herself, fighting her fears, trying to be fair. He should have called his plan off right then, but he didn't. He waited.

"She's the best person for the job?" Susie asked, her expression bleak.

"I think she is," he said.

She lifted her chin. "Then there's no choice," she said, suddenly determined. "You have to hire her."

"And you'll be okay with it?"

"I'll deal with it," she said staunchly. "Don't worry about me."

Because he wanted so badly to make the deal with the bank come together, Mack ignored all the promises he'd made to himself earlier and chose to take her at her word.

Still, he felt compelled to add, "If you

ever have a moment's doubt about this, just say the word and she'll go."

"Do you love me?"

He held her gaze. "You know I do."

"Then I won't have any reason for doubts, will I?"

The words were brave, but there was no mistaking the flicker of worry in her eyes. It gave Mack pause, but in the end he convinced himself that hiring Kristen was the right thing to do. Making this newspaper happen was not just for him. It was for him and Susie, and for whatever family they were able to have down the road. The decision was for their future. The past simply couldn't enter into it. He wouldn't let it.

Susie told herself she was fine with Mack's plan to bring an old lover into town. She had his ring. She had his devoted attention. But it was a lot harder to remember all that once the bank had approved the loan and he was fully engaged with actually getting the business off the ground. It was even harder once she'd gotten her first glimpse of Kristen Lewis.

"She's a blasted cover model," Susie griped to Shanna while having coffee at

Shanna's bookstore. "Have you had a look at her? What was I thinking?"

"You were thinking that she was the key to getting this newspaper venture off the ground," Shanna reminded her. "Mack laid everything out for you. If you had reservations, you should have spoken up. He gave you every opportunity to do that."

"And I would have sounded like some insecure woman who was terrified that someone was going to steal her man. I couldn't do that, not with him looking at me like I held the answer to his entire future."

"Don't be dramatic," Shanna scolded. "That's Bree's domain. She's the family playwright."

Susie sighed and sipped at her cappuccino. For once it wasn't making her stomach flip over. It might be decaf, but it was better than nothing. She'd missed these afternoon gabfests with her friend, though not so much Shanna's straight talk that called her on everything.

"Invite her to dinner," Shanna suggested.

Susie stared at her incredulously. "You want me to invite Mack's ex-lover into my home?"

"You want reassurance, don't you? Get a good look at how they act together. Mack loves you, sweetie. I think you'll see that their relationship now is strictly professional. He knows an entire town will come down on him hard if he allows anything else."

Susie permitted herself a grin. "That might be fun to watch. Maybe I should tip off Matthew and Luke, or even Uncle Mick, and let them have at her."

Shanna shook her head. "You are a perverse woman."

Susie laughed. "Apparently so. Okay, enough about me. How are you feeling? Is the pregnancy progressing the way it's supposed to?"

"Everything's right on schedule," Shanna said, beaming. "We might be able to tell the baby's gender on the next sonogram, but Kevin and I are arguing about whether we want to know. He's all for waiting. I want to know now, especially if it's a girl." Her expression lit up. "We are going to have so much shopping to do, if it is. I can hardly wait to start buying frilly little pink dresses. This family already has too many rambunctious little boys."

"Don't forget Caitlyn and Carrie. Once upon time, they were little angels, but now they're twin troublemakers," Susie reminded her. "I can hardly wait to see how Abby and Trace cope with them once they hit their teens."

Shanna chuckled. "Something tells me that Trace is going to be one of those fathers who scares off every boy who comes to the house. He might be their stepfather, but he's the kind of dad who pays attention to everything those two are up to. Since he works at home, they certainly won't be able to sneak anything past him." Shanna's grin spread. "Abby's counting on that, I think."

She hesitated, then added carefully, her worried gaze on Susie as she spoke, "She's thinking it might be a good time for them to have a baby. They're talking about it. I think she's finally convinced that Trace isn't going to demand she quit her job the second she gives birth the way Wes did when the twins were born."

Susie felt a momentary twinge of jealousy at the news, then forced a cheerful expression. "That's great!"

Shanna regarded her apologetically.

"I'm so sorry, Susie. It must be hard on you hearing all this baby talk."

"It was when you first told me you and Kevin were expecting, but I'm past that now," Susie assured her. "There's no point in looking back. I can't have my own biological children, but as soon as things settle down and my treatments are behind me, I'm going to talk to Mack about starting the adoption process."

"How does he feel about that?" Shanna asked. "Did you discuss it before your surgery?"

Susie nodded. "He said he was open to the idea. It can be a lengthy process, so I don't want to wait too long to get started. Connor said he'd help me try to find some kind of private adoption if that's the way we decide to go. His old law firm in Baltimore has some experience with those."

Shanna looked genuinely pleased for her. "Oh, sweetie, I'm so happy for you. That would be fantastic! You and Mack will make amazing parents."

"You might mention that to him sometime. He's not so sure about his own parenting skills, given his lousy examples, but

I think he'll be a great father precisely because of what he went through."

"Childhood experiences certainly mold us into the adults we become," Shanna agreed. "Sometimes for the better, sometimes not. I think Mack is one of those who learned from all the mistakes his parents made."

"I agree," Susie said. She stood up. "I'd better get home, though I'm honestly not sure why I'm rushing. If Mack even makes it home before I'm asleep, he grabs a quick bite and is right back out the door."

Shanna frowned. "Are you okay with that?"

"It's great to see him so excited about work again. He's throwing himself into getting this paper off the ground. I just wish I could be involved somehow. Maybe then I wouldn't be freaking out quite so much about him spending all this time with the gorgeous Kristen."

"Tell him that," Shanna advised. "Be a part of it, if that's what you want, Susie. Don't let him shut you out, even unintentionally." A wicked gleam lit her eyes. "Or you could greet him in one of those scraps of lingerie I bought for you. That ought to keep him from heading right back out the door."

"Are you suggesting I use sex to keep my husband's attention?" Susie asked, not sure whether to be indignant or intrigued by the idea.

"It's a surefire solution," Shanna said. "Worked like magic with Kevin when he started spending a little too much time in Annapolis working with Thomas's foundation." She rested a hand against her belly. "How do you think we wound up pregnant?"

Susie chuckled. "That's quite a recommendation," she agreed, then hugged her friend. "Thanks for listening."

"Anytime. You know that."

Susie headed straight home, pulled the sexy black lingerie from her drawer and eyed it speculatively. But when she went to put it on, it no longer fit. The steroids she'd been taking had added pounds. More than she'd realized, in fact. Looking in the mirror at the material that now stretched far too tightly across her butt, she felt tears welling up in her eyes. Nor did the scrap of lace in front do much to conceal the abdominal scar from her surgery. The bra wouldn't even hook in back.

She grabbed her favorite terry-cloth robe from the closet and belted it tightly as the tears streaked down her cheeks. She was still sitting there when she heard Mack's key turn in the lock.

"Susie!"

She brushed uselessly at her cheeks. "In here," she said. "Give me a minute. I'll be right out."

But he didn't wait. He walked in, caught a glimpse of her face and his expression fell.

"What's wrong?" he asked, panic threading through his voice.

Unable to reply, she held up the lacy panties as if the sight of them alone would explain.

Mack merely looked puzzled.

"They . . ." Her voice caught on a sob. "They don't fit. Nothing sexy fits."

She saw the relief in his eyes and knew then just how badly she'd scared him, though he was clearly struggling to sympathize.

"I'll buy you ten new pairs of panties tomorrow," he offered.

She frowned. "That is so not the point."

"Then what is? I'm trying here, Susie, but you have to help me out."

"I'm fat. I wanted to be sexy and seduce you, but now I can't."

He shook his head. "You are far from fat. You're still the most beautiful, sexiest woman I know. Frankly, all that lace just got in the way. I was terrified of ripping it to shreds." He slipped a hand inside her robe. "Give me a good, sturdy terry-cloth robe anytime. No straps. No tricky hooks. I just have to loosen the belt a little." He suited action to words. "Then slide it down one shoulder."

His gaze fell on her exposed breasts. "And there you are," he said, his breath hitching in a way that reassured her as his words hadn't. "Ripe, gorgeous and all mine."

"Oh, Mack," she whispered, shrugging out of the robe and clinging to his shoulders.

He was right. Lingerie only got in the way. This, his skin against hers, was all that mattered—that and the unmistakable love she saw shining in his eyes.

* * *

Mack hadn't realized until sometime in the middle of the night that he'd never called Kristen to let her know he wasn't coming back to the paper. Not that he owed her an explanation. He was the boss, after all, but they'd planned to go over the website design one last time to make sure every element was exactly right. They hoped to go live with it next week, and there were still plenty of decisions left to be made. Though he trusted her judgment in this area, he wanted to be involved in every aspect of the paper's launch online and in print.

There was already a lot of buzz about it around town. Local businesses were even more eager than he'd anticipated to have an outlet for advertising their products and their sales. Realtors loved having access to both online audiences and those who still preferred to get their news and their housing options from a paper. Mack was feeling more and more confident about the venture's prospects.

When he walked into the offices he'd found just off of Main Street in a row dominated by accountants, insurance agencies and other service-oriented businesses,

Kristen glanced up from her computer. She frowned when she saw him.

"Decide to play hooky last night?" she asked lightly, though there was no mistaking the edge in her voice.

"I should have called," he apologized. "Something came up."

"I'll just bet it did," she said knowingly. "Your wife got jealous of all the time we're spending together."

Now it was his turn to frown. "Susie's not like that. She's totally on board with what we're doing. She knows it takes a lot of hard work and long hours."

"But when you left here, you were planning to come back. Why the change of plans? What did she do? Something to make you feel guilty, I'll bet."

Mack didn't like the direction of the conversation. It hinted of a possessiveness that was totally inappropriate. Even though he might be oblivious to a lot of what went on in women's minds, he was smart enough to read between the lines.

"Kristen, what's this really about? I thought you and I had an understanding. You moving to Chesapeake Shores and taking this job is strictly professional.

There's nothing between us anymore. If you think otherwise, if it's going to be a problem, then we need to reassess the situation."

She inhaled sharply at his direct words, then sighed. "Sorry. I did sound like a jealous shrew there for a minute, didn't I? You're a newlywed. Of course there are going to be times you want to be with your wife. I just wish you'd called to let me know. I hung out here for hours."

"You're right about me letting you know. I'll be more considerate in the future."

She hesitated, then met his gaze. "Working with you like this, it's harder than I expected it to be," she admitted. "I thought all those old feelings were dead and buried, but I guess they're not, after all. I'll do my best to make sure it doesn't become a problem."

"Maybe if you met Susie, had dinner with us or something," he began in an attempt to try to give her some perspective on exactly where she stood in his life.

She was shaking her head before he could finish. "Not just yet, okay? I'm not quite ready to deal with you and the whole wedded-bliss thing."

"But Kristen, I am happily married. That's reality."

"I know. I get it. That doesn't mean I want my face rubbed in it just yet. I will respect the boundaries, though." She sketched an exaggerated cross across her chest. "Promise."

"That's good enough for me. But if this gets too uncomfortable for you, say the word and I'll do whatever it takes to help you land another job. I'd hate not having you here, because you're the best at this whole internet news business, but I don't want to screw with your head."

She grinned at that. "My head's just fine, thank you. You may be sexy and intriguing and all that, but there are other fish in the sea. I just need to get my stilettos on and go fishing."

Mack laughed. "Now, there's an image that'll make a man's heart take a dive. If you drove a pickup, you'd be some guy's ideal."

She rolled her eyes at that. "My convertible suits me just fine."

"That'll work, too," Mack said. "Want me to fix you up?"

"Absolutely not," she said, looking genuinely horrified. "The day I need an ex to start finding my dates for me, I'll throw in the towel and surround myself with cats."

"Something tells me that's not going to be your fate," he said candidly. "If you'd get out of this office for a couple of hours, you'd have the men of Chesapeake Shores swooning all over you."

"Good idea. Where do the singles in this town hang out?"

"The bar at Brady's draws a good singles crowd on the weekends. We get a lot of sophisticated out-of-towners there, too."

She nodded. "Brady's tonight, then," she said cheerfully.

But the shadows in her eyes suggested she wasn't nearly as happy about the prospect as she tried to sound.

15

Laila rolled over in bed, debated waking Matthew and decided against it. It was easier to slip out in the middle of the night without his entreaties that she stay. In fact, it was getting more and more difficult for her to leave him at all. She'd tried to do it back in the fall, to walk away from what she knew was a terrible mistake.

She'd refused to join his family on Thanksgiving until Jess had pressured her to come. Even after she'd agreed to attend the awkward holiday meal, she'd tried to keep some distance between her and Matthew. He'd challenged her on it, they'd argued and she'd left. She'd been a little surprised that no one in the family had picked up on that. Then again, the focus had been on Mack and Susie and the obvious tension between them.

Even after last night—yet another amazing night—she knew she had to end it. Right now it was all about making love, about the way Matthew made her feel like an incredibly sexy, desirable woman, but she could envision a time when it could turn into something more. That scared her to death. Matt was too young to be ready to settle down and she was starting to hear her biological clock ticking so loudly it could probably be heard across town.

"Laila?" he murmured sleepily just as she pulled on her boots.

"Go back to sleep," she said softly. "I'll see you in the morning."

Most nights that was all it took to have him wrapping his arms around a pillow and falling straight back to sleep, but apparently not tonight. Instead, he climbed out of bed and pulled on his boxers, giving her a momentary glimpse of a body that made her heart stutter. He walked over and stood in front of her, put his hands on her shoulders and looked directly into her eyes. His, as blue as midnight, were entrancing. Right now they were also troubled.

"This has to stop," he said.

"What?" she asked, not wanting to be drawn into the conversation she knew was inevitable.

"You sneaking out of here in the middle of the night like you're ashamed of what's going on between us," he explained impatiently. "Would it be so terrible if someone saw us leaving here together in the morning?"

"You know it would be," she said. "It's not about being ashamed, Matthew. It's about being prudent. This is Chesapeake Shores. You know the kind of talk it would stir up. In my position at the bank—"

"Damn the bank!" he said fiercely. "This is not about the bank, Laila. It's about you and your crazy idea that what we have can't possibly go anywhere."

"It can't," she said simply.

"Tell me why."

"Because . . ." She faltered. She could have listed a hundred reasons why their relationship could never work, but knew he'd find a way to counter every one of them. He was good at that, at making what was happening between them seem rational and potentially enduring. She just knew better than to buy it. Not a single one of her relationships with far more suitable men had lasted. Why on earth would this one?

As he waited for her reply, he was clearly growing more exasperated.

"If you throw the age thing in my face, I'm not sure how I'll react," he burst out finally. "I swear I sometimes think I'm more mature than you are."

Laila felt the sting of his words. "That's a lousy thing to say."

"Hey, I'm ready to step up and acknowledge what we have. I care about you. This isn't just a fling for me. How about you? Can you say the same?"

Laila hesitated a little too long.

"I thought so," he said. "Well, great as the sex is, I'm not settling for just that. Go ahead and leave. You can call me when you decide you're interested in more than my body."

She actually thought she heard a trace of hurt in his voice, but that couldn't possibly be. Matt was the kind of guy who never had anything more than flings. He should be thrilled by this no-strings relationship of theirs, her desire to be discreet, to avoid complications. At one point he had been. Clearly, though, that wasn't the case any longer.

"Matt, what's really going on here?" she asked, confused by his desire to change the rules.

"I just told you. I'm tired of having you treat this as some kind of back-alley affair," he said. He leveled a look into her eyes and added, "Either we go public and give it a chance to turn into something real, or I'm done."

His words rattled her more than she'd imagined possible. Did she really want this to end? It was certainly the sensible thing, but when she thought of the empty, lonely nights she'd had before this relationship had started, she felt sick inside. The question, though, was whether her feelings had anything at all to do with Matt himself or whether any intelligent, attractive man would have filled the void. She needed time to figure that out.

"Maybe that's a good idea," she told him.

"Calling it quits, I mean. It sounds as if we could both use some space to figure out what we really want."

He scowled at the suggestion. "I already know what I want, but if you don't, then by all means, take all the time you need."

He started pulling on clothes, his movements jerky. "Let's go."

"Where are you going?" she asked, watching as he grabbed his keys and headed for the door.

"I'm taking you home."

"Matt, it's two blocks. I can walk."

"Not in the middle of the night you can't," he declared, his scowl daunting. "I don't care how safe Chesapeake Shores is, at 3:00 a.m. we're not taking any chances."

"I've walked home before."

"Sure, when you've successfully slipped out without waking me. Well, tonight I'm awake, and I'm driving you home, or walking with you, or walking twenty paces behind. Take your pick."

She regarded him with frustration. "Geez, you're stubborn."

"Not a news flash, darlin'. Now, what's it going to be?"

She relented. "You can walk with me."

"Thank you," he said with exaggerated gratitude.

"Starting the car might wake the neighbors," she added, knowing perfectly well it would provoke him.

He rolled his eyes. "Whatever."

They made the two-block walk in silence. Laila felt the tension between them getting thicker and thicker. By the time they reached her two-bedroom bungalow on Primrose Way just off Main Street, she was so rattled she couldn't get her key into the lock.

"Let me," Matt said, nudging her aside.

When the door swung open, Laila started to slip past him, but he blocked her way. She met his gaze, saw the anger blazing there. Or was it passion?

"This isn't over," he said quietly. "Not by a long shot."

"I'm sorry."

He smiled then, even though it didn't quite reach his eyes. "No need to be. I've always loved a good challenge."

Before she could move, he kissed her soundly, then headed down the block, whistling softly. It was an airy little tune, Irish, if she wasn't mistaken, a reminder of the O'Brien stubbornness, perhaps.

The sound faded as he turned back onto Main. Only then did she go inside and close the door. Leaning against it, Laila breathed a sigh of relief. She'd done it. She'd called it quits. Again. Or he had. It hardly mattered which of them had first said the words. The whole thing had never made a lick of sense in the first place.

Then she thought of the way Matt's lips had felt against hers just now—knowing, persuasive, determined. She thought of the immediate heat that had stirred at his touch, and knew with absolutely certainty that Matt had gotten it just right. They were far from done.

Matt showed up at Susie's just before dinnertime. "I come bearing gifts. Does that earn me the right to stay for dinner?"

Susie grinned at her brother, then caught a glimpse of the rolled-up pages he was carrying. She knew an architect's drawings when she saw them. "Our house?"

"Just some preliminary sketches, but yes."

"Gimme," she said eagerly, wiggling her fingers to grasp the pages.

"Not until you invite me to dinner," he said, holding them aloft. "What are we having?" He sniffed the air. "I don't smell anything cooking."

"Mack's bringing home Chinese. I'll call him and tell him to add another order of egg rolls, some sweet-and-sour soup and whatever else you want if you'll hand me those drawings now."

"Call first," Matt said. "You might back down if you don't like the drawings, and I'm starved."

Susie laughed, but she made the call and told Mack about her brother's impromptu visit. "And hurry, Mack. There's something you have to see."

"What?"

"You'll see when you get here."

He hesitated. "Look, as long as your brother's there, why don't I bring Kristen along?"

Susie froze. "Tonight? You want to bring her here now?"

"It just seems like the perfect opportunity for you to get to know her. Maybe she and Matthew would hit it off."

Susie thought of the drawings of their dream house that her brother had brought. She didn't want to share those with her husband's ex-lover. "Not tonight," she said tightly.

"You've said that every other time I've suggested it, too."

"Then maybe you should take the hint," she said, slamming down the phone.

She looked up to find her brother staring at her worriedly. "What was that about?"

"Nothing to concern you," she said, trying to inject a chipper note into her voice.

Matthew clearly didn't buy it. "Susie, what's going on? Are you and Mack having some kind of problem?"

"No," she said at once, determined not to stir up his protective instincts. Next thing she knew the entire family would be on the warpath. While that might be satisfying on some levels, it wasn't the way to handle any issues in her marriage.

"Do I need to have a talk with him?" Matthew persisted.

"Absolutely not. Now, let me see those drawings."

"Don't you want to wait until Mack gets here?"

"There's no telling how long he'll be. Show me," she commanded.

Matthew rolled out the drawings on the dining-room table, then stood back while she studied them. She'd seen enough architectural plans in her lifetime to know exactly what she was seeing. She blinked back tears.

"Oh, Matt, it's perfect. It's exactly the way I envisioned it."

"Four bedrooms and a study, just the way you wanted. There's a lot of glass facing the bay upstairs and down, so the light should be amazing." He gestured toward the foundation. "I've used fieldstone here, and a grayish-brown siding with white trim. I think it'll make the house blend into the woods surrounding it, so it looks almost like part of the landscape."

"And you can avoid tearing out all of the beautiful old trees?"

"Of course. We'll do as little damage to the area as possible. I didn't grow up around Uncle Thomas without learning a thing or two about protecting the environment."

The front door opened then and Mack

walked in, saw the two of them huddled over the drawings and crossed the room. "What do we have here?" he asked as he set aside the bags of takeout.

Susie ignored the remnants of her earlier annoyance and beamed at him. "Plans for our house on Beach Lane," she told him, then quickly added, "They can be modified if there's anything you hate or anything I didn't think of. Matt wanted to do them for us as a wedding present."

Mack nodded. "It's an amazing present," he told Matthew, though Susie heard the reservation in his voice. "Let's take a look."

Susie left it to her brother to explain the drawings while she got out plates and silverware for their dinner. She set the far end of the table, and Mack pored over the drawings at the opposite end.

"Well?" she prodded eventually, studying his expression. "What do you think?"

He met her gaze. "Is this the house you want?"

She nodded. "I think it's perfect."

"Then it's the house we'll build," Mack told her. "We won't be able to get started on it right away. Every dime I have is tied up in the paper."

Susie started to tell him that her father had offered to front them the money, but now wasn't the time. Mack would turn the offer down flat, especially if she made it in front of her brother.

"I know, but it's great to have the design ready to go when we are," she said enthusiastically.

Mack nodded. "Absolutely." He clapped Matthew on the back. "Thanks. You did a great job. It's an amazing present."

"I was happy to do it," Matthew said, looking from Mack to her and back again. "Look, I know I planned to stay for dinner, but I think I'll take off. You all probably don't get a lot of time together these days. I shouldn't intrude."

"Don't go," Susie pleaded. "I promised you dinner."

"I'll just take my egg rolls and soup home," Matthew said. "No big deal." He leaned down and kissed her on the cheek. "See you soon."

He left before she could summon up another argument. She whirled on Mack.

"Why did you run him off?"

He stared at her incredulously. "Me?"

"He obviously felt the tension between us."

"Probably because he knew you'd hung up on me earlier," Mack said. "Why did you do that, by the way?"

"Because I couldn't believe you wanted to bring your ex-lover over here to meet my brother. I don't want her in our personal lives, Mack. It's too much."

With that, she burst into tears and left the room, cursing herself for being so foolish and letting him see how just the mention of Kristen was so upsetting to her.

Mack followed her into the bedroom, then sat down beside her.

"Susie, I thought you were okay with her being here," he said.

"I was," she murmured. "I am. Theoretically, anyway."

She looked up and caught the beginnings of a smile on his lips. "Don't you dare laugh at me."

"I'm not. I'm just thinking about how Will pegged it exactly right."

"Will? What does he have to do with anything?"

"He told me you'd say what I wanted to hear, then regret it later."

"I'm sorry. I know I'm being unreasonable. And I probably would feel a thousand times better if she were involved with someone else, but my brother, Mack? Come on. That's a little too close to home."

He shrugged. "And probably a pipe dream anyway, if he's involved with someone else."

Susie frowned. "I wonder about that. He hasn't mentioned anyone recently."

"He's not likely to," Mack said, his expression grim.

"What is that supposed to mean?"

"Just that he seemed determined to keep the relationship under wraps."

"He did, didn't he? I wonder why that is?"

"Probably because he knows it's doomed," Mack said direly.

Susie sat up. "There it is again. You know something, don't you?"

Mack touched her cheek. "Still not at liberty to say."

"But you must not approve if you were so eager to set him up with Kristen," she persisted, trying to pry it out of him bit by bit.

"It's not up to me to approve or disapprove," he said, "and that is all I intend to say about that. Do you think you can stop being mad at me long enough to go in there and take another look at those house plans? I'd love it if you'd walk me through them, tell me exactly what you're envisioning."

"It's all there on paper, pretty much the way you described it to me that day at Beach Lane a few months ago. I've added a few ideas of my own, but it's your house, Mack."

He draped an arm around her shoulders and drew her close. "No, it's *our* house, Susie. And we're going to make a lot of memories there, enough to last a lifetime."

She leaned against his chest and closed her eyes. "I want to believe that, Mack. I really do."

"Then believe it," he said. "Hold on to it with everything in you. It's one more reason to keep fighting the cancer with all you've got."

Right now, in his arms, that was easy enough to do, but tomorrow, when those poisonous chemicals were dripping into her body once again, it would be a whole lot harder to hold on to the dream.

Mack had just stepped out of his car in front of the newspaper office a couple of hours after dinner when his brother-in-law came out of the shadows, his expression grim.

"What's going on with you and Susie?" Matthew demanded. "Don't lie to me and tell me everything's fine. You could cut the tension tonight with a knife. And I was there when she snapped at you on the phone and hung up. What was that about?"

"I'm not discussing my marriage with you," Mack said. Only the knowledge that Matthew truly cared about his sister kept Matt from saying more about his brother-in-law's interference in something so personal.

"So help me, if you've done something to hurt her, I'll break your neck. Don't you know she can't take any stress right now? She has to save all her energy for fighting the cancer."

"I know that," Mack said.

"Then why are you deliberately upsetting her?"

"Let it go, Matthew. Susie and I will work things out."

Matthew frowned. "That tells me there's something that needs to be worked out. What is it?"

Just then he glanced toward the newspaper office and caught a glimpse of Kristen through the window. He muttered an expletive under his breath. "It's her, isn't it? She's the problem."

"Kristen is not a problem. She's creating the paper's web presence. That's it."

"But Susie's freaking out about her, isn't she?" He gave Mack a disgusted look. "Man, do you know nothing about my sister? She's always been insecure where you're concerned. Having your ring on her finger should have changed that, and maybe without the whole cancer thing it would have, but come on." He gestured toward Kristen. "You bring a woman who looks like that into the middle of your life *now*? Are you crazy? Even I would have had better sense."

"My relationship with Kristen is totally innocent," Mack said, "and I certainly don't have to justify my hiring decisions to you."

"Did you run it past Susie?"

"As a matter of fact, I did."

"So you knew it could cause a problem and you did it anyway," Matthew said, regarding him with dismay. "What were you thinking?"

"That I wanted this paper to be a success, and Kristen could help me make that happen," Mack said. "Susie agreed. Now, go home, Matthew. I have work to do."

Matthew cast another look inside. "I'll go, but so help me, Mack, I'd better not find out you've been cheating on my sister."

Mack regarded him solemnly. "It's not going to happen, Matthew. I give you my word on that."

Matthew didn't look entirely appeased, but he nodded eventually. "Okay, then."

Mack hesitated, then thought of his earlier plan to introduce Matthew and Kristen. "Want to come inside? You can meet her and see for yourself that nothing's going on."

"I'll pass," Matthew said a little too quickly.

"Not interested?"

"I'd have to be dead not to be a little intrigued," he said, casting another surreptitious glance through the window. He shook his head. "No way. I've got enough female problems on my plate these days without adding anyone else into the mix."

Mack seized on the opening. "Are you and Laila having problems?"

"What we're having is a stupid, unnecessary separation," Matthew said. "Her choice. Or maybe mine. It got a little muddy when it came right down to it."

"Then it's over?"

"Of course not. She just thinks it is."

Mack chuckled. "You know I had my doubts when I first figured out what was going on between the two of you, but I'm starting to rethink that. Laila may be exactly the right woman for you. Like Susie did with me, Laila's not going to let you get away with a thing."

"Tell me about it," Matthew said. "Of course, unlike you, I've let her know how I feel from the get-go."

"Which is?"

"I think we're a perfect match," he declared, then shrugged. "She seems a little skeptical. She's convinced she's robbing the cradle or some stupid thing like that. And she's worried sick about what people will think."

"In her position, that's a real consideration."

Matthew scowled at him. "Not you, too? She works for a bank. She's not a nun."

"Banks are not frivolous businesses," Mack reminded him. "Customers expect a certain amount of dull, steady stodginess from the people who handle their money."

"That's what she said," Matthew admitted, his expression thoughtful. "I suppose I wasn't listening because I found the whole argument too archaic to be believed."

"Maybe this is one of those times when you need to trust Laila's judgment."

"And let her use that as an excuse to run me off?"

"No. Let it guide you on the approach you need to take with her. Make sure no one can misinterpret this as some kind of fling." He gave his brother-in-law a hard look. "Unless that's all it is."

"It's not for me," Matthew insisted. "I think we have something really good going, or we would if she'd just give it a chance. She's the one who seems into the whole fling concept. It's a little insulting, as a matter of fact."

"Then change that."

"How?"

"Stop hiding it from everyone. Bring it out in the open."

"Don't you think I want to?" he asked with evident frustration. "She's the one who's insisted on keeping the whole thing a secret. That's why we fought at Mick's on Thanksgiving. I was sick of it."

"Why'd you go along with it in the first place?"

"At first, I suppose it added a little edge to everything. You know, the whole thrill of trying not to be caught. Now, though, that's getting really old. I want people to know we're together." His expression turned wistful. "I want to take her to dinner at Brady's, to stop avoiding her at family dinners on Sunday so no one gets suspicious, to bring her over to have dinner with you and Susie."

"And Laila knows that?"

Matthew nodded. "Apparently it scares her to death."

Mack grinned. "I'd take that as a good sign, then."

"How do you figure that?"

"Sounds to me like she's afraid she's falling for you, and once the cat's out of the bag and no one has a heart attack when they find out, she'll be out of excuses for keeping you at arm's length."

Matthew's expression brightened. "You think so?"

"Based on my limitless experience with women, I'd say so. That's the point at which I always ran the other way. Since Laila's the woman you think you want, you might want to stick around. I'd say everything you want is within reach."

"Susie gave you the same kind of runaround, didn't she?"

"Oh, yeah," Mack said. "Dragged it out for years, too. She taught me the value of patience and persistence."

"Not my best traits," Matthew said. "I've always been very big on instant gratification."

Mack chuckled. "So was I, but I promise you'll learn, my friend. Anything worth having is worth waiting for."

It had certainly worked out that way for him. And no one, especially not Kristen Lewis or the meddling O'Briens, was going to get between him and Susie now.

16

Susie stood in front of the bathroom mirror, a fistful of her bright red hair in her hand, and started crying. She'd been told this was a possibility, but she'd been in treatment for a few weeks now and her hair had seemed fine. She had dared to hope it would continue that way.

She glanced back at her image and saw that Mack had walked up behind her. She met his gaze in the mirror and saw his dismay before he could mask it behind the facade he always wore when dealing with the unavoidable evidence that she was undergoing cancer treatments.

"You always said you hated your red hair," he said in a halfhearted attempt at a joke as he stepped up behind her and wrapped his arms around her waist.

"I didn't mean I wanted it to fall out," she said, choking back a sob.

"I know, sweetheart, but it's going to grow back," he soothed. "The doctor explained that to you. So did the women in that support group you joined, right?"

She nodded. "It was just such a shock. I thought it would happen right away, and when it didn't, I guess I started taking it for granted that I'd be one of the lucky ones."

He kissed the back of her neck. "I think the bald look might be kind of sexy. Or you could get a bunch of wigs in different colors and test-drive a whole new you every day. It would be like coming home to a different woman every night."

She gave him a wry look. "Are you bored with the one you have already?"

"I could never be bored with you," he assured her. "In fact, why don't I play hooky from the paper so you and I can spend the day together? We'll take a picnic and Matthew's plans and spend some time at Beach Lane."

Susie knew he was trying to cheer her up, and she appreciated the effort, she really did, but right this second she wanted to crawl back into bed and hide.

As if he'd read her mind, Mack said, "Hiding out here all day is not an option. If you don't want to spend the day with me, call Shanna. Maybe she can get someone to cover for her at the bookstore and the two of you can go shopping. Or call your mom. Spend some time with her."

"Shanna has a doctor's appointment today," she said dully. "They're going to find out the sex of the baby."

Mack turned her until she was facing him. "And that's tearing you up inside, isn't it?"

She nodded. "I want to be thrilled for her and Kevin. I *am* thrilled for them, but I want babies, too, Mack."

"Do you want to meet with an adoption attorney? Because we can do that," he offered. "Connor said he'd arrange it whenever we were ready."

She searched his face. "Are you ready for that, Mack?"

"I have some doubts," he admitted. "But I want this for you. You're going to be an incredible mom. I figure you'll more than make up for whatever my shortcomings are as a dad."

For a moment she was tempted to make the appointment. Thinking ahead to having a child of their own would give her something positive to hold on to. In the end, though, she shook her head.

"It's too soon," she said. "What if the treatments don't work?"

Mack didn't pretend not to understand. "They're going to work," he said with confidence. "But if you think we should wait till we're sure, that's okay, too. You're the boss here."

She rested her hand against his cheek. "I love you, Mack. I'm not sure I could get through this without you."

"Of course you could," he said firmly. "You're the strongest woman I know. Now, what's it going to be today? What will it take to cheer you up?"

She thought of what had brought her down—the sight of that handful of hair in her hand. "Get some scissors and a razor," she said determinedly. "I'm going to find a scarf."

"And then?"

She smiled at him, albeit shakily. "You're going to shave my head. Won't that be fun?"

His eyes widened. "Are you sure?"

"It's inevitable," she said with a shrug. "Why not face it head-on and take charge? And then, if you're not embarrassed to be seen with me, we can have that picnic over at Beach Lane. We might have to eat in the car to keep from freezing to death, but we can pretend it's our first meal in our new home."

"Hopefully our real new home will have heat," Mack said.

She grinned. "Check the plans. Meantime, let's play beauty parlor. Bet you thought the day would never come when I'd let you near my head with a sharp instrument."

"You're right about that."

Suddenly she recalled an incident years before. She'd been over at Mick and Megan's playing with Jess, who was a couple of years older, maybe six or seven. Already the rivalry between them had been fierce. Jess, a devilish glint in her eyes, had suggested they play beauty parlor. Susie, clueless, had eagerly gone along.

A few minutes later clumps of her hair had been scattered across the front porch. Nell had found them and raised a holy ruckus, sending Jess to her room and Susie straight to a real beauty salon, where an attempt to style her hair had left her looking like a pixie or maybe a miniature punk rocker.

"Wait!" she said to Mack when he'd retrieved scissors and the razor.

"What? Have you thought better of this?"

"In a way," she said. "You've been hinting around for a while that Jess and I need to make peace. I'm calling her to come over and do this."

Mack looked uneasy. "You want Jess to shave your head?"

Susie nodded. "She came close to leaving me bald when I was four. Maybe this will remind her of that incident and we can put it behind us. It'll be a first step."

Mack looked doubtful. "Are you sure about this? What if she messes it up?"

"How's she going to do that?" she asked reasonably. "Bald is bald."

"Okay, if you say so. What about the picnic?"

"I'll call you later. Will that work?"

"I'll make it work," he said. He winked at her. "I can't wait to be dazzled by the new look."

"Dazzled might be a little too much to hope for."

He shook his head. "You always dazzle me," he said solemnly.

Susie watched him go, then sighed. Mack's ability to say something sweet like that just when she needed most to hear it was one of the reasons she loved him so much. Sometimes, though, especially these days, it was very hard to trust the words, or even the well-meaning actions.

As soon as she heard the apartment door close behind him, she called the inn and asked for her cousin.

"Hey, Jess," she said. "I need a huge favor."

"Sure," Jess said, though there was the faint hint of a reservation in her voice. "What do you need?"

"Could you come over here? It might be easier for me to explain it in person."

"Now?"

"If you're not too busy."

There was the slightest hesitation, but then, being a true O'Brien who showed up when a family member was in need, she said, "No, of course I'm not too busy. I'll be there in fifteen minutes."

"Thanks." Susie smiled as she hung up, envisioning her cousin's reaction when she discovered they were about to reenact one of the moments from their past . . . and hopefully turn a negative childhood memory into a positive moment of genuine bonding between two adult women.

By the time Jess knocked on the door, Susie had set up a chair in the kitchen, put newspaper on the table and on the floor. She'd laid out the scissors and razor, along with some soft soap and a bowl of water. She had a towel ready to wrap around her shoulders.

She opened the door and greeted her cousin with a smile. "Thanks for coming."

"Not a problem, but I'm not sure why you called me. Wasn't Shanna available?"

Susie winced at the remark. It was proof of just how much distance there was between them, that Jess would assume Shanna would be her first choice for anything important. That it was true was even more telling.

"Actually, when this came up, you were the first person I thought of," Susie said. "Well, besides Mack. He would have done it if I'd wanted him to."

"Okay, you've got my attention," Jess said.

"Come on in the kitchen," Susie said, leading the way.

Jess caught a glimpse of the table and paused. "Susie, what's going on?"

Susie met her cousin's confused gaze, took a deep breath and blurted, "My hair's falling out in clumps. I want to take charge and shave my head, and I want you to do it."

Jess regarded her with dismay. "Why me?"

"Remember when you were six or seven and practically scalped me?" she asked her with a grin. "I figure you have just the experience I need."

Jess looked mortified. "Oh, my God, I think I'd blocked that from my memory. Gram was furious." She regarded Susie worriedly. "Are you still holding it against me? Is that what this is about?"

"Not half as much as all the things you've held against me through the years,"

Susie said pointedly, then held up a hand. "I'm not blaming you. I know some of the things the family said and did had to hurt you. Even though it wasn't my fault, I got why it made you resent me. But we're all grown up now, Jess. Our husbands are best friends. I want us to get over the past and move on, maybe even be friends."

"And we're bonding over my shaving your head?" Jess asked skeptically.

"Something like that. How about it? Will you do it?"

Jess still looked hesitant. "You trust me to do this? Maybe you should go to a professional."

"Like I told Mack earlier, bald is bald. You can't mess this up, Jess. I'm looking at this as some kind of rite that'll make us closer."

"What if you hate the way you look?"

"Believe me, that won't have anything to do with the haircut." She sobered. "My hair's falling out, Jess. I have to do this. I have to be in charge of something. Surely you know how that feels?"

Jess nodded slowly. "More than you can imagine." She started to touch Susie's cheek, then pulled back and said briskly,

"Okay, let's do this. Put on some music, something empowering, I think. I'll pour us a couple of cups of tea. Wine might be more liberating, but it's probably not wise under the circumstances."

Susie laughed. "Now you're getting into the spirit of it."

When the music was blaring and they were sipping Gram's favorite Irish breakfast tea, Jess made her first snip, and a fistful of red curls landed on the newspaper spread on the floor. Susie's breath caught in her throat for just an instant.

"You okay?" Jess asked. "It's not too late to stop. I can even up the other side and you'll look fairly decent."

"Nope. It all goes," Susie said. "I'm going to picture Sinead O'Connor while you cut."

"You'll probably need to go out and get a tattoo for that image to really work for you."

Susie thought about it. "Maybe I will."

Jess seemed startled by her offhand response. "Seriously?"

"You never know. I wonder what Mack would think if he discovered a little butterfly somewhere interesting."

"If you do it, I will," Jess challenged. "Will could use shaking up."

Susie laughed. "I imagine you keep Will pretty stirred up without coming home with a tattoo. He's the happiest I've ever seen him, you know. He looks a little dazed most of the time."

Jess sighed. "Me, too. I don't know why I fought it for so long."

"Fear, I imagine. That's what kept me from admitting how I really felt about Mack. I was so scared I'd never be able to hold on to him after all those other women that I didn't even want to try. It was safer to accept just being his friend."

"Fear," Jess echoed. "That was exactly it. I was so afraid Will wouldn't be able to cope with all my flaws, but the reality was that he knew every one of them and loved me anyway." She lathered up Susie's now-unevenly-shorn head, then asked, "Ready?"

Susie closed her eyes and took a deep breath. "Ready."

Though Jess was gentle, every scrape of the razor across her scalp brought tears to Susie's eyes. When Jess noticed she was crying, she uttered a gasp of dismay.

"Am I hurting you? I'm trying to be so careful."

Susie reached up and caught Jess's hand. "You're not hurting me," she promised, then added with a rare burst of anger, "It's the cancer that's hurting me. I hate this, Jess. I hate what it's done to my body, what the treatments are doing to me now. I can't admit that to anyone else. Everyone's trying so hard to be upbeat and brave. Mack's been a rock through this. I can't let them down by falling apart."

Jess moved in front of her and hunkered down, her arms resting on Susie's thighs. "Then you can fall apart with me," she said simply. "Believe me, I get what it's like to want to scream, to be scared of letting everyone down. I've done it so many times. So from here on out, if it gets to be too much, you call me. Understood?"

Rather than abating, Susie's tears came in a torrent. Jess simply gathered her in her arms and rocked her until she was spent.

And for the first time in their tenuous relationship, Susie knew with absolute certainty that this wasn't something Jess

Sherryl Woods

would ever hold over her head. They'd
breached that horrible divide between
them. Maybe there were some silver linings
to what she was going through, after all.

Mack leaned back in his chair and looked
at the mock-up of the *Bayside Chronicle*
with satisfaction. The masthead was traditional, but the font he and his graphics
artist had chosen gave it a modern look.
Though he'd wanted to use color, the budget simply wouldn't allow it. Not now, at
any rate. And he'd concluded that putting
color in the first edition to make more of a
splash would only raise people's expecta-
tions that subsequent issues wouldn't be
able to deliver on. It was better to start as
they intended to continue.

"It looks fantastic," Kristen said, leaning
over his shoulder to stare at the computer
screen. "Mack, you must be so excited.
Next week you're actually going to launch
a newspaper, one that's all yours! That's
amazing."

He glanced up, caught the scent of her
seductive perfume, felt the draw that had
once seemed so natural and familiar. He
jerked back immediately.

"It's pretty cool," he said as he stood up and began to pace.

"Why don't we go out and grab a bite to eat?" she suggested. "We can make it a celebratory lunch. My treat."

He shook his head before she'd completed the thought. "Sorry. I already have lunch plans."

She regarded him skeptically. "Really? It's already after one. What time were you supposed to go out?"

"We didn't set a firm time. I'm waiting for her call."

She frowned then. "You and Susie?"

"Of course. Who else?"

"I don't know, Mack. You used to have a whole string of women at any given time when you were in Baltimore."

"Times change," he said.

"So, since I've finally accepted that it's inevitable, when am I going to meet this wife of yours, the woman who finally managed to tame the wild and carefree Mack Franklin?"

"I'm sure she'll be at the launch party this weekend," he said. "I know she's anxious to meet you."

"Really?" Kristen said skeptically. "I

wouldn't be, if I were in her shoes. In fact, I'm not so sure how eager I am being in *my* shoes. I'm starting to get used to the idea of you being with someone who really matters to you, but it's been difficult." Her gaze narrowed. "Of course, I'm assuming she knows about our past. She does, doesn't she?"

"We discussed it before I ever offered you the job," he said.

"In the interest of full disclosure, of course," she commented.

Mack frowned. "Kristen, what's the deal? You're sounding weird again, almost jealous."

"Am I? How silly of me. I certainly have no right to be, do I?"

"No, you don't. I thought you were going to get out and meet some new people."

"How much time have you actually spent at Brady's, Mack? There aren't a lot of single men around, at least none who measure up to the one who got away."

He ignored the veiled reference he assumed was meant to describe him. "Are you unhappy here, after all? Do you want to leave?"

She sighed and sat in the chair he'd vacated. "Not really. The job is challenging. I want us to become a huge success. I don't like leaving anything half done."

He thought he saw the real problem. She was in a new place with no friends and she was spending all her waking hours at work, with him. He needed to find a way to fix that. Hopefully the launch party would be the first step. She'd really get to meet all of the town's movers and shakers. He had no doubt that she'd fit in, at least with anyone who wasn't a suspicious O'Brien determined to protect Susie's turf.

"You need to spend more time outside this office," he said. "Once we get past the launch, you'll have time to meet people and get involved in everything going on around town."

"That'll help, I'm sure," she agreed, though without much conviction.

He looked up just then and spotted Jess in the doorway. "Hey," he said. "What brings you by? I thought you were with Susie."

"I was," she said, then glanced toward Kristen with a frown. "I am. She's in the car. She said something about the two of you having plans."

"Why didn't she come in?" he asked, then could have kicked himself for his stupidity. "No big deal. I'll be right out. My car's in back. If you brought lunch, you can transfer it into that. Susie has the key."

Jess nodded, gave Kristen another hard look and walked back out.

Mack turned to find Kristen watching him curiously. "That was weird. Why didn't your wife come in? And who was the avenging angel she sent in her place? If looks could kill, I'd be dead on the floor right now."

"You're exaggerating. And Susie wasn't avoiding you, if that's what you were thinking. Things are a little tough for her right now. She doesn't always feel great."

Kristen's jaw fell. "She's pregnant? Is that it? Please don't tell me you're having a baby already, Mack. You've barely gotten married. I didn't think you'd ever do that, much less have children."

"She's not pregnant," he said. "Look, I can't get into this with you right now. Susie's waiting."

"Well, maybe you should explain before we cross paths at the launch party—that is unless you don't care if I blurt out the wrong thing."

"I assume you have better manners than to blurt out anything insensitive or inappropriate," he said. "We'll talk tomorrow. Take the rest of the day off. You deserve it."

"Sure thing," she said, an unmistakable note of bitterness in her voice. "There's nothing that excites me more than the idea of doing nothing in a town with nothing to do." She winced as soon as the words were out of her mouth. "Sorry. That sounded awful. Just chalk it up to a bad day, please. I'm not usually such a bitch."

"I know that," he said. "That's one reason I'm so worried. I don't want this situation to turn you into one."

She drew herself up, squared her shoulders and forced a smile. "Not to worry. I won't let it happen. I'm tougher than that."

Mack gave her another considering look, then left to meet his wife. Even though Kristen had made no overt passes, she'd made it plain that she was still available to him. Once again he wondered if bringing her here had been a dreadful mistake, just as everyone had told him it was from the beginning. He'd been so sure Susie could handle it, that *he* could. To be totally honest, he'd never even considered whether Kristen could.

But then he thought of the paper they were about to launch and knew that if it succeeded, in large measure it would be due to Kirsten's digital talents. How could he possibly regret that?

When Mack opened the driver's side door of his car and slid in, he tried not to look taken aback at his first glimpse of Susie with a colorful scarf wrapped securely around her head like a turban. The look made her eyes seem huge, her cheeks more well-defined.

"What do you think?" she asked tentatively, touching nervous fingers to the scarf and regarding him hopefully. "It's not too awful, is it?"

He forced a smile. "It's not awful at all. In fact, the look suits you. You look as if you've recently left a harem and are in a particularly seductive frame of mind."

As he'd hoped, she laughed. "Yeah, that's me. The ultimate temptress."

He sobered at once. "You are, you know. I'm not sure I can wait till we get to Beach Lane to get my hands on you."

She rolled her eyes at that. "You're overplaying your hand." The words were no sooner out of her mouth than she seemed to go perfectly still.

Mack tried to follow the direction of her gaze, but she turned so quickly, he couldn't be sure what had caused the reaction. "Susie, what's up? What just happened?"

"Is that her?" she asked. "Is that Kristen?"

Mack stilled. "Where?"

"At the back door. She was watching us. Tall, willowy blonde. That is her, isn't it? I saw her once, but from a distance. She has quite a following at Sally's. I hear none of the men can speak for at least five minutes after she's picked up her lunch and left."

He glanced toward the building, but the back door was closed. "Whoever it was has gone now. More than likely it was Kristen, though."

"She was spying on us," Susie said flatly. "Or trying to get a glimpse of me."

"She was probably just making sure the

back door was locked before she leaves," he said, determined to put an innocent spin on it. He even believed what he was saying. Kristen wasn't the kind of woman who'd spy on them. She was too sure of herself, too full of pride to risk being caught and made to look foolish or needy.

"If you say so," Susie said, her doubts plain. "But if she turns up at Beach Lane, she and I are going to have it out. I may be sick, but I can still take her down."

He was wise enough to hide his smile. Susie would definitely come out on top in any sort of physical confrontation. Kristen would never resort to rolling around in the mud the way Susie would. She'd be too worried about the dry cleaning bill for her designer clothes.

"You sound a little too eager, Susie," he chided. "The woman's done nothing to you."

"She slept with you, didn't she?"

"A long time ago."

"That doesn't mean I have to be happy about it."

He laughed. "No, it doesn't mean that." He let his smile fade, then looked into her eyes. "I'm yours now, Susie. That's the only thing that matters. The past is over and done with. You're my present and my future."

She sighed, but she didn't look entirely convinced. "I remind myself of that every day," she said. "You're the biggest blessing in my life. Without you—"

Mack cut her off. "There won't be a day without me," he said adamantly.

She looked shaken by his vehemence. "You must get sick of me sounding needy. I'm sorry."

"You don't have anything to be sorry about. And you're the least needy woman I know. You went for years showing me just how little you needed me. Frankly, it was tough on my ego."

That brought a faint smile to her lips and put some color back in her cheeks. "It was an act, you know."

He reached for her hand and held it, then brought it to his lips. "But a darned convincing one. From here on out we just have to remember that we need each other. No more games, Susie. Not ever."

"No more games," she promised.

Mack had to wonder, though, if it was ever possible to go through life without a game or two. For instance, there was the one he played every single day, the one in which he tried not to let Susie see how terrified he was of losing her. That was a game he couldn't afford to quit. He kept hoping if he pretended he was confident and brave about the outcome of her cancer, sooner or later he'd actually believe the words he was saying.

So far, though, it wasn't really working all that well. And seeing her just now with the scarf tied around her shaved head reminded him all too clearly of the stakes of this particular game he was playing.

17

Mack wasn't entirely shocked when he arrived at work the next morning to find Jess waiting for him. Thankfully, Kristen hadn't come in yet, because he had a sneaking suspicion she was the reason for Jess's visit.

"This is a surprise," he said cheerfully, unlocking the front door and letting her in. He flipped on lights and put his briefcase on his desk. "Let me get the coffee started, and you can tell me why you're here."

She gave him a scathing look. "You know why I'm here. I walked in on something yesterday, and I didn't like it. I considered letting it go. I even told myself it was none of my business. I've never been a big defender of Susie's because, frankly, she didn't need it. Now I think she does."

Mack met her gaze evenly. "Your point?"

"Is there something going on between you and that woman?"

Mack didn't pretend not to understand. There was no point in insulting her intelligence. And this was what he'd wanted, wasn't it? For Susie and Jess to get closer. He just hadn't expected his best friend's wife to get in *his* face about *his* marriage.

"No," he said evenly, deciding that now was not the time to mention their past. It was, after all, in the past. "There is absolutely nothing between Kristen and me beyond our work."

"Well, the tension in the air yesterday came from something else. I recognize sexual attraction when I see it. I swear to God, if you do anything that's going to upset Susie when she's fighting for her life, I will personally take you apart."

Mack smiled. "It won't be necessary."

"That's what Will said, but I didn't believe him. I wanted to hear it from you."

"And now you have," he said. "What's the verdict?"

Her gaze was assessing as she surveyed him. "Well, I've known you to play around, but I've never known you to lie. And my husband's opinion counts for a lot, so I'm going to give you the benefit of the doubt."

"Thank you," he said solemnly. "All of this is quite a turnaround coming from you. You've never been one of Susie's biggest fans."

"I had an epiphany yesterday. I realized she was never the enemy. I just needed someone on whom I could focus all my anger, and she worked for me. She was such a blasted paragon, you know? Smart as a whip, athletic. She did everything right."

"And you didn't," he suggested gently.

Jess sighed. "And I didn't."

"You discovered all that while shaving her head? You did a good job, by the way. I like the look."

"Me, too. She has the kind of face that can pull it off. I'd be jealous, except the reason for shaving her head sucks."

"It certainly does," he agreed. "Are we okay, Jess?"

"For now, but I'm keeping my eye on you at the launch party. If I see anything amiss, you and I are going out back for a little come-to-Jesus talk."

Mack smiled. "I'd almost like to see that."

Jess chuckled, but her own smile immediately faded. "Susie is going to be okay, isn't she?"

"It's what we're all praying for," he said. "We won't know anything until after she finishes the treatments, though."

"Are you doing okay?"

"I'm hanging in there. I'm not the one with the tough assignment."

"I don't know," Jess said. "I think it must be awful watching someone you love going through so much. I know Will's the shrink in the family, but I'm around to listen if you ever need a sounding board. No judgments, I promise."

"Thanks, Jess, and thank you for coming over here to stand up for my wife."

"You know I'm just the tip of the iceberg, right? If you get out of line, the O'Briens will nail your hide to a wall."

"Believe me, I don't need reminding of that."

She nodded, looking satisfied. "Okay, then, my work here is done." She crossed the room and kissed his cheek. "You and Susie should come over for dinner when she's feeling up to it. Will and I would love that. It can be on a moment's notice, whenever she's having a good day."

"We'll plan on it," Mack said, then watched her go.

No sooner had Jess left than Kristen appeared. "Is she gone?" she asked dramatically. "I assume she came over here to warn you away from me."

Mack laughed. "How'd you guess?"

"I told you I saw murder in her eyes yesterday. Is she coming to the launch party?"

"Of course. She's the owner of The Inn at Eagle Point. They're catering the launch."

Kristen winced. "I guess I'll have to watch what I eat, then, won't I?"

"Probably not a bad idea," he admitted. "Now, let's go over the story log for our first editions. We'll have to allow for any breaking news, but I think we can nail down the features."

"Sure," she said, pouring herself a cup of coffee. "But first I want to apologize for yesterday. I know I forget about the boundaries from time to time, but I'll try really hard to play by the rules from here on out. I don't want to be the other woman, and it's too late for me to be anything else." She met his gaze, her expression wistful. "Isn't it?"

"It's too late," Mack confirmed.

"Okay, then," she said briskly. "Let's plan that first edition."

Mack had hired a high school student as a stringer to cover local school sports. He planned to write about professional sports himself, along with writing the editorials. His general assignment reporter would be on board this weekend, and he had three people who would contribute feature articles on a part-time basis. It was a skeleton crew, but he thought they could manage for the time being.

His sales team had been in place from the beginning, and they'd been drawing in more advertising than he'd anticipated. The first edition was going to be a healthy one, with two full sections jam-packed with ads and great articles. The website was interactive, so readers could comment, and allowed for video streaming of local events and important meetings.

As he and Kristen went over every detail for the launch issue, Mack's confidence grew that the *Bayside Chronicle* was going to work. He knew there would be challenges ahead, but he could envision doing this for a lifetime, becoming a part of Chesapeake Shores in a way he'd never imagined possible as the kid from a troubled home who'd desperately wanted to belong.

As they wrapped up the meeting, he met Kristen's gaze and grinned. "I think we've done it," he said optimistically.

She grinned back at him. "I think we have," she agreed, and held up a hand for a high five. "We're a good team, Mack."

When she said it, though, the wistful note was no longer in her voice. It was clearly an acknowledgment of their professional accomplishment and nothing more.

At least, he hoped that was the case.

Susie was sick and tired of being sick and tired. The minute Mack left for work, she showered, dressed and headed for the real estate office. It was time she got back into her routine and reclaimed her life. It was one thing to fight cancer and conserve her energy. It was quite another to hibernate.

She chose a bright pink scarf she would never have dared to wear with her red hair, wrapped it around her head and studied herself in the mirror. "Daring," she concluded, grinning. "It says I'm back."

But when she walked into the office, her father took one look at her and paled. She'd forgotten he hadn't seen her since she'd shaved her head.

"Hey, Dad," she said jauntily. "I decided it was time to come back to work. Otherwise I'll never straighten out the mess you've probably made of all my files."

He blinked hard and tried to muster a smile, but there was no mistaking the tears brimming in his eyes. Susie walked over to him. "Don't you dare start crying," she commanded, hugging him fiercely. "I'm okay. It was just hair."

"And you always hated it anyway," he said, his voice choked with emotion.

"That's what Mack said."

"It wasn't as if your opinion was a secret. I always thought the real reason Jess chopped off your hair when you were a kid was because you begged her to."

Susie laughed. "I most certainly did not, but I did ask her to do it this time."

Her father looked surprised. "Really? You and Jess have made peace?"

"We're trying," she said, not sure if the fragile truce would hold. Years of bitterness and resentments couldn't be cured in a day, no matter how well-meaning both parties were.

"I'm glad. You need Jess and the rest of Mick's girls in your life. They're strong women. They'll provide good backup. Just because Mick and I don't always see eye to eye doesn't mean you should keep some kind of distance between you and them on my behalf. If I've ever given you the impression I expect that, I'm sorry."

"You haven't done that. I held myself aloof out of some misguided sense of loyalty, but I know it was unnecessary. And I think I'm finally realizing how important women friends and family are. We've always been a strong family but it was at Gram's insistence. I'm just starting to figure out why she was so determined to keep us close-knit despite all the issues between you, Mick and Thomas."

"It took me a while to get that myself," Jeff admitted. "But when this cancer thing came up, it felt mighty good to walk into that hospital waiting room and find my brothers there."

Susie pulled up a chair. "So, tell me what's going on around here. What do you need me to do first?"

Her father frowned. "Are you sure you're up to this?"

"I need to be here, Dad. At home all I do is sit around and worry about whether the chemo is working."

"Okay, but here's the deal. You stay until you get tired. Then you go home. I don't care if you're here an hour or six hours, okay?"

"Got it. I'll pace myself, I promise."

"Okay, then, why don't you go over that new lease for a pet boutique on the corner of Main and Shore Road."

Susie regarded him with admiration. The space was large and, therefore, pricey. In this economy it had been a tough sell for start-up businesses. "You leased that space? Fantastic. And we need a fancy pet store in town. From what I can see around here, people pamper their pets more than they do themselves." She paused, frowning. "They're not selling puppies or other pets, are they? I hate those puppy mill operations."

"No, though they will offer connections to all of the legitimate breeders in the region. And they've already worked something out with the rescue shelters so they can post pictures of the pets they have up for adoption. I think they plan on having regular adoption days, too."

At the mention of adoption, Susie felt a tug at her heart. "If only it were that easy to adopt a baby," she said.

Her father regarded her worriedly. "Isn't it too soon for you to be thinking about that?"

She nodded. "I know. Mack and I agreed to wait until we know—well, until the future's a little clearer."

"You could always take in a puppy in the meantime," Jeff suggested in an attempt to be helpful.

She shook her head. "Not in the apartment. That'll have to wait for the house, and who knows when we'll get that built."

"I told you I'd front you the money, and I know Mick would put a crew on it the second you ask. Matthew told me he'd drawn up the plans."

Susie shook her hear. "Thanks, Dad, but Mack would never hear of it."

"Have you mentioned to him how much it would mean to you?"

"No. Right now it would amount to the kind of manipulation I hate. If I mention wanting anything, he'll move heaven and earth to get it for me, whether he thinks we can afford it or not. I don't want him to go against his principles to pay for our house. Besides, right now he's totally focused on getting the paper up and running. We can discuss the house again once the launch is behind us."

"There's a lot of buzz around town about the paper, that's for sure."

"Are people excited?"

"They can't wait. I've bought quite a few ads myself for the properties we're handling. I think the online component has attracted a lot of businesses. That woman he has creating the website seems to know what she's doing."

"Have you met her?" Susie asked curiously.

"I've seen her a time or two in Sally's. She turns heads, that's for sure." As soon as he said the words he looked vaguely guilty, as if they'd been some kind of betrayal.

"So I hear," Susie said neutrally, determined not to let the offhand comment throw her. "I'd better get to work. Right now I feel as if I could tackle the world, but it won't last."

"You call it quits whenever you need to," he reminded her.

"Will do, Dad."

She went to her desk, viewed the daunting pile of folders awaiting her attention and dug in. She found the pet store lease, went over it, checked for any loopholes, then called the prospective renter to let him know it was ready to be signed.

Though her energy was flagging by lunchtime, she felt ecstatic over making it through an entire morning. She knew she needed to call it a day, and was organizing her files when Mack walked in the door. He gave her a chiding look.

"I thought the reports of you being back at work had to be all wrong. What'd you do, sneak out of the apartment as soon as I left?"

She grinned. "Something like that. It feels so good to be back. I almost feel like the old me again."

"Except more exhausted," he guessed. "You look tired."

"I am a little," she admitted. "I was just getting ready to head home." She regarded him hopefully. "Unless my handsome husband would like to buy me lunch before I go. What do you say? Panini Bistro? Sally's? Anything that doesn't involve a can of soup in our kitchen."

"Are you sure you feel up to it?"

"I think I can keep my eyes open for another half hour, especially if you'll fill me in on the plans for the launch party. Is there anything I can do to help?"

"I just want you there by my side, since you're the inspiration for this. You can bask in all the glory and take all the credit."

She laughed. "That'll be fun, but it hardly seems fair, since you've done all the hard work."

"Let's go to Sally's and I'll tell you all about it. Will and Jake will be there. Mind if we join them? I've bailed on them a few times too many lately."

"Of course not. I'd never interfere with tradition."

When they walked into Sally's, Susie tried to ignore the shocked expressions she glimpsed on the faces of people she hadn't seen in a while. When she reached the booth in back, Jake and Will both stood and gave her resounding kisses. To their credit, whatever their reactions to her appearance, there was no outward evidence of anything more than delight at seeing her out and about.

"You look good," Will said. "Jess told me about the new hairdo. She felt honored that you asked her to help."

"Did she tell you why I thought she was the perfect choice?" Susie asked, grinning.

Will laughed. "She did. Now, tell me how you're feeling."

"Better than the times when I feel like I've been run over by a bus," she said candidly. "But I do not want to talk about me. I want to hear about you guys. Jake, how's the baby?"

His face lit up. "Trying to walk. As cute as she is when she pulls herself up and then falls back on her little padded butt, the thought of trying to keep up with her once she can actually walk scares the dickens out of me."

"You're not the one who'll be trying to keep up with her," Susie reminded him. "Bree will."

"That's what you think. She's told me she can barely contain her in her playpen at the flower shop now. Once the baby's walking, Bree says she's going to work with me on my landscaping jobs so she can roam the wide open spaces. I almost think my wife is totally serious."

"She probably is," Will confirmed.

Sally came over to take their order. Her only acknowledgment that anything was wrong with Susie was the reassuring squeeze she gave her shoulder. "Okay, hurry up, you guys. I don't have all day to stand around while you make up your minds," she said with her usual brisk manner.

When they'd all placed their orders, she winked at Susie. "You're a brave woman for taking on these three at the same time.

I have no idea how Bree and Jess put up with them."

"We're very lovable," Jake told her.

"Couldn't prove it by me," Sally said.

Their meals came within minutes. By the time Susie had finished half of her tuna salad sandwich, she was too tired to lift another bite to her mouth. Mack took one look at her and stood up.

"I need to get this beautiful woman home. She's been out gallivanting too long."

"I'll drive myself," she protested.

He leveled a stern look into her eyes. "Not a chance."

"Let the man pamper you," Will advised. "It doesn't come naturally to him, so he needs the practice."

"Bite me," Mack said. "And you can pay for lunch while you're at it."

"My pleasure," Will called after them as Mack guided Susie out of the restaurant.

"That felt almost normal," she said as she sank gratefully into the passenger seat of Mack's car.

"Almost?"

"Didn't you see the way some people were staring when we walked in? I felt as if

I were on display, the poster child for cancer or something."

"You handled it well. You didn't let on that it bothered you."

"I guess because I understood. I've reacted the same way when I've run into someone who's obviously undergoing treatment. I felt tongue-tied. I mean, what are you supposed to say?"

"'Hello' seems like a good place to start," Mack said.

"But 'hello' can start a conversation, and then what? Do you avoid the subject or talk about it? It's tricky." She sighed. "I suppose I need to get used to it. Otherwise the launch party is going to be pretty awkward."

"I'll be right there with you every second," Mack assured her. "And it's going to be packed with family and friends. You don't have a thing to worry about."

"Right," she said. "Besides, it's your night. It's not about me."

"It wouldn't be happening if it weren't for you," he corrected as he pulled up at their apartment.

"Don't park. I'll be fine going in," she

told him. She leaned across the console and kissed him. "Thanks for lunch."

"Thank Will."

"Yes, but you were my very sexy escort. Maybe all those people at Sally's were staring at you, rather than me, after all."

"I'm sure that's it," he said drily. "Love you. See you around six."

Susie stood on the curb, then bent to lean in through the passenger window. "It's been a good day, Mack. Who knew I could be so grateful for getting to spend a few hours at work and having lunch at Sally's?"

"Maybe it's a good reminder to all of us to count our blessings when they're happening," he said. "You're at the top of my list."

"And you're at the top of mine," she said, then watched him drive off.

Her good mood lasted all the way inside and up to the bedroom and then her head began to swim. The dizziness washed over her in nauseating waves.

Struggling, she barely made it to the bed before her knees gave way. She was reaching for the phone to call for help when the walls seemed to close in, the light seemed to fade. And then nothing.

When Mack walked into the darkened apartment at six o'clock and heard not a single sound, his pulse started to race and his heart began to thud.

"Susie!"

He ran to the bedroom, switched on the light and saw her sprawled half in and half out of the bed, still wearing the coat she'd had on earlier.

"Oh, dear God," he murmured, rushing to her side and feeling for a pulse. It was faint, but it was there. "Susie!" he said again, giving her a gentle shake, even as he dialed 9-1-1 with a hand that shook so badly he could barely clasp the phone.

The next half hour passed in a blur as the paramedics tried to revive Susie, then settled for stabilizing her so she could be transported to the hospital. Mack called Jeff and Jo, then followed the ambulance.

By the time he reached the emergency room, Susie was already in a cubicle surrounded by doctors and nurses.

"You need to wait outside," a nurse told

him. "Let the doctors figure out what's going on."

"She's recovering from ovarian cancer," he told her. "She's on chemo. Has anyone called Dr. Kinnear or the oncologist?"

"We will if we need them. We have all of her records," the nurse informed him gently. "We'll take good care of her."

Mack was pacing the waiting room when Jo and Jeff arrived, followed quickly by Nell, Mick and Megan.

"Abby and Bree are on their way," Megan told him. "So are Will and Jess."

"Has there been any news?" Nell asked.

Mack shook his head. His gaze kept being drawn to the closed doors behind which they were doing who knows what to his wife. Could their life together end like this, so unexpectedly? Surely fate wouldn't be that cruel.

"I knew she was overdoing it today," Jeff lamented. "I should have sent her straight home."

Mack understood the regret he was feeling. He was carrying a load of it himself for taking Susie to lunch, rather than home. Still, he kept hearing her words echoing in his head.

"She needed to be at work today," he reassured Jeff. "When I dropped her off at home, she kept telling me what a great day it had been, and that she'd almost felt like her old self."

Jeff wasn't consoled. "Still, it was too much for her. I should have insisted that she leave."

Jo gave him a chiding look. "Do you imagine our daughter would have listened to a word you said? Her mind was made up. Mack's right. She did exactly what she wanted to do today."

"But if something happens because of it . . ." Jeff argued.

They all knew what he was trying so hard not to say—if Susie died—but no one dared to utter those words. Surely death was too high a price for having one day doing what she enjoyed.

"Stop it, all of you!" Nell commanded. "Susie will be just fine. This is a little set-back, nothing more."

Mack hoped that was the case, but his faith wasn't as strong as hers. As if she understood that, Nell crossed the room and pulled him down beside her.

"She's going to be okay," she assured him. "Believe that. Hold on to it."

He regarded her bleakly. "I'm trying."

She patted his hand. "Well, fortunately I have enough faith for the both of us. Susie's a strong woman, and she loves you too much to leave you now when your life together is just getting started."

Mack heard the words, absorbed the confidence with which they were spoken as a thirsty man soaked up rain. He struggled to match Nell's belief. He believed in Susie. He believed in them. He hoped that was enough.

18

"Susie's white blood count has fallen dangerously low," Dr. Kinnear explained to the assembled O'Briens a couple of endless hours after Susie had been brought into the hospital. Her oncologist was by his side, nodding. "We need to keep her in here for a few days, try to build her blood back up."

Though he wasn't sure he wanted to know, Mack forced himself to ask, "What about the treatments?"

"Everything stops for now," the oncologist said, his tone firm.

Charles Price might not have Dr. Kinnear's

comforting demeanor or his charm, but his professional skills were excellent. Mack had researched his credentials thoroughly. He had to trust the oncologist now.

"But isn't that risky?" Jo inquired hesitantly, her eyes filled with worry.

"It would be riskier to continue before we know she's able to tolerate another round," Dr. Price insisted. Dr. Kinnear concurred.

"It's a setback, but there's no reason for panic," Dr. Kinnear assured them. "This happens."

"Is she awake now?" Mack asked. "Does she know about this?"

Both doctors nodded. "We've talked to her and explained things," her gynecologist said. "As you can imagine, she's not happy about delaying treatment. Try to convince her this isn't a death sentence. She's scared it could be."

"So am I," Jo admitted, looking increasingly shaken. Nell and Jeff moved to put their arms around her.

"Nobody's allowed to think like that, or at least to say anything remotely like that around Susie," Mack said fiercely. "She needs us to believe she's going to beat this. It's up to us to keep her spirits strong."

"That's absolutely right," Dr. Kinnear said. "Mack, why don't you spend a little time with your wife. Jo, if you and Jeff want to pop in after that for a minute, go ahead, but the rest of you should wait for tomorrow. And keep the visits brief. Susie needs rest. I imagine I don't need to remind you not to visit at all if you have a cold or anything else contagious. She's highly susceptible to infection right now. The nurse will explain all the necessary precautions to you."

Mack took off down the hall, but when he reached the door to Susie's room, he halted in his tracks. He was leaning against the wall, trying to gather his composure, when Will arrived.

"You want to talk a minute before you go in there?" Will asked.

Mack shook his head, tears stinging his eyes. "What is there to say?"

"Exactly what you said not five minutes ago, that everyone needs to believe Susie's going to beat this. She needs *you* to believe it most of all."

"I'm scared, Will." It was not an admission he'd made often, not even when he'd been a kid and his mother had vanished for days at a time. Instead, back then he'd focused on keeping the authorities from finding out, because he'd known intuitively they'd have taken him away from her if they'd known. Only Will and Jake had guessed about those terrifying incidents and somehow had found a way to get him invited to their homes for extended visits. He'd always wondered how they'd known, or why their parents had gone along with those visits without questions.

Now Will put a reassuring hand on his shoulder and just stood there, solid in his understanding and support. Thankfully he didn't utter a lot of platitudes that Mack wouldn't have bought anyway.

Finally Mack drew in a deep breath, gave his friend a grateful look, then opened the door.

Susie was so pale, her color seemed no deeper than the white sheets on the hospital bed. An IV was pumping blood and who knew what else into her system. Her eyes were closed. She looked so lifeless, so unlike the animated woman with whom he'd fallen in love, Mack was once again taken aback. If it had been even remotely acceptable, he might have turned tail and run, but of course he couldn't. Susie needed him now more than ever.

He pulled a chair up closer to the bed, sat down and took her ice-cold hand in his. Then he shut his eyes and prayed as he never had before in his life.

"Please, God, let her be okay. She doesn't deserve this, and, to be honest, I have no idea what I'd do without her. The same goes for her family. We all need her, God. Please, please, make this turn out okay."

"Mack?" Her voice was raspy with sleep, but it was enough to have his eyes snapping open.

"Hey, beautiful," he said, leaning closer. "How're you doing?"

"Not so good," she confessed. "I feel weaker than a newborn kitten. What happened?"

"Dr. Kinnear and the oncologist said they explained to you about the low white blood count."

She looked confused, but then her eyes cleared. "Oh, yeah, that's right. When can I go home?"

"I'm not sure. They want to get your blood count up a bit."

"But I'll be out before the launch party, right? I can't miss that."

Mack had made a decision earlier, though he hadn't mentioned it to anyone. "I'm postponing that."

Alarm filled her eyes. "Mack, no. The paper has to come out."

"The paper will come out, right on schedule, but we can have the party later. I'll speak to Jess. I'm sure it won't be a problem. And the family can make the calls to everyone. They'll understand. I'm not doing this party without you, and it'll be too much for you right now."

To his surprise she didn't argue, which told him just how beat she must be.

"If it's what you want to do," she said wearily. "I'm sorry."

"Don't you dare be sorry. You didn't wind up in the hospital on purpose. This is just a little bump in the road. Nothing more."

She searched his gaze as if she feared he wasn't telling her everything. "Are you sure about that?"

"Swear to God," he assured her. "The doctors aren't worried. They said things like this happen, so we're not worrying. Understand?"

She gave him a look filled with sorrow. "You certainly didn't bargain for this when you asked me to marry you."

"I bargained for having you in my life in sickness and in health," he corrected. "We're going to tough it out through this sickness, and then we're going to have the rest of our lives to do all the things we ever dreamed of."

She managed a faint smile. "There you go, cheerleading again."

"That's my job. You fight this disease. I hold pep rallies."

"Mack," she whispered, her gaze locking on his.

"What?"

"I want to build our house now."

It was the last thing he'd expected her to say. "But—"

"No buts," she said adamantly. "I know all about the cost, but we can work that out. My dad and Uncle Mick will work with us."

"Come on, Susie," he pleaded. "I don't want to be indebted to your family."

She continued to hold his gaze. "I swore to myself I wasn't going to persuade you like this, but I have to do it."

"Do what?"

"Use whatever means necessary." She held his gaze. "You love me, don't you?"

He saw where this was heading. He also knew there was no way he could refuse her anything she wanted. And he knew she knew that, as well. If she was playing her trump card, it had to matter to her.

"Of course I love you," he said.

"Then do this for me. If . . ." She sucked in a breath, then spoke determinedly. "If I don't beat this cancer, I want to have spent at least a few nights in our dream house with you. I want you to have memories of us living there together, no matter how briefly. I understand all the reasons why you don't want to ask my family for help, but please, just this once, Mack, put your pride aside and do this for me."

He saw how much this meant to her. He even understood her desperation. He studied her hopeful expression and knew he couldn't deny her this one wish, even if asking for financial help went against every principle he had.

"It's that important to you?" he asked.

She nodded.

"Okay, then, I'll do it on one condition."

Her eyes lit up. "Anything. What is it?"

"No more talk about dying, Susie. It tears me up inside."

Her expression sobered. "We might have to face it, Mack. We need to be prepared."

"Not now," he insisted.

"Please be realistic."

"If the time comes, I will be. I promise you I will listen if you need to talk. I won't deny the reality, but we're not there yet," he said fiercely. "Not yet!"

He felt tears dampening his cheeks, but he made no attempt to brush them away. It was Susie who reached up and touched his face tenderly.

"No matter what happens, Mack, please know this. You've given me a lifetime. You've made me happier than I ever imagined I could be. Whether I live a few more months or we're together for many, many years, I'll have been blessed."

Mack tried to keep it together. He really did, but he knew if he didn't get out of that room right now, he was going to lose it, and he didn't want to upset Susie.

"I'll be back," he said, standing up suddenly. "I'm going to get your parents. I know they want to say good-night."

He found Jo and Jeff nearby. He was so choked up, he could only gesture for them to go in. Jo regarded him with concern, but when he waved her off, she went into her daughter's room with Jeff.

Mack headed for the chapel, hoping he could find the peace and composure there that had eluded him in Susie's room. To his surprise, he found Nell already there. She smiled a welcome, then patted the pew beside her. When he was seated, she silently took his hand in hers, allowing him to draw on her strength, and together they prayed.

Susie's fighting spirit came back as her blood count and energy rose. She wanted to go home, and had been telling everyone who'd listen that she'd do it against medical advice if the doctors didn't get a move on and release her.

"You'll leave here early over my dead body," Mack said grimly when she made the announcement to him when he finally managed to drop by late one evening.

He tossed something to her—a rolled-up

newspaper, from the look of it. Suddenly all thoughts of fleeing the hospital vanished. Sitting in the chair beside the bed, she reached up and flipped on the nearby light.

"This is it?" she asked excitedly. "The first edition of the *Bayside Chronicle*?"

"That's it. Hot off the press. It'll be on newsstands and in mailboxes around town first thing in the morning. I came straight here after we finished the press run."

She tore off the plastic wrap and spread it open on her lap. "Oh, Mack, it looks amazing," she said. "Honestly. I think it has the very best front page I've ever seen. It looks so inviting and readable. The pictures are great. Who took them?"

"A couple of the freelance people," he said, then added more hesitantly, "And Kristen."

Susie stilled. "She does a little bit of everything, doesn't she?"

"She was just pitching in," he said, a defensive note in his voice. "We're all doing things that eventually will be assigned to other people."

"I know. I didn't mean to make an issue

of it," she said. She patted the chair beside her. "Sit here while I read every word," she told him excitedly.

"You don't have to read it now."

"But I want to. This is amazing, Mack. To think that you started this from scratch."

"Let's hope everyone in town will be as thrilled as you are."

"You sound doubtful. Why is that?"

"The editorial," he admitted, his expression chagrined. "I took the mayor to task over not keeping up with the parks. Some of them are looking pretty ragged, and spring's just around the corner. Kids should be able to play in them on nice days, and couples should be able to go for a stroll. Right now I wouldn't want to see a stray animal out in those weeds."

"Hey, it's your job to call the mayor on stuff like that."

"No one ever has before. He might be a little sensitive to finding the criticism in the paper's first edition, especially when he can probably argue that budget cuts have forced his hand."

She waved off his concern. "Uncle Mick rakes him over the coals on a regular basis. Believe me, if Mick hasn't been all over this already, he will be now. He'll back you a hundred percent."

"That reminds me," Mack said. "I spoke to Mick and your father about the house. As soon as you're feeling up to it, we're all going to get together and finalize the plans."

Susie regarded him with astonishment. "Really? You're going to let them get started?"

He nodded. "We've worked out a payment plan I can live with. It's almost spring, the perfect time for breaking ground. At least, that's what the two of them tell me. They say we'll be in the house by the end of summer, maybe sooner if Mick doubles up on the crews."

Susie's excitement dimmed a bit. There it was, the hint that her time might be fleeting, the sense of urgency to get this done. None of them would say the words, but they all knew what could happen.

"That's great," she said, but without much enthusiasm.

Of course Mack noticed. "Don't look like that," he said gently. "Nobody thinks you're dying."

"They'd be crazy if they didn't," she said candidly.

Mack stood up and began to pace, just as he always did when he was agitated. His eyes flashed angrily. When he faced her, he was clearly furious. "Susie O'Brien Franklin, I don't ever want to hear you say something like that again." He frowned down at her. "Do you understand me?"

She recognized that there was unspoken fear behind the anger. "I'm not giving up," she assured him. "I won't, Mack."

He released a sigh and sat back down. "Sorry I yelled at you."

She nodded. "I know. Let's make a pact here and now. We both have permission to yell when one of us sounds like we're giving up, okay?"

"Works for me," he said. "Now, you need to get some sleep, and I need to make sure these papers get distributed."

"Are you planning to hand out each one personally?" she inquired, trying to hide a grin.

Mack looked sheepish. "I probably won't go that far."

"Good, because if you start doing that,

I'll never see you, and just so you know, that's not acceptable."

He leaned down and lingered over a kiss. "It's definitely not acceptable," he agreed. "See you in the morning."

"Only after you've been to Sally's to bask in all the accolades," she said. "I want to hear every single word."

Mack nodded. "I'll bring croissants, coffee and gossip. How's that?"

"Perfect."

"Sleep well," he said. "I can't wait to get you back home and into our bed."

"Believe me, I can't wait to be there. Not only is this bed uncomfortable, it doesn't have you."

Mack hesitated, then gestured toward the bed. "Climb in," he said.

"What?"

"Climb in," he repeated.

When she'd done that, he managed to slide in next to her and draw her close. "I'll be here till you fall asleep," he promised.

With his arms around her, she fell into the first untroubled sleep she'd had in days.

"I'm so damned angry all the time," Mack said at lunch the next day. Despite the newspaper selling out its first edition, despite all the phone calls and messages of congratulation he'd received, he hadn't been able to bask in any of it.

Will regarded him sympathetically. "Are you mad at Susie?"

"Of course not. She didn't ask for this disease."

"As long as you've got that straight, then I'd say what you're feeling is perfectly natural," Will told him.

"But come on, it can't be good walking around like a time bomb that's likely to explode at any second. I'm afraid if somebody says the wrong thing or does something to set me off, I'll go for the jugular."

"You want something to calm you down? I'm sure a doctor would prescribe something."

For an instant Mack considered asking for some sort of antidepressant, then shook his head. "No, there has to be a better way to deal with what I'm feeling. The worst part is knowing that Susie's handling so much more, and *she's* got it together."

"Really?" Will asked skeptically. "Or is she just hiding it from you?"

Mack thought about the question. "She

may be hiding it from me," he conceded. "I've seen Jo leave her room in tears a couple of times, so maybe she's letting her feelings out with her mother. The same with Shanna. She's been a rock for Susie. And Jess is stepping up, too. She's been by the hospital every day, always with some silly gift that makes Susie laugh. I know you're partially behind that. I appreciate it."

"I'm not sure I did that much. I think Susie's illness gave Jess a new perspective on their relationship. I think she finally saw that even the so-called golden people have their crosses to bear. No one's immune."

"Still, it's been good for Susie to know there are people she can count on."

"And people she can talk to," Will added.

"She ought to be able to talk to me," Mack said in frustration. "I feel like I'm letting her down. I want her to be able to share her feelings with me. I need to know when she's scared, or when she's not feeling strong enough to fight. How else am I supposed to help her? But I have to admit when she looks at me with unmistakable fear in her eyes, it tears me apart. I'm not sure how much help I am then."

"You can't help her all the time. Be grateful she has family and friends around to back you up. Nobody goes through something like this exactly the same way. They find comfort and strength where they need it."

"I just feel so blasted helpless," Mack complained.

"The truth is, you are," Will reminded him. "The doctors and God are in charge here."

"I don't like being the outsider," Mack grumbled.

Will allowed himself a smile. "You're hardly that. You're the one holding her at night, the one she looks to when her heart needs a lift. She counts on you in ways you probably don't even realize." He gave Mack a knowing look. "Or is that the real problem? That you know she's counting on you for all those unspoken needs of hers, and you're afraid of missing something important and letting her down?"

Mack regarded his friend with astonishment. "You're good," he said approvingly.

"That's why my sessions are so expensive. Lucky for you, you get off with buying me lunch."

"I'll throw in dessert," Mack offered. "You're worth at least that much."

Will chuckled. "Not necessary. Gail keeps leaving these decadent desserts in the fridge at the inn. Who knew I could get addicted to pretty much having a personal chef around? I swear I've gained ten pounds since Jess and I got married. I never knew what a chocoholic I am."

"Then you're the only one who didn't know it," Mack taunted. "I can recall a lot of Halloween candy bars going missing from my sack and Jake's when we were kids."

Will tried to look offended, but in the end, he laughed. "Caught me. I'm surprised the two of you didn't beat me up."

"You were the tall, skinny one. We figured you needed 'em."

Will's expression sobered. "Mack, one last word about your situation with Susie. I think you're handling it all just fine. It can't be easy, but you've stepped up. From the minute you found out what was going on, you've put Susie first. I admire you for that. Just keep on doing what you've been doing. You'll get through this okay."

"I wish I had as much faith in me as you seem to have."

"I've had years to figure out the kind of

man you are," Will said. "There's not a doubt in my mind that you'll do whatever needs to be done."

Mack sighed. "I'm certainly going to give it my best shot."

Laila took one look at Susie's haggard face and felt her heart twist in her chest. She'd been meaning to stop by for days, had intended to get to the hospital, but the whole situation with Matthew had made her skittish around all of the O'Briens. Once Susie had gone home, though, she'd known she couldn't put it off any longer.

"You look amazing," Susie said when she let Laila in. "I want some of whatever you're eating and drinking these days." She gave her a considering look. "Or does that glow come from something else?" Her eyes lit up. "Are you in love, Laila Riley?"

Laila flinched guiltily and felt the color rise in her cheeks.

Before she could reply, Susie's eyes grew even wider. "You are, aren't you? Sit down right this second and tell me everything. I'll make some tea."

"Shouldn't you be in bed?" Laila asked. "Or at least resting?"

"I've spent too much time in bed lately. What I need is the latest dish on your life. Talk to me."

As Susie busied herself with the tea, Laila considered how much to reveal. She didn't think this was the time for the truth, though Susie more than anyone else might have exactly the perspective she needed.

"I'm not hearing deep, dark secrets," Susie chided as she set a steaming cup of tea in front of her.

"I have none," Laila fibbed. "I'm afraid my life is dull as can be these days." It was actually true, since she'd sent Matthew packing.

Susie studied her intently, then shook her head. "I'm not buying it. There's something going on. I don't know why I didn't notice right away, but you look a little sad. It's in your eyes. Did some fool break your heart? Was it somebody you met through Will's dating service?"

"You couldn't be further from the truth," Laila insisted. "Now, let's change the subject. I came over here to see how you're doing. I'm sorry I didn't get by the hospital."

"The doctors didn't want a lot of people

traipsing in and out of my room, anyway. Talk about being bored. Try lying in a hospital bed for days with hardly any visitors and about three functioning TV stations. I think they bought the extreme budget cable plan."

Laila laughed. "That must be the one I have at my house. Do you know I hear it's possible to get all sorts of things on demand, but I'm terrified if I buy that package, I'll never leave the house again. Throw in a cat and I'll be the town spinster everybody whispers about."

"No chance of that," Susie told her. "If Will can't find you the right guy, I'll get on it as soon as I'm back to full speed. I have instincts about these things. In fact, I always envied Uncle Mick a little. He always seemed so sure about matching up his kids. I think I have that same skill, and with two brothers still unattached, it's time I put it to good use."

Laila paled at the mention of Matthew and Luke. What would she do if Susie got it into her head to start introducing Matthew to a whole string of beautiful, accomplished women? Worse, what if Matthew didn't resist?

The sick feeling in the pit of her stomach told her quite a lot about how she really felt about Susie's brother. She'd tried for weeks now to convince herself that what they'd had was no more than a casual fling, that it didn't stand a chance and that ending it was the only sensible thing to do.

Apparently her efforts hadn't worked. Just envisioning him with someone else made her want to break things. That wasn't good. It wasn't good at all.

"I need to run," she said suddenly.

Susie regarded her with confusion. "Is everything okay? Did I say something wrong?"

"Absolutely not," Laila assured her. "I just remembered someplace I need to be. I'll be back to see you later this week. In the meantime, if you need anything, anything at all, call me. I mean that, okay? We're practically family."

As she said the words, she suddenly realized just how much she wanted them to be true in a way Susie couldn't possibly understand. Was she brave enough to claim what she wanted? Or did she even know what that really was?

Before she went to Matthew and turned both of their worlds upside down, she needed to have a long, honest talk with herself and know with absolute certainty that she wanted what he claimed to want. Because if the two of them ever got on the same page, even for a minute, there'd be no turning back.

19

When Matthew called to say he'd finalized the last details they'd discussed for the house on Beach Lane, Susie had been so eager to see the plans on paper, she'd invited him for dinner. Only after she'd uttered the invitation did she realize it had been days since Mack had mentioned the house. What if he'd changed his mind about letting her dad and Uncle Mick help or, worse, what if he'd agreed to go along with building only to appease her and had since had second thoughts? This dinner could be an uncomfortable mistake.

Oh well, better to get it out in the open if

he was having second thoughts, she reflected.

"Suze, is everything okay?" Matthew asked, showing surprising perceptiveness. Maybe this woman he was seeing, whoever she was, was a good influence on him. He seemed more attuned to nuances lately.

"Everything's fine," she said, pushing aside her doubts. When a brainstorm hit, she seized it. "Hey, why don't you bring along this woman you've been dating?"

"Not a good idea," her brother said at once.

"Why not?"

"She's probably busy."

"Probably? You won't know for sure unless you ask her. Come on, Matthew," she pleaded, warming to the idea. "You're going to have to come out of hiding sooner or later. Better to do it with me than have the rest of the family get wind of this secret relationship and pounce all over you. I can provide backup when the time comes. Having me in your corner will be some kind of secret weapon."

Still he hesitated. "Let's do it another time, Susie. We need to focus on these plans tonight. It might be awkward having a fourth person in the mix."

Now he'd stirred her curiosity. "Why would it be awkward?"

"I'm just saying, I don't think she'd feel comfortable."

She was suddenly struck by a worrisome possibility. "You're not dating Kristen, are you?"

"Who's Kristen?" he asked blankly. "Oh, do you mean that woman who's working at the paper with Mack?"

"Yes, that one," she said drily. "Please don't try to tell me you haven't noticed that she's gorgeous. I thought every male in town was worshipping her from afar at least."

"So I've heard," he admitted, though without even a hint of interest. "Other than knowing she's a thorn in your side, I haven't paid much attention to her."

Susie found that oddly reassuring. If her brother, who'd always chased after every beautiful woman who crossed his path, had been immune to Kristen, perhaps she was exaggerating her allure.

Or perhaps it meant that Mack—despite his seeming willingness a while back to set Kristen up with Matthew—had sent out some sort of hands-off message. She pushed that troubling thought from her head to focus on her brother. Why was she making up problems when her husband had told her repeatedly that there were none? She was not going to let herself be that insecure woman.

"Okay, let's get back to the woman you *are* dating," she said. "Ask her to dinner. If she says no, I'll respect that, though I'll definitely wonder why she doesn't want to be seen with you. That'll be a huge black mark in this ledger I'm keeping about the women you date."

"You have no idea what women I date," he countered.

"Believe me, I know more than you think I do. Luke is a blabbermouth. Somehow you've kept this latest fling from him. It's driving him a little crazy."

"Luke ought to be worrying about his own love life and staying out of mine," Matt grumbled. "I'll have to pound that lesson into him when I see him. The kid's getting entirely too annoying lately."

Susie smiled. "Luke's hardly a kid. He'll graduate from college this spring."

"And I'd like to know how," Matthew said. "Have you ever seen him crack a book?"

"Photographic memory," Susie said. "Now, *that's* annoying. His messing in your love life is just amusing."

"You didn't think it was so funny when Luke and I messed around in yours."

"True," she agreed. "Life just isn't fair that way, is it? Big sisters have all sorts of perks that brothers don't get. Now, I'll expect to see you at seven with a date."

He sighed. "I'll call you if she can't make it."

"Something tells me she'll make time for this."

"Why would you say that?" he asked, sounding frustrated by her confidence.

"Because you don't date stupid women. She'll recognize a command performance when she sees one," she teased. "See you later."

She hung up, pleased with herself. Not only was her curiosity finally going to be satisfied tonight about her brother's new woman, but she'd found the perfect buffer to keep Mack from overreacting if he wasn't pleased that they were all but ready to break ground on their house.

When Mack walked into the house at six, hoping to grab a quick bite with Susie before getting back to the newspaper office, he found the dining-room table set for four. He frowned as he walked into the kitchen, where the aroma of garlic permeated the air.

"Smells good in here," he said, nuzzling Susie's neck as he said it. "And I'm not just talking about dinner."

"You like the new perfume?" she asked. "It has a grapefruit citrus thing going on. They say it turns men on."

"I don't know about the perfume, but you always turn me on," he said, "which makes the prospect of company for dinner darn inconvenient."

"It's just Matthew and his girlfriend," she said over her shoulder as she bent to check on the lasagna that was baking in the oven.

Mack stilled. "Really? He agreed to bring her to dinner?"

"Reluctantly," she admitted, "but yes."

"Oh, boy," he murmured under his breath.

Susie stood up and faced him. "Okay, I've let you get away with keeping my brother's secret for weeks now. You obviously know something, so spill it."

"No can do," he said, holding up his hands and backing up a step. She had methods of persuasion that no man could possibly resist. The military should know about her tactics.

"Mack Franklin, if you know something and it's going to cause an uproar, you'd better fill me in right now. It would not be good for me to be blindsided tonight."

"I wish I could. In fact, I wish I could be here when this plays out, but I need to get back to the office."

Her gaze narrowed. "Oh, no, you don't," she commanded. "Tonight's my night. We agreed that one night a week—Friday—was mine. Period. No exceptions."

Mack regarded her blankly. "It's Friday?"

Susie rolled her eyes. "You ought to glance at a calendar once in a while. Yes, it's Friday. It has been all day."

"I'm sorry, but we're right in the middle of—"

"I don't care," she said adamantly, cutting him off before he could offer some creative reason that would make her feel guilty if she didn't let him head back to work. There were always reasons these days. Good ones, to be sure, but she didn't intend to start a pattern that would wind up destroying their marriage. "If Kristen's expecting you back, call her and tell her you can't make it."

"I could suggest she join us," he said, treading carefully. It was painfully obvious that the two women were never going to trust each other, much less like each other. So far circumstances had kept them as far apart as humanly possible. Sooner or later, though, that had to change. Maybe tonight would be just the night.

"It might be good for you to spend a little time together socially," he suggested tentatively. "You know, before the launch party we rescheduled for next week."

"Not tonight," she said flatly.

He frowned at her grim determination. "Susie, I wish you two would at least try to make peace. Kristen's here to stay. You knew about the past before I hired her. You said you could deal with it."

"I thought I could," she said. "Then I

caught a glimpse of her and started hearing about her from everyone in town."

"She's beautiful, so what?"

"I don't give two figs how beautiful she is," she said, in what he perceived to be a bald-faced lie. "It's the fact that she still wants you that grates on my nerves."

Mack felt his blood turn cold. There it was in a nutshell. The terrible part was that Susie had nailed it. Kristen had made it clear more than once that she was willing to pick things up where they'd left off years ago. "Nothing is going to happen between me and Kristen," he said flatly. "You know that. I love you. I married you. End of story."

"But you didn't bargain for a woman who's bald and gaining weight from steroids and has the stamina of a slug," she said.

"Seems to me you're feisty enough right now," he replied. He took a step toward her, but she held up a hand. "I was just going to say that I think you're beautiful."

"And we all know that you're a charming scoundrel," she said. "Especially if you think it will get you out of a sticky situation."

Mack had no idea how to respond to that. "Do you honestly believe I'm the same superficial guy I was five years ago?" he asked, trying not to let her see how hurt he was by her comment.

She hesitated for a moment, then sighed and shook her head. "I know better," she said softly. "But then I look in the mirror, see what a mess I am, and I get scared, Mack."

"You don't need to be," he said quietly, holding her gaze. "You're it for me, Susie. What can I do or say to prove that to you?"

She gave him a smile tinged with sadness. "Nothing," she conceded. "The doubts are all in my head. I'll just have to figure out a way to manage them."

This time when he reached for her, she let him pull her into his arms. In so many ways she was strong and confident. It was easy to forget how scared she was, how many insecurities had come with the cancer. Sometimes all he could do was hold her and pray that she could feel his love surrounding her. Because the very last thing he would ever knowingly do was to hurt her. She was his life.

Laila stared at Matthew as if he'd grown two heads. He'd certainly lost his mind.

"You want me to go with you to dinner at Susie's?" she repeated incredulously.

"That's the plan," he said cheerfully. "We're due there in fifteen minutes."

"You really are crazy, aren't you?"

"Actually, you're the one who might be the tiniest bit delusional if you think there's a way out of it," he said. "Susie's determined. She seemed to think you'd recognize a command performance when you heard about it."

"But of course she had no idea she was talking about me, did she?" Laila retorted. "So, what? Off we go and walk in there with no warning?"

"She knows we're coming," Matthew corrected.

"She knows you're coming with a date," Laila corrected. "She has no idea that woman is me."

"It's not a big deal," Matthew insisted. "She likes you."

"As a friend," she said impatiently. "Not as someone who's dating her baby brother."

Matthew scowled. "I'm hardly a baby, Laila."

"Oh, you know perfectly well what I mean.

And why are you just telling me about this now, fifteen minutes before we're due there?"

"Actually it's more like ten minutes now," he said. "And I didn't want you to have a lot of time to get all flustered and turn me down."

"I'm surprised you didn't get me in the car, drive over there and then mention it as you were parking," she said, regarding him with dismay. "Matthew, you know this is a terrible idea. We're not even dating right now anyway. We agreed to take a break. We'll be creating an uproar for no good reason."

"I don't see it that way. I figure we'll get this out of the way. You'll realize that if Susie's fine with us together, then the whole family will be fine, too. Remember Connie and Uncle Thomas? They were in a tizzy that people might guess, but in the end everyone took that in stride, even Gram. This is the same kind of thing."

"Older men date younger women all the time. They even marry them. Besides, Connie wasn't that much younger. She and Thomas were old enough to know their own minds."

"Actually it's about the same age

difference as there is between you and me," he said. "And I really hope you're not suggesting that I'm too young to know what I want."

She avoided that minefield. If Matthew *thought* he knew himself, who was she to try to convince him otherwise? No, this was about maturity, plain and simple.

"Except I'm the older, more mature one who should know better," she said. "I *do* know better."

"You're just resisting because you think you should," he argued. "You know we're really, really good together."

"I don't know any such thing," she insisted.

He stepped closer, rubbed a thumb across her lips, sending seismic shudders through her. "Really?"

"Stop it," she commanded. "This is about more than sex."

"I agree."

She paused and frowned. "You do?"

"Well, of course. If this were only a fling, it would have run its course by now. I'm the master of flings. I know all about their expiration dates."

"That is so not a recommendation in my

book," Laila said, regarding him with exasperation.

Matthew chuckled. "It only bothers you because you can't deny this is serious. Come on, Laila, take a risk. Let's trot this relationship out for a test run."

"You sound as if you want to take a sports car off the lot for a spin."

"No, I want to have a pleasant dinner with my sister, her husband and the woman I care about. Since you know all the parties involved, it shouldn't be that scary." He glanced at his watch. "We're down to five minutes, by the way. Do you really want to be late and start off by insulting our hostess?"

"Insulting Susie is the least of my concerns. What about Mack? How's he going to react?"

"He already knows about us," Matthew admitted.

Laila felt her knees start to give way. "He does?"

"He's a bright man. He figured it out weeks ago."

"Dear God in heaven," she murmured.

"So, you see, Susie's the only one in the dark," he pressed. "Is that really fair?"

Laila rolled her eyes. "Oh, when you put it that way, how can I possibly refuse?" she said bitingly.

Matthew brightened. "Okay, then, let's do this."

"You knew all along I'd eventually cave in, didn't you?" she asked as they left the bank and headed for his car.

"I have a lot of faith in my powers of persuasion," he admitted, "but you're unpredictable, so no."

Laila stopped in her tracks. This was an unexpected twist. "You think I'm unpredictable?"

"Oh, yeah," he said. "I certainly never know what to expect with you."

And with those words, Laila fell just a little bit more deeply in love with this totally inappropriate man. No one had ever described her as unpredictable before. All her life she'd heard—had thought of herself as—staid, stodgy, even dull. She was a banker, for goodness' sakes, and before that she'd been an accountant. She thrived on making numbers add up. It wasn't exactly a career that made for scintillating dinner conversation. A part of her had always wanted desperately to be interesting, a risk taker, unpredictable.

If Matthew O'Brien saw her as the woman she'd always dreamed of being, then maybe it really was time to stop fighting this so hard.

Susie went to the door at what had to be her brother's knock, put on her most welcoming smile and opened the door, only to see Laila standing just behind Matthew. For a moment it didn't make any sense.

"Laila, I had no idea you were dropping by tonight," she said without missing a beat. "You're just in time for dinner. I hope you can stay."

Matthew cleared his throat. "Um, Laila's with me, Suze."

Susie blinked. "With you?" she repeated. When the truth dawned on her, she simply stared.

"You can close your mouth now," Laila said wryly. "There's no need to go into shock."

"I'm just . . . I'm surprised," Susie murmured, trying to wrap her mind around this turn of events. Matthew and *Laila?* How could that be? Laila was sensible. She was smart. She knew his track record. Surely she knew better than to put her heart on the line with Susie's scoundrel of a brother.

Mack joined them in the foyer and she whirled on him. "You could have warned me," she said, giving him a poke in the ribs with her elbow.

He shrugged. "I told you it wasn't my news to share. Come on in, you two." He kissed Laila's cheek. "Don't worry, the shock will wear off eventually."

Laila eyed Susie skeptically. "You sure about that?"

Mack nodded. "Susie has amazing recuperative powers, don't you, sweetheart?"

Susie shook herself out of a near trance. "Of course. I'm sorry. It was just so unexpected to see you standing there. Laila, why don't you come help me in the kitchen? Matthew, you can show Mack the house plans."

Laila cast a desperate look in Matthew's direction, but she dutifully followed Susie.

Susie closed the kitchen door, poured a

glass of wine and handed it to Laila. "When did this start?"

"A few months ago," Laila told her, taking a sip, then quickly following with another. "We ran into each other a couple of times and got to talking. Then he asked me out, sort of a no-big-deal thing." She blushed. "And then it turned into kind of a big deal. I thought it was just about the sex." She winced, then swallowed the rest of the wine. "Sorry."

"Believe me, I know all about my brother and his flings," Susie said dismissively. "I just never thought you'd be one of them."

"He says I'm not," Laila told her. Her expression turned hopeful. "I'm almost starting to believe him."

Susie regarded her with real worry, even as she poured more wine. Nothing loosened the tongue like a little alcohol, and she wanted to get to the bottom of what was really going on between these two. She loved her brother, but she cared about Laila, too.

"Laila, come on," she chided. "You know my brother's track record with women."

"You mean the way you knew about Mack's?" Laila retorted.

Susie flinched at the direct hit. "Yeah, exactly like that," she conceded. "But Mack and I were always friends."

"You seem to forget that I've known Matthew about as long as you've known Mack."

"But he was just a kid for a lot of that time," Susie argued. "In many ways, he's still a kid."

"Not the way I see him," Laila said. "He's surprisingly self-confident, focused and determined."

Susie couldn't deny that he'd seemed that way lately. Was that due to his relationship with Laila? Could he really be ready to settle down? Hadn't she herself noted earlier that he seemed more sensitive, possibly due to a good female influence?

"Just don't put your heart on the line," Susie pleaded, unable to hide her worry. "I know my brother. So do you. He might not be ready for anything serious. And you're not the kind of woman who does casual well. I know you're ready for marriage, kids, the whole nine yards. You deserve a man who's ready for that, too."

Laila looked oddly resigned. "You're not telling me anything I haven't told myself," she admitted. "I've tried to walk away. I've sent Matthew away. In fact, until today I thought this latest separation might stick."

Susie stilled. "Until today?"

"Your dinner invitation," she reminded Susie. "Matthew apparently saw it as the perfect excuse to turn up in my office and practically kidnap me."

"You didn't want to come tonight?"

"Oh, I wanted to. I just thought it was a terrible idea."

"And now?"

"I still think it was probably a terrible idea, but I'm starting to relax."

Susie chuckled despite herself. "Maybe that has something to do with the two glasses of wine you've chugged down since we came into the kitchen."

Laila stared at the glass in her hand. "Two?"

"Yep."

She groaned. "Now the man has driven me to drink."

Susie shook her head. "That was probably me. Sorry. I'm all over the shock now. You know I love you, and it would be fantastic if this works out. I'm just a little worried for you."

"Not for your brother?"

"Are you kidding? He'd be lucky to wind up with an incredible woman like you."

Laila laughed. "First he calls me unpredictable. Now you call me incredible. I don't know if it's just that O'Brien charm at work, but you're all turning my already slightly dizzy head."

Susie linked arms with her. "Let's go in there so I can get a better look at the two of you together. It's going to take some getting used to before we spring this on the rest of the family."

"I think I'd like to wait a long, long time for that one," Laila said.

"Come on, we're not that daunting," Susie said, then sighed. "Okay, yes, we are, but we already love you."

"The O'Briens are not my only concern," Laila admitted. "Have you met Trace? My brother is amazingly overprotective when it comes to my social life, especially recently. He freaked out about the whole dating-service thing, then had a genuine conniption when he finally heard about that stalker Will had inadvertently introduced me to via Lunch by the Bay."

Susie beamed at her. "Here's the good

news. Compared to all that, my brother is actually a paragon of virtue. Trace will probably be thrilled to turn you over to him."

Laila stared at her for a moment, then suddenly giggled. "I may be a little loopy from the wine, but that actually makes sense to me."

"Okay, now that you have my stamp of approval, you can return the favor by coming with me and going into raptures over my brother's plans for my dream house on Beach Lane. Mack might be a little bit on the fence about the idea. I need you in my corner."

"The least I can do," Laila agreed.

But when they walked into the living room, they found Mack totally absorbed with the design as Matthew went over it with him. He glanced up at Susie and beckoned her over.

"This looks amazing to me," he said, drawing her down beside him. "What do you think?"

She couldn't tear her gaze away from him long enough to spare a glance for the plans. "You still want to build the house?"

"Absolutely," he said, then frowned. "Did you think I might back out?"

"I wouldn't blame you," she said. "It's a lot to be taking on right now."

"It is," he agreed. "But it's an investment in our future."

She looked toward her brother, saw Laila snuggled comfortably at his side, and concluded that a lot of future plans were coming together tonight. It was turning out to be one heck of a dinner party, with some fairly astonishing twists.

20

Susie was standing in line at Sally's waiting to pick up a takeout order for herself and Shanna when she spotted Mack coming through the door. The woman laughing at something he said and staring at him adoringly was Kristen. Susie recognized her from her few previous glimpses through the window at the newspaper office and one photo that had appeared in the launch edition. She was even more stunning in person.

The woman could easily have wandered straight out of the pages of a *Sports Illustrated* swimsuit issue, Susie thought with a sinking sensation in the pit of her stomach. One glance at the lithe, sophisticated woman and she immediately felt frumpy and small-town. If she could have ducked down behind the counter to avoid an introduction, she would have, but O'Briens simply didn't run from their fears.

"Susie!" Mack said, his eyes lighting up when he caught sight of her. "I didn't expect to see you here." He dragged Kristen over. "It's about time you two met," he said with forced cheer. "Susie, this is Kristen Lewis."

Kristen's expression, which had been filled with warmth just seconds ago, seemed vaguely frozen now. "Susie, I've heard a lot about you."

Though the words were spoken pleasantly enough, there was no disguising her shock as she took in the scarf tied securely into a turban on Susie's head.

"Mack raves about your work," Susie said, injecting the words with as much enthusiasm as she could muster. "The website looks fantastic, and I hear it's getting an astonishing number of hits."

"Thanks. I still have some fine-tuning to do, but I think it's going to be an important component of the paper's success," Kristen replied. "I can't tell you how much it means to me that Mack gave me this chance. I just love working with him."

"I'm sure he's a great boss," Susie said, grabbing her bag of takeout from Sally's hand and shoving a twenty in her direction. She was already backing away from the counter. "Sorry, but I need to run. I promised Shanna I'd be back with lunch."

Mack regarded her with disappointment. "Couldn't you drop it off next door and then come back and join us? I'm sure Shanna wouldn't mind."

"Afraid not," she said, then found herself planting a possessive kiss firmly on his lips. "See you at home later. Love you."

"Love you, too," he called after her.

She made her way to the bookstore with her thoughts in turmoil. Had she made a mistake not sitting down with them and observing their interaction for herself, maybe staking her claim on her husband? She chided herself for the ridiculous thought. Her ring was on his finger and his on hers. The claim was in plain view for anyone to see, if they wanted to.

At the bookstore she walked straight

past Shanna, yanked out a chair in the
café section and sat down, then started
pulling food from the bag with jerky movements. Shanna appeared and sat across
from her, regarding her warily.

"Long wait at Sally's?" she inquired
tentatively.

"Nope. Just a little unexpected encounter with my husband and his star web-
master."

"Oh, boy!" Shanna murmured.

"I swear to God, I wanted to tear her
hair out, every long, gorgeous strand of it."

"That could just be a reaction to you being bald," Shanna suggested hopefully.

Susie scowled at her. "No, it was a reaction to the way she looked at me, as if I
were no competition at all, and the way
she looked at Mack, as if he were the great-
est thing since sliced bread." Her scowl
deepened. "Which he is, of course, but
he's *my* man."

"Of course he is. How did Mack look at
her?"

Susie paused in her tirade to think back.
"Actually he didn't look at her much. He
was watching me, probably trying to figure

out if I was going to explode or turn into some jealous shrew right before his eyes."

"Or maybe he was looking at you because he loves you and can't tear his gaze away from you."

"I'm not one of those romance-novel heroines," Susie snapped. "At least not right now. Look at me. I'm fat and bald."

Shanna had barely picked up her sandwich, but she put it back down. "Stop that this instant!" she commanded, her gaze intense. "There's no denying that you're bald, but you're far from fat. You've just filled in a little. You were too skinny before."

"Nothing fits," Susie complained. She gestured to her clothes. "Look at me. I'm wearing old jeans and a baggy T-shirt. You should have seen Kristen in her expensive linen slacks, her fancy silk blouse and a pair of stiletto heels I couldn't wear for an hour, much less to work. She had on a gold-and-diamond bracelet that probably cost more than my entire wardrobe."

Shanna gave her a knowing look. "If you're only worried about her outfit and her jewelry, we can go shopping tonight after work. I guarantee we can find you a few things that will put her wardrobe and accessories to shame."

Susie sighed. "It's not about the clothes. At least not entirely. I just feel frumpy and undesirable." She gave Shanna a plaintive look. "Have you ever read about women who are sick and tell their husbands they want them to move on, who even try to handpick someone for them?"

Shanna gave her an amused look. "You are so not that woman," she said.

Susie allowed herself a faint grin. "I'm not, am I? I mean, I'd want Mack to be happy if I died, but I'm much more likely to leave a list of the women he should avoid. Kristen would be at the top of the list."

"Maybe underneath all that polish, she's a nice woman," Shanna suggested gently.

"No," Susie said. "I saw the way she looked at Mack. She'd snatch him from me in a heartbeat and never look back. Now that she knows I have cancer, she probably figures she can bide her time and grab him when I'm gone."

"Will you please stop talking about what's going to happen when you die?" Shanna pleaded. "You're not going to die."

"Let's get real," Susie said bleakly. "The odds are not in my favor."

"So help me, if you start thinking like that, you won't need to worry about the odds. I'll strangle you myself."

Susie laughed. Maybe it was kind of a macabre humor, but being able to laugh about her situation felt good. She squeezed Shanna's hand. "Thank you for letting me vent."

"Anytime. You know that. Now, about that shopping—I still think we should do it. The rescheduled launch party is in a few days. You need to walk into that event feeling like a million bucks."

"You're probably expecting too much from a dress," she told Shanna. "But I'm game if you have the time."

"For shopping?" Shanna replied. "I can always find time for that. We'll get you a party dress, and I'll buy a million more things I don't need for the nursery."

"How does Kevin feel about these shopping binges of yours?"

Shanna grinned. "I doubt he's overjoyed, but taking back half the stuff a few days later keeps him occupied and makes him feel as if he's won. In the end, I wind up with the essentials I'd wanted in the first place."

"Sounds like the perfect compromise," Susie congratulated her.

"The essential ingredient in any happy marriage," Shanna agreed. "I'll pick you up at six-fifteen. Does that work?"

"I'll be at the house. If I'm going on a spending spree, I'll need to rest up this afternoon."

"Perfect. I'll see you tonight."

Susie gave her friend a fierce hug. "You're the best friend ever, and the best sounding board."

"It's what I'm here for."

And thank heaven for it, Susie thought as she walked back to the real estate management office. An hour ago she'd been having herself an excellent pity party. Now she had her perspective back and her good humor. That still didn't mean her opinion of Kristen had changed.

Susie had barely settled behind her desk again, when her brother Luke appeared. He'd come home from college for a long weekend so he could attend Monday's launch party for the newspaper. Like his older brother, there was rarely a party that he missed.

"I was at Sally's a little while ago," he announced as he perched on the corner of her desk. "Who was the hottie in there with Mack?"

Susie froze. "I assume you're talking about Kristen," she said, trying to keep her tone casual. "She's his digital guru. She's running the paper's website."

"Looks and brains, too," Luke said approvingly. "I wonder if she's dating anyone. Do you know?"

"I only met her myself earlier today. I have no idea what sort of social life she has."

"How about an introduction?"

She regarded him impatiently. "Since when have you ever needed me to run interference for you? Besides, if you want an introduction, you're asking the wrong person. Speak to your brother-in-law."

Something in her voice must have alerted him that he'd hit on a sore subject. His gaze narrowed.

"Is she causing problems between you and Mack?"

"Don't be absurd," she said, though without much conviction.

Luke looked as if he wanted to ask more, but she cut him off before he could. "I really do not want to talk about Kristen Lewis."

In fact, if they didn't change the topic soon, she very well might burst into tears and totally humiliate herself. "Don't you have someplace you need to be, Luke? Go."

He stood up, but he looked uncertain. "Suze, are you okay? You look like you're going to cry."

"I am so not going to cry over that woman," she declared fiercely. "Now, will you please get out of here."

"I'll beat Mack up for you," Luke offered, perhaps a little too eagerly. "Or her, if she's the one you're really angry with."

"Thanks, but I don't think that will be necessary," she said, smiling despite herself. Her brothers might be major nuisances 99 percent of the time, but when they came through for her that other one percent, they made her feel as special as any princess on earth.

After Luke had gone, she tried to bury herself in paperwork, but she couldn't seem to shake the feeling she'd had for a while now that in encouraging Mack to start his own newspaper, she'd pushed him right out of her life and into someone else's arms.

"You never told me your wife had cancer," Kristen said, an accusing gaze directed at Mack.

Mack had been waiting for this ever since their encounter with Susie at the café, but at least Kristen had waited until they'd returned to the relative privacy of the office before bringing it up. Clearly she felt as if this were news she'd had a right to know. He didn't see it the same way.

"Possibly because I didn't think it was any of your business," Mack replied. "It has nothing to do with the newspaper or our professional relationship."

She looked as if he'd slapped her. "I thought we were friends," she said softly, then stood up. "My mistake."

Before he could answer, she'd grabbed her coat and headed for the door. "I'll be back later to finish up, hopefully after you're gone."

Mack stared after her and uttered a curse. The day was getting better and better. He'd seen the defeated expression in Susie's eyes earlier when he'd introduced her to Kristen. All she'd seen was a beautiful, well put-together, healthy woman, and turned it into a competition in which she fell short. Now he'd angered Kristen because she felt as if he'd deliberately left her out of the loop.

"Problems?" his brother-in-law inquired, walking into his office with a familiar, irrepressible grin on his face.

"Don't test me, Luke. I'm not in the mood."

"So I gathered. I heard that curse you uttered about two seconds after Kristen stormed past me as I was coming in the front door. Trouble in the news business?"

"Something like that," Mack said, determined not to get into this with a kid who hadn't even graduated from college yet.

"Funny thing," Luke said casually. "My sister seems to be in a pretty foul mood, too. It must be catching."

Mack stilled. "You've seen Susie?"

"I just left her office." He studied Mack with a deceptively neutral look. "Care to explain what's going on?"

"There is nothing going on," Mack said.

"Okay, here's my guess, for whatever it's worth," Luke said, ignoring Mack's obvious attempt to end the topic. "The beautiful Kristen wants you. Susie's ticked off about it. And you're caught between a rock and a hard place, because you love my sister and you need Kristen."

Mack regarded him with astonishment. "Not bad for an amateur. Maybe you should talk to Will about joining his practice, especially since everyone knows that your current major in history will never be put to practical use."

Luke shrugged. "I like history. It got the school off my back." He gave Mack a shrewd look. "So, do you want my advice, after all?"

Mack felt ridiculous accepting the offer, but he had to admit he was at a loss. Maybe a fresh perspective would help.

"Go for it," he said reluctantly.

"Set me up with Kristen. I'll keep her distracted. You can focus on keeping my sister happy."

Mack was speechless. He might have expected something like this from Matthew, but Luke was still a kid. "You're too young for Kristen," he protested. "She'll eat you alive."

Luke gave him a confident grin. "Not a

chance. I've been studying you and my brother for a long time. I've learned from your mistakes."

"Mistakes?" Mack echoed quizzically.

"Trust me, you've both made plenty. I can hold my own with the Kristens of the world."

Mack hid a laugh. "So this would be some sort of magnanimous gesture on your part to protect your sister, save our marriage and keep the paper operating smoothly?"

"Something like that," Luke said. "What do you think?"

The eagerness in his eyes was what made Mack acquiesce. Every man needed a chance to play knight in shining armor from time to time. If Luke's desire to do that saved Mack's hide in the process, so much the better.

"Kristen won't make it easy for you," he warned.

"Of course not. She thinks she wants you," Luke said. "I can persuade her she doesn't."

Mack studied him curiously. "And then what? Don't you have to go back to college in a few days?"

"Graduation's less than a month away," Luke reminded him. "I can come home weekends till then. Don't worry. I'm up to this. Something tells me I've been in training for it all through college, and that professor last semester—"

Mack stared at him. "You were dating a professor?"

"Well, technically I guess she was an associate professor, but yes. Anyway, I think she was probably the perfect warm-up for Kristen."

"You amaze me," Mack said. "But I thought I heard something about you planning to go to Europe after graduation. I believe you've described it as the trip of a lifetime. What happens to your brand-new relationship then? Will I have to pick up the pieces of Kristen's broken heart?"

"Absolutely not. Actually I'm going to Nice and Monaco. I think Kristen would fit right in."

"She has a job here," Mack reminded him.

Luke gave him a disgusted look. "It's two weeks, bro. Find a substitute. Do you want me to bail you out of this mess or not?"

"I would be incredibly grateful," Mack admitted. "You'll have to pardon my skepticism, though. I know Kristen, while you haven't even met her."

Luke held out his hand. "Address, please."

"You're going over to her house?" Mack asked, shocked by his audacity.

"Do we have time to waste?" Luke inquired.

Mack scribbled out the address, then shook his head. This crazy plan of Luke's just might work, though he had this awful feeling he was tossing a baby minnow right into the path of a circling barracuda. At the moment, though, he couldn't be entirely sure which was which.

Susie came home from her shopping trip with Shanna feeling marginally better. She'd found some dynamite clothes that Shanna assured her would leave Mack tongue-tied. She'd even tried on dozens of wigs and found a short cap of golden-blond curls that worked with her complexion and made her look like a different woman. Rather than Little Orphan Annie, she looked more like Sharon Stone after she'd taken scissors to her own blond hair and cropped it short.

She was surprised to find Mack at home. He'd been staying so late at the office, she'd been sure she'd have time for a leisurely bubble bath before greeting him in another of those sexy negligees Shanna had insisted she buy.

He looked up from his paperwork and smiled. "You must have had fun," he said, noting the number of packages she was carrying.

"I haven't shopped like this in years. Shanna is like some fashion drill sergeant. She bossed me around from store to store, refusing to settle for anything that wasn't absolutely perfect and a bargain to boot. Kevin should thank me."

"Why?" Mack asked, looking blank.

"She was so focused on me, she never got around to splurging on the baby. Apparently she's gone a little overboard lately and he's spending his spare time returning the excess."

Mack chuckled. "Something tells me that's her strategy, to buy more than she wants, so he'll be happy if she lets him return a few things."

Susie regarded him with astonishment. "How'd you figure that out? Kevin hasn't."

"It's probably easier for an outsider. Now, come over here and show me what you bought."

She shook her head. "Sorry. They're surprises."

He looked vaguely disappointed. "Then just come here and tell me about your day. Don't run straight off to bed."

"I wasn't going to. I'd planned a bubble bath and something special for you for later."

"Really? I'm intrigued."

"Give me a half hour?"

He nodded. "Take all the time you need. I have plenty to do. I still have an editorial to write for next week's edition."

"Write fast," she told him, and headed for the bedroom.

She put away her purchases, except the negligee with spaghetti straps. The silk skimmed over her curves in a creamy cascade.

She took her bath, donned the silky confection, then adjusted her new blond wig. She added just a whisper of mascara and a bit of lip gloss.

When she walked back into the dining room, Mack glanced up from his laptop. His eyes immediately filled with appreciation.

"You look like Carole Lombard in one of those old movies," he said. "You're gorgeous, Susie. You honestly take my breath away."

She smiled at his words, but it was the barely banked desire in his eyes that convinced her.

"Come here," he murmured, a hitch in his voice.

"I think I'd rather you came over here," she said.

"I'm not sure I can stand up."

She regarded him skeptically. "Seriously?"

"Seriously," he confirmed, though he did stand unsteadily and made his way toward her.

She all but floated into his arms. She knew she would remember the look in his eyes for a long time to come. She was beginning to need that look the way plants needed water. It made her feel like a woman. No, it made her feel like a *desirable* woman, and these days that was a difficult pinnacle to attain. Some days she despaired of ever feeling like that again. Today had been one of them.

The admission made her think once more of Kristen, the woman who'd intentionally or not made her feel less than whole, less than her best.

"Mack, I'm sorry for that whole scene with Kristen at Sally's. I should have been more gracious."

"I thought you did amazingly well."

"It's just that she's—"

"Hush," he murmured against her cheek. "Let's not bring her into our house, into our bedroom. Besides, she's not going to be a problem anymore."

Surprised, Susie pulled back and looked into his eyes. "You fired her?"

"No," he said, still trying valiantly to distract her by nuzzling her neck.

"She quit?" That would be even more astonishing . . . and wonderful, she admitted candidly to herself. Mack wouldn't feel nearly as guilty if Kristen walked off the job.

"No." His lips drifted to the valley between her breasts.

Susie's breath caught, but she wasn't

quite ready to let the conversation drop. "Mack, tell me what you meant."

"Luke's fixing things."

She backed away so fast, she almost stumbled. Mack had to steady her. "You got my brother involved in this?"

"Actually he came to me and volunteered."

She stared at him incredulously. "To do what exactly?"

"I didn't ask, but I imagine seduction is pretty high up in his plan."

"But he's never even met her. He begged me for an introduction. I said no."

Mack grinned. "I guess that's why he came to me. And apparently he'd gathered that Kristen makes you feel insecure, because he formulated his request as a way to protect your honor and our marriage."

Susie just stared at him. "And you let him?"

"Hey, it works for me if it'll reassure you and keep her focused on something other than me."

"Then you admit she still has the hots for you? Thank heaven. I was beginning to think you were one of those clueless men who got lured in because of a nonfunctioning brain."

"My brain is functioning just fine," Mack said, clearly offended.

"Apparently not, if you sent Luke to take care of this. He's a kid, Mack."

Mack shook his head. "Trust me, not so much."

"She'll rip his heart out," Susie predicted. "And if that happens, I'll never forgive you."

"Hey, Luke is a grown man. He wanted to do this. I don't know if he was thinking with his hormones or his head, but I have confidence he can handle Kristen. I didn't at first, but I saw something in him that we've all been missing. He's got his act together, possibly more so than either Matthew or I did at his age. He claims he learned from watching our mistakes. Surprised the heck out of me, since I thought I, at least, was so smooth."

"I hope you're right," Susie said, not entirely convinced. "I don't want him to get hurt."

"And he doesn't want you to get hurt. He's doing this as much for you as he is for his own nefarious reasons. I think it's sweet that he wants to be your knight in shining armor."

Sweet? Susie could think of several other words to describe it. *Insane* came to mind.

"Do you think we could forget about your brother and Kristen?" Mack asked longingly. "I have this beautiful blonde stranger in my arms, and I want to get her into bed."

Susie looked into his eyes. "Stranger, huh? Do you do this sort of thing often?"

"Are you kidding me? If my wife found out, she'd kill me."

She beamed at him. "And don't you forget it," she said sweetly as she wrapped her legs around his waist and covered his mouth with hers, then let herself get lost in the fantasy.

21

Susie walked in the door for Sunday dinner at Uncle Mick's and immediately felt the swirl of tension in the air.

"What's going on?" she whispered to Abby, who was closest.

"Trace just figured out that his sister is involved with your brother," she replied in a hushed tone. "We're all waiting for the you-know-what to hit the fan."

"Laila actually came with Matthew?" Susie asked, not even trying to hide her surprise. "I thought they intended to keep their relationship under wraps a while longer."

Abby whirled on her. "You knew?"

Susie winced at her cousin's stunned reaction. "Not for long. And I only found out after I insisted he bring the woman he was seeing to dinner. When Laila showed up at my door, I thought it was just some weird coincidence."

Abby propelled her onto the porch. "And?" she demanded. "Is Matthew just fooling around, as usual? Trace will kill him if he is. You know how protective he is of Laila."

"I actually think Matthew's fallen hard for her. The way I understand it, they've been together for a while now. They've split up at Laila's request, but the breakups haven't lasted. That tells me the feelings are mutual and getting stronger."

Abby looked stunned. "Well, I'll be. Good for Laila. I'd better go back inside and try to keep my husband from punching Matthew's handsome face."

Susie smiled. "I'm sure we'd all appreciate that."

She followed her cousin inside just in case any additional help was needed, but to her amazement, Laila was the one who seemed to have things well under control. She was right up in her brother's face.

"You do not get to make these decisions

for me," she said, poking Trace in the chest. "I'm a grown woman."

"A woman who's apparently lost her mind. Matthew's a nice enough guy, but he has a track record with women, Laila, and it's not good."

She gave him a disgusted look. "Don't you think I'm very well aware of his track record? Don't you think I've taken that into account? I'm not stupid, Trace. Nor am I self-destructive."

Matthew stepped forward, rested a calming hand on her shoulder, a gesture that drew a furious scowl from Trace. Matthew ignored him.

"Laila, it's okay," Matthew soothed. "Maybe your brother and I should take this outside and have a private conversation. He needs to know I'm serious about this relationship."

Susie couldn't be sure who was more shocked by the comment, Trace or Laila. She was relatively stunned herself. She was almost certain the word *serious* had never crossed her brother's lips before, at least in connection to a woman.

"Serious?" Laila echoed.

Matthew gave her an incredulous look.

"Haven't I told you the same thing a hundred and one times?"

"Yes, but I always thought it was so you could get me into bed."

Trace nearly choked and his eyes blazed. "I swear to God . . ." he began, but this time it was Abby who put a restraining hand on him.

"Let him talk," Abby commanded.

"Laila, I love you," Matthew said earnestly, then looked around the room with an air of defiance. "There, I've said it in front of all these witnesses, who'll for darn sure hold me accountable for the words."

"I certainly will," Trace said heatedly, but at another touch from Abby, he seemed to deflate. "Okay, I'll back off, but so help me, Matthew . . ."

"Yeah, yeah, you'll bash my head in or worse," Matthew said with a grin. "Believe me, I get where you're coming from. I said the same thing often enough when Mack was hanging out with Susie."

Susie looked around for her husband, who'd come inside earlier. Now he seemed to have disappeared.

Just then Shanna approached, her expression filled with concern. She leaned down and whispered in Susie's ear, "Do you have any idea what's going on around here?"

Susie regarded her blankly. "You mean besides Matthew and Laila coming out as a couple?"

Shanna nodded.

"This is as far as I've gotten," Susie admitted. "You mean there's more commotion?"

"Oh, yeah. Luke's in the kitchen with Kristen. Mack looks like a cornered man. And Gram's antennae are on full alert."

"Oh, sweet heaven," Susie murmured. "What was my brother thinking?"

She was halfway to the kitchen when Mack came striding out, silently grabbed her arm and steered her in the opposite direction.

"You don't want to be in there right now," he said tightly.

"You mean because of Luke and Kristen?" she inquired sweetly.

His eyes widened. "You heard?" he asked, then groaned. "Of course, you did. Shanna could hardly wait to get out of there and find you, am I right?"

"Yep. How bad is it?"

"Your grandmother is a saint. I could tell

she had a thousand and one questions, mostly for me, but she managed to restrain herself. All she said was that perhaps I should find you." He gave her a hopeful look. "I'm thinking we should leave now. What do you think? I've had about all the fireworks I can handle for one day. You?"

"I think if we leave, it will say way too much about how I let that woman get to me," Susie said. "We're staying." She gave Mack a hard look. "And *then* I'm going to kill my brother for showing the judgment of a gnat."

Fortunately from Mack's perspective, once everyone was seated for Sunday dinner, there was so much chaos that Susie and Kristen could barely even see each other, much less exchange words. Luke was safely out of Susie's reach, as well. Most of the attention seemed to be on Matthew and Laila, anyway. No one seemed to know quite what to make of them as a couple.

As the meal wore on, Mack kept a close eye on his wife. She looked a little pale to him. He attributed it to her treatments, but it could have been the unmistakable tension in the air. The second they'd finished dessert, Jo appeared at Susie's side and whisked her away, suggesting she, too, had seen the strain on Susie's face.

Will joined Mack. "An interesting day, don't you think?"

"It's been hell," Mack said.

"How's Susie holding up?"

"She's trying, but being in the same room with Kristen is harder on her than I anticipated. It doesn't seem to matter that she's here with Luke."

Will chuckled. "How'd that happen, by the way?"

"Long story," Mack said, glancing toward his brother-in-law, who was leaning close to whisper something in Kristen's ear. He couldn't tell if her amused expression was because of what Luke was saying or because she found the whole situation hilarious. Knowing Kristen, she was probably going along with Luke's pursuit for her own reasons. Mack didn't want to think about what those might be.

Jo suddenly appeared at his side. "Mack, I think Susie needs to go home and get some rest," she said quietly.

He regarded his mother-in-law with alarm. "Is she okay?"

"Just exhausted, I think. And I know she's worried sick about her test tomorrow."

Mack stared at Jo blankly. "Test? What kind of test does she have tomorrow?"

Jo looked surprised. "She didn't tell you about the PET scan? They're checking to see if there's been any improvement with her cancer. It's an important milestone, Mack."

Mack felt as if he'd been sucker punched. "She never said a word."

"Oh, dear, I'm sure she just didn't want to worry you," Jo said guiltily. "She knows you have a lot on your plate lately."

"Nothing that's more important than her health," he said adamantly. "Thanks, Jo."

On his way to find his wife, he tried to get his temper in check. How could Susie keep something this important from him? It wasn't as if it was the first time, either. She'd tried to keep the cancer from him in the first place. Hadn't she learned any-thing from that about trusting him to be supportive?

Sure, he was busy, and maybe she

thought she was being considerate, but what did it say about their marriage that she thought he wouldn't want to know, that he didn't deserve to know? For the first time since their rushed wedding, he wondered if they'd made a mistake after all. Clearly when it came to the important things in their lives, when it came to trust and communication, they were further apart than ever.

Susie's nerves had finally gotten to her. She'd been so exhausted by the end of the meal, it had taken everything in her just to stand and walk away from the table. Mack had been oblivious, but thankfully her mother had noticed and gotten her out of the dining room and into one of the spare rooms where she could lie down for a few minutes. If she'd crashed in front of the family, it would have been okay, but her pride couldn't have taken the humiliation of passing out in front of Kristen.

When the door opened and Mack stepped into the room, she sat up, startled.

"How did you know where I was?"

"Your mother told me. She said it was time to get you home."

There was a tone in his voice she'd never heard before, a distance. Or was it a barely restrained hint of anger?

"Mack, is everything okay?"

"Everything's fine," he said, though his tone was unconvincing. "You up to walking, or shall I carry you? We can slip out through the kitchen."

"I'll walk," she said, studying his grim expression. She considered pressing for an explanation for his odd mood, but she wasn't sure she was up to hearing the answer.

They rode home in silence.

Inside the apartment, Mack said, "Go on and hop into bed. I'll bring you some tea."

Susie nodded. "Thanks."

Before she could walk away, he added, "And then we're going to talk."

She paused. "About?"

"After I get your tea," he said, and left her standing there.

If she hadn't been so tired, she might have argued, but the stress of the day had caught up with her. She took off her clothes, put on her favorite nightgown and crawled between the sheets. The second her head hit the pillow, she fell asleep.

When she woke, the room was filled with

shadows, and Mack was sitting beside the bed, his expression unreadable.

"Your tea's cold by now," he said. "I'll fix you another cup."

"No," she said softly. "You're obviously furious about something. Let's talk about it."

He hesitated, then asked, "Are you sure you're up to it?"

"I'm okay. The nap helped."

He sat back down, then regarded her with a mix of frustration and resignation. "What kind of marriage do you think we have, Susie?"

Her heart plummeted at the blunt question, at the despair in his voice. "We've hit a few bumps, but a good one, I think, given all we've had to deal with."

"I'd have said the same thing until I spoke to your mother earlier."

"What on earth did Mom say to make you question that?" she asked, genuinely mystified.

"She says you have an important scan tomorrow, one you never bothered to mention to me." He regarded her with dismay. "Why would you keep something like that from me?"

"It wasn't like a big secret," she insisted.

"I never intended to keep it from you. You've just been so busy, and tomorrow night's the launch party. You delayed it once because of me. I didn't want you to start worrying and do that again. The test's no big deal. Mom said she'd take me."

"No big deal?" he repeated with barely contained anger. "This test is going to tell us if the chemo has helped, right? You don't think that's a big deal?"

She winced at his tone. "The *results* are a big deal, not the test," she said, trying to explain her logic. "I won't know those right away. I would have wanted you there with me when I got those."

"Really? How am I supposed to believe that? I thought we were in this together, Susie. All the way."

"We are," she said quietly, understanding the depth of the mistake she'd made. She'd left him out of something critical to their future. Good or bad, those results would determine what their life would be like going forward. "I'm so sorry, Mack. I thought I was doing the right thing."

He shook his head. "You don't need to protect me, Susie, or keep things from me, or make decisions for me. When it comes to us, when it comes to your health, I get to decide if something is inconvenient or unimportant. And I'm here to tell you right now that *nothing* is unimportant and *nothing* is inconvenient. I'll be at that test with you tomorrow." His declaration sounded like the challenge he'd meant it to be.

"Okay."

"And please remember this. *I love you,*" he added emphatically. "I don't give two hoots about a stupid party. What time is the test?"

"Eight o'clock," she admitted, feeling even more foolish.

"At night?" he asked, bemused.

She shook her head. "In the morning."

He regarded her with astonishment. "And you thought a test at 8:00 a.m. would cause me to postpone a party taking place at six in the evening?"

She winced. "It doesn't make much sense when you put it that way. I just didn't want you worrying."

"Well, I am worried, and it's not about the test. It's about us. Is this because a part of you still thinks I'll run if the going gets tough?"

Was that it? she wondered. On some

level was she still worried that the Mack who never stayed with anyone for long would take the easy way out? No, absolutely not, she told herself. She knew better. She'd seen firsthand the undeserved loyalty he'd shown to his mother. He'd never bail on her, either, not when she needed him.

Or was that her real fear, that if the news was bad, he'd stick by her side out of pity rather than love? Maybe so, she thought with a sigh of regret. Admitting to her insecurities, though, simply wasn't an option.

"Mack, you've been my rock through all of this. Please don't think for a minute that I don't understand how hard it's been."

"Hard's not the problem, Susie," he said, holding her gaze. "I can do hard. What I can't live with is you shutting me out."

"It won't happen again," she vowed.

Despite her promise, he sat there in stony silence for so long, she thought maybe he really wasn't going to forgive her for her insensitivity, for her lack of faith in him. Finally, though, a sigh shuddered through him.

"Promise me something, Susie, a cross-your-heart kind of promise."

"Anything."

"From here on out, we share stuff, good

and bad. Otherwise, we don't stand a chance."

She heard the solemnity behind his words, and it scared her to death. "I promise," she whispered.

He crawled into bed beside her and took her in his arms. "I hate fighting with you," he murmured.

"I hate being fought with," she told him, nestling her head against his shoulder. "But we'll probably do it again."

She could feel his smile against her cheek.

"More than likely," he agreed.

"But we'll be okay," she said with rare certainty.

"We'll be okay," he concurred. "Always."

She knew that like all married couples, they'd be tested. Probably more than once. She just needed to hang on to Mack's declaration of forever no matter what hurdles they faced.

Laila drew in the first decent breath she'd taken all afternoon and faced Matthew. "Well, that was fun," she said sarcastically. "My stomach's in knots. How about yours?"

Matthew gave her a wary look, then said, "Think of it this way. We'll never have to do it again."

"You planning to leave town?"

"I meant for the first time. Everybody knows about us now. They'll chew on it for a while. I imagine we'll have to fend off plenty of well-meaning advice, but then the dust will settle."

Laila regarded him incredulously. "Excuse me, but have you met your family? Or mine, for that matter?"

Just as she spoke, her cell phone rang. A glance at caller ID indicated it was her brother. She shoved the phone back into her purse.

"Who was it?" Matthew asked.

"Trace," she admitted.

"Isn't it going to tick him off more if you don't pick up?"

"More than likely."

"And that's okay with you?"

"At the moment, it is."

The next time the phone rang, she didn't even take it out of her purse. The third time, she yanked it out, then snapped, "What do you want?"

She winced at the sound of her mother's voice. "Sorry, Mom. I thought it was someone else."

"Your brother, no doubt," her mother said.

"I gather he's filled you in on today's events," Laila said, resigned to a lecture.

"Today's events don't interest me," her mother said. "I am, however, very interested in this relationship that's been going on right under my nose for months now. Sweetheart, what are you thinking? Matthew is young enough . . ." Her voice trailed off.

"To be what?" Laila inquired, glancing at the man in question. "My son? Hardly. I assure you he's of legal age."

"Well, of course he is. You're not a fool, dear."

"Thank you for that, I suppose."

"So when are you going to bring him by here, so your father and I can spend some time with him?"

"Mother, you've known Matthew all his life."

"Not as someone you're dating," her mother retorted. "I'd suggest you make it soon, because your father is blustering about the damage this will do to the bank's reputation when word gets out about it."

Laila turned a grim look on Matthew. She'd anticipated something like this. Well, she'd borne her share of unwanted humiliation and interrogation today at the hands of the O'Briens and her brother. Now it was his turn.

"No time like the present," she said with grim determination. "We'll be there in ten minutes."

She hung up to find Matthew regarding her warily. "Where are we going to be in ten minutes, or do I even need to ask?"

"My parents would like us to drop by," she said sweetly. "And if you ever hope to borrow a dime in this town, I suggest you don't do anything to further offend my father."

He frowned at the suggestion. "Why would I offend him?"

"You're dating his precious daughter," she reminded him. "That's offense enough. Now you need to make him believe it's serious."

"No problem. I've already told you and everyone else it is."

"I'm not even sure *I* believe that. Trust me, my father's going to be a tougher sell."

"Tougher than Trace?" he asked.

"My brother was practically a single-handed welcoming committee by comparison."

Matthew grimaced. "Gee, now I'm really looking forward to this."

She gave a nod of satisfaction. "Good. Now you have some idea of how I felt walking into Mick and Megan's today."

"So this is payback?"

She smiled sweetly. "Something like that."

"You are a very perverse woman," he commented.

"Thank you."

"I'm not sure I meant it in a good way."

"Doesn't matter. It gave a boost to my spirits," she said happily.

When they pulled into the driveway of her family home, Matthew actually looked a little pale. It took him a long time to cut the car's engine. Laila let herself out of the car and walked around to the driver's side.

"Come on, kid. I'll protect you."

He scowled at her as he left the car. "That is so not amusing."

"I thought it was hilarious," she said with a smile.

The impressive front door swung open

as they approached, and her mother stood in the foyer wearing an expensive knit suit, low heels and with every hair in place. Just a casual Sunday at the Rileys, Laila noted, thinking of the mishmash of attire at the O'Briens and the chaotic atmosphere. Though Carrie and Caitlyn had free rein here, even Abby's irrepressible twins seemed to understand this was a somber house.

"Hello, darling," her mother greeted her with a peck on the cheek. "Matthew, very good to see you. It's been a long time. Are you out of college now?"

Laila shot her a poisonous look. "Mother!"

"It's my younger brother, Luke, who's about to graduate," Matthew said, looking more amused than petrified or insulted.

"Oh, of course. How silly of me! Let's go into the parlor. Mr. Riley's in there catching up on all the Sunday papers."

Laila rolled her eyes. Who had parlors anymore, anyway? Her mother seemed to be trotting out all of her most formal Southern manners and references for the occasion.

"Look who's here, dear," her mother announced when they walked into what was usually referred to as the family room to distinguish it from the formal living room they rarely entered.

Lawrence Riley put down his paper and stood up. He frowned as he gave Matthew a once-over, then gave Laila a halfhearted hug.

"What's this I hear about the two of you making a spectacle of yourselves?" he inquired directly.

"Gee, Dad, no how are you? No nice to see you?"

"I believe in getting to the point," he said. "This nonsense can't continue."

Now Matthew frowned. "What *nonsense* would that be, sir?"

"You and my daughter cavorting around town making damned fools of yourselves. It doesn't look good. She'll be a laughing-stock. It'll reflect badly on her judgment and, in turn, on the bank."

Matthew looked as if he might explode. Before he could, Laila stood up. "Thank you so much for your support, Dad. As always, it's been a pleasure. We'll run along now."

"Hold on just one minute," her father commanded. "You don't walk out on me, young lady. I'm your boss."

"Oh, pardon me for thinking that in this house you were my father," she retorted. "If you want to discuss this in your capacity as my boss, I'll see you in your office tomorrow morning." She hesitated, then said, "Or maybe not. Maybe I'll just quit now and save myself the aggravation."

"Laila!" her mother protested, looking shocked.

"Come on, Matthew," Laila said, ignoring her mother. "Let's get out of here."

"If you walk out of here right now, don't bother showing up at work tomorrow," her father shouted after her.

"Didn't you hear me? I just quit," she shouted right back.

Matthew stopped her in the foyer, his expression filled with worry. "Laila, come on," he cajoled. "Settle down. You don't want to do this."

"Oh, but I do," she corrected. "Let's face it. Dad never wanted me in the job in the first place. Now I've given him the perfect excuse to get rid of me. I've just made his day."

"But you love the job. That bank is a family business. Don't let him force you out, not over our relationship. It's just going to take a little time for him to get used to the idea."

"Why do you care whether I quit? Are you worried I'll blame you for ruining my life? Or expect you to marry me and take care of me? I won't. This is liberation day!"

He still didn't look as if he believed her. "Look, if you want to leave, I'm behind you a hundred percent, but don't do it in haste. Think it through."

"Oh, this has been a long time coming," she said. "I should never have taken the job in the first place. Dad wanted Trace to have it, but my brother manipulated him into accepting me. As good as I am at the job—and believe me, I am damned good—it's been a bad fit all along."

As they talked, she could hear her mother trying to cajole her father into re-considering his stance. "Listen to them," she said. "Why would I want a job that first my brother and now my mother have to beg to get for me? There are other banks."

"You're going to regret this tomorrow," Matthew said.

Laila thought about it and realized he was wrong. She felt lighter than she had in months. No question that she loved the bank, that she'd wanted desperately to be worthy of taking over someday, but there were other banks where her talents and expertise would be appreciated, not maligned. And the management at those banks wouldn't give two hoots if she were dating Matthew.

She actually managed to smile when she looked into his eyes. "No," she told him. "I won't. No regrets at all. In fact, I feel like celebrating. Since I barely choked down two bites at Mick and Megan's, you can buy me dinner at Brady's."

Matthew chuckled. "You constantly amaze me."

"Right this second I amaze myself," she said. "And you know what? It feels really, really good."

22

Susie felt like some kind of minor celebrity with an entourage when she arrived for her scan on Monday morning. Not only were her mother and Mack with her, but her father and grandmother had shown up, as well. When Matthew walked into the waiting room, she scowled at him.

"This is crazy," she said. "I don't need all of you here holding my hand. I'm not going to know anything when the test is over."

"Who says I'm here for you?" Matthew said. "I could use a little family support of my own this morning."

Susie immediately studied him with concern. "Did Laila break it off again? Who could blame her after yesterday?"

"No, we're solid enough," Matthew said. "But she quit her job at the bank last night."

"Why on earth would she do that?" Susie asked.

"We dropped in on the Rileys, at her mother's request. It was basically an ambush. Her father didn't take the news of our romance very well. He went on some tirade about how it would reflect badly on the bank, and she lost it. I tried to talk her out of doing something rash, but she blew up, quit and walked out."

"Oh, my," Gram said. "Serves that stuffy old man right."

"I agree," Jeff added. "Lawrence Riley's going to ruin that bank with his old-fashioned thinking. Laila was the best thing that ever happened to the place."

Susie turned to Mack, who looked vaguely thunderstruck. "What's wrong?"

"Do you think Lawrence can pull the loan for the paper? After all, Laila's the one who pushed it through."

"Absolutely not," Jeff said. "The paperwork's been approved. As long as you make your payments, there's not a thing

Lawrence can do, at least not without causing a major ruckus in this town. The community's already a hundred percent behind you, Mack. Everyone I know is talking about what a difference it's making to have a local paper."

"Dad's right," Susie reassured him.

"Focus, people," Matthew said. "What am I supposed to do about Laila? I know she acted impulsively, but this is all my fault. I refused to listen when she said people might overreact to the two of us being together."

Gram shook her head. "Laila's a woman who knows her own mind. If she's in love with you and you with her, then there's nothing wrong about what's going on between you." She gave him a hard look. "Though personally I'd feel better about it if I saw a ring on her finger. That would take the wind out of that old man's sails, too."

"I think we can all agree about that," Susie said, mostly to watch the quick rise of color in her brother's cheeks. "How about it, Matthew? You going to make an honest woman of Laila?"

Matthew gave her a chiding look. "You

say that as if the thought might never have crossed my mind. I'd marry her in a heartbeat, but I don't think she's ready for a proposal. She'll probably turn me down flat, especially right now. I actually had a plan, a timetable, but this has thrown it into chaos."

Susie studied her brother curiously. She'd never thought Matthew considered much beyond whatever suited him at the moment. "What kind of plan?"

"You know how you've been talking about the whole family going to Ireland once you're finished with treatments?" he said.

"I'm thinking about next Christmas," Susie confirmed. "It's going to be Mack's and my honeymoon."

Matthew rolled his eyes. "Only you would invite a crowd along on a honeymoon."

She grinned. "That was Mack's reaction, but he's getting used to the idea, aren't you, sweetie?"

Mack shook his head. "Resigned to it is more like it."

"Anyway," Matthew said, "I thought I'd try to talk Laila into coming along. I'd propose in Ireland, on Christmas Eve, in fact."

"What a lovely thought," Gram said, looking misty-eyed. "I can hardly argue against waiting now, can I?"

Just then the technician came out and called Susie's name.

For a few minutes she'd been so caught up in her brother's drama, she'd almost forgotten why everyone was gathered yet again in a hospital waiting room.

Mack gave her hand a squeeze. "It's going to turn out great," he assured her.

Unable to speak around the lump in her throat, she merely nodded. She barely heard the other words of encouragement uttered by her family as she went into the back with the technician.

What happened next had the power to change everything, to give her a future . . . or to snatch it away.

As expected, they'd learned nothing from the technicians or doctors at the hospital. Mack kissed Susie goodbye as she left for work with her father after the test, and headed for the newspaper office, where he found Jess and her crew turning the place into party central. She'd rearranged the desks to create an open space for guests to mingle. It was evident no work was likely to get done around there today.

The minute Jess spotted him, she dropped what she was doing and crossed the room.

"How'd the test go?" she asked, her eyes filled with genuine concern.

"No news," Mack said. "It could be a day or two before the doctor gets the report."

Jess frowned. "Why do they insist on doing that? They know how freaked out everyone is by tests like this. Somebody should be there to read them on the spot."

"I couldn't agree more," Mack said, thinking of the panic lurking in Susie's eyes as she'd left the hospital. She'd put on a brave front, but anyone who knew her could tell how terrified she was. "Let's not talk about it. How are things here?"

"Coming together very nicely," Jess said, her pride evident. "Bree's bringing flowers in a couple of hours. That will dress the place up. Gail has the food under control at the inn. We'll have that here and ready to go by five-thirty before the guests start arriving. The champagne is already chilling."

"Including some of the nonalcoholic variety?" he asked, thinking of Susie.

"Of course."

"Is there anything you need me to do?" he asked, feeling oddly at loose ends and not liking it. Too much time meant he could start thinking about that blasted test, just as Jess had said.

"No. Why don't you get out of here? Take your wife out for lunch or something."

"She's probably better off at work. It'll keep her mind off the test results."

Jess rolled her eyes. "Nothing's going to take her mind off those. Yours, either, so you might as well try to distract each other. Something tells me you could be pretty good at it, if you put your mind to it."

He grinned. "Thanks for the vote of confidence."

Struck by a sudden idea, he made a call to Matthew, who confirmed that they had in fact broken ground for the Beach Lane house and were over there working on the foundation.

"Jess, do you think Gail would whip up a fancy picnic basket for Susie and me?"

Her eyes immediately lit up. "Of course she would. I'll call her now and it'll be ready by the time you get there. We always have the perfect gourmet ingredients on hand, in case our guests want to take something down to the beach. Even this time of year, there are a few hearty souls who'll bundle up and go for a hike along the water."

"Tell her I'll be by in a half hour, and call Bree and ask her if she'll make up a bouquet of some kind for Susie. I'll grab that on my way to Susie's office."

Jess kissed him on the cheek. "I love seeing this romantic side of you. Will must have coached you."

Mack laughed, thinking of the tips he and just about everyone else in town had given Will when he was courting Jess. "Yeah, that's it," he said.

He went home and found a blanket, then picked up the elaborate basket that was crammed full of delectable treats and a bottle of sparkling cider. Bree had put together a small bouquet that was perfect for a beachside picnic. Mack hid it all in the trunk of his car, then walked into the real estate office.

Susie looked up and regarded him with concern. "What's wrong?" she asked at once, fear in her voice. "The doctor didn't call you, did he?"

"No, I haven't heard a word. I came to distract you."

"But I just got here," she protested. "I need to get some work done."

"Are you really able to concentrate?"

"No," she admitted. "I've been staring at the same lease for an hour."

"Then you won't be missed," he declared. "Do I need to clear this with your father?"

"Dad's not even here."

"Okay, then, there are no roadblocks. Let's go."

Though she still looked hesitant, she grabbed her purse and followed him outside, locking the door behind her.

"Where are we going?" she asked.

"You'll see. Someplace special."

As he made the turn onto Beach Lane a few minutes later, she gasped. Construction sounds were audible even before they reached the end of the road.

"Our house!" she exclaimed excitedly.

"It's officially under construction," he confirmed. "And we are going to have our first meal there."

She turned to him, her eyes alight. "Seriously?"

"Would I kid about such a special occasion?"

He pulled off the road under a giant oak that was just beginning to get its leaves. "I'd love to eat at the site itself, but it'll probably be safer if we go onto the beach," he said. "I brought along an extra sweater if you're cold."

"The sun is perfect," she said, her eyes wide as she took in the bustling scene. "I wish I could climb up in a tree and see it from above. From this angle it's hard to picture what they've actually accomplished so far."

"The rooms aren't exactly identifiable yet, are they?" he agreed. The framing hadn't yet begun. "But they're making great progress, according to your brother. He said he dropped by this morning, and they're right on schedule. Another week or two and it will start to look like a house."

"I can't wait," she said, holding his arm as they made their way past the heavy equipment and piles of construction supplies.

When they were on the beach, about

fifty feet from the front of the house, the noise suddenly stopped.

"Matthew asked them to take a break for the next hour, so we can enjoy the peace and quiet," Mack told her, then turned on the CD player he'd grabbed at the last second. A Jimmy Buffett collection set exactly the right mood for a lazy, beachside outing even on such a chilly early-spring day.

"You think of everything, don't you?" she said, looking pleased.

"I hope I always do," he said as he spread the blanket on the sand. When he set the bouquet of flowers on the ground, her smile spread. "Bree must have done that. She knows how much I love daisies."

"So do I," Mack said. "They remind you of sunshine. You told me that once."

Susie reached eagerly for the picnic basket. "Oh, my. Gail has outdone herself. We'll never eat all this." She immediately plucked out the slices of chocolate cake. "This first."

Mack laughed. "So you're a proponent of the dessert-first philosophy?"

She nodded. "Absolutely. This cake is far too decadent not to savor every single mouthful."

"I love how much you savor things," he said quietly.

For a moment she fell silent. "I think I do even more now, because I don't know how long I'll have left to enjoy them. Why can't people remember to do that all the time, to live in the moment? None of us know how long we have. I just happen to be facing my own mortality."

"Sometimes that's what it takes," Mack said.

"But it shouldn't be that way," Susie said.

Looking into her shining eyes, seeing her enjoyment of every little detail about being here, about the meal and the flowers, Mack nodded. "No," he confirmed. "It shouldn't be that way. Blessings are meant to be counted every day, not just on Thanksgiving or when we're bargaining with God."

She studied him curiously. "Have you done much of that? Bargaining with God, I mean? Heather said Connor did when she had her accident."

"I get exactly where Connor was coming from," Mack conceded. "And I've had my share of conversations with God lately."

"Me, too," she admitted.

Mack pulled her back to rest against his

chest. "Your grandmother swears He's listening."

Susie nodded. "I believe that, too. I have to."

"Then we're going to be okay," Mack said with more confidence than usual.

They simply had to be.

It had been one of the most wonderful afternoons of Susie's life. Mack had driven her home to get ready for the party at the paper, changed his own clothes and hurried off. Until she was alone in their apartment, she'd hardly spared a thought for the test results all afternoon.

When the phone rang, she wasn't even thinking about them. When she picked up, though, it was Dr. Kinnear on the line. She sat down hard on the edge of the bed.

"You have the test results," she said, unable to keep the dread out of her voice.

"I do, and it's good news, Susie. The chemo has worked almost as well as we'd hoped. It has the cancer in check."

Her emotions went from high to low in a heartbeat. "What does that mean, in check? Am I in remission or not?"

"There are a couple of places that still

concern us, but it's looking very, very good. We want to wait a bit, let you recover some, and then do another round of the chemo."

"So the cancer's not gone?" she said, deflated. Despite all the caution she'd expressed aloud, she'd allowed herself to be hopeful.

"No, it's not gone, but there's every reason to be optimistic," the gynecologist told her. "The oncologist says it's quite remarkable for the first round of treatments to go so well."

She thought of the nausea and other side effects of the chemo. Could she do all that again? She sat up straighter and thought of the stakes. Of course she could. If it meant having a life with Mack, she could endure whatever it took.

"Thank you for letting me know," she told the doctor.

"Come in next week and we'll come up with a timetable," he said. "This is good news, Susie. It may not be exactly what we'd hoped for, but it's very positive."

Susie tried to remember that as she dressed for the party. She zipped herself into the knock-'em-dead dress Shanna had helped her find, put on her blond wig

and was about to do her makeup when
she glanced in the mirror and decided,
what the hell? She took off the wig and
tossed it aside. It wasn't fooling anyone,
and she was proud of getting through this
first round of treatments with her spirit in-
tact.

She rubbed the faint bit of fuzz on her
head and grinned. Like a newborn baby's,
she decided, thinking the comparison was
apt. Maybe she didn't have a free-and-
clear prognosis, but it wasn't dire, either.
And that was like a rebirth of sorts. It was
one of those blessings she and Mack had
been talking about earlier, a moment to
savor before the hard work once again
commenced.

Mack looked around the newsroom at
the crowd that had assembled to wish him
well and for a moment he actually felt
something suspiciously like tears sting his
eyes. These people, many of whom had
once written him off, were here because
he'd accomplished something, because
his newspaper was making a contribution
to Chesapeake Shores, a town that had

surrounded him with love and ultimately given him the love of his life.

He searched the crowd for some sign of Susie, but apparently she hadn't arrived yet. Kristen slipped up beside him and linked her arm through his.

"We did it, Mack! The paper and website are already the talk of the town. There's even been some buzz in the newspaper world. I've fielded a few calls today from other papers wanting ideas for integrating print and the internet."

He looked into her sparkling eyes and grinned. "Are you going to take off and start your own consulting company now?"

She frowned at the suggestion. "Is that what you want me to do?"

"No, I need you right here, but I know it hasn't been a comfortable situation for you."

She gave him a smile tinged with sadness. "It's getting better."

He studied her curiously. "Because of Luke?"

She chuckled. "Luke's a charming diversion. Nothing more."

"Does he realize that?"

"Absolutely. He's only pursuing me to protect his sister's turf. It's working out for both of us, at least for now."

Mack glanced away from her and spied Jess heading their way. He gently extricated his arm from Kristen's before she could reach them. Kristen chuckled.

"Ah, it's the avenging angel," she said.

"Isn't there someplace you need to be?" Jess demanded, her tone unfriendly.

Kristen stood her ground. "Last time I checked, I worked here."

"That could always change," Jess said, casting a meaningful look at Mack. "Couldn't it?"

Mack held up a hand. "Settle down, you two. This is a party."

Jess looked as if she had a lot more on her mind, but she glanced around the room. "Where's your wife?"

"I haven't seen her yet," Mack admitted. "I should probably call the house to make sure everything's okay."

"I'll do it," Jess offered. "You should be mingling." She cast a pointed look at Kristen. "So should you. Separately."

Mack watched Kristen begin to circulate, then regarded Jess with amusement.

"You didn't have to step in, you know. There's nothing going on between Kristen and me."

"With women like that, there's always something going on."

"You saw her at your parents' place. She was with Luke."

Jess rolled her eyes. "Oh, please, she's toying with him. Or he is with her. Nobody bought that act. Now, go and talk to your guests. I'll track down Susie."

Reluctantly, Mack left her to it.

A half hour later, he finally spotted his wife hovering on the fringes of the crowd. In that unguarded moment she looked withdrawn and very much alone. Apparently none of the O'Briens had seen her yet.

Wanting to share the night's success with her, he began working his way through the room, but everyone had congratulations to offer, a toast to make. It was slow going.

The next time he glanced her way, she was gone. Jess, however, was nearby.

"I was trying to get to Susie, but she's vanished again. Any idea where she might be?"

Jess pointed to the buffet table, where

Susie was with Shanna and Kevin. "Have you even spoken to her since she arrived?"

"I've tried, but I keep getting waylaid."

"Something's off with her tonight," Jess said.

Mack frowned. "What do you mean?"

"It's in her eyes. She just looks sad. I know I'm no expert on Susie, but it worries me, Mack. Find her. See if you can get to the bottom of whatever's wrong. If you can't spare a few minutes, I'll put Will on it."

Mack shook his head. "I'll take care of it, Jess. Thanks."

But as he was about to make his way to Susie, the paper's freelance photographer, Jerry Hastings, dragged Kristen over and insisted on a picture of the two of them. "The next edition won't be complete without this. And Kristen's going to want it for the website, too."

"Sure," Mack said, though he was impatient to get to his wife.

"I think the occasion calls for a celebratory kiss," Jerry called out as he snapped away.

Kristen gave Jerry a wry look. Mack

shrugged. As he went to press a kiss to her cheek, she turned her head and he caught her on the lips. The kiss lasted less than a heartbeat, but he knew the instant it ended that it had been a dreadful mistake. He looked toward the last place he'd seen Susie, but as he'd feared, she was gone. A survey of the room revealed no sign of her.

"Dammit!" he muttered. Surely she knew that kiss had meant nothing. It was one of those public relations moments.

Even as he tried to convince himself of that, he could envision it from Susie's perspective. A kiss on the cheek might have passed muster for PR purposes, but Kristen had deliberately tried to turn it into something else. Worse, it would likely show up online and in the paper's print edition unless he made a production out of keeping it out. That could stir its own sort of controversy, with people speculating about why he'd objected so vehemently.

"Susie missing?" Kristen inquired, not looking entirely displeased by the idea.

"What were you thinking just then?" Mack demanded. "Not only was that kiss bad PR because it insinuated there's something more between us, but you crossed a line, Kristen. You know what's going on with my wife and you deliberately did something you knew would hurt her."

For a fleeting instant he thought he detected shame in her eyes, but then she shrugged.

"It wasn't a big deal," she insisted. "I can't help it if she thought otherwise."

"If you honestly believe what you're saying, then you're not the kind of woman I always thought you were."

"You were with me because I was sexy, Mack. My high moral standards had nothing to do with it."

"You're wrong. I liked you, Kristen. It was never just about the sex. For all of my faults, I never slept with anyone just because they were easy."

She looked momentarily taken aback by that.

"I have to get out of here and find my wife."

"You can't leave now," she said, looking shocked. "This party's a professional obligation."

"And I have a personal obligation that's more important," he declared. "Make sure our guests have a great time."

Unfortunately, when he went looking, Susie was nowhere to be found.

23

Susie knew almost the second that she walked out of the newspaper offices that she was making a mistake, but her pride simply wouldn't allow her to turn around and go back.

That very public kiss between Kristen and her husband had been humiliating. Even if she knew without a doubt that Mack had no feelings for Kristen, there wasn't another person in that room likely to believe it.

A braver woman—a woman who'd been told she was in remission, for example— might have been able to walk across the room with her head held high and stake her own claim. Susie wasn't that woman. Not tonight, anyway. Tonight she was facing a whole boatload of insecurities.

She'd never had to fight that hard for anything in her life. Jess had been right when she'd noted that things had always come easily for Susie. Until Mack. And even he was a piece of cake compared to beating cancer. Now she was in the battle of her life, *for* her life. She had to give her full attention to that, or nothing else would matter.

As always, when her spirit was crushed, she ran to Gram's. All the adults in the family had their own keys to the cottage. It was meant to be their refuge, whether Nell was there or not. Tonight, of course, she was at the party with everyone else.

Susie let herself in, brewed a pot of tea, then settled on the sofa, thinking of another night just like this one when she'd done the same thing to escape from the painful truth—that she didn't really trust Mack to stick by her side. Oh, she'd told him she did. She'd even convinced herself of it for a time, and allowed Will to persuade her that Mack was a steadfast guy, despite his track record with other women.

Though it was a pleasantly warm spring evening, she shivered at her dark thoughts and wrapped the quilt more tightly around her.

It wasn't long before the front door opened and Gram came in, her expression filled with worry.

"I thought I might find you here. You caused quite an uproar by leaving the party without even speaking to your husband."

"He seemed to be otherwise occupied," she said bleakly.

Gram gave her a chiding look. "Oh, please, you know better than that. There's only one woman on this earth for Mack Franklin, and you're it!"

Susie wasn't entirely consoled by her grandmother's certainty. She was too caught up in her own misery to be entirely rational. "Things change."

Her grandmother's gaze narrowed. "What's changed? Not Mack's feelings. I know that for a fact. Nor yours."

Susie drew in a deep breath, then blurted, "My cancer's not in remission." She felt hot tears scalding her cheeks. "I was so sure I'd beaten it, Gram. I prayed so hard."

Nell immediately sat beside her and

gathered her into her arms. "Oh, my sweet child, that doesn't mean you've lost the war, just that there's more fighting to be done."

"I know. And I'm willing to do whatever the doctor suggests, but how can I drag Mack through more of this? I need to let him go." Even as she said the self-sacrificing, supposedly noble words, she knew she wouldn't do it. She needed him more than ever now. Maybe it was selfish. Or maybe it was the depth of her love, but she wasn't ready to let go.

Nell sat back and shook her head at Susie's words. "Now, that is without a doubt the silliest bit of logic I've ever heard. Mack doesn't want to go anywhere."

"We both know down deep that he thought the chemo would cure me."

"He *hoped* it would. He prayed that it would. We all did. That doesn't mean one of us is just going to write you off and move on to other things, or to other people. That's what this self-pity is really all about, isn't it? Kristen, and the kiss?"

At Gram's words, Susie sat up, let indignation flow through her. "Did you see that woman? She's nothing but a brazen slut. I don't care how valuable Mack thinks she is to the paper. And what about Luke? She kissed my husband right in front of him, too. Maybe he was only dating her for my sake, to keep her away from Mack, but what if he fell for her?"

Gram merely looked amused. "I doubt Luke's heart is broken. Yours shouldn't be, either. That kiss was the act of a desperate woman. It meant nothing to Mack. If anything, it probably demonstrated the kind of woman she is."

Even though in her heart she knew better herself, Susie wasn't quite ready to let the incident go. "I didn't see Mack shoving her away."

"Because your husband knew that causing a scene would only make matters worse. He had quite a lot to say to her afterward, though. I don't think I've ever seen him so angry."

Susie felt a moment's delight in that news, then shrugged. "It doesn't matter. Kristen's not the problem. Not really. Oh, she's a healthy alternative to me, but I know Mack doesn't love her."

"If you understand that, then I don't see the problem," Gram said. "Please don't be one of those self-sacrificing people who walks away from something just because you think it's for the best, Susie. Mack has a say in your future, too. And he's not the kind of man who turns his back on something just because it's hard. You know that. It's one of the reasons you love him. What happened tonight is a little blip. It's insignificant, and in no way does it measure up to enough to cause the two of you to split up for good. If you let that kiss—or even the cancer—have that kind of power over you, then you're not the O'Brien woman I thought you to be."

Susie managed a smile. "You always believe that O'Briens have more strength than other mere mortals."

Gram grinned. "Because we do. Now, you mend fences with that man of yours. I intend to go to Ireland next Christmas, and you're going to be right there celebrating the holidays with me. I won't have it any other way." She gave Susie a sly look. "Besides, you promised."

Susie rested her head on her grand-mother's shoulder, feeling better for the tough love that wouldn't allow her moment of self-pity to cause her to do something rash. "Then I guess I'll have to live up to my promise, won't I?"

"I'm counting on it," Nell told her in no uncertain terms.

Laila had watched Susie slip out of the party, her expression stoic, but the tears gathering in her eyes giving away just how hurt she was by the kiss Kristen Lewis had planted on Mack.

"What is wrong with men?" Laila inquired irritably of Matthew.

"Hey, I haven't done anything wrong," he said. "As for Mack, he was hardly to blame for that kiss." He glanced around the room. "Have you seen Luke? I should probably find out how he's taking it."

"Forget Luke. It's your sister you ought to be worrying about."

Matthew's expression darkened. "She saw it? I didn't think she'd shown up yet."

"Oh, she was here, and it hurt her, Matthew."

He heaved a sigh. "Why don't you find her? I'll check on Luke. And then we can all give Kristen a piece of our minds."

"As much as I would love to gang up on that woman right now, let's focus on Susie."

After they'd circled the entire room with

no luck, Jess informed them that Susie had taken off and Mack had gone after her.

"That's good, I guess," Laila said. "I hope he can make this right."

"He will," Jess said with confidence. "Now let's try to get these people out of here without causing a scene. I want to get over to Mom and Dad's. The family's going over there to wait to see whether Mack can get Susie to listen to reason. Are you guys coming?"

Laila wasn't sure it was a good idea, but Matthew immediately said, "Of course we are."

Jess nodded. "Then I'll see you there. Try to be diplomatic when you're encouraging the guests to leave. And whatever you do, do not let Kristen find out there's going to be an after-party at my folks' place."

After Jess had moved on, Laila regarded Matthew curiously. "Are you sure you want me to go to Mick and Megan's?"

Matthew gave her an impatient look. "We're together, aren't we? Why wouldn't I want you there?"

The tightness in her chest eased at the

determination and certainty she heard in his voice. "Then this really is turning into something serious between us?"

He grinned, sending her heart into a happy cartwheel. "I told you it was."

"I'm unemployed," she commented.

He laughed. "As if that matters to me. Whether or not you work is entirely up to you. Personally I kind of like the idea of you being there waiting for me if I decide to pop home in the middle of the day."

She regarded him with amazement. "You actually mean that, don't you?"

"I do."

"Well, I happen to like working. I love banking, and the second one of these feelers I've put out pays off, I'm not going to be at your beck and call anymore." She grinned. "Until then, I suppose we could make the most of my availability."

"I'm glad you're able to see the obvious benefits of the current situation," he said solemnly.

"Maybe you should consider working from home," she added.

For an instant he looked startled, but then he gathered her into his arms and twirled her around. "Now you're getting into the spirit of this. I always knew you had a wild and reckless streak."

Laila seized on those two words—*wild* and *reckless*—and added them to the collection she was holding close to her heart. With Matthew it wasn't that she was turning into someone no one would recognize. He'd simply unleashed new facets of her personality, helped her to become the exciting, well-rounded woman she'd always longed to be. How could she possibly help loving him for that?

Unlike the last time Susie had gone missing, this time Mack had a pretty good idea where to find her. Like all the other O'Briens, Susie counted on Nell for not only a safe haven, but solid, no-nonsense advice.

With his heart thudding dully in his chest and after assuring himself that Susie was nowhere in the building, Mack left the party and drove directly to Nell's cottage.

En route, he couldn't help thinking about the last time he'd made this trip looking for Susie. He'd been greeted by the worst possible news, that she had cancer. Now it was entirely likely that the news would

be no better. She might be prepared to tell
him their marriage was over. Just the
thought of it was enough to make him a
little crazy. He couldn't let that happen. He
couldn't lose her.

Darkness had fallen before he reached
Nell's. There were lights in the windows,
and smoke from a late-spring fire was curl-
ing from the chimney. Only the absence of
Christmas lights twinkling on a tree made
it appear any different from the last time
he'd arrived here on a mission to prove to
Susie he loved her.

When Nell responded to his knock, she
took one look at him and relief washed
over her face. "Thank goodness," she murmured, hugging him fiercely.

"Is she okay?"

"She's heartsick," Nell responded. "Now
that you're here, that'll change." She reached
for her coat, which was hanging on a peg
by the door. "I'm going up to Mick and Megan's. I think I'll spend the night there. Susie's in the kitchen, unless she's heard your
voice and gone scurrying off to the guest
room. Don't let her run you off, Mack. She's
going to try. She thinks you want your freedom or that you deserve it, or some cocka-

mamy thing like that. I can't say much for her logic right now. Whatever she tries to say or do, remember that she loves you."

Mack clung to that thought as he pressed a kiss to Nell's cheek, then went in search of his wife.

He found Susie, as predicted, in the kitchen, her hands wrapped around a cup of tea, her expression bleak.

"Go away, Mack. There's nothing left to say. Not tonight, anyway. I need more time to think."

He kept his temper in check. "Thinking, under the circumstances, is overrated. If you ask me, there's plenty that needs to be said," he corrected. "Not that you said a single word to me before taking off from the party. Bottom line, if you've run out of words, I'll go first."

She blinked at his determined tone, but she didn't offer a single comment.

"Okay, then," he said. "I know now that bringing Kristen here was a huge mistake. Maybe at some other time it wouldn't have been, but she was like some kind of nagging burr under your saddle from the day she hit town."

When she opened her mouth to speak,

he cut her off. "Let me finish. I thought what we had was strong enough to handle the presence of a woman who means nothing to me, but I was wrong. Under other circumstances, I think that would have been true."

He gave her an earnest look. "You know what's in my heart, Susie. You always have. Somehow, though, Kristen being here made you think you couldn't trust that. Or maybe it got all twisted up with whether or not you were going to beat the cancer, whether I was with you out of pity, who knows? Anyway, I made up my mind tonight that she's going. I'll tell her first thing tomorrow. I didn't tell her before I walked out on the party, because somebody official needed to stay there and keep everyone happy."

Finally she lifted her head and met his gaze. "But the paper needs her," she said, looking guilty.

"Not half as much as I need you. I won't ever have you questioning that again, Susie. Not for a single second. You're my motivation, my inspiration and my heart." He studied her gaze, saw the barely concealed relief in her eyes, the faint hint of hope.

"My test results came back," she said softly.

Mack felt his pulse slow. "And?"

"I'm not in remission," she admitted. "I'm going to have to have more treatments, Mack. I don't know if I can ask you to go through that."

"You're the one who's taking the treatments, Susie. You've got the tough job. I'm just the cheerleader. It's what I signed on to be, and I'm not about to give up now."

"How can you face all that again?" she asked.

"Look, I'm sorry the news isn't what we'd hoped for, but if you can deal with more chemo, so can I," he insisted. "Especially if it means more time with you. You'll beat this yet, Susie. There's no other option."

She searched his face for what felt like an eternity before throwing herself into his arms and burrowing her face into his neck. "I didn't want to leave you, you know. In some twisted way I was trying to give you a chance at the future I didn't think I'd be able to give you. The whole time I was saying the words, though, I was praying you wouldn't go. I guess I'm just not that unselfish, after all. I want every minute we can get."

Mack closed his eyes, felt a tear slide down his cheek. "The only future I want is with you," he told her. Her tears mingled with his. "We're going to make it a great one."

Susie nodded, looking heartened. "The best."

Mack reached into his coat pocket and pulled out a thick bundle of papers he'd been saving in case he needed one final bit of ammunition to win her back. As it turned out, maybe they were more about giving her hope, something to look forward to. He handed them to her.

"What are these?" she asked, her eyes alight with curiosity.

"Open the envelope and see for yourself," he said. "They were meant to be my final bribe to keep you with me."

When she drew out the airline tickets, a smile spread across her face. "Our honeymoon, the one you promised me," she exclaimed.

"Ireland for Christmas," he said. "Take a good look."

"Oh, my gosh! There are tickets for Gram, Mom, Dad, Matthew, Luke, all of us."

"And Mick and Thomas have their tickets for everyone else," he said. "It's been quite a production keeping this a secret from you. O'Briens are lousy at keeping their mouths shut. It's a very good thing you've been distracted lately. Otherwise it might have taken a miracle to make sure no one let anything slip."

"You did all this for me," she marveled.

"And for Nell. She's been my staunchest supporter lately. I owed her."

"She must be over the moon," Susie said. "When we talked earlier, she reminded me that I'd promised her this trip, and told me I was not to let her down."

"You could never let her down. Or me. You've given me everything I ever hoped for, Susie."

"A sick wife with no prospect for a family?" she asked wryly.

"A beautiful, loving wife, who *is* my family," he corrected. "I had a call from Jess on my way over here. I think the rest of the family is gathering up at Mick's, hanging out to see if we've worked things out. Shall we join them?"

Susie rested her hand against his cheek. "Not just yet. I think we've got some celebrating of our own to do. I love you, Mack."

"Not even a tenth as much as I love you," he responded. "Loving you has made me whole. Despite the fact that we don't have children, might never have them, you've given me a family, Susie."

For just an instant, a shadow fell across her eyes. He touched her chin, forced her to meet his gaze.

"I mean it. We're surrounded by this huge wonderful family. And if we decide we want kids of our own, we'll make that happen. Connor has that adoption attorney on speed dial." He stroked her cheek. "There's absolutely nothing we can't do."

She smiled slightly. "You still can't make Gram's pot roast without burning it," she said. "I despair of that ever happening."

"But you can," he said. "Which only proves my point—together there's nothing that's beyond us. We fit, Susie. We always have, always will."

And thank God for it.

Epilogue

The house on Beach Lane was finished by the end of summer. Mack still wasn't used to returning each day to a real home, where the woman he loved would be waiting for him. The spacious rooms, the spectacular views, the coziness of the furnishings that had been lovingly chosen by Susie were a far cry from the cramped apartments where he'd grown up.

When he arrived after work on Friday, their decreed "date night," he found Susie in the kitchen surrounded by boxes of takeout. Her head snapped up and a guilty expression crossed her face when she saw him.

"Uh-oh," she said. "Now you know my dirty little secret."

"You mean the fact that Jess has had Gail at the inn preparing these Friday-night dinners for you to pass off as your own?" he teased.

She immediately stood a little taller, radiating indignation. "That is so not true."

"Really?" he said, eyeing the empty containers. "If I were a lawyer, I'd call those boxes evidence."

"Well, not everything is what it seems," she retorted. "The food is from the inn, but I prepared it, albeit under Gail's watchful eye."

Mack crossed the kitchen and peered at the food she'd been dishing onto plates. It certainly looked edible. "You cooked?" he asked warily.

She nudged him in the ribs with her elbow. "Stop it. You've been eating my cooking for weeks now, and you've lived."

He thought of the meals, mostly simple and basic, but definitely with more taste than anything Susie had been capable of a few months ago. He'd been certain he had Jess and Gail to thank for those. Or, in some instances, Nell. He wrapped his arms around Susie.

"You've been taking cooking lessons," he said, oddly pleased that she would go to such lengths to please him. "Amazing."

She turned in his embrace until she was facing him, her eyes almost level with his. "I wanted our Friday nights to be special. My repertoire is still pretty limited, but I'm getting there. Gail and Gram have both been helping."

"I thought I detected your grandmother's hand in there somewhere."

"The pot roast and the chicken and dumplings," she confirmed.

With Susie nestled in his arms, Mack took the time to study her. Her hair had started to grow back, still red and, if anything, even curlier, much to her dismay. Tonight it seemed to him there was an especially bright sparkle in her eyes.

"Is something going on?" he inquired.

"You mean besides this fabulous dinner, which we're about to eat on the porch?"

"Yes, aside from that."

She grinned. "You'll have to wait and see. It's a surprise for after dinner."

He dropped a kiss on her forehead, another on her cheek, a third on her neck.

"Bet I can get it out of you sooner," he murmured against her heating skin.

"Stop," she commanded, laughing and pushing him away.

"You are definitely in an odd mood tonight." He paused, then glanced at the calendar that hung on the wall. Understanding dawned. "The doctor! You saw the doctor today."

Though she looked a little disappointed that he'd guessed, she nodded.

"And?" he asked, hardly daring to hope that her long ordeal with the chemo might finally be over for good, that she might be cancer-free. He'd wanted to be there with her, but she'd been adamant that she wanted to hear the news on her own, wanted time to digest it, good or bad. He'd argued to no avail.

A slow smile spread across her face and actually reached her eyes. "I'm clear," she revealed, a hitch in her voice. "There's no cancer, Mack."

Mack drew in a deep breath for what felt like the first time in months. Tears welled up in his eyes, spilled down his cheeks.

"They're sure?" he said, still not daring to believe.

Susie nodded. "As sure as they can be. I'll be monitored closely, but we have a chance, Mack, a real chance at the future we want."

Mack pulled her back into his arms, letting the tears fall freely as he rested his chin on her shoulder. "I already have the future I want," he murmured. "It's right here in my arms, Susie. You're all I'll ever need."

She was his past, his present and, now, thank God, his future. Forever no longer seemed as if it had an expiration date.

"Do you have any idea at all how much I love you?" Susie whispered.

"It can't be any more than I love you," he said, kissing her. All thoughts of dinner and being on the porch for the sunset fled. Everything that mattered was right here.

* * * * *

QUESTIONS FOR DISCUSSION

1. For years Susie O'Brien declared that she would never date a player like Mack Franklin. Instead, she settled for being his friend. In the book, though, Susie is ready to change the rules, but finds that it's next to impossible. Have you ever established boundaries in a relationship, then regretted it? Were you able to change the dynamics from friendship to something more? How?

2. What are the risks if you do take a chance on getting involved with someone who's been a friend? Have you ever taken that next step, then lost the friendship when things didn't work out? Was it worth it? Or were you able to recapture the friendship? If so, how?

3. Susie's diagnosis of ovarian cancer is devastating. Aside from medical treatment, what do you think is most important in her ability to fight the disease?

Her relationship with Mack? Her inner strength? What role do you believe a positive attitude plays in healing? Have you had experience with this?

4. When Susie is first diagnosed with ovarian cancer, her doctors recommend not waiting for surgery in order to harvest any viable eggs. They also encourage her not to take the more cautious approach of removing only the affected ovary. This guarantees that she and Mack will never have children of their own. Have you ever faced such a difficult decision? What did you do? If not, how do you think you would have proceeded? Would you have followed doctor's orders or insisted on a more cautious surgery in the hopes of having children?

5. Susie and Mack go forward with the surgery the doctors feel will give her the best chance for survival. Do you think Mack's concerns about being a father play any role is his encouraging her to do this? Or is he totally focused on Susie's survival?

6. Along the same lines, Mack comes from a very troubled background. How do you think that affected the relationships he had before Susie? And what role do you think it plays in keeping them apart for so long? Or is that not-dating stance totally Susie's thing?

7. When Mack hires Kristen Lewis to work for his newspaper, there are red flags everywhere. How did you feel about that decision? Should he have anticipated the problems, especially with everyone speaking out about them? Or should Susie have been more candid about her own doubts? Have you ever gone against the advice of family or friends and lived to regret it?

8. Susie and her cousin Jess have had a very competitive relationship throughout their lives, mostly because things came so easily to Susie, while Jess always had to struggle. Have you ever had a competitive relationship with a sibling or other family member or even a friend? How have you dealt with it?

9. Initially Susie and Jess's tense relationship poses potential problems for their spouses, Mack and Will. Have the feelings of a spouse ever caused problems in an important relationship in your life? How have you worked it out?

10. When Susie's first round of chemo doesn't put her into remission, she's completely thrown by the news. With her optimism and hope shaken, she offers to give Mack his freedom. He absolutely refuses. But not all men are like Mack. Have you known people whose marriages have been broken by an illness— one affecting either of the partners or a child? Are there steps that can be taken to keep a marriage strong through such difficult times? What role does faith play?